Praise for

T0160295

Pas de deux

Pas de deux doesn't disappoint: the writing is excellent, the pace is ideal, the characters are layered and, yes, relatable, including the secondary characters, from Caitlyn's groom Wren, to Addie's friend Teresa and, of course, Dewey the horse. One of the many things I loved in this book is the way the MCs deal with problems. They do this very adult and very rare-in-lesfic thing: they talk to each other. This book is proof that miscommunication isn't required for drama. Neither is a breakup. Well-fleshed characters with very human hang-ups bring all the angst and drama necessary. It's all the more interesting here as *Pas de deux* is part enemies-to-lovers romance, part second chance, depending on whose point of view is playing.

-Les Rêveur

This story is not the traditional enemies-to-lovers romance, and I love that. Noyes really puts emphasis on how skewed memories can become as you get older, and how an experience may appear different to another person who had the exact same one. Even if you are unfamiliar with dressage, Noyes' writing is still spot on and delivers the same compelling, fun, and intriguing story with loveable characters of both the two-legged and four-legged kind. This love letter to a sport she obviously has a passion for is so evident and I felt honored to have her share her passion with me and every reader who picks it up. If you love horses, enemies-to-lovers, or even just Noyes' stories in general, this one will definitely be a favorite on your list.

-The Lesbian Review

This romance hit two main tropes. For one main character this is a second chance romance, for the other character, this is an enemies to lovers romance. I loved the two different sides of how the character saw things and I think it gave the book a little zip that caught my attention from the beginning. I was very happy that while this was first person, the POV is actually from both main characters. It was perfect for this book especially since both mains can't even agree on their past. Seeing how each character thought and why, was the right choice for this romantic story. As long as you are a fan of horses, or at least are okay with them, then I would absolutely recommend this one. Noyes writes really well and makes smart choices so that is why she is one of the best.

-Lex Kent's Reviews, *goodreads*

Reaping the Benefits

The story is quite eccentric with its paranormal context but in fact is a pure romance at heart with a nice dose of humor. The book is written in third person, from the point of view of both protagonists, which is not common for Noyes, but it is executed perfectly. With all main elements done well, this makes an awesome read which I could easily recommend to all romance fans.

-Pin's Reviews, *goodreads*

I've read many love stories that entertain the idea of soul mates, but this one does something even more interesting. This one explores the depth of love and its ability to transcend death. This story plays with the idea that love has no limits or boundaries. Its exploration provides a unique setting for this heartfelt romantic tale. At its core it remains a romance. The love story between Jane and Morgan is tender and sweet. It's so cleverly and delightfully done; I've never read anything quite like it before. Noyes possesses the ability to see a story where others don't and turn that into something unique and captivating. She uses rich storytelling and engaging characters to enthrall and delight us.

It's fresh and original. It's everything you crave when you want to dig into a great romance. I highly recommended it.

-Deb M., *NetGalley*

I'm spectacularly smitten with Death, to be specific with E. J. Noyes' personification of death as Cici La Morte in this new and most wondrous book. Cici is not one of the main characters but she is the fulcrum about which the whole plot rotates. She simultaneously operates as a beautiful symbol of our fascination with the theme of death and loss, and as a comedic but wise Greek chorus guiding Morgan through the internal conflict threatening to tear her very soul apart. All of E. J. Noyes' previous books have had emotionally charged first-person narrative, so I was curious how her switch to writing in the third person would play out here, but it really works. Despite many lighthearted and genuinely funny moments I found that this book not only had E. J. Noyes' signature ability to make me cry, but also fascinating ideas and philosophies about grief, loss, and hope.

-Orlando J., *NetGalley*

E. J. Noyes never disappoints and this book is another added to one of my favourites. What I love about Noyes is every book is different and unique from the other which is what makes her such a special writer. The way she has me completely entrenched into the story has me wanting to read or listen to her books over and over again, it's addictive. I highly recommend the book.

-Catherine C., *NetGalley*

E. J. Noyes is an amazing writer. I have read all of her books and no two books have even a remotely similar plot. She constantly pushes herself to be a better writer. This book is no exception. This book was such a fun twist on what everyone normally thinks about life, death, and the afterlife. I loved the dialogue between the characters as well as the plot development. It was a lot of fun to read!

-Jenna F., *NetGalley*

This very unique story line turned into a beautiful story that had me experiencing a multitude of emotions, from humor to heartbreak and everything in between. The paranormal aspect works beautifully in the novel. Ms. Noyes made the supernatural aspect of the story seem like a normal part of life. The characters are well developed. The ideas of life, death, and the afterlife are handled in a manner I would have never thought about, but which works well in the book.

-Betty H., *NetGalley*

If you're looking for a lesbian romance, but with a twist of something different, I recommend *Reaping the Benefits*. It's sweet, sexy, and fun.

-*The Lesbian Review*

Wildly unique and completely unexpected, *Reaping the Benefits* wasn't a hard sell given the expertise with which the author has been able to entertain me with every book published. The letting go of reality to fall into a paranormal underworld is a most unusual backdrop for a love affair but here we are, and I enjoyed every minute of it. Despite the uniqueness of the scenery and its characters, Morgan and Jane's developing attraction eventually directs Morgan to contemplate everything. The intensity of her introspections coupled with her musings with Death is as bizarre as it is incredibly interesting. This author never fails to entertain me in the most unusual ways that leaves me ruminating over her words long after The End.

-Cathie W., *NetGalley*

Alone

E. J. Noyes is easily one of the most gifted writers pulling us into whatever world she creates making us live and feel every emotion with her characters. Definitely, loudly, vehemently recommended.

-Reviewer@Large, *NetGalley*

Alone is an absolutely stunning book. This book is not a 5-star, it is well above that. You don't see books like this one very often. Truly a treasure and one that will stay with you long after the final page.

-Tiff's Reviews, *goodreads*

For being one of my most anticipated books to read in 2019, this one sure had a lot of expectations to live up to! I can say with full authority that it met or exceeded every single hope that I had. Noyes has done it again, cementing her place as a "must-read" author. *Alone* lived up to all the hype, and is easily one of the best books of 2019!

-Bethany K., *NetGalley*

There are only a handful of authors that I will drop everything to read as soon as a new book comes out, and Noyes is at the top of that list. It seems no matter what Noyes writes she doesn't disappoint. I will eagerly be waiting for whatever she writes next.

-Lex Kent's Reviews, *goodreads*

There are only a few books out there so compelling they seem to take control of you and force you to read them as quickly as possible. You can't put them down. You just want the world to go away and leave you alone until you can finish this story. *Alone* by E. J. Noyes is that book for me. This novel is absolutely wonderful.

-Betty H., *NetGalley*

Not only is this easily one of the best books of 2019, but it has worked its way onto my personal all-time top 10 list. There is not one formulaic thing going on, and it's "unputdownable."

-Karen C., *NetGalley*

I cannot give this anything more than five stars, but damn I wish I could. I would give it 15.

-Carolyn M., *NetGalley*

Ask, Tell

This is a book with everything I love about top quality lesbian fiction: a fantastic romance between two wonderful women I can relate to, a location that really made me think again about something I thought I knew well, and brilliant pacing and scene-setting. I cannot recommend this novel highly enough.

-Rainbow Book Reviews

Noyes totally blew my mind from the first sentence. I went in timidly, and I came away awaiting her next release with bated breath. I really love how Noyes is able to get below the surface of the DADT legislation. She really captures the longing, the heartbreak, and especially the isolation that LGBTQ soldiers had to endure because the alternative was being deemed unfit to serve by their own government. I applaud Noyes for getting to the heart of the matter and giving a very important representation of what living and serving under this legislation truly meant for LGBTQ men and women of service.

-The Lesbian Review

E. J. Noyes was able to deliver on so many levels... This book is going to take you on a roller-coaster ride of ups and downs that you won't expect but it's so unbelievably worth it.

-Les Rêveur

Noyes clearly undertook a mammoth amount of research. I was totally engrossed. I'm not usually a reader of romance novels, but this one gripped me. The personal growth of the main character, the rich development of her fabulous best friend, Mitch, and the well-handled tension between Sabine and her love interest were all fantastic. This one definitely deserves five stars.

-CELEStial books Reviews

Turbulence

Wow... and when I say 'wow' I mean... WOW. After the author's debut novel *Ask, Tell* got to my list of best books of 2017, I was wondering if that was just a fluke. Fortunately for us lesfic readers, now it's confirmed: E. J. Noyes CAN write. Not only that, she can write different genres... Written in first person from Isabelle's point of view, the reader gets into her headspace with all her insecurities, struggles, and character traits. Alongside Isabelle, we discover Audrey's personality, her life story and, most importantly, her feelings. Throughout the book, Ms. Noyes pushes us down a roller coaster of emotions as we accompany Isabelle in her journey of self-discovery. In the process, we laugh, suffer, and enjoy the ride.

-Gaby, *goodreads*

This was hot, steamy, even a little emotional...and I loved every second of it. This book is in first person. I know some don't care for that, but it works for this book, really. Always being in Isabelle's head, not knowing for sure what Audrey was thinking, gave me almost a little suspense. I just love the way Noyes writes. I know I am fan-girling out a bit here, but her books make me happy. All other romance fans, I easily recommend this. I just hope I don't have to wait too long for another Noyes book.

-Lex Kent's Reviews, *goodreads*

The entire story just flowed from the first page! E. J. Noyes did a superb job of bringing out Isabelle's and Audrey's personalities, faults, erratic emotions, and the burning passion they shared. The chemistry between both women was so palpable! I felt as though the writer drizzled every word she wrote with love, combustible desire, and intense longing.

-*The Lesbian Review*

Gold

This is Noyes' third book, and her writing just keeps getting better and better with each release. She gives us such amazing characters that are easy for anyone to relate to. And she makes them so endearing that you can't help but want them to overcome the past and move forward toward their happily ever after.

-The Lesbian Review

This book is exactly the way I wish romance authors would get back to writing romance. This is what I want to read. If you are a Noyes fan, get this book. If you are a romance fan, get this book. I didn't even talk about the skiing... if you are a skiing fan, get this book.

-Lex Kent's Reviews, *goodreads*

If the Shoe Fits

When we pick up an E. J. Noyes book we expect intensity, characters with issues (circumstantial and/or internal), and a romance that builds believably. Considering this is *Ask, Tell* #3 we expected all of the above layered with epic seriousness. We were pleasantly surprised and totally floored by the humor in addition to what was already expected!

-Best Lesfic Reviews

Go Around

Other Bella Books by E. J. Noyes

Ask, Tell
Turbulence
Gold
Ask Me Again
Alone
If the Shoe Fits
Reaping the Benefits
Pas de deux

About the Author

E. J. Noyes is an Australian transplanted to New Zealand, which may be the awesomest thing to happen to her. She lives with her wife, a needy cat, and too many plants (and is planning on getting more plants). When not indulging in her love of reading and writing, E. J. argues with her hair and pretends to be good at things.

Go Around

E. J. Noyes

BELLA
B O O K S
2021

Bella Books, Inc.
P.O. Box 10543
Tallahassee, FL 32302

Printed in the United States of America on acid-free paper.

First Edition - 2021

Editor: Cath Walker
Cover Designer: Kayla Mancuso

ISBN: 978-1-64247-325-4

PUBLISHER'S NOTE

Acknowledgments

Like so many people these past eighteen months or so, I've often found myself a little adrift, and trying to write novels with so much swirling around wasn't easy. I would never have produced anything if not for a bucketload of supportive pals and people who knew stuff and, most importantly, were happy to share that stuff with me.

Kate, thanks for being the best Pocket American a gal could ask for. Every time I wobbled, you were there, and I'm so grateful for your friendship and support.

Thanks to That Person who asked That Other Person questions about the Federal Air Marshal Service, and then thanks to That Other Person for answering the questions for me. Cryptic, no?

Claire, I often think nobody is as excited for my new works as you are, and that excitement is so vast that it takes away all my doubty feelings about works-in-progress.

Anna, thank you for answering all my random questions about LA and how TV stuff works. I'm ready for that drink when you are.

Cath, after nine books together, you've taught me so much—not only about how to make novels better, but how I work best. And I say, without hyperbole, that working with you is my favourite part of the writing process. Thanks for fixing this one when I couldn't.

Bella Crew! Copy and paste from all my previous book acknowledgments.

Pheebs… Oh boy, this year, hey? It would have sucked much without you by my side. Your endless patience, support, and love make the world keep spinning for me. You know I'd follow you anywhere, but I'm glad you didn't make me go too far. I lurve you.

CHAPTER ONE

Sloane Markwell's handgun was pointed at Kanzi's face. "You know how I feel about giving people second chances," she said, her tone conversational. "But after seeing how well you dealt with the shipment delay this week, I've…reconsidered." Her expression was mockingly benevolent, as if the man should recognize just how rare this second chance was and that he should be groveling in gratitude.

Kanzi swallowed, the irregular bob of his Adam's apple betraying the panic he kept from his face. After a quick moment of eye contact, he dropped his gaze. "Yes, boss. Thank you, boss."

"Good. Remember my kindness." Sloane's pale blue eyes were hard as she flicked her wrist, the gesture indicating in no uncertain terms that he should move and do it quickly. "Now get out of my sight."

Kanzi dipped his head in submission and after backing up a few steps, turned to walk away. His strides were short and quick, as if he expected her to shoot him in the back and was barely able to keep himself from sprinting away. A ridiculous fear. Everyone in Sloane Markwell's crew, hell, everyone in the city knew she would never do something as cowardly as shoot a man in the back.

The sound of Kanzi's shoes echoed through the warehouse as he rushed away from Sloane and the four men shadowing her. Nobody moved. Nobody spoke. Until Kanzi was halfway to the huge sliding doors that led out into the alley and Sloane called, "Kanzi?"

He stopped and slowly turned around, his eyes locked onto the suppressor Sloane was casually screwing into the barrel of her gun. Both Kanzi's hands came up to shoulder height. "Boss...I—" He laughed nervously. "C'mon."

"Yes," she mused, her mouth quirking sardonically. "I'm the boss. Which means I know *everything* that happens around here. And I know it was you who told the Carmichaels. That was dumb. I loathe worms. And now you're worm food." She raised the gun and fired two shots into his chest. Kanzi dropped to the floor and Sloane walked over to where he lay gasping and writhing on the concrete. She stood in the pool of blood spreading out from underneath him and fired another shot. Kanzi went still.

Sloane inhaled deeply, stared at the body for a few moments then gave a small nod as if satisfied. She spun to face the men. "Is anyone else feeling disloyal?" she asked, waving the pistol around. When none of them answered, she unscrewed the suppressor and holstered the gun on her hip. "No? Good. I've already ruined one pair of shoes tonight." She made a vague gesture with the suppressor before tucking it into an inner pocket of her designer leather jacket. "Get rid of that mess. And do it fast. We have a shipment coming in and I need to make myself presentable for my evening of...entertainment."

Sloane spun around and walked away through the high stacks of plastic-wrapped bricks filling the warehouse, the sound of her stilettos clicking sharply against polished concrete. The camera lingered on her ass then panned down to the three-inch heels that made her legs look out...of...this...world. She left a trail of bloodied footprints as she walked. Click, clack, click, clack. The screen went black.

My blinking feels too fast, like my brain can't process what I've just watched. The episode was so intense, so incredible that the only words circling through my brain at top speed are, "Holy shit." The usual next-episode trailer rolls, telling me *Greed* will return next week for its final episode of the year and promising things are going to get bigger, more exciting, and more dangerous. It seems Sloane Markwell, a.k.a. undercover LAPD detective Jessica Meares, has a problem with her handler-slash-partner. He's worried about her, worried she's too deep into her Sloane Markwell persona, and feels like he doesn't know who she is now.

I try to ignore that too-close-to-home sentiment to focus on the teaser of Meares' badass fight scene in the next episode. I wonder if she'll shoot her handler too and shed her detective skin once and for all to dive fully into her undercover drug-lord role. That would be an epic cliffhanger for the Christmas break.

Once the credits start rolling, I turn off the TV and lean over to Bennett who's lying in a dog bed by my feet. For a few moments I'm unable to say anything and when I finally manage words, all I get out is a rushed, "Holy fucking shit, Bennie. I cannot believe Meares just smoked Kanzi. I mean, he totally deserved it but I did *not* think she'd go through with it. That'll seriously complicate matters with the department. Like, it's homicide, even if she's undercover, right? Because it was so not self-defense. Fuuuck," I breathe. "So good."

Without raising his head resting on his massive paws, my Rottweiler-boerboel cross gives me his best side-eye. This time with a little eyebrow lift that clearly conveys he thinks I'm being dramatic and that he wishes I hadn't stopped rubbing my bare feet along his back and sides for scratchies. Bennett is used to my outbursts during our weekly viewings of *Greed*—the award-winning television drama about a vice detective who went undercover to infiltrate a drug ring, rose quickly through the ranks with the help of departmental arrests removing key players until she eventually took over the crew, and over the course of the past one and a bit seasons found her morals blurring at the edges.

Every Tuesday night when we watch the show together, I wonder if Bennett recognizes Meares-slash-Markwell. Or, as he knew her when he last saw her a year and three months ago— Elise Hayes.

Elise. Hayes. The woman who used to sneak Bennie morsels of prime steak while she was preparing it for my dinner. The woman who bought him his most favorite toy in the world, the rubber elephant. The woman who would drag him out in all weather for a walk because she insisted it was good for both their mental health. The woman who thought he should be allowed on the couch and our bed, because his super-duper comfy doggo beds weren't good enough, and who made this point repeatedly despite our agreement when Bennett arrived as a puppy that he was going to be far too big to fit comfortably and I wanted to sleep, not squirm around one hundred and sixty pounds of dog all night. The woman who walked out on me and that dog because she wasn't ready to show the world she was in love with a woman.

Quick FYI? It's hard to get over your ex-girlfriend when your breakup came out of nowhere and you're still in love with her. It's even harder to get over her when you see her *everywhere* advertising the country's top-rated drama show and when said show is actually really damned good and you watch it every week. Apparently, I'm a glutton for punishment.

Bennett wouldn't understand what happened but I know he knew how miserable I was in the months following the breakup. My huge dog is a huge baby and when I was in my post-breakup funk he turned into an even huger baby, probably due to my general meh mood and because Elise was his second mom and he loved her. Maybe he still does. I know I do, even though I know how pathetic it is to be in love with your ex, especially when you've accepted what happened and moved on. Kind of.

I finish my drink and after upending the glass into the dishwasher come back to find Bennett still in his bed by the couch with his head on his paws. When I indicate he should come to me, he stands and yawns then stretches first with a bow then one hind leg at a time. But he doesn't move toward me. It's his classic reaction to nighttime potty, like he thinks if he doesn't move then maybe I'm not serious and he can just go back to his bed.

"Bennie, come on. Time to put out the trash, and you need a walk." And I need to take a walk to shift my brain from Elise or I'm going to have weird and uncomfortable dreams about her all night, which sometimes happens after watching her show. My subconscious is a shit.

Bennett's slow approach is the epitome of *I was comfortable, do I really have to go outside?* I point at the door. "Yes, we're going out. I don't need you waking me up at three a.m. because you gotta go pee. I've got a full day of work tomorrow." I slip into laceless sneakers and clip the leash to his collar while my dog manages to make me feel like a monster. Yeah, Bennett, I get it. I'm the worst dog mom in the world for caring about your needs and health. I never wanted to be a dog mom but when my brother left his puppy with me almost five years ago, I was stuck with the gig.

Bennett makes a perimeter check for his nemesis, Mr. Opossum, and apparently deeming us safe from the beast, sits down to wait for me to put the trash out. I hook the handle of his leash over a fence paling so he won't get in my way while I deal with my eighty-two-year-old neighbor's bins. On top of one of Mrs. Obermeier's trash bins is a Tupperware container of baked goods, with AVERY written in Sharpie on the lid as if I wouldn't know it was for me. This week it's blondies. She knows my sweet spot. The weekly trash-for-treats is a good system, one we've had almost since I moved in and is maybe part of the reason I haven't moved out of my house of memories.

Once I've set two households' worth of trash out, I nab Bennett and with the Tupperware under an arm to load me with provisions for a mid-walk snack, we begin our usual nighttime route around the block so he can smell every single thing we pass before finally peeing. For a dog who tells me nightly how much he doesn't want to go out before bed, he really seems to enjoy going out before bed.

I hear a distant plane overhead climbing to cruising altitude after its departure from Los Angeles International Airport and make a mental note of tomorrow's workday. I've got a full day in the air, and waiting in airports, an out-and-back flying LAX to ORD return—what we call the seven-thirty-seven-thirty where we depart LAX at seven thirty a.m. and land back at LAX at seven thirty p.m. It'll be an ordinary day for those traveling around the country. Just as it is for me every time I step into a plane cabin to keep those on board, and those on the ground, safe.

We loop past the park and onto the main street and while Bennie is preoccupied with a tree, a yellow hydrant and a bus shelter I sneak a blondie out and eat half in one bite. I've just tucked the Tupperware back under my arm when a truck roars past, the wind catching the hair half-heartedly pulled into a ponytail and sticking it to my face. I turn away from the street and spot something new on the bus shelter. They've changed the poster and now it's an ad for *Greed*. My ex-girlfriend looks like a million bucks and is holding what looks like a million bucks. Sigh. I really can't escape her.

I almost choke on the remainder of the blondie I'd stuffed into my mouth to hide it from Bennett and with cheeks bulging, try to chew and swallow while juggling a baggie of dog shit and the Tupperware while I pick bits of hair from my mouth. If anyone saw me now? Well, let's just say…thanks, universe, for reminding me who is doing better after the breakup.

CHAPTER TWO

The scene outside Chicago O'Hare is miserable and threatening a storm. I cross my fingers that the weather doesn't worsen and delay my flight back to LA. Not only have I sat in the lounge on my laptop for a very boring three hours, but I promised Bennett we'd go for an evening run when I got home. To him, my promise is more of a threat and he's probably doing some doggo rain dance to ensure delayed flights. If Bennett were human, let's just say he'd spend more time in the weights room than on the treadmill. In addition to my run plans, I've had a long and tiring day and after I shake the flights out of my body with some exercise I want to order pizza and fall asleep on the couch mid-PlayStation session.

My flight is called and I send my usual thanks to every deity responsible for getting flights away on schedule. Sorry, Bennett, but we're going for a run. I take my place at the front of the line for priority boarding and check I look somewhat presentable. As I shuffle forward, I fiddle with the small leather wallet that holds my Federal Air Marshal Service ID, ready to discreetly show it and my boarding pass to the crew member admitting passengers. They'll already know who I am and the crew in the cockpit will be aware I'll be on board.

My professional and objective opinion is that the Southern Air cabin crew are the hottest of all the airlines I fly with regularly. At the aircraft door, the attractive early-thirties woman who checks my boarding pass and sights my FAMS ID doesn't betray by a look or word that she knows who I am or that she's expecting me. After she murmurs something to the captain and first officer, both turn around to get a look at me and I get a dual nod in response. With a broad smile, the flight attendant directs me to my seat, offers me a drink—which I decline—then moves on to let the rest of the passengers board.

This flight, I'm up front in first instead of back in coach and while I get comfortable for another four and a half hours in a plane seat, I sneakily scan the cabin and boarding passengers to make sure nobody stands out and there's nothing making my gut feel off. Everything seems normal. Already winning. I catch the eye of a greasy, balding businessman seated across the aisle from me. He leers, his eyes lingering on my breasts before his gaze comes up to mine so he can be sure I've noticed what he's done. Oh, I noticed. When I refuse to look away, as he'd probably expected a woman to do, he squirms and fakes rummaging around in the seat compartment in front of him. I return to pretending to read the emergency instructions card.

He's a creepy asshat, sure. But a terrorist? Unlikely.

The plane is three-quarters boarded, and I've swapped the emergency card for a book I won't read during the flight, when I hear a familiar voice at the cabin door laughing and joking with the cabin crew. Oh god. The voice sends a cold shudder down my spine and an unexpected rush of adrenaline dampens my armpits. Onscreen, Elise sounds different to the way she does in the flesh—her normal speaking voice is lower and lazier, almost drawly—but I'd know the sound of her anywhere.

I haven't heard her in person for over a year and the sound of that honeysuckle voice sends a rush of memory through me. It's the voice asking me to buy strawberries while I'm at the store, calling down the hall to ask if I want coffee, laughing because her hair has tangled in her sweater again and she needs my help, or cuddling me from behind as I made breakfast exactly the way she loved it. It's intimately familiar to me as the voice of a woman underneath me, straddling me, on top of me. It's the voice that begged me to make her come and then told me how much she loved fucking me and that it'd never been like this with men. And it's achingly familiar as the disembodied voice from the other side of our bedroom door, telling me she was sorry she couldn't be who I wanted her to be and apologizing for her weakness.

I scrunch down into my seat, lift my book a little higher and turn slightly away from the aisle. I'm desperately hoping she hasn't seen me but then that familiar voice is the surprised one to my left asking, "Avery?"

I look up, trying to pretend that I'm stunned to see her and not like I'd known she'd boarded the moment I'd heard her talking at the door. But she's the actress, not me, and I'm sure she sees right through me. Mercifully, I sound normal and not squeakily panicked when I say, "Hey, Elise. How are you?"

The smile my ex-girlfriend gives me is genuine, not the false one I've seen her throw out thousands of times to others. Her smile always made my insides do funny little flip-flops and now is no different. She takes off her sunglasses, the way she always does when she wants to be polite so people can see her eyes during a conversation, and tucks the glasses into the neckline of her boat neck top. Her eyes, a clear pale blue like water from a glacier, shine with excitement. "I'm really good. You? You... look great."

That small gesture of her removing her sunglasses pleases me and then my pleasure annoys me because I shouldn't be pleased about her being polite to me. I shouldn't care. I make myself return her smile though it probably doesn't seem as genuine as hers. "I'm..." Confused, shocked, annoyed, upset and a million other emotions. "...fantastic."

"I'm glad to hear it," she says. She sounds sincere. After a pause Elise points to the window seat on my right. "This is me."

You have got to be fucking kidding. The irony is amazing.

Since the breakup, I've been on more flights than I can count and had thought my odds of not seeing her on a flight ever again had risen to *pretty good*. And here she is, not only on my flight but seated right next to me and flying from Chicago of all places. We met when we were seated next to each other on a flight from Chicago a little over six years ago, back when she was bit-parting in television shows and starring in a few small-budget movies and still photo modeling and half-heartedly dating guys. As soon as she'd buckled herself in, she'd leaned close and admitted she's a nervous flyer and talking helped her forget about her fear of falling from the sky. Then she'd added an apology for the fact that I was her captive audience for the flight.

And I'd forgotten my usual self-consciousness around beautiful women and told her I wouldn't mind being her captive audience, that I flew regularly for work and could tell her all the weird noises and bumpy bits which were just part of flying and that I wouldn't mind talking her through it. Elise had gripped my arm like it was a lifeline through takeoff and leveling out and when she finally let go, I felt like she'd taken part of me with her. Fighting the unsettling sensation, I'd prompted her to tell me about herself. The stream of consciousness that spilled out had me hanging on her every word. We talked—or rather she talked and I mostly just listened—about music, books, movies including her movies and the bit part roles she'd had on television, her picture modeling and how her modeling agent had wanted her to do runway work but her legs were apparently disproportionately short for that type of full-body work.

She'd patted her legs as if thanking them for saving her from the runway. My gaze had strayed to those legs and I'd swallowed hard and pondered how someone might think them too short when they were fucking magnificent. A few weeks later that opinion was solidified. And in the weeks and months and years that followed I realized those magnificent legs were the perfect length to wrap around my waist when I had her on the kitchen table.

When she'd finally relaxed enough to stop blathering, she asked what I did. I told her I owned a software company—dressed in jeans, scuffed cowboy boots, a gray tee and blazer, the lie worked. I looked like the casual nerd who grew wealthy but never outgrew my wardrobe.

After we'd settled into a solid relationship and were living together, I'd had to come clean and we laughed and joked about how good an actor I was. Elise had shyly asked me to teach her to shoot and some basic self-defense to help her prep for those kinds of action-based roles. Now, every time I watch an episode of *Greed* and see how comfortably she handles firearms or engages in some staged fight, I mentally pat myself on the back.

Grinding my molars together helps dispel those memories and brings me back to this moment which may be the most awkward of my life. I dog-ear my page, stand and move into the aisle to let her slide into the window seat. Her arm brushing against mine makes me shiver. She's changed her perfume, thank god. Even now, the passing scent of *D&G Light Blue* on a woman has me surfing a wave of longing that's quickly followed by a wave of nausea that dumps me sprawling on the beach.

Once I'm seated and buckled in again, I pick up my book and deliberately open it, smoothing out the bent corner. Elise laughs and stows her handbag under the seat in front. It's the same everyday handbag she had when we were dating—a huge, butter-soft red leather tote that seems like it fits half her possessions in it. "I see you still don't know how to use a bookmark."

I spare her a glance and a smile. "It's a waste of paper." She knows my opinion on bookmarks. Waste of paper aside, I always lose them. Except the one she made me, a piece of cardboard with a dragon that she drew on it, which is in a drawer in my house. It's special and I never put it in a book. I don't know why I didn't toss it out.

She opens her mouth like she's about to start our old teasing argument about me ruining books, then quickly closes it again. I can almost see the thoughts passing through her mind until she settles on how it's not for her to tell me how to live my life anymore. We sit quietly as people file past and get seated, and after a few minutes, she sighs. The sound is a whisper, almost as though she tried to hold it back but failed. "You'd think I'd be used to it by now, but I still don't like flying." The admission is quiet, like she doesn't want anyone to hear her admit this weakness, even someone who knows more of her weaknesses than just this one fear.

A nicer person would probably take their ex's hand, pat her arm or try to soothe her with kind words, but my limbs are leaden and my tongue too big for my mouth. I make a noncommittal *hmmm* sound. The cabin is getting noisy and on top of the usual sounds of people moving through the aisles and taking seats, is an odd stop-start of people talking, recognizing Elise, pausing their conversation, then picking it back up again. It makes the air hum with a weird, disjointed vibe and adds ten levels to my discomfort.

But nobody approaches her and I'm glad for this small mercy. She'd have to lean over me to sign whatever was being offered or take a photo with the fan and then she might touch me and I couldn't stand it. Unasked, a memory of her touching me lingers in my thoughts. The first time when she was so sweet and tentative. And then she was bold and adventurous and wonderfully insatiable.

I'm unsurprised by the faint hint of arousal her presence has elicited. Not wanting her was never the problem. Even at the end when it was all falling apart, I still wanted her. Maybe I wanted her a little too much and more than she wanted me. Maybe her manager's suggestion that dating a *civilian* wasn't good for her image, especially not when I was a woman, was just a convenient excuse to dump me. These thoughts aren't helpful and I shove them aside.

"You're working?" Elise asks quietly.

I don't look up from my book. "Yep." Suddenly everything feels wrong in the place I always feel right. In this seat, I know my place and my purpose but now I'm adrift. I pull my attention away from the page and am startled that the first-class cabin is almost full and the captain is making his announcements. My job is to pay attention and she has me so off-kilter that I've failed my most basic task.

Elise shifts and crosses her legs, bouncing her foot. Luckily, she's in jeans and boots and not a dress or skirt. If I saw her legs, I'd probably say something that's inappropriate to say to your ex. She really does have fantastic legs. I force myself to not look at them. Elise pulls two hairbands from her wrist and drags masses of curly, shoulder-length chestnut hair up into a loose topknot, her elbow bumping my shoulder as she fixes her hair. She hasn't changed her hair product and the scent of it hits me like a gut punch.

She's unusually silent for the taxi and takeoff, though she's gripping the armrests like they're keeping her from melting to the floor. As the plane begins to level, she murmurs, "Thank fuck." Elise releases her grip on the seat fractionally. "I would give half my paycheck for someone to invent a fast way of traveling that's not flying."

I can't help asking, "Why are you in Chicago?" It's weird for her to be away from her home in Los Angeles. Or at least I assume she still lives in LA because I know *Greed* films there.

Her eyebrows shoot up, perhaps at my question or that I'm speaking to her without prompting. "Final chemistry test for an indie part I'm chasing. The director is based in Chicago and she hates Hollywood so everyone has to go to her. And every time I've been, she throws a dinner party." Elise smiles self-deprecatingly. "I'm a little hungover. My manager had the good sense to make an excuse and fly home last night."

She doesn't look hungover. She looks flawless as ever with her face bare of makeup, except for her ever-present eyeliner. Without makeup, the smattering of freckles across her nose and cheeks is exposed and this reminder of her as My Elise instead of Superstar Elise makes my stomach ache. On camera they cover up her freckles which I've always thought odd. She needs nothing covered up. Elise's features are delicate yet bold and sometimes when I'd look closer at her, it felt like none of them should fit together to make such a perfect picture. But they *do* fit, making an unmistakable beauty.

If you search for a stock image of Beautiful Woman, it'll be Elise. If you search for a stock image of Scandinavian Woman, you'll see me—blond and blue-eyed, pale skin, average face, average height, nothing remarkable. In the beginning I couldn't understand how someone who looked like Elise was interested in someone who was just regular like me. It didn't take long to realize she's the epitome of the cliché "It's what's on the inside that counts." She's a good person—kind, warm, funny, caring, passionate—who happens to be wrapped in an incredibly attractive package. A good person who couldn't be honest with the world. And I still can't make those pieces of the puzzle of our breakup fit in any logical place.

I loathe awkward silences and after a few moments of deliberation, decide spending the flight avoiding speaking with or looking at her is going to take far more effort than if I just get over it for a few hours. I chance a look at her and realize she's already looking at me. Her caught-in-the-act expression makes me smile. "Congrats on the Emmy."

"Thanks." Elise doesn't feed me the usual bullshit spiel you'd hear in an interview or the like, about what an honor it was just to be nominated. Instead, she laughs softly and leans closer to whisper, "Totally didn't think I'd get it. I mean, I was nominated with Margie Emmy-Golden-Child Hament and my nomination was for first-season work. Those wins are super rare, even for amazing shows like *Greed*." There's no smugness, only pride, when she says *amazing*. She should be proud.

"I don't watch it," I say airily. "I just saw the Emmy thing in the news." It's the hugest of lies, obviously. I've watched the show every week since its premiere and not because I'm hung up on Elise but because at first I was curious about it and she's a phenomenal actress. Of course, irony meant I discovered from the pilot that I really liked the show. A drama about a kickass female undercover detective leading a crime organization and her growing moral struggle—what's not to like? Plus there's the clothes the wardrobe department drapes her in. Part of me hates it, part of me can't help remembering when she'd dress up for me.

"Oh." She studies me for a moment, then glances down at her hands. "Avery, can we talk?" she asks the seat in front.

"We are talking," I remind her and deliberately turn the page of the book I'm still not actually reading.

Elise doesn't answer, so I look at her. The moment we make eye contact, she does the eyebrow raise thing that always makes my stomach do a slow excited roll. It's withering and exasperated and playful all bundled up in one eyebrow movement that requires no words to get her meaning across. "You know what I mean," she says.

Of course I do, but... "I don't think there's anything to discuss and even if there was, here's not the time or place. And besides—" I gesture vaguely to where she'll know my pistol is holstered and lower my voice to just above a whisper. "I'm working, remember?"

Despite my assertion, she keeps pushing at me. "Maybe I could call you, or we could meet up for coffee and just...talk? I feel like we never really talked about what happened."

I almost laugh at that obvious statement. We absolutely didn't talk about it—she told me how it was and then left. I was nothing more than a bystander. But I don't laugh. I can't do anything but stare at her.

Elise exhales lengthily and her voice drops until it's barely audible. "I miss you. So much."

Exasperated at her persistence and seeming cluelessness, I drop my book onto the tray. The sound bounces off the cabin walls and I sense people looking at me. I ignore them to blurt, "Jesus, would you just fucking drop it? Please."

Elise gapes and her face changes from shocked to hurt to angry in the space of three seconds.

Within moments, a female flight attendant appears, leaning over me to talk to Elise. "Is everything all right, Ms. Hayes? If you're bothered, I'm sure we can arrange another seat for you." She shoots me a dirty look, as though this whole thing is my fault. "The first-class cabin is a little full but I'm certain we can find a way to accommodate you comfortably for the rest of the flight." The unspoken meaning is clear—is the angry woman causing problems for you, Ms. Celebrity? This one must have been in the galley during boarding and doesn't know who I am.

Before Elise answers, she graces me with an expression I know all too well. It's her *Oh boy, can you believe this person?* look. For the briefest moment it's as though we've gone back fifteen months, and if we stepped back in time and were alone, she'd be rolling her eyes and we'd be laughing about it. But we haven't, and we aren't, so we don't.

Elise needs to do damage control, lest someone recognize this for what it is—an ex-lover's tiff, with another woman. When Elise looks up at the flight attendant the transformation of her expression is instant. I've forgotten how quickly she can switch personalities when she needs to. Her voice gets higher, softer and her body language changes to openness, drawing the woman in. "Oh no, it's perfectly fine. Just engaging in a hearty political debate with my seatmate," she lies, smooth as anything. She offers a bright smile and something unexpected. "Turns out I'm wrong. But thank you so much for your concern."

It's interesting watching her lie because she never lied to me. Every moment we spent together she was the real Elise, and that was the issue and where all our problems had begun. The real Elise was afraid to come out and despite her talent she could no more pretend otherwise than I could have won an Emmy.

I sigh inwardly, knowing someone is probably already spilling sneaky photos and captions all over Twitter, Instagram, and Facebook. By the time we've landed, every form of social media will have me listed as "Antagonistic Political Activist" or something equally inane. I'll be demonized and ridiculed as the woman who argued with Elise Hayes on a flight from Chicago to LA. Oh well. I can deal with that. A quick glance around tells me that, surprisingly, nobody is photographing us. A small mercy. The last thing I need or want is attention.

Elise, on the other hand, likes attention. The only thing she wouldn't like would be if someone reported that she'd been seen kissing a woman. Her biggest fear, greater even than flying, is being found out as someone who is attracted to women. When we started dating it wasn't really an issue, but apparently with great success comes great closeting.

I want to tell this Barbie Doll leaning over me to mind her own business. Point out how intimately I know the woman beside me. But I can't. If nothing else, I've always respected Elise's fear, her need for privacy, and her almost desperate desire to hide that part of herself. I don't agree with it but I would never betray her, even when it's been the cause of all my angst for the past fifteen months.

I hold my tongue and plaster my best contrite look on my face. An apologetic non-apology. Then I ask for coffee to make the attendant go away. Elise stretches her legs out then draws them back to rest her feet flat on the floor. There's plenty of space, but she seems cramped and uncomfortable. I know it has nothing to do with me being beside her and everything to do with flying. Or maybe it really is me that's making her uncomfortable.

Her white-knuckled grip on the armrests has returned and pulls some of my anger away. I almost touch her. But it's not for me to calm her now and not for me to touch her in public. Slowly, the tension seems to drain from her and she reaches down to collect a fat stack of papers from her handbag. From the corner of my eye I recognize it as a script and it takes all my self-control to not peek at it, in case it's a script for *Greed*. We sit in silence except to talk to the flight attendants who are certainly paying Elise more attention than any other passenger. Every now and then, Elise changes position and apologizes for touching me. I want to tell her it's fine and make a joke about how much we used to touch, just to break the tension. But I can't.

She said she wanted to talk, presumably about things we did a lifetime ago, what she did, and I wonder why *now*? Why not *then* when it really mattered? We've made it almost three-quarters of the way through this hellacious flight when Elise turns slightly sideways to face me. She nudges me with her knee. "Avery?"

"Yeah?"

"I'm sorry." She puts her hand on mine. I stare at the contrast of her tanned Mediterranean heritage against my paler skin. So much about us contrasted but it's part of why we worked so well. Until we didn't. That's not entirely true; we always *worked* but we couldn't make it work. I didn't want to be in the dark for the rest of my life and she wouldn't step into the light with me. The hand withdraws as if my skin burns her. "I shouldn't have pushed."

"Mmm." I want to say more but there's really no point. And even if I wanted to, there's no space here for us.

A person looms over me and after a moment of their hovering, I look up and raise my eyebrows. He's the pale, early-twenties guy seated a row back and across the aisle in the window seat. He's gotten up to use the lavatory twice and been in his backpack three times. He ignores me to address Elise. "Excuse me, Ms. Hayes?" His voice is unusually deep and doesn't seem to match his youthful face. Sweat beads at his hairline and a droplet is trying to slide down his jaw. I almost snicker at how nervous he is.

Elise glances up from the script, an automatic smile already fixed in place. "Yes?"

He waves his phone around and he's clearly trying hard to keep his voice from shaking. He's not having much luck. "I'm so sorry to bother you, but would you mind taking a photo with me?"

Elise gives him her red-carpet smile. "Of course, I'd be happy to." She sets the script back into her handbag and unbuckles her seat belt. "What's your name?"

"Troy. Troy Bridges." His voice lifts hopefully at the end. "I'm a huge fan of yours." His earlobes and neck are bright red.

"Well thank you, Troy. That's very sweet of you." Elise looks to me, her left eyebrow lifted.

I suppress an eye roll and stand up so she can pass to take a photo with him or sign whatever it is he wants signed or hear about how much he loves her show and the movies she's been in and blah blah blah. When we were together, knowing Elise had fans from her film and modeling work never bothered me, but it's boring when you're the uninvolved party. And here I am again somehow, uninvolved and bored. I'm going to the restroom, otherwise I'll have to stand around looking like an idiot until they are done. If I want to use the first-class lavatory up the front near the galley, I'll have to scoot past Elise and her fan so I decide to take a walk to the back of the plane and see what's what.

After quickly confirming nothing's amiss, I dawdle back up front. When I open the curtain to the first-class cabin, Elise and Fanboy are still talking but she's moved slightly back so she's standing where my legs would be. I hear her dry, uncertain laugh and know exactly what it means. He's made a suggestive comment and she's uncomfortable about it but won't be rude and tell him to fuck off. Sometimes she's far too nice for her own good. We used to laugh that she needed to go to classes to learn to be more of a bitch.

Elise looks away from her fan, her eyes sweeping the space until she finds me. She holds eye contact with me for a few seconds, then turns it back to the guy, and then back to me again. I can read her expression, know the nuance in the lift of her right eyebrow and the way her eyes widen. I know everything about her and right now, she's asking me something that she never asked me. She's asking me for help, for me to bail her out, and the unspoken question in her expression is as serious as I've ever seen her.

I rush forward and when I'm about five feet away, the guy says something in a low hiss and grasps her forearm. Elise tries to pull away but can't because he's still holding her in a tight grip. That's it. No physical contact if she doesn't want it. I don't care who he is, who she is, who she once was to me. He's touching her when she doesn't want to be touched.

He reaches into his pocket and my hand goes automatically to my holster, but just as I get my hand on my gun, he grabs Elise in a headlock and drags her out into the aisle and toward the front of the plane. He holds her in front of himself and she's flailing, digging her heels in, trying to grab the seats or someone's hand as she passes. But just as suddenly as she fought, she goes limp.

It takes me a moment to realize why she's stopped fighting. Why everyone seated near the front of the plane is getting out of their seats and moving away. Why her eyes are wide with fear when they find mine again. He has something in his hand, pressed into the soft, beautiful skin of her neck, right at the place I've put my lips a thousand times. The spot that makes her groan when I run my tongue over it.

"I have a knife," he snarls.

Wonderful.

CHAPTER THREE

A thousand things barrel through my mind, the thoughts crashing into each other, bleeding together and making it hard to concentrate. I inhale slowly, hoping the influx of air will help me reset and focus. I see plastic in his fist, but not the blade which must be lying flat against the inside of his forearm. Smart. He can use the pressure of his arm to keep the blade against Elise's neck. But how the fuck did he get a blade past pre-flight security?

An ordinary pair of small craft scissors would maybe have caught a TSA agent's notice but remarkably aren't prohibited for carry-on. A broken-off ceramic knife blade could be carried on his person and probably not set off scanner alarms, but it can't be that because I see plastic. So it seems someone in the Transportation Security Administration fucked up on a day they really shouldn't have fucked up.

He's pulling her back into him which is forcing her up on her toes to get away from the pressure of his arm and the blade at her neck. The way he's holding her is blocking me from getting a clear shot. I drop my hand, leaving my gun holstered.

I've always trusted my instincts and right now they tell me he's going to freak out and do something stupid if he sees a gun. If I need to, I can draw it in a split second.

The flight attendants have herded everyone out of the first-class cabin and closed the curtain behind us, hiding us from view of the rest of the plane. Thank god Southern Air has a solid bulkhead and thick curtain separating the cabin classes so what I'm doing up here won't be seen by everyone on the plane. I hear one of the cabin crew, the younger first-class attendant, on the phone informing the cockpit of what's going on in first. There's anxious chattering in the cabin behind the curtain and the flight attendants are trying to calm everyone.

Those are the things I know. Now I need to know more. I have to set aside Elise and concentrate on the things I've spent years training for. She looks petrified, and even from here I can hear her ragged, gasping breathing. She won't stop looking at me and her eyes are so wide and I can't think about her as *Elise*. She's just a hostage and if she's wounded or killed in service of me saving a planeload of people then that's what has to happen because she's not the priority but fuck she is a priority and I can't think like this.

Is he a decoy and something serious is about to go down on this plane? My gut says no but I still turn slightly sideways so I can see anyone who might approach from the back of the plane. Here, it's just me, Elise, and him. Elise. Elise... I can't think about her. I don't discard her but put her safely into a compartment in my brain where I know she's there, needing my consideration, but where she's not going to distract me.

I hold my hands slightly in front of myself and near my sides. "Hey there. Why don't you calm down and tell me what's up, uh...Troy?" I creep closer and closer with each word but keep enough distance so he won't be spooked. A quick glance over each of my shoulders confirms nobody's approaching from behind.

He's talking too quietly for me to make out his words, but whatever he's saying has Elise panicked. Or even more panicked than she already is, considering someone has her at knifepoint.

"Troy?" I ask quietly.

Finally, he answers. "What?" When he looks at me, the thing that strikes me most is how normal he looks now. His nervousness has melted away. He's not crazed or agitated. He's calm and methodical, like this plan of his is going exactly as he wants.

I need to be calm and methodical too so I can disrupt his plan. "I think you're making this woman uncomfortable. If you tell me what you want, maybe we can work something out."

"She's mine. I want her." He frowns and adjusts his statement. "We do. She's going to be ours."

Mine. Ours. I chew the words over and after a few moments realize with horror this isn't random. He wants Elise. *Wants her.* It clicks into place like zooming Tetris blocks. She's not his, not at all. Knowing Elise as I do, seeing her interact with him earlier and watching this scene, I know there's *no* way she's willingly participating in any of this. He's having a delusional fantasy about being in a relationship with Elise.

When she was just getting started with *Greed*, Elise told me about the interaction primer she'd been given to teach her how to deal with overzealous fans, stalkers, and those who fall into unrealistic fantasies about relationships they think they have with celebrities. She'd laughed and told me, "As if I'm ever going to be famous enough for that to happen."

And I'd replied immediately, "Everyone is going to absolutely love you."

Well, Elise, seems it's happened. And I wish to hell I hadn't said that.

I make eye contact with Troy and keep my voice as blandly neutral as I can. "Yours? She's your girlfriend? This isn't a very nice way to treat her. Why don't you let her go and you guys can go back to your seats and talk calmly about it? What do you want?"

"Maybe it's not *nice*, but maybe she'll listen to me now. I'm sick of her ignoring my letters and emails." He drags Elise back another few steps and she emits a sound like a shriek and a cough in one. His left arm is around her waist, his right around her neck to keep the blade against her skin. He's still holding her so she's blocking every clear torso shot I could make, not that I think he's factored someone like me into his plan. He's just doing what he can to control her and the situation, and to him I'm probably just an annoying, meddling thorn in his shoe.

I could go for the headshot but I can't risk now being the time my top one percent of all Federal Air Marshal's marksmanship fails me. If it was anyone else, and this was more than just a celebrity fan incident, I might consider it. But it isn't, so de-escalation it is. Judging by the hand the blade is in, he's right-handed. His forearm is slender, but dances with lean muscle. He's about two inches taller than Elise's five-nine which means he's four inches taller than my five-seven. But he's not solid, not ripped, more big-cat lean and lithe.

"Troy?" I ask again, "What do you want?"

"When they land the plane, we're just going to walk away and nobody is going to bother us."

Yeah, that's not going to fucking happen, buddy. "Okay. Why don't you just ease up here and let this woman go and I can maybe tell a flight attendant to talk to the captain to make sure he knows you and your…friend aren't to be bothered."

"Good. Do that." His words are punctuated with jerks of the arm around her waist.

Elise squeaks and he snarls something in her ear. My eyes are fixed on the plastic handle in his hand and I can't stop the vision playing out in my mind where he cuts her, of her neck being sliced open and arcs of blood spraying out. But if he wants her to leave with him then logic dictates he doesn't want to hurt her. Yet. But he might slip and cut her or I might fuck this up and she might get killed or hurt and fuck I can't think about this.

Elise opens her mouth as if to say something but I shake my head very slightly to try and tell her not to talk. Do not engage him. Please pay attention to me, Elise. She blinks very slowly and I know she's understood what I've tried to tell her without words.

I take another small step closer. "Right. But I think the captain is more likely to do what you want if he's not worried about one of his passengers being harmed. So why not let her go and you two can sit in the front row just over there until we get things squared away."

"No."

That was pretty much the answer I expected. Elise is the only leverage he has and he's not just going to give her up. But if I want to get control of this clusterfuck then I need to get her away from him. To get her away from him, I need to shift his focus to me and the only way I can think of to make myself a target is to insult her. If he's deluded about this *relationship* he thinks he has with her then me telling him Elise is nobody special should piss him off big-time. So...I'm going to have to lie about how boring and ordinary Elise is.

I feign nonchalance. "What's so great about her?" I force the ridiculous thoughts from my head, the ones that spool out to list everything I know to be special about Elise. The only thoughts I should have right now are how I'm going to win this.

His jaw goes slack with disbelief then hardens to determination. "This is Elise Hayes. Emmy Award winner? Star of the number-one show in the country? Only the greatest actress of this century." Each word is matter-of-fact, underscored by a hard edge of conviction, and unfortunately punctuated with a press of the blade at her neck that makes Elise flinch.

"Ohhhh." I lean a little closer and fake a squint. "Elise Hayes from that show...what's it called? Umm...*Greed*? Hmm, I thought she looked familiar. Kind of. She's not that attractive in real life though, probably why I didn't recognize her." I make a point of staring at Elise, hoping she knows how much I'm lying. Her mouth twitches.

Troy mumbles something I don't catch but that sounds like he thinks I'm the worst person for not knowing who Elise is. I take another step forward. I'm still too far away. "You want *her*? I mean, she's not a very good actress." I hold up my hands like I'm apologizing. "No offense, Ms. Hayes." I know Elise will forgive me for disagreeing with his assessment that she's the greatest actress of this century. She's incredible, but she's no Hepburn or Streep or Hayworth or Dench.

"Shut up," Troy snarls.

I bulldoze forward, unfortunately only with my words. "Come on, I mean that episode where Meares-slash-Markwell and Oliver had that showdown?" The laugh I force is dry and appropriately humorless. "Didn't believe it for a second. She's supposed to be this badass detective pretending to be a badass drug lord and she can't even control some random piece of shit trying to undermine her and turn people against her in her organization."

Elise's mouth falls open. Yeah, okay, you caught me. I watch the show. Every single fucking episode. "And yeah, I mean she's not short, but she's tiny. There's *no way* she'd be able to take down all those burly guys." I try not to think about the fact that she's stronger than she looks and can effortlessly reverse our positions to flip me onto my back and ride me.

Troy's jaw bunches. "Shut. Up! You fucking shut up."

I don't. "And those skanky clothes she wears? Makes her look like a slut, not a badass crime boss. I mean, it's no surprise why they hired her, right? I guess she doesn't have enough star power to speak up about those outfits." I refuse to drop eye contact, willing him to focus the weapon on me. Come on, come on. I shrug and try to drive it home. "I just don't believe it. And when you add all that to her mediocre acting skills…" I raise both hands as if indicating my case is rested.

Finally, he does what I want, the arm around her neck loosening as he repeats, "Shut up!"

Not a chance. I try not to look at Elise's neck, afraid I might see she's bleeding. "Okay, sorry. I mean, I'm just trying to understand why you want someone who's not even *that* pretty." It's one of the biggest lies I've ever told. Elise is a fine wine that only gets better with each passing day. Hers is a beauty to be painted—straight nose, aristocratic chin, arching cheekbones, full sensuous mouth, the perfect curves of eyebrows over bright blue eyes that could never hide any emotion from me. Deliberately, I avoid looking into those eyes. If I look, I know I'll see all her emotion there and I'm going to lose my focus. I'm going to think about the consequences of fucking this up.

The muscles in the forearm wrapped around Elise's body tighten. "You shut your fucking whore mouth." He releases his grip from around her neck and points the blade in my direction. It's then I realize there is no blade, it's just a narrow plastic ice scraper. "You're a fucking idiot, you—"

It takes a millisecond to grab my baton, flick it to full extension and crack down on his wrist. The moment he drops the scraper I lunge, grab that arm and step behind him to wrest the arm up and into his back. I keep pressing, keep twisting his shoulder and elbow and wrist into an unnatural position until he cries out and releases Elise. The moment I know she's free, I drop him to the ground.

Elise makes a sound as she falls too, a grunt and a shriek rolled into one gut-wrenching noise. But I can't do anything about her. Not right now. I have to get him away from her. Despite what must be obvious pain from me disarming him and his face smashing into the armrest on his way down, he's squirming, shouting, and cussing. I pin him facedown with my bodyweight and his arm locked in a hold behind his back as I growl into his ear, "Federal Air Marshal. Do not move."

Despite my command, he keeps squirming and I dig my knee into his kidney until that pain seems to override everything else and he's finally still. I want to pound his face into the floor over and over again until his face is broken and pulpy. I want to hurt him until he pisses himself and feels the same fear I do. But I don't. I cuff his wrists, drag him to his feet, and push him into a seat in the front row. His nose is bleeding, obviously broken. Naughty armrest…

"Sit," I growl. "If you open your mouth for any reason other than breathing, I'm going to gag you. If you move, I'll break your ankles. If you try anything at all that's not just *existing*, I'm going to shoot you. Do you understand?"

His eyes widen and after a long moment he nods. Perhaps that wasn't the wisest thing to say—if he reports me, I'll probably be disciplined. Right now, I don't care. He's crying, snot mingling with tears and the blood trickling from his broken nose. All his conviction and bravado have evaporated like a contrail in the summer sky. I imagine the wrist I whacked and maybe broke is quite painful with a handcuff around it, especially pulled behind his back. Too bad. The cabin seems to come alive like a beehive with crew members appearing from everywhere to assist.

I raise my voice above the noise. "I need restraints." Within a minute someone hands me the thick straps used for those who become belligerent in the sky. The female flight attendant who sighted my ID as I boarded helps me strap one around Troy's chest to pin him to the seat, another around his bicep and then the ankle restraints. I yank them extra tight but still check they won't cut off circulation. He's oddly still and compliant now. I don't know if he's shocked, scared, or seething.

When I'm sure he's not going anywhere I turn my attention to Elise who sits slumped on a seat across the aisle and a few rows back, while cabin crew flutter around her, trying to offer assistance. I pick up the piece of plastic and study it. The scraper edge seems sharper than normal which would have felt like a knife against her skin. I put it in my inner jacket pocket then part the small crowd using my elbows and a muttered, "Move please."

When I stand beside her, Elise looks up at me, blinking slowly as though she's a newly formed human trying to work out what eyes do. Elise is holding her neck and a thin stream of blood seeps through her fingers, but it's not enough to trickle down. It pools on her ring finger, running along it to her knuckle as though moving through an aqueduct. Those fingers I loved so much, the shape of them and their beautiful nails. Fingers that have touched every part of me. Fingers that have intertwined with mine and carried me away with her.

I place a hand on her shoulder, the other on top of the hand she has pressed to her neck. My voice softens from its earlier growl. "You're okay, Ellie. It wasn't a knife, just an ice scraper."

"I'm too scared to take my hand off it," she chokes out on a whisper. "It felt sharp like a knife. I can feel blood."

"It's okay, honey. I'm right here with you." I can't stop touching her. I lay my hand on her cheek, forcing her to look at me. "It's going to be okay," I promise. I say it over and over again, as though I could somehow make it so just by saying it.

"You called me Ellie," she whispers.

It's such an inane statement that it takes me a moment to work out why she's mentioned it. "What about it?"

"Nobody else ever called me that. Just you."

If we were anywhere else at any time else, I might tell her the reason only I call her Ellie is because she's only mine. A mid-forties woman materializes by my elbow, shouldering me out of the way as she explains, "I'm a medical doctor." Those four words ease the rage I feel at being roughly maneuvered away from Elise. The doctor glances around. "Someone get me a first aid kit, please."

Satisfied Elise is safe, I move to check Troy. Still handcuffed and restrained in the front seat, still breathing, still quiet. But his eyes are murderous. I'm sure mine are too and the moment he makes eye contact he looks away from me to the ground. My rage rises again and I'm certain if I wasn't in a public place, he'd be nothing more than an unconscious heap on the ground. The thought is both satisfying and frightening. I've never considered myself capable of such a thing, but I know now that I would do it. For Elise, I'd do it. Even when she's not mine anymore. I look away from him again, desperate to settle myself, and my gaze falls back on Elise.

I move to her, careful not to interfere with the doctor, and quietly ask, "What happened?"

Her breathing stutters in and out. "He was just talking to me, the usual creepy suggestive shit. When you came back he said he wanted me to come sit by him and when I said no thanks, that I had my own seat, he grabbed me by the hand and started dragging me. I tried to pull away but then he...he..."

Ellie's expression is one I've seen before and requires immediate action. I turn around. "She needs a barf bag, *right now*."

A flight attendant gets a bag in front of Ellie just in time and once she's done retching, Ellie flashes me a grateful look. I wonder how many people know that Emmy Award-winning actress Elise Hayes is a pain and adrenaline puker. Our second date, a hike to Switzer Falls, she fell on the way back to the car and badly twisted her ankle when we were a quarter mile from the trailhead. Sitting on a rock, staring at her swelling ankle and the bleeding grazed mess the trail had made of her knee and shin, she'd looked at me with an odd, white-faced expression. Before I could decipher the look, she vomited all over my shoulder while I'd been crouched in front of her.

Later in the week she joked that despite puking on me, and the fact I had to strap her ankle then piggyback her out in nothing more than a sports bra with my pack on my front, I'd still wanted to sleep with her. Because after we'd both cleaned up at my place after the hike, I'd done just that.

I blink the memory away.

The doctor is talking to Elise, her words calm and easy. I can't hear what she's saying but Elise nods, smiles shakily, and visibly relaxes. The doctor peels open a dressing and quickly replaces my ex's fingers with it. In the moment of changeover I see the slice on her neck isn't deep at all, just a scratch really. Still, she's injured and I'm outraged and scared.

I keep staring, waiting for a massive blood stain to appear. For her neck to burst open in a gush of bright red blood and kill her while I'm standing here helpless. But nothing happens. She's trembling, clutching a fresh barf bag as people fuss around her. The stewardess who thought I was pestering Elise won't stop looking at me, and her expression moves between awe, shock, and contriteness. She steps beside me and whispers in my ear that the pilots want to speak with me.

"Thanks. Can you tell them I'll be up there in a few minutes?"

She nods and goes toward the galley, presumably to phone the captain with my message. I double check Troy is secure then walk down the aisle to where Elise has been moved into the last seat of first class. She's been watching me approach and when I crouch beside the seat, she reaches for my hand, gripping it like she's afraid of being pulled away from me. "Hey."

"Hey." I squeeze her hand. "Everything's fine, Ellie. He's secure and he's not going to hurt you again. He can't even look at you from where he is. And if he says anything, even asking for a drink, I'm going to shove a sock in his mouth and duct tape his mouth closed. Real duct tape, not the soft and easily removed movie stuff."

That makes her smile, though it's more a quick acknowledgment of amusement rather than her relaxing. "Okay. Okay. Thanks." She's moved from trembling to shaking, her muscles twitching and jumping. "Are you staying here with me?"

"I can't, hon—" I catch myself before the unconscious endearment slips out. "I have to stay up there with him."

She pauses. "Sure, I understand."

"But you've got the doctor and the cabin crew will be with you to help you with whatever you need."

Elise buries her teeth in her lower lip. "Mhmm."

I bury the urge to kiss her forehead, to cup her face, to pull her against me. I want nothing more than to gather her in my arms and hold her close until she calms down. To tell her it's all okay and I'm here and I'm not going to leave her and she's safe. But I can't. I squeeze her shoulder and move away to check on my charge.

"What—" he begins, his voice thin and wavering.

I cut him off with a flat, "No. No talking. I will duct tape your mouth closed."

He opens his mouth as if to respond, then at my glare, presses his lips together again.

The doctor materializes by my side to check him out and agrees he's broken his nose. "Can we ice it?" she asks me.

"No. Sorry." Totally not sorry. He can breathe, he's fine.

Her lips set in a thin line, but she nods. The rules around this guy are my rules now. I address Troy Bridges. "I'm going to talk to the captain and if I hear you've misbehaved, there's going to be an issue. Am I clear?"

He pauses for a long moment then, with clear reluctance, nods.

After a quiet conversation with the captain, I agree we can continue on to LAX instead of trying to get clearance to land somewhere closer. It's not that much farther and a diversion with a plane full of people just to get this guy into lockup twenty minutes earlier is going to cause issues for the airline. Bridges is secure and quiet, I have control of him, and there's no reason to make the airline figure out what to do with a planeload of people dropped short of their destination, as the captain quietly reminds me in that "I don't want to have to explain why I cost the airline money" way I've seen before.

Most importantly, Elise doesn't need immediate medical attention. The thought of her needing *any* medical attention sends a fresh surge of unease through me. If she'd been injured I'd have demanded the pilots put the plane on the ground immediately, even if they had to land it in a cornfield. I suppress that demand, but not another. "I want local law enforcement there to meet me when we land and if they aren't I'm going to handcuff him to the landing gear and leave him there. And I don't care if someone takes off again with him still attached to the wheel."

The captain and first officer exchange a look. The captain nods. "I'll make the call."

"Thank you. And could you please ask the cabin crew to reallocate the first-class cabin throughout the rest of the plane." I don't want any of them seeing me taking him off the plane and making the connection to my role. "I'll let you know if I need anything else."

Bridges doesn't look at me when I sit next to him. A small mercy because the thought of his face makes me nauseated. I leave my seat belt unbuckled in case I need to move quickly, and finally rearrange my clothing which rumpled during the scuffle. The captain makes an announcement that there's been an on-board incident but everything is fine and we're on schedule to land as normal if everyone would return to their seats. He apologizes to those in first class who have to scatter themselves in coach for the remainder of the flight. I wish I could go back and sit with Elise who hates landings almost as much as takeoffs and who's undoubtedly also scared and upset. She has the doctor beside her, but does the doctor know how afraid she is and that the best way to keep her calm during a landing is to talk to her?

It's a smooth landing and reasonably short taxi for LAX, and the moment we're at the gate I stand up. "I'm going to unstrap you now. If you—"

"If I move you'll shoot me or duct tape me. I got it." Despite his situation he still manages to look withering.

Fucking smartass. I remove the straps keeping him pinned to the chair then drag him to his feet and pass him to the two burly law enforcement officers who came in the moment the cabin door opened. Once he's in their custody I take my laptop bag the flight attendant collected for me and turn back to see if I can spot Ellie. She's leaning out into the aisle, watching me. Her expression is unreadable but she raises her hand as if saying goodbye. Another goodbye. I make myself smile and wave before I exit the plane. And all I can think of is how I wish I'd told her…

It doesn't matter now.

CHAPTER FOUR

I'm put in a small, comfortable room that feels like a cross between an office and a hospital waiting room. A young poster boy for law enforcement brings me a cup of decent coffee and tells me the vending machine has been fritzed since last week so there are no snacks, sorry. He sounds almost distraught, like vending machine visits are the highlight of his day. I empathize.

I've informed Rowan, my direct supervisor, of the incident and he's promised to call back once he gets a preliminary report. There's nothing to do but wait until I'm needed for my statement, which means I'm stuck in this room with nothing to do but think. And I do just that. I go over and over what happened, trying to find a point at which I could have handled it differently. Every time, I come to the same conclusion—I couldn't have, not without escalating the situation or adding extra casualties. It was a good outcome, the perp is in custody and nobody is seriously hurt.

But Elise *was* hurt.

Elise. I can't stop thinking about her. I don't know if I should call her and check if she's okay, leave her alone, or what the hell to do. I don't know if she's here giving her statement or at a hospital or at home, wherever her new home is. I've almost decided on calling her when I remember I don't even know her number. She got a new one after our breakup and the only reason I know this is I tried to call her to let her know her mail kept arriving at my place. In the end I called Elise's manager, Sandra, who took care of it. I could call her manager now. She should remember me, "The reason for all her troubles," as she once labeled me. As if having a closeted client was the worst part of her job and I was somehow responsible for it.

That number is disconnected and a quick Google tells me Sandra is no longer in the talent-managing business but moved to Barbados last year. Interesting. And frustrating. I'm trying to figure out what more I can do when one of the law enforcement guys pokes his head into the room to tell me they're ready for me to give my statement about my arrest of Troy Bridges. Right. Work, not personal life.

By the time I've finished my interview and dealt with the masses of paperwork generated by taking someone into custody, it's almost eleven p.m. While I was waiting around, I used some apps to turn on lights in the house and release snack kibble from the auto-feeder to tide Bennett over until I can get home. But I haven't managed to get myself anything for dinner. My stomach has long passed growling or nausea and is now just an empty well that reminds me I haven't had anything but coffee since the lounge waiting for my flight from Chicago.

I take a twenty-minute detour to my comfort food truck to grab a burrito, and eat it one-handed while driving home, ignoring the filling spilling onto my pants. Today has already been a complete fucking mess so why not add another messy thing to it. A fleeting thought of a cold beer or five passes through my head and I take a few moments to acknowledge the thought, the reason for it, then set it aside. That's one mess I don't want.

My phone rings halfway through my very late dinner. Rowan. I suck my burrito-y finger before I stab the speaker button. "Hi."

Rowan launches right in before I can say anything more. "Sorry for the late call but I just heard from local law enforcement and wanted to check in." His naturally gruff voice softens. "You sure you're okay, Weston?"

"Fine. Except with all the fracas I left my book on the plane." Not that I was actually reading it or would read it during a mission flight, but I might pick it up at home on a day off.

He laughs. "I'll buy you a new one. Nice work, by the way. I haven't seen anything on the news about this yet."

"Thank the Southern Air crew. They kept it locked down pretty tight."

He laughs again, this one deeper and mirthful. "Ah yes. Is there nothing they can't do?"

"Apparently not." Everyone in the field office knows about my obsession with the Southern Air crew, and every year when we run our stupid and shallow "Who's the best, a.k.a. hottest, cabin crew" pool, I'm the only one who puts Southern Air. "I swear they were even smiling while they handed me the restraints."

"Weston, everyone smiles when they look at you. You're sunshine and lollipops personified."

"Aw thanks," I say around a mouthful of carne asada. "But, given who was involved, I'm expecting it to leak to the media. Could we get our PR people on it so I'm just a 'helpful bystander,' not a Federal Air Marshal?"

"Already dealt with. Southern Air is releasing a sanitized statement about an incident on one of their flights and know how to handle your involvement when the journalists come knocking. If any of the passengers feel the need to speak to the media, Southern Air will have gotten in first with you just being a brave and nameless assistant."

"Thanks. I really like my job and I don't want to have to wear glasses and a fake nose every time I fly because I've been outed."

He chuckles. "So noted. I gotta ask, why didn't you shoot if it was a clear hostage situation?"

"I didn't shoot because there was no clear or safe shot. He was shielding himself with…the hostage." The mouthful I've just swallowed feels like a lump of clay in my chest. "I made a judgment call and decided I could de-escalate it verbally. He was exhibiting clear signs of a delusional obsessive fantasy around a relationship with Elise Hayes and I thought I could get his hostage away before restraining him. And I did."

"Yes you did. It was nicely handled."

"Aw thanks. Am I getting a raise?"

"That's above my paygrade." His standard, joking response whenever any of us ask the question. "Listen, I wanted to give you a heads-up. He said a few things during his interview that's got LLE's spidey senses tingling. The Feds are likely going to get involved."

My own spidey senses tingle. "Why?" Not that I don't want the Bureau to nail this guy to the wall, but because FBI involvement means this is more than a simple assault case. More than a simple assault case in which my ex-girlfriend was the victim. Fuck.

Rowan confirms my suspicion immediately. "Looks like there's more to it. I only got the basics but there's apparently been a network of escalating cyberstalking around the victim as well, and Bridges implied he's involved with those guys. So, in addition to the charges from today's adventure, it's going to take the Feds a little time to dig around and see what they can unearth with the other stuff."

Cyberstalking. Fuck again. The word *guys* pings around my brain and reminds me of something Bridges said. She's going to be *ours*. Fuck again squared. "Has Elise Hayes pressed charges?"

"Mhmm, she has. Word is they're going with aggravated assault and interfering with transportation, and then they might layer some other charges on top of that. And *then* it could be intertwined with this Internet group he says he's maybe possibly but not gonna admit outright to being part of, so first they've gotta see if he's telling the truth about that or not. If he is part of it, then it's about how it ties into today, or if it's a separate investigation for multiple suspects, or what else the fuck is going on."

"Terrorism group?" Even as I say it I feel ridiculous. Nothing about him screamed terrorist, domestic or otherwise.

"No. Just another group of guys with delusional fantasies about celebrities. This sort of shit really sticks in my gears."

"Mmm." It's all I can say, because if I start on how fucked up and invasive and creepy and gross I find it, I'll never be able to stop.

"But also, another heads-up, this guy's father is a hotshot criminal defense attorney with Parker, Lawson and Butler so I'm pretty sure one of his daddy's colleagues will scream misdemeanor and have him out on bail tomorrow. And you just *know* the defense's angle will be that he had some sort of mental snap. We really need to make this watertight. Hope your paperwork was A-grade shit."

"Fucking brilliant," I sigh. "And of course it was A-grade paperwork. If there's a problem it won't come from my end." Now I *really* need to get in touch with Elise and tell her to be careful, to get a restraining order on the guy. Not that I expect a piece of paper to stop someone like him, but if he violates it then it'll give us extra in the case against him. Give *them* extra in the case. My job is done. This isn't my problem anymore.

"The system works," Rowan says dryly and with not a small hint of sarcasm.

"Yeah, yeah. Thanks for letting me know. I assume we'll be told what they think we need to know. Can you keep me in the loop?" I peel back the foil to access more burrito.

"Probably, and yeah, sure. But why are you so interested? Get a little starstruck on the flight?" he teases.

I almost choke on my mouthful. "No. Just being a diligent government employee following up on my arrests. And that whole probably having to testify thing."

"Right. What I know, you'll know."

"Great. Thanks. See you tomorrow." Once we've ended the call, I finish the rest of my dinner in a few huge bites and clean spilled bits from my lap.

To put the cherry on my shit-day cake, some idiot with a near-new black BMW has parked in front of my three-bedroom California bungalow, blocking my bins. They're lucky pickup day was today, not tomorrow, or with the mood I'm in I might have keyed their stupid car for blocking my trash collection. I deathstare the car as I drive past and once parked, I crouch under my closing garage door and cross the driveway to collect Mrs. Obermeier's empty bins and put them back.

As I walk back across my driveway for my own bins, the driver door of the BMW opens. My heart rate spikes, my hand goes automatically to my holster. Even as I'm doing it, I recognize how stupid and paranoid it is. Nobody cares about me, nobody would be coming here for me. But the adrenaline I've been suppressing all day has suddenly escalated tenfold.

The adrenaline releases when someone I never expected to see at my house ever again slips out of the car. Elise's profile is shadowed by the streetlights but I would know her anywhere. I drop my hand from where I'm about to remove my firearm, and close the gap between us. "Ellie? What are you doing here?" My relief at seeing her makes my words rush and I can't stop my hands from gently grabbing her biceps, my thumbs from sliding up and down as if they're desperate to make sure she's real. "Are you all right? I've been trying to figure out how to contact you. I wanted to make sure you're okay. Not check up on you or be creepy or anything, just…I've been super worried."

Her smile is fleeting and her expression one I recognize well—the one where she's anxious and trying not to let it seep through. "Yeah, I'm okay. Mostly. I think." The smile grows as she gently thumbs the edge of my mouth. "I see you still don't know how to drive and eat at the same time. Late-night burrito from Leo's?"

Even after all this time apart, she still knows me so well. Right now I feel like the last fifteen months were just fifteen days. Seeing her here, standing and talking and being so…alive, makes me forget myself. Makes me forget the last year. I move my hands to her face and in the streetlight, study her closely. Her olive skin is pale and she now has a proper medical dressing on her neck, but she seems otherwise all right.

"I—" What wants to come out of my mouth is how glad I am that she's okay, how utterly terrified I was that she'd been hurt. "I tried to call to make sure you're okay, but I don't have your number and Sandra's number isn't in service and I didn't know what else to do."

"Yeah. A lot's changed in the last year or so." She laughs shakily. "But obviously not your address. Thankfully."

I try not to stare at her neck and fail. "Are you sure you're all right? Does it hurt?"

"I'm fine. Really," Elise adds at my apparently dubious expression. "Listen, I know this is kind of out of line and out of the blue, and it's incredibly late, but I really need to talk to you." She lightly touches my cheek. "May I come in?"

The question is so unexpected that I just nod and say, "Sure."

CHAPTER FIVE

As I fit the key in my front door, I tell Elise, "I'll just need to let Bennett out. There's only so much pee the wee-wee mats can handle." It feels like an unnecessary bit of information, because she's lived in this house with a dog who stayed indoors while we were both at work all day. But I need to talk to cover the awkwardness.

"Sure, no problem." She's right behind me and as I unlock the door and disable the alarm, her fingers brush the back of my jacket as if she's afraid I'm going to race through the door, slam it, and leave her outside. Bennett rushes to greet me as he always does and when he spots Elise, he freezes with a front leg hovering in midair and his tail straight up.

Laughing, I tell him, "S'okay, Bennett, you big dork. Look closer."

I've barely finished speaking before Elise exclaims, "Bennie! Hello, my guy! I've missed you!"

The moment she talks, Bennett rushes over and erupts into a frenzy of leaps and squirms and licks before starting zoomie laps around the house. I let him complete two and a quarter laps—mostly because the sound of Elise's laughter is incredible—before I ask him to chill. He's too big to be cavorting around like this and has reached the body-tilting-sideways around corners stage and begun to skid out, and it's only a matter of time before he loses control and takes out a piece of furniture or pees in excitement.

Elise drops to her knees and opens her arms, and Bennett almost knocks her down with the force of his approach. She hugs him tightly, scratches his back, kisses his face, rubs his ears, and laughingly pushes him away when he tries to lick her ear. Unlike cat-person me, Elise has always been a dog person and when my brother, Tristan, dropped Bennett off out of the blue and asked me to watch him for a few days, Elise had jumped in and said we'd love to watch Baby-Bennett before I'd been able to complain about what a pain it would be.

She'd loved taking care of the puppy, babying him and continuing the basic obedience training Tristan had started. She fed Bennett, worked on his house training, pouted at me when I insisted the puppy had a perfectly wonderful and comfortable dog bed and blankies in our room, and didn't need to sleep in our bed. When I'd received that phone call two days after Tristan's visit, Elise had bundled up four-month-old Bennett and come with me to identify my brother's remains. And when we got home again, Elise had Bennett squirmingly sitting on her feet as she'd snuggled into me, held my hand, and wiped my cheeks while I read Tristan's suicide note because I couldn't make myself do it alone.

Elise had made sure Bennett was well-cared for when I was grief-stricken and trying to arrange things so that my parents didn't have to deal with it from afar. She took care of me and I'd never felt so loved and supported as I did in those months. After she left I kept thinking about that time and wondering if it was real, why she would bother putting so much of herself into our relationship if she wasn't even invested enough to put us before her career.

Bennie finally stops his eruption of excitement and settles into dopey adoration mode, leaning against Elise, stretching his head up to rub against her hip with a goofy doggo smile firmly in place. Elise pauses her ear rubbing and glances up at me, a smile of her own spreading across her mouth. "Sorry. I guess I didn't realize 'til now just how much I missed him."

Missed my dog but not me. I clear my throat and force a smile of my own. "Looks like he missed you too. I'll just let him out back then give him something to eat. Make yourself comfortable and help yourself to anything." It feels weird to be telling someone I used to share the house with to act like she lives there.

Bennett is both busting to get out and also apparently really wants to get back in to see Elise, because after bolting out the door he makes two super-quick stops in the yard then sprints inside, leaving me to clean up after him. Normally he'd want to play fetch or tug of war for a while, but apparently Elise is more important than a game or spending time with me.

Back inside, I'm not surprised to find Elise crouching on the floor by the kitchen table, hugging my dog, kissing between his eyes, and generally fussing over him. Bennett seems more enthused about being with Elise than being fed so I decide he'll be okay waiting a minute or two. "Gimme a sec to put my stuff away and clean up after Bennie's day inside."

The pair of them are so engrossed in their reunion that they barely acknowledge I've spoken. It only takes me a few minutes to get rid of today's pee mat, move dog toys out of the thoroughfare and securely lock my work gun away. When I come back into the kitchen, rolling up the sleeves on my shirt, I spot Elise and Bennett still engaging in their "I'm so pleased to see you" ritual. The image makes me smile. "You hungry?"

Elise looks up, eyes creasing with amusement. "Me or the dog?"

"I know he probably is, but I meant you."

It takes her a few seconds to answer and it's a shy, musing, "I'm not sure."

"That means you are. Just let me feed Bennie and then I'll make you something to eat."

The moment I open the knee-high tub of kibble beside the fridge, Bennett abandons Elise and rushes to sit beside the end of the counter where he gets fed. Elise laughs and stands up, propping her elbows on the counter. "Nothing's changed."

"Not a bit. And you know, I *still* can't get him to eat anything except his special organic human-grade food. Thanks for introducing him to that super-expensive dog cuisine." I know she'll take it in the teasing tone I've intended, because we used to banter and fake-bicker back and forth about her bringing home the expensive stuff one day and how Bennie refused all brands of wet food except that one from that day forward.

"My pleasure." Grinning, Elise indicates Bennett, who is intensely focused on me spooning his wet food onto his kibble. "Look how healthy and shiny he is though."

Smiling, I carry the bowl across the kitchen and set it down. There's no point in rebutting, as I used to, that he could be just as healthy and shiny for fifty bucks a week less. Bennie waits until I've stepped away and indicated he can go nuts before he digs in.

"Right. Food for humans now." I frown when I think about the contents of my fridge which, if Elise's diet is the same as it was the last time she was in this house, would be boring and problematic. She's been a vegetarian since she was twelve. "Sorry, since you uh, left, we turned back into a house of omnivores. If I'd known you'd be around I would have prepared better. I mean there's food for you but nothing exciting."

She smiles fleetingly. "You couldn't have known I'd turn up on your doorstep. It's totally fine. Anything is fine."

"Grilled cheese and tomato it is." As I pull things from the fridge, I ask, "So, what did you want to talk about?"

There's a long pause before she murmurs, "I need a place to stay."

The quiet statement is so not what I expected, and I drop the tomato and package of cheese to the counter. The tomato rolls to the edge and I grab it before it splats onto the floor. "Oh." Carefully, I set the tomato back. My mouth has gone dry and I rub my tongue on the roof of my mouth until saliva flows. "I assume the place you want to stay is here."

Elise's response is uncharacteristically shy. "Yes. Please. I'm so sorry, I just didn't know where else to go. After what happened today, I need to lie low for a while. Be somewhere that isn't my place because some people know where I live." Her words are running away from her. "Everyone I know is out of town for winter hiatus or working on other projects in other cities or countries. I really don't want to get on a plane right now to go hide out somewhere, and I can't go home. I'm sorry, I just couldn't think of anywhere else. Not anywhere private."

I fumble the handle of the knife in the block before I manage to get a grip. "Why can't you stay at a hotel?" Despite my effort to be neutral, the question sounds accusatory and sarcastically obvious.

"Because the moment some employee who thinks privacy rules are flexible and don't *really* need to be adhered to puts my picture on the Internet, there will be swarms of people there. Including those people I don't want around me." She leans down to pat Bennett who's finished dinner and has glued himself to her side.

I slice tomato thickly, just how she likes it. "Right. What about getting an Airbnb?" It's not that I don't want her staying with me, but I don't want her staying with me. I've only just started to get my life back in order after the mess she left it in when she walked out, and I don't need or want the confusion of having her around. I care about her and want her to be safe and to feel comfortable. Just not with me.

"I thought about it and went to make an account while I was at the hospital. But then I saw the 'add a picture so your host will recognize you' thing. Kind of defeats the purpose of lying low."

"Right." I blow out a loud breath. "Well, this really is the perfect place for you to hide, isn't it? Nobody knows I exist, so they'll never look for you here." I mean for it to sting, to remind her of what she did, why she left, but I'm surprised to realize that it stings me too.

"Avery—"

"No, it's fine, really." I'm sure she sees right through my lie. It's very late, I'm tired, today has been shit in every sense of the word and this has just topped it off. I try to gather slippery thoughts. "Why exactly do you need to hide? People really know where you live?"

She nods slowly. "There's been a few uncomfortable fan incidents recently. Some creepy letters and emails and social media posts. Then after today…" Elise trails off, her expression turning distant. She shakes her head, as if trying to shake out the thoughts stuck in there. "I need to hide from the public eye for a few weeks, for my own sake. And Rosemary and Paul are a little spooked." Her mouth quirks as she gestures at the sandwich press on the counter behind me. "You need to turn that on."

I do as she says. "Who are Rosemary and Paul?" I'd already gathered some of what she's said from my conversation with Rowan about FBI involvement, but I set that knowledge and anger aside to get some facts.

"My new manager and agent. I fired Sandra and Bert about nine months ago. Sandra fled to Barbados to avoid a stack of lawsuits and Bert died of a heart attack three months ago."

"Good," I say before I can stop myself. "I mean, not the dying and the lawsuits but that they're no longer part of your team. They were fucking toxic." For her career and her personal life.

"I know," Elise murmurs. "I wish I'd realized that sooner. For both our sakes." She says the last part so quietly that I'm not sure I heard her correctly. The look she gives me tells me I did.

I force my brain back on track as I slice cheese thinly, again, just the way I know she loves it. "What are you going to tell your team about where you are?" I offer her some cheese.

"Thanks." She folds the slice in half and eats it. "I'll tell them I'm staying with a friend until things settle."

"You've probably had plenty of practice at that, telling them you're just *staying with a friend*, right?" The moment I say it I want to take back those hurtful words that just fell from my mouth, but I can't retract them. Still, she deserves an apology because it's ruder than I should have been. "Sorry. That was cruel."

"It's fine," she murmurs. "I know what you're saying. Or not saying." The edge of her mouth twitches.

"Do you think those things you mentioned are related to what happened today?" As much as I want to, I can't let on what I know and that I also know the FBI is getting involved.

She nods, shivers, then catches herself, wrapping her arms tightly around her midsection. "Mmm. The cop guy I talked to tonight said it seems likely."

Her obvious anxiety melts some of my frustration. "What is it?" I only just hold on to my *sweetheart.*

"Today was the first incident like…that, but the cops think there's going to be more. I mean there's more fan guys obviously, but they think it's going to uh, escalate to more events like today. If they don't figure out who and where they are and get a handle on it, that is."

My burrito asks if it can come back up and I have to take some slow breaths to calm myself. What she's alluding to is more than what Rowan said. "What do you mean exactly? Don't dance around it, Ellie. Tell me everything." My words sound so personal and I turn them about to try to bring it back to neutral, uncaring. "I might be able to help out if there's some sort of investigation." It's not true, but it makes me sound less desperately caring.

"There's a whole group of them, like some sick stalker fan club. They call themselves the Hayes Horde." Though her expression is neutral, all her emotion is in her voice—fear, upset, disgust.

"Why haven't the cops or FBI been involved before now?" A slow boil of fury simmers in my gut. This should *never* have gone this far, to the point of a fan attacking her, especially not if Ellie's management team were aware of these guys and what they've been doing.

"They have been. But the guys haven't done anything really serious or big before today. Just the usual creepy fan stuff, sporadic things but nothing that ever felt too significant. Just enough to feel gross. We report the ones that cross a line to the police and they said to keep files and records, and they're keeping a file too."

"Stuff like what?"

"Letters, emails, a couple of lewd photoshopped pictures, vague kind of blackmail threats but nothing that's concrete. We block all the emails and Rosemary dutifully reports the ones that should be reported, but—" She shrugs. "It hasn't felt truly scary until now." Her lips tremble. "Now…now I feel like I don't want to go out."

I wonder what she's not telling me or maybe even what she doesn't know. "I'm so sorry this is happening, Ellie. And that stuff is illegal. You have a right to feel safe wherever you are and not harassed in any form, over the Internet or through mail or in person." It sounds so ineffectual. "I heard from my supervisor that you pressed charges against him. Did they talk to you about restraining orders tonight?"

"Mhmm. The cop called a judge tonight and got me an emergency protective order against—" She pauses and inhales slowly, deeply. "Against Troy Bridges that'll last for a week, I think? He did explain it to me, but I couldn't take it all in."

"Smart cop. The EPO is basically an immediate restraining order, like a buffer to give you time to get to the courts and get a temporary restraining order which will last until a court date where you'll get a permanent restraining order. Assuming that's what you want to do." I stop myself from telling her that it's what she should do. She's not mine to give advice to anymore.

Her breath is shaky. "Good. I'll take a look at what I need to do for that." She bites her lower lip, then softens to nibble the skin. "I don't want him anywhere near me. Ever again."

"I know. And I think it's the right way to proceed." I want to caress her lips gently, to stop her from nibbling. But I can't. I turn slightly away. "How long has this sort of stuff been happening?"

"Started not long after *Greed* first aired. But the Hayes Horde specifically? Seven months or so. It's just the usual delusional fan messages from them, always signed with their name and HH. After today, Rosemary said she's going to make sure there's extra security for me when I'm back on set. If it keeps going then I'll have to think about hiring a bodyguard." She makes herself smile. "I'll be a regular A-List celeb with my big, beefy bodyguard."

I can't make myself return the smile. "If it's gone this far then I think that's a very good idea." I hate that she might have to go that extreme just because some delusional basement dwellers won't leave her alone.

She shrugs, like she's trying to seem nonchalant but I know she's very chalant. "As much as I hate it, I agree. They seem to know what I'm doing and where I'm going to be. Today being the perfect example."

That pulls me up. "What do you mean? He knew you were going to be on today's flight?"

"Yes," she says instantly.

"How the hell did he know that?" It's not like she's the President and has her daily schedule put up online for one and all to look up.

"I have no idea, but the best guess from the law enforcement I talked to before I drove here is someone hacked into Rosemary's computer and has been taking note of my travel plans. Along with other things." Elise looks like she's about to vomit again. "When he had me—" She stops abruptly, then swallows and licks her lips. "When he had me on the plane, he said he's been sending me letters and emails and asked if I liked the pictures he'd sent and that he wanted to take some of me, real ones, not just pretend."

"Oh, Ellie. Fuck. I'm so sorry." I reach over and take her hand, and she grips mine like it's a tether.

She pauses to inhale slowly. "He got so angry, he said I've been ignoring him, that it's my fault, that he's been following me for months, and *finally*, he managed to get near me."

"That must feel horrible and scary." My statement is so weakly ineffectual but I just don't know how to comfort her in this ex-girlfriends dynamic.

"Yeah." She gives me a smile, along with some trademark Elise Hayes optimism. "It could be worse, really."

I decide to play along, though my brain's already run all the scenarios of how exactly it could be worse. "That's true. When's hiatus finish?"

"I'm back on set eleventh of January."

Given that it's only the first week in December I try to sound casual when I ask, "How long do you think you'll need to stay here?"

"A few weeks maybe. At least until I'm back at work and I'm settled into that routine. If that's all right?"

"Sure." Even with everything lingering between us, knowing now that she's in actual danger, I'd never make her leave. I've dealt with awkwardness and discomfort before and I can do it again for a few weeks. An unsettling thought intrudes. It's unlikely, but maybe this guy somehow knows about me and Elise from before and might guess she's come here to hide. I push the thought aside. Elise wasn't a big-name star when she was with me, and she was so careful to keep her private life private. The chance of someone knowing she's here is tiny and with Bridges currently enjoying some of the state's hospitality, he couldn't have followed her.

"I'll need to get food," I say inanely.

"It's fine. I'll do an online grocery order in the morning for some things to tide me over." She gestures to the steaming, sizzling sandwich press. "That's ready."

I take my time assembling the sandwich, shake salt and pepper over it, and close the press. "The wi-fi password is the same and the gym and everything else is the same as last time you were here. Just…make yourself at home, eat and drink whatever you want, of course."

"Thanks. I will."

I turn away and pretend the sandwich press needs monitoring, just so I don't have to look at her. Once her dinner's done, I pass it across the counter to her, along with a glass of sparkling water. "I'll leave you to eat that. I really need a shower." A glance at my watch tells me it's well past midnight and though I'm desperate to go to bed, I can't just leave her.

The sandwich is already halfway to her mouth. "Sure." After a beat, she adds a quiet, "Thank you."

CHAPTER SIX

In the safety of my bedroom, I quickly strip out of my clothes and toss them in the hamper. My shower is borderline too hot, but I want that discomfort, I need it to wash the day from my skin. I need to wash away the emotion that's been dredged up by everything that happened today. Compartmentalizing is not only part of my job, but it's also something I've always found easy. Until today. These things on their own would be easy to place into separate compartments—seeing Elise for the first time since the breakup, her incident, her arrival on my doorstep— but cumulatively they've broken down my usually solid walls and left me feeling like I'm teetering on the edge of a cliff.

I pull on sweats and a tee, and am about to leave the room when something twigs. After a few moments of consideration I pull off my tee and put on a bra. Elise is where I left her and still being kept company by Bennett who's pressed against the leg of the breakfast-bar stool, either still in his *I love you* phase or hoping for dropped cheese. Probably both. I make sure I say a quiet, "Elise?" before I approach.

She turns slightly to the side. "Mmm?"

"You okay?" I glance at the plate, which is empty aside from the crusts. Elise doesn't like bread crusts. I should have remembered that.

"Yeah. Thanks for the late dinner." She offers me a smile. "You were right. I needed to eat something."

"No worries." I drop the crusts into Bennett's bowl, which makes him briefly abandon Elise to hoover them up, and climb up onto a stool beside her. "So…what are your plans exactly? Are you going to hide out fully in here for a few weeks and never leave the house? Or will you go out?" Christmas is in three weeks and while her being here won't interfere with my nonexistent personal plans, I'm sure she's got something arranged.

Elise rests an elbow on the counter. "I think I'll hide out for a few days until I don't feel like things are going to jump out of the shadows at me. Then I'll have to go back to normal. Or normal-ish." Her teeth graze her lower lip. "It's more just that my home address is known, and not just to these people but to anyone who knows how to Google such things. It's secure, but I still don't want to be there alone."

Secure. I think about the security of my house, which I've always considered safe. Only my backyard is fenced, not that a fence is really that much of a deterrent. But I do have an alarm, sensor lights and cameras, deadbolts, and security screens on my windows. And Bennett, if he can be called *security*. "I can understand that. But I don't think locking yourself away in here will be good for you." Ellie loves the outdoors, sunshine, cool breezes, movement, being with people.

"I won't spend the whole time just hiding inside." She brightens a fraction, her expression turning almost slyly teasing. "I have to go out to exercise and see the sun, and I need to do my Poké-chores. This house is a dead spot for Pokémon and PokéStops and if I sit around here instead of going out, my progress is going to hardcore stall."

I suppress my guffaw. "I can't believe you still play Pokémon Go."

She lightly punches my arm. "Hey, you have your games and I have mine."

"True." It would be so easy to get into a familiar back-and-forth about our different hobbies and how we used to spend time together but doing different things. We have as much not in common as we do in common and when we first started dating, those discoveries were fresh and exciting. I idly wonder if she has any new hobbies, but just as quickly tell myself it doesn't matter.

After a quick study of my face, Elise climbs off the stool. "Mind if I take a look around and refamiliarize myself with everything before bed?"

Nothing in this house has changed and knowing me, she'd know that. But my ex-girlfriend is very good at reading a room and changing the mood to make things more comfortable for all present. So I nod my agreement, shelve my relief at the subject change, and slide off my stool.

She's quiet as she wanders through my house and after a quick peek into the guest room where she'll stay, Elise goes straight to the living room with Bennett following close behind. I love that he's reattached himself to her so readily—at least I know he'll keep her company and comfort her when I'm not around, or I just…can't. Elise lightly traces her fingertips over the closed lid of the antique Steinway & Sons grand piano I inherited from my grandfather. Elise is the only one who's played it since. She peers at her fingertips but I know she'll find no dust because I keep the instrument meticulously clean. "When did you last have this tuned?" she asks.

"Beginning of August last year." Right before she left. I don't play the piano, have never been able to play anything beyond basics like "Chopsticks" and the top notes bit of "Heart and Soul," both of which she taught me. I should have just sold the piano when we broke up, as my grandpa intended when he left it to me, but I've always liked the way it looks in my house—even if it does take up a huge chunk of the room. And if I'm honest with myself, I like remembering Elise playing it in the evening while I listened. She'd tell me what she'd just played until eventually I'd learned to recognize the composers and which of those composers went along with her moods.

She runs her hand over the Steinway's closed lid again, the movement slow and luxurious, as if she just can't help herself and touching the piano is giving her some sort of pleasure. "May I?"

"Of course." I help her raise the lid and prop it open, and wonder what mood she's going to telegraph through her music.

Elise peers at the guts of the piano then raises the fallboard—which I mistakenly called a lid until I met her and was gently schooled on piano terminology—from the keys, carefully, respectfully. She lightly plays her fingers over a few keys, her head cocked to the side. A wry smile. "Not *too* badly out of tune."

She'd know. I've skimmed articles and interviews where she occasionally mentions piano as one of her hobbies. What she never mentions is that she's played since she was three, and that she spent years at Julliard. She had a choice, and chose music over acting, but after her Bachelor of Music she moved into their drama program and completed that degree as well. Talented is an understatement when talking about Elise. I found out about her music during our first date when she came to my place, saw the piano, and asked so politely and so excitedly if she could play. Once she'd wowed me with a Bach piece that almost made me cry, she explained how she was so damned good. She seemed more excited about her music than acting.

I press the last key on the left. Sounds like a piano note to me. "I'll call and get it tuned for you this week. He doesn't do many old pianos so he should be here in a day or two."

"It's fine. I'll cope."

Laughing, I disagree, "No you won't."

As she settles on the stool, she smiles back at me and says, "You're right. I won't." She pauses for a few seconds with her hands resting in her lap before she begins playing. Her head bobs every now and then which I know means something sounds really wrong to her ear. I can't hear it, but I do know what irritates her is my out-of-tune piano, not her playing. She's perfect.

She plays for about five minutes, a soft and sweetly meandering piece of music, while I lean against the wall just out of her line of sight. When she's finished, I murmur, "Chopin." One of her go-tos when she's melancholy, along with Debussy. After her day, I understand the feeling and wish there was something I could do to ease it.

"Mmm. 'Nocturne Number Twenty in C Sharp Minor'," she says once she's pulled her hands back. "I'm surprised you still recognize it." Elise spins around on the stool, the tentative smile turning into a fully formed one. "I needed that. This piano feels like an old friend." After carefully closing the fallboard, she stands and points to the small bar tucked into the opposite corner of the room. "Is any of my alcohol still here?"

"Yes. I had…company, but there should be some left. Sorry," I add when I remember it was hers and I shouldn't have let someone else drink it, even if left-behinds are fair game after a breakup.

"Apology not needed." Her expression tells me clearly that she knows exactly what I meant by *company*. I want to explain that since she left me I dated exactly two women for exactly six weeks total combined, and every minute of it felt like I was walking barefoot on Lego bricks.

She reaches under the bar and pulls out an unopened bottle of Syrah. "You want a glass?"

"No thanks, I'm good."

She pauses, not bothering to mask the expression of panic passing over her face. "Fuck. I'm so sorry. That was totally thoughtless, just an automatic question and the dumbest one at that. I know you're…" Elise pauses, her cheeks puffing with air.

Laughing, I finish her sentence. "A teetotaler?"

She grins. "Yes, that. If I'd allocated a moment's brainpower to it, I'd have known that's not really something that would have changed."

"It's okay." And it really is. "Not your thing to worry about."

Her voice drops to intimate softness. "But it is, Avery."

I suppose she's right. She was with me when I used to drink, and drink too much. Far too much. But after my alcohol-dependent brother killed himself, I made a choice that I wasn't going to take the same path he did. Elise supported me as I tried to find new ways to deal with my work stresses—the irregular hours, the short notice for assignments, the misogyny and sexism and inappropriate comments, the lack of mental health support. She even stopped her usual few-glasses-a-few-times-a-week until I was established in my new no-booze routine and had assured her that I really had no issues with her drinking. I just didn't want that for myself any longer. I've always been an all or nothing person, which I suppose bled into our relationship as well.

She clears her throat and rummages around in the bar utensils pot, peering under the small counter overhang, opening a drawer then closing it again. It finally twigs what she's looking for. Her corkscrew. "I donated all of them," I say. "Sorry. They weren't any use for me." When she lived here we had two of almost all our small utensils like corkscrews, peelers, scissors, and certain serrated things like bread knives. My left-handed ones and her rights. No point in keeping the rights when she was gone.

Elise's mouth twists like she's tasted something bad. "Oh. Of course."

I open another drawer and extract my corkscrew to open the bottle for her. And I wonder if she knows just how hard it was for me to get rid of those utensils. I take a step back, desperate to move away from...this. "I'll clean that wineglass for you." It doesn't need cleaning but I need to distance myself from her. Away from memories I don't feel like reliving right now. In the kitchen, I carefully wash, rinse, and dry the glass, taking more time than I need to get it clean so I can calm myself. It doesn't really work, but I can't stand at the kitchen sink for an hour just scrubbing.

Elise pours herself a small glass of wine, takes it to the couch, and sits on *her* side—the right-hand side which is closest to the piano. Bennett sits by her legs, practically on her feet, so he can lean into her with his head on her thigh. She strokes his face and stares at the piano, her gaze slightly unfocused as if she's thinking deeply about something. After her horror day, I would have expected her to gulp down her drink but she sits quietly, sipping thoughtfully.

The silence stretches beyond comfortable and I fill it with inanity. "You having to stay with me kinda feels like the plot of a romance movie. Irony really."

Elise turns sideways and the smile she graces me with is pure Hollywood charm. At another time it might have melted me, but now it makes me feel weird. "What? You think after we spend some time together we'll realize we made a terrible mistake splitting up, and fall back into each other's arms?"

The quirk of her mouth makes her look both teasing and uncertain, as if she was trying to tell a joke that felt so uncomfortable she couldn't even fake it. If an award-winning actress can't even pretend that the idea of us being together isn't loathsome then what hope did we have? Still, I know that when we were a couple it was real and right, so it seems she's bought into her own narrative for not being able to be with me because of other people's prejudice.

"Maybe that, but also no, not that." I force a laugh. "I was thinking about *Second Chance.*" The movie released this summer where Elise and movie hunk of the moment played childhood sweethearts who met again as adults and the predictable movie thing happened and they lived happily ever after with a dog, station wagon and two-point-three kids.

She gapes for a moment before rushing to say, "You saw it? But you *hate* rom-coms."

"Mhmm, yes I did, and no, I'm still not a rom-com fan. Someone took me to see it. It was…a fun movie." In case you've ever wondered, going on a first date with someone to see a movie in which your ex-girlfriend plays the lead is *beyond* awkward. Especially when you can't elaborate on why you just didn't really get into something which, by all accounts, is an excellent movie for what it is.

"Someone," she muses. "I'm glad you're dating."

I don't bother asking how she's managed to make that leap from me going to the movies with someone to me potentially dating. I don't get a chance to refute the fact because after a quick glance around she says, "I'm not intruding with that, am I? I don't want to be in the way if you'll have company." There's a strange hesitancy to her words. It's possible she feels weird about me dating—I know I still feel weird about her dating—but more likely, and knowing Elise, she just doesn't want to intrude.

"I'm not dating anyone. At the moment," I add, in a sudden desperate and childish attempt to make it seem like I've *totally* been dating and being a normal person, not working too much and trying to figure out what my new, single life should look like.

Her shoulders drop and in a rush she says, "Me either. Otherwise I could have gone there. If it wasn't public that is."

So many responses spin through my head, like "What about those pictures of you at basketball games with Tomas Silva or the pap-snaps I saw in an airport lounge magazine where you looked super cozy with Marcus Rutherford?" Instead, my response is a quiet, "Oh. Okay then."

Ellie looks like she wants to say more but instead, she finishes her drink and after scratching Bennett's neck, stands. "I think I might be ready for bed. I've got some bags I need to bring in." She pauses. "Do you mind coming out to the car with me?"

"Sure. Just let me move some things out of the way first so you can put your car in the garage." I feel like I have to explain that with only one car there's no need for me to keep the space that used to be hers free. After I've cleared my mountain bike, road bike, and ski tuning station out of the way, I walk her out to her BMW and watch while she parks carefully beside my Prius. After I help her with her rolling suitcase and duffel, I pause at the guest room door. "I think I'm going to go to bed too. Is there anything you need before I turn in?"

Elise peers around the room before her gaze comes back to rest on my face. "I think I'm okay. Thanks though. For everything." Her voice tightens. "For what you did on the plane and also what you're doing now."

"No problem." I linger longer than I should, trying to get the words in my brain to form in my mouth. But they won't. The words that do form are inadequate, pointless. "Okay, I'll leave you to it. Sleep tight. You know where I am if you need anything."

Elise's smile comes quickly, as if she knows what I want to say but can't get out. "That I do."

Bennett comes right up to the edge of my bed and nudges my hand as he does every night before he goes to sleep. I've never been sure if he wants pets or is checking on me before he becomes unconscious until morning. Either way, I rub his head and ears, and receive a hand lick as payment before he huffs and snuffles into a comfortable position in his bed in the corner.

Unsurprisingly, it takes me far longer to fall asleep than usual because my brain is still slowly walking the loop of my procedures on the plane as well as everything Elise revealed. Her stalkers, the fact nobody has done anything about them, her wanting…needing to see me, how quickly I've fallen back into the easy sensation of her being here despite the undercurrent of weirdness and awkwardness. Over and over. Around and around.

When I wake to Bennett nosing my hand with the obvious intent of waking me, my first thought is he needs to go out. "Bennie? I let you out before bed," I mumble. "You sick?" I've just grasped the covers to shove them off when I hear Elise's throat clearing quietly. I sit up, eyes straining in the darkness to find her. It's just past four a.m. Mmph.

"Sorry," Elise murmurs. "He saw me at the door. I don't think he needs to go outside." The fact he woke to Elise moving about makes me wonder if he isn't as dead to the world as he seems when asleep. That, or he's hyperaware of Elise being in the house again.

"Ah." I lean over to rub Bennett's ears. "Then you really don't need to pee, Bennie?"

His response is to nose my hand again before he settles back into his bed. I push myself fully upright and reach for the bedside lamp, blinking as my eyes adjust. Ellie is framed in the doorway. "What's up? You okay?" Dumb question. If she was okay she would be asleep in my guest room, not visiting my room at four in the morning.

"Not really, no. I can't sleep." Her voice is soft and almost childlike. "I keep having nightmares and then waking up."

I'm pretty sure I know what she'll say, but I ask the question anyway. "What about?"

"Being grabbed, choked, stabbed." Elise inhales shakily. "You getting blown up."

"Does your neck hurt?"

"No. The dressing is annoying as hell, but it's fine. Just feels like a cat scratch." She gestures to the space beside me. "Can I... sleep here? With you?"

Perfect. Sharing a bed with my ex. But I'd be an absolute monster if I said no after everything she's experienced. I'd also be a liar if I said that I hadn't thought about her coming back to my bed nearly every night in the last fifteen months. I can totally handle platonic sleeping next to someone. "Sure."

She carefully slips under the covers without touching me and, as always, bashes the pillow into submission. She's using new lotion or face care products and smells differently from how she should. But underneath that new scent is a familiar, comforting one. After her nighttime shower, Ellie always shakes scented talcum powder into her armpits, instead of putting on deodorant. I can imagine the spots of talc dotted around the bathroom sink and floor. The thought of Elise now when she's famous, popping into Walmart to buy her two-packs of talc as she's always done, is oddly comforting. Some things change. Other things never will.

The cliché would be that I sleep like a baby with her in my arms, but the opposite is true. I lie awake like a plank of wood, then doze for a little while, then wake again a few hours later when I decide it's time to get up. Elise, on the other hand, sleeps without moving.

Or she pretends to.

CHAPTER SEVEN

I slip out of bed and after checking Elise, curled up on her side as she always sleeps, grab clothes and sneakers and let Bennett out into the backyard. While hiding in the laundry, I change from pajamas into workout clothes then go into the yard to clean up after my dog and play games and roughhouse with him. Unlike last night where Bennie was desperate to get to Elise, he's now happy to chase his Kong toy around the yard like a gigantic puppy.

After fifteen minutes of playing fetch, I leave him with his tether-tug toy—a thick, solid piece of chew-rope on the end of a long pole that rotates around as he pulls and swings himself around. When he was smaller, he loved me swinging him around by a stick or piece of rope in his mouth, but he quickly got too big for that.

Back inside the house, I lock myself in my small home gym and after thirty minutes and almost five miles on the treadmill, I'm dripping sweat. I towel myself down and reach for my bag mitts, then reconsider. No. I want to feel it today. After ten minutes at the freestanding punching bag I'm gasping for breath and have raw grazes on my knuckles. I move to Bob in the corner.

Bob doesn't complain when I send a sharp right across his jaw and counter it with an elbow to the chest. Bob never complains, which is one of the benefits of a punching dummy. My body is full of rage. It sits in my fists and no matter how hard I clench them, it remains in there. Rage isn't an emotion I often encounter in myself and I'm not entirely sure how to deal with it. I'm not even sure exactly where it's stemming from, but my top contenders are:

The thing that happened yesterday.

Elise waltzing back into my life like she never left it.

Elise being here.

My own stupid feelings about letting her stay.

But even as I accept why I'm so angry, I know that being angry isn't going to help anything. I wish I could be like Elise and meditate my feelings into more comfortable ones—it would be less painful—but I can't. By the time I've finished my hour-long workout, I feel calm enough to function without feeling like I'm going to scream.

Before I shower, I make a quick phone call to confirm there's nothing urgent in the office or in the air for the rest of the week and that I can take a few personal days to give Elise some support. I know she has friends, but I also know she won't let them come here because it might somehow give away her secret. That barely suppressed upset wants to bubble up again and I force it down. The past is done and there's nothing I can do to change it. Except have feelings about it when it's brought up again and shoved in my face. That's totally normal, right?

When I walk into the kitchen dressed in sweatpants and a hoodie instead of the usual starched shirt and pantsuit combo I wear to the office, or one of my many flight-day outfits, Elise's expression turns hopeful. After a full, albeit quick and not pervy, up-and-down inspection, she asks, "You're not going in today?" Her gaze lingers on my hands and I know she understands the raw skin. But she says nothing about it.

"Nope. I've taken today and tomorrow off. Thought I'd—" I pause to figure out how exactly to word my answer. After a few moments of thought, the truth is what comes out. "I'd...make sure you're okay. Relatively speaking," I add when I realize how stupid I sound thinking she could be okay after yesterday.

Her face relaxes. "Thank you. I think I'm okay, relatively speaking. I'll have to go in for another interview with the uh, whoever is handling this. And ask them what happens next with the assault charges and all that stuff." She pushes out a self-deprecating laugh. "I was so out of it yesterday that I didn't really pay attention to who was in charge of it all." The laugh fades. "All I could think about was that you'd taken him and they were going to keep him so he couldn't come back again."

"He's not going to come back again, Ellie. We're all going to make sure of that." I almost feel like I'm about to drop to a knee to pledge something to her, such is the intensity of my statement.

Her expression turns serious. "I know you will." She glances away, as if she can't deal with the emotion in the room. "I also need to get that other restraining order done, but I'll have to get my brain in gear first."

"I can help you with forms and stuff if you like? Or your management team or a lawyer can."

"Thanks." Elise moves quickly to the coffee machine, as if she can't stand being still. She's moving around my kitchen like she still lives here, and I'm not entirely sure how I feel about it. I like that she's so comfortable here, but at the same time it makes me feel almost cheated, like we haven't acknowledged what happened between us and now, never will. Passing me a mug of coffee she asks, "Do you know who will be in charge of all the police-y stuff?"

I bend the truth of what I know. "My gut feeling is that it will get passed to the FBI, especially if he's involved in this fucked-up stalker club, and also after what he did. I really don't know how they'll choose to handle it but I'm sure they're all over it. They'll make sure you're safe. Remember, even with the emergency protective order he can't come near you, he can't contact you, he's not allowed to buy any firearms or keep any he might already have." I can't guarantee it, but the last thing she needs to hear right now is that maybe this guy will be out on bail in a day or two. Or that he already is.

"Right." She plasters a fake smile on her face. "According to a text I got this morning from Rosemary, there's going to be a Zoom meeting with network people tomorrow so they can figure out how to handle extra security on set when I go back in the new year. Also working out any publicity angles we might have to spin in case someone leaks what happened and that it was me." She glances at her phone. "So far it's just the statement from Southern Air, but I've no doubt my name is going to be in the news soon."

"Okay, well, just let me know what time you're meeting and I'll be sure to keep quiet. So you're not disturbed or so people don't think…" My thought fades and I can't finish the sentence.

"I have female friends, Avery," Elise says evenly. Her expression is just as even, like she's landed on "neutral" in her repertoire.

"Right. Of course."

Her lips part then close again. Elise turns away from me and begins inventory on my fridge and pantry. With her back to me, she asks, "Is there anything you want, grocery-wise, before I place an order?"

My brain stalls on this most basic question. After a minute of me umming and ahhing and mumbling, "Let me think," Elise laughs and cuts me some slack. Her tone is diplomatic, with a hint of teasing. "I see you're still an impulse grocery buyer. Why don't I just order what I think we need to fill the kitchen with food for both of us." She worries her lower lip with her teeth. "Have your eating habits changed since…then?"

"Not really. But I did eat eggplant."

Elise throws both her hands up triumphantly. Her smile is luminous. "Heyyyy! I did it. I told you I'd convert you one day."

"Well, it was just once." When we were together, I ate mostly vegetarian because it's really good and was easier than making two separate dishes. But I drew the line at eggplant.

Once a week we had what we used to call Freebie Night, with separate meals for each of us. The menu on Freebie Night never changed. I'd have meat Elise grilled—despite not eating it, she somehow always cooked steak better than I could—and Ellie would invariably make something where eggplant was the star. And we'd sit across the table from one another and make pretend faces at each other's meal. I can't imagine doing that with her right now, in this awkward, figuring-out-where-we-stand phase of our life.

"What changed your mind?" she asks as she sets out things for her breakfast.

It takes me a moment to get my brain out of the past and back to this conversation. I almost tell her the truth that someone I went on a few dates with had cooked for me and I'd eaten eggplant without realizing. "I had it in a meal. Not something I'll voluntarily eat again. Taste-wise it was fine I guess, but I still think the texture's a bit weird."

She grins. "Only if you don't do it right. And the whole point of it is that it just takes on whatever flavor you give it. I'm going to make you a couple of fabulous eggplant dishes. You'll be singing my praises." After a pause and a too-bright smile Elise says, "I'll even leave the recipes so you can make them once I'm gone." She turns away again to rummage in the fridge.

"I'd like that," I murmur. "How'd you sleep?"

She confirms my suspicion about her just pretending to be asleep in my bed with a wry, "I didn't really. I was mostly just meditating. Every time I dozed off I'd wake up feeling anxious."

"I'm so sorry, Ellie. This should never have happened to you."

"No, it shouldn't have," she agrees. "But…if it *had* to happen, I'm glad you were there with me when it did."

I bite my tongue on the unemotional response of "I was just doing my job" and offer her my truth. "I'm glad I was there too. I'm sorry I said you weren't pretty."

Elise choke-snorts on the cherry tomato she's just popped in her mouth. When she stops laughing, she says, "It's okay, really. I've been called worse things." The mirth fades. Her fingers flutter against the dressing on her neck. "You were brilliant. He...didn't hurt you, did he?"

"Not at all."

"Good."

For breakfast she makes her usual scrambled egg packed with sautéed veggies, though with the status of my crisper it's less packed with veggies and more just sadly adequate. While we eat we have the basic catch-up conversation we should have had last night. Ellie pushes her coffee to the side to cool a little. "How's work?"

She knows I can't talk specifics. "Same as always, maybe a bit more intense some days." I bounce my eyebrows and am glad she seems to have taken the joke. "How about you?"

"Yeah, same too I guess." Elise grins. "Maybe a bit more intense as well." She forks up egg and mushroom. "Did you have a good Thanksgiving?"

"Not bad. I was in the air all day but no dramas. Mrs. Obermeier made me come round when I got home to collect a plate of food and also piled me up with leftovers to get me through a few days. How about you?"

"I see your neighbor is still a saint. I had dinner with Steven." She smiles. "The usual."

I mash and spread a banana over my toast. "How is he?"

She nods as she speaks. "Doing really well, gained some weight finally. He had a small stroke..." Her eyebrows furrow. "Uh, about a year ago but it doesn't seem to have caused any new damage. I pulled him out of that respite home not long after that. Just...they weren't taking care of him the way they should have. I bought him a home in Coto de Caza, had some renovations done for his needs and he's got two full-time staff, one day and one night to help out with cooking and showering and stuff. We still go out for burger night once a month, and he comes on set here and there when it's a non-pyrotechnics day. But you know him. He doesn't want his little sister meddling about in his life." She laughs. "Unless it's to buy him a sweet bachelor pad of course."

I offer a conspiratorial wink. "Of course." Elise's brother, Steven, had suffered a traumatic brain injury during the Iraq

War and required constant assistance with his daily schedule. Elise and Steven's parents had been murdered in a gas-station robbery gone wrong when Elise was fifteen, and Steven's care had fallen to Ellie. In a world where everything seems to be news fodder, she's somehow managed to keep this portion of her private life private. Or maybe I'm just still not good at ferreting out celeb gossip.

Elise tests her coffee then quickly sets it back down. "A couple of his friends from the respite home moved in too. They split costs for all the household things and those guys have their own part-time caretakers too. Stevie loves it, says it feels like college but with less girls and less beer."

Laughing, I agree, "Sounds like it." I'd met Steven many times—as Elise's friend—and we'd always gotten on like a house on fire. He was a gamer before his incident and after his TBI he used gaming as physical therapy to help with concentration and maintaining fine motor skills. Whenever I'd visited him, he'd kicked my ass in multiple video games until I'd had to admit my ego was too bruised to play with him anymore. He'd been gleeful and not at all gracious about his victories, and we moved to playing tabletop games where I evened our gaming scores. "I'm glad he's doing well."

"Same. That's all I've ever wanted really, for him to live his best kind of life. That's what I was thinking when I—" She shakes her head like she's shaking the thought out of her brain. I know exactly what thought just passed through her mind. She was thinking of being able to keep working so she could provide care for her big brother. It was probably the only thing that stopped me from hating her for what she did. When she speaks again, she's changed direction. "How are your parents?"

"They're great. Busy as usual and trying to do too much."

"Where are they this year?"

I have to think. "Uhhh, Ukraine. Before that they were in Jordan and Syria. They'll be home in the new year for their usual whirlwind US trip to lay eyes on me and visit Tristan before they're off again." The moment I was old enough to live on my own, my parents had abandoned their hospital jobs in Arizona where I'd grown up and now both worked for Médecins Sans Frontières.

Mom had tried to recruit both her kids into the Doctors Without Borders program before she realized neither of us had the aptitude or fortitude for medicine and we would not be fulfilling her vision of a happy family of four doctors. Tristan and I had both gone into law enforcement—me to the Federal Air Marshal Service and Tris worked his way up until he was a detective in the Sex Crimes Unit in Portland. Maybe he should have stayed a beat cop. Maybe he would have been able to handle that work better than the stress of Sex Crimes and he'd still be here instead of in a grave in the family plot in Arizona.

Elise's smile is almost shy. "I've kind of missed them."

"I miss them too. Until they're staying here for a week and then I most certainly do not."

Elise laughs. "True. But we always managed."

"That we did," I agree. My parents adored Elise, which helped ease any possible tension when they'd make their annual We Don't Like Hotels And Our Daughter Has A Guest Room trek from wherever they'd been working.

She pushes eggs around her plate. "Do you have plans for Christmas?"

"I'll be in-air in the few days before and I've put myself down to be on call on Christmas Day." Because I have no family or partner it makes sense for me to take any last-minute mission flights sent our way. And most importantly, it means I can use the "I worked Christmas" card to guilt my other team members into taking shifts for me when I need some time off. I'd done the same thing last year. "So…maybe working, maybe gorging on gingerbread cookies and watching *Die Hard*."

Elise reacts exactly as I expect. With an eye roll and, "*Die Hard* is not a Christmas movie."

And I react exactly the way I know she'd expect. "For the millionth time, it so is. It's set at Christmas, therefore it is a Christmas movie. Even Google says it's a Christmas movie. And we all know the Internet never lies."

Instead of her usual comebacks, which would inevitably include comparisons to *The Muppet Christmas Carol* and *It's a*

Wonderful Life and every single "traditional" Christmas movie ever made, she just smiles and says, "Sometimes it does. Last year I apparently shoplifted a dress, screamed at a barista for giving me oat milk instead of almond milk, donated a quarter of my salary to help orphans in Chile, was involved in some massive illegal undercover gambling thing, and stopped a child from being hit by a bus."

"I have no idea how you actually managed to work around all that."

"Me either," she says dryly. "At least I'm simultaneously a good and horrible person, according to Internet lies. Well, most of it was lies." She grins then turns back to her breakfast.

"Let me guess, the helping orphans donation was true?"

"Kind of. The least lie-ey of all." Her shrug is casual. "Not really a quarter of my salary."

It was probably half her salary. "Mmm. What about your Christmas plans? You're spending it with Steven?"

"Yep, same as always. He'll probably kick me out right after he opens his gift." At my eyebrows-raised query she elaborates, "A PlayStation Five."

I drop my toast to the plate. "You are fucking *kidding* me. I've been trying to get one of those consoles since pre-order but they sell out faster than Taylor Swift concerts. I think I'd have more luck getting a ton of uranium at this point."

Ellie laughs and repeats a line I've heard before. "Some things are easier when you're on television every week."

"Evidently." She probably just asked someone for a PS5 and they fell over themselves to give it to her.

She studies me, and her expression makes me think she knows exactly what I'm thinking. "I got it from Best Buy on pre-order. Just happened to sneak in with a mouse click at the right time, or so I've been told from every jealous person on set who knows I got one."

"And here I was thinking I was the one with the good reflexes. I clicked that 'add to cart' button so fast and so many times on so many different sites my finger nearly cramped, and still missed it. D'you think Stevie would mind if I dropped by to see him sometime?"

"I'm sure he'd love to see you. And share his PS-Five with you," she adds slyly.

"Well that too. I can't wait for him to kick my ass in full 4K high-definition graphics."

Elise's mouth quirks. "I'd forgotten about that. He really did used to kick your ass at games. And he was always so proud of it too, like he used to text me to remind me about it. We both know he's not good at holding back." Her expression melts to contemplative. "At any rate, I'm sure he'd be super happy to see you, gaming or no gaming, and with or without me."

Going to see Elise's brother without her feels borderline bizarre, despite the fact Steven and I were always friendly. The emphasis being on *friend*, which is what he probably thought I was to Elise. I swallow the last mouthful of my breakfast and make myself smile. "Well, I guess I know what I'm doing with these few days off. Gotta get some games practice in."

Smiling, Ellie uses her fork to point down the hall in the direction of the gaming cave. "Then I'll know where to find you."

After lunch, she does.

The gaming cave is my sacred space, filled with not only my comfy couch, my PlayStation and the huge television that I'm too embarrassed to admit how much I'd paid for, but also posters, figurines, and collector's editions of all my favorite games. Most of my free time when I'm home is spent indulging in bad posture and swearing at the screen. I'm doing just that, playing *Vindauga*—an installment of one of my favorite video game franchises, *Assassin's Guild*—and trying to stealthily infiltrate a hideout while bastard enemy guys keep spotting me and either killing me or making me retreat, when Elise slowly moves into my periphery.

"Is that *Rhetra*?" she asks quietly. There's a hint of delight in her question.

I have to suppress my cringe. Elise is the face model and voice actress for the just-released installment in the series—*Assassin's Guild: Rhetra*. The excitement I'd been cultivating since first hearing about the new game had deflated more quickly than the Hindenburg when news broke that my ex was basically the main character. Every gaming blog has her motion-captured face plastered all over it and eventually I had to stop reading them because I couldn't stand seeing it. I'd bought the game to complete my set but it's remained on the shelf where I put it the moment I brought it home.

I spin the joystick to rotate the camera to the front view of the character so she can see I'm playing a female Viking, not a female Greek warrior. An unexpected bout of embarrassment flares when I tell her, "No. It's last year's installment. *Vindauga*."

Elise tries to catch her expression before it reveals her feelings, but she drops it. She's hurt. "Oh."

I hasten to unhurt her. "I did buy it. It's over there on the shelf."

She frowns as she runs her fingers over the plastic-wrapped box that holds a hard copy of *Rhetra* along with some replica items from the series like the *Golden Guide* and the *Talisman of Life*, as well as a collector's edition game artwork book. She speaks to the shelf. "You haven't even opened it." The question is not so much a question as a statement that seems to hold hurt and accusation all in one mouthful.

"No."

She's still facing away from me when she asks, "Did you hate me so much that you couldn't even play it? Couldn't even open it?"

"For the millionth time, Ellie, I don't hate you. I never hated you. Not even after you left."

Now she turns around. "You don't hate me, but you can't play a game in which I voiced and motion-captured the face of the main character for?" Her forehead furrows. "I don't get it. It's not *me*. I only auditioned for the job because of watching you play for hours at a time. I know how much you love that series and I wanted to surprise you."

It had surprised me. Knowing the timelines for game development, I'd realized Elise must have started some of the basic face capture stuff when we were together. Nondisclosure stuff aside, she hadn't even mentioned she was working on a video game. Which meant that around the piano lessons she gave to supplement her acting income, which was sporadic back then, she'd been sneaking off to work on a game she knew I'd love.

I struggle to explain myself in a way that doesn't seem like I just don't want to see her. "Being you as a character where I'd hear you constantly and see your face in cut-scene cinematics and every time I turned myself around in the game just felt too raw. And too weird. I couldn't make myself do it."

She folds her arms over her breasts, the fingers of her free hand breaking free to gesture. "So, you can't play a fictional video game person that looks and sounds like me. But you can watch me looking and sounding like me in a television show."

"That's different."

"How so?"

"Because when I'm watching *Greed* it's just me watching you act as a character. I'm not pretending to be someone who has your body. It just felt too weird to be so immersed." I pause and admit, "And listening to all the grunts and groans and whatever other sounds I know you'll make during combat felt too… intimate." Listening to those sounds, recalling them in other contexts is just too much.

Elise smiles like a patient parent. "It's a *character*, Avery. It's not really me, you know. It's my face but they gave me facial scars and made my eyes brown and made me taller and waaay ripped. I mean, have you seen her abs on this box?" She doesn't mention her sound effects.

I move the joystick around, making my character wobble. "I know, but it just felt like too much."

"I can understand that. But you still bought it," she points out.

"Well, yeah. You know how I feel about supporting creators." I pause and wonder if I should admit what I'm about to admit. "Plus, I thought good sales would translate into more voiceover and game work for you if you wanted it. I know one sale isn't world changing, but…"

Now her smile turns tentatively hopeful. "Maybe it will. I wouldn't mind more of that work, even though it was exhausting to fit in the voice work around filming *Greed*. I…after we broke up, doing the voice acting was not fun. I kept thinking of you gaming." She forces her smile into extra brightness. "Hopefully, if we spend a little time together now it might make it easier? I know how much you love that franchise and I'd hate to think of you not playing because of me."

"Maybe," I venture. But I'm pretty sure it won't make it easier.

Elise laughs. "You know, even I've played it."

I try not to laugh myself. "And how'd that go?"

"Confusingly," she admits. She sounds almost gleeful about it. "I died *a lot*. I ran into things a lot. And I threw away some important questing item. Twice. I think they used the footage of me making a fool of myself for some marketing stunt thing."

The visual makes me cackle. Elise's favorite games are those she can play on her phone or tablet, like her Pokémon Go thing. But she was always interested in watching me gaming and when she asked if she could play, I tried to teach her. It ended pretty much the same way she's just described. "I might have to dig that up from the Internet and have a laugh."

"You could. Or you could just open it up and let me have a go at it now and laugh at me in person."

I can't figure out why she's so set on me engaging with *Rhetra*. "Why do you want me to play this game so badly?"

"It's my first full main character voice role and I'm really proud of it, and I think it's great." Elise's eyebrows come together. "The bits I saw during gameplay that is. I don't know, I guess I just thought you'd really enjoy it. I'm sure you won't really think it's like me. I've got an accent too, remember?"

"That makes it even worse," I say dryly. "Though I had suspected as much, given this game is set in Ancient Greece. You know how I feel about you and accents." As in they turn my insides to mush.

Her mouth opens and I just *know* she was about to say something with an accent. Apparently, and fortunately, my alarmed expression stops her and with a wry grin, she closes her mouth again. Elise plus accent equals melted Avery. It always has. Around the grin she tells me, "I'm sure you can imagine kind of what it sounds like."

"Mhmm. I'm sure I can." I've heard snippets, and even those short sound bites left me feeling so simultaneously anxious and excited that I didn't know what to do with myself.

"Okay then." She carefully straightens the *Rhetra* box on the shelf. "My grocery order will be here soon so I guess I'd better make room in the fridge and pantry. I'll leave you to your adventuring."

CHAPTER EIGHT

Elise cooked dinner—a delicious lentil Bolognese created with the spoils of her grocery order—which means I'm on dish duty. While I rinse plates, pots, and pans, she hops up onto the counter and crosses her ankles, gently bumping her heels against the cabinet doors. It's such a familiar pose, her sitting up there to my right while I clean up after she's cooked, that a wave of nostalgia sweeps over me. I run my hand through the stream of too-hot water, trying to squash the feeling.

When I turn, plates in hand to stack them in the dishwasher, Elise says, "I was thinking maybe we could go for a hike sometime soon?" Her smile is dry. "My cabin fever is getting out of control."

"Sure." Laughing, I add, "Cabin fever? It's only been one full day, honey. Maybe we need to find some coping strategies to get you through the next few weeks." I cringe internally and hope she hasn't noticed the endearment that slipped out. Being with her again makes me feel like nothing has changed. "If you feel okay going outside then you don't have to keep yourself cooped up here. Just be cautious when you're out. And you could always take Bennie for a walk if you want something to help keep people away." Most people swerve to avoid my giant marshmallow of a dog, which is always amusing.

Elise grips the edge of the counter and leans forward, teasingly toeing me in the butt. "I've found a coping strategy. Going for a hike."

"Right." I close the dishwasher door and wash my hands. "So when and where?"

"When? ASAP. Where?" Her voice drops until it's a low murmur. "Switzer Falls."

My stomach does a rollercoaster drop. Our second date was that trip-and-puke hike to Switzer Falls. Then it became one of our regular trail spots. I try to make a joke. "Haven't puked on anyone recently and feeling the urge to change that?"

"Actually, I think I got a little on that doctor on the plane, so I'm good for another few months."

"She's probably honored to have been the recipient of Emmy Award-winning puke."

Elise grins. "Maybe she is. I should have charged her for the pleasure." The grin softens but doesn't fade. "You okay with Switzer?"

Okay with the location, yes. Okay with the surge of memories I know it's going to dredge up, not so much. But I've been living with memories for a while now, so what's wrong with a little reminder here and there? Especially if it helps her. "Sure. We can go on the weekend?"

"Perfect."

"Yep, great." I straighten the dishtowel. "I'm going to—" Do something, anything but be right here. "Just, uh, check the doors are locked."

Elise snags my arm as I move past her. "Avery…"

I don't resist as she pulls me to a stop and tugs my arm until I turn to face her. Elise opens her knees to give me room and when I stand between them, she closes her legs until her knees lightly rest against my hips. The pressure isn't forceful or constricting but she's letting me know very clearly that she wants me right where I am. I think I want me right where I am.

She studies me intently, as if trying to decipher what I'm thinking. "I meant what I said on the plane. I've *really* missed you." Elise's hands slide up my biceps, over my shoulders, up my neck until she's cupping my jaw. Her thumbs delicately brush back and forth over my skin, and I suppress a shudder. "Do you remember our first kiss?" she quietly asks. "I think about it all the time. How you brought me back here, cleaned up my scrapes, lent me clothes and a brand-new toothbrush. How shy you were, like you weren't sure if I wanted to kiss you or not, when I'd wanted to kiss you the day we first met and I thought you knew that." She tilts her head to indicate the space around us. "It was right here. Do you remember?"

I remember it vividly. We'd both showered after the hiking puke incident and her hair was still wet. It plastered itself to her neck in long strands that I carefully moved aside when I couldn't keep myself from kissing her neck any longer. She'd smelled fresh, tasted spicy like my cinnamon toothpaste, and everything had felt so right that the deep ache of want I'd been holding back had immediately eased. "That's not fair," I whisper hoarsely.

"I know." But she asks the question again. "Do you remember?"

"Yes."

"And the last time we made love." Elise swallows hard. "There was so much love, despite it all."

I want to shake her for saying this now, for dragging memories and feelings from that box I've kept them shut up in. "Yes," I agree. "There was." My voice feels hollow in my ears, even though I know what I'm saying is anything but hollow.

She takes my left hand, studies my thumb and forefinger. "When I'm alone, I think about you fucking me, think about me fucking you. And I make myself come with that image in my brain. I remember these calluses." Elise sucks first my thumb, then my forefinger, slowly, her tongue sliding along each digit. After all this time she still knows exactly how to press my buttons. "Gaming and trigger calluses. You still have them. I remember how that rough part of your finger used to feel, contrasting with the softer skin of the rest of your finger, as you touched me."

"Damn you," I choke out. And then I pull her face down, and kiss her. The moment I feel her lips against mine I'm struck with the same nervous excitement as the first time we kissed. That excitement had quickly run out of control and she'd begged me to take her to bed. I did, but not until I'd had her on the kitchen counter first. This excitement feels slightly more settled, but still intense, and I know if I'm not careful it's going to run out of control again.

She opens her mouth to me, inviting me in, and I accept. I suck gently on her lower lip then lightly slide my tongue against hers. The sound she makes is so familiar, a quiet sigh and groan all in one. Her legs wrap around my waist, arms around my shoulders as if she's terrified I might back away from her and leave her wanting.

"I've missed you," she repeats, her lips a breath from mine. "I've missed this."

"Me too. But nothing has changed for you." My protest is weak. "This is only because of what happened on the plane." She's been frightened and wants to be comforted by something she knows. Something safe.

"You're wrong, Avery. So wrong. *Everything* has changed." Her thumb moves roughly over my lower lip before she kisses me again, softly, as if wanting to ease that rougher touch.

She tastes exactly as I remember and I can't help myself, I open my mouth and let my tongue glide over her lower lip. Elise's moan is barely audible. I close my arms around her and drag her forward. She tightens her legs around my waist, gripping me as I pull her down from the counter.

Ellie digs her heels into the back of my thighs to keep me with her as I push her back into the edge of the counter. I know it's wrong. I know we shouldn't be doing this. But I can't stop myself. I still love her. I never stopped loving her. But I'd thought I'd finally reached a point where I didn't need her anymore. Right now, with her clinging to me, her hands tangled in my hair, pressing herself into me, her rough kisses driving me crazy, I know how stupid I was to think I didn't need her.

I take a fistful of her hair, pull it gently to make her arch her neck so I can have access. I focus on the non-bandaged side of her neck, suck her skin, lightly nip under her ear then lick the spot I've just bitten. "Are you—" I don't quite know how to ask if she's safe, if she's been with other people and if I should be worried about that. I desperately want to bury myself in her wet heat and the thought that I can't do that, that I can't taste her again, makes my throat tight.

Ellie intuits what I'm trying to ask. She carefully disengages herself to drop to the floor, keeping one leg hooked around my thigh. "Yes," she gasps. "Please. Please."

As I work at the ties on her sweats I murmur, "When was the last time you let a woman taste you? Let a woman fuck you?" I run my tongue from the base of her neck to under her ear.

She inhales sharply. "No one since you."

Abruptly, I pull away. "Really?" It seems unfathomable that she's gone unloved for all this time.

Elise's eyes are wide, begging me to believe her. "I'm telling the truth. After I…left, I couldn't stand the thought of anyone else's hands on me."

"I've seen photos of you with—people." I want to grind my teeth at the thought. Not of a man touching her, but of *anyone* else touching her. That jealous flare makes me feel vaguely ill. I've never been the jealous type, even when we were together. But especially now, I have no right. She's not mine anymore and if she wants to have someone new in her bed every week then it's not for me to have feelings about.

Ellie runs her hands through the hair brushing my shoulders. "Everyone needs friends. Tomas and Marcus are beards, Avery. Men to keep the media interested and stop speculation. I hate it, but you should know how it works."

I do. I know all too well and I hate that publicity machine. When Elise got the role in *Greed*, I watched her manager send her out to get public coffee or have public meals with Elise's male friends to sow the seeds of heterosexuality. And I stayed home and wondered when it would be my turn to be out with her in public as a couple. Not long after I'd wondered that, I got the answer.

I rumble out an indistinguishable sound and she places the softest kisses along my cheekbone before gently biting my earlobe. Then she presses herself to me, grinding against my pelvis as her words choke out. "You know I've never lied to you about us. Not once."

"I know," I say, my throat tight with that thought.

"Nobody's touched me since you, and that's a very long time. God, I want you. Please." Her hands are frantic in my hair and her lips move restlessly over mine. "Let's worry about all the other stuff later, please. Can we do that? Right now, I just need you. Please, just fuck me. I want to feel your mouth on me, your fingers inside me, I need your body on top of me."

I don't think I've ever wanted anything as badly as I want her now. But it's such a bad idea. Hell, it's the *worst* idea. It's only going to confuse things, make everything topsy-turvy. But the familiarity of her draws me in and makes me forget all the bad ideas. I suck her neck then bite until she groans. It's going to leave a mark on her and I don't care. Ellie doesn't either and her low moan of pleasure at the small amount of pain I've inflicted is all the confirmation I need.

I'm going to take her hard and fast like she wants, then once she's soft and sated I'm going to take her to bed and have her slowly. I'm going to take my time rediscovering everything she took away from me. I'm going to fuck her exactly how she loves it and make her remember what it's like to be with a woman. I'm going to taste her until she comes again in my mouth.

Her gasps are of frustration, not pleasure, because I can't get my hand inside her sweats, can't get to what I want. I take a step back so I can strip her sweats and panties from her, then pull her to the floor on top of me. Sliding a hand between us, I find what I'm seeking. Find her wet and hot and wanting. Elise braces her hands on my shoulders, her fingernails digging in through my clothes. She grips fistfuls of my shirt and pulls, trying to get me to sit up. The moment our torsos touch, Ellie wraps her arms around my shoulders and settles herself so she's straddling me. Her kiss is frantic, needy, like she's trying to tell me through this kiss how desperate she is.

Unexpectedly, unwantedly, I think about that last time we made love, hours after she told me she was leaving. I'd gone to bed, numbly trying to process how my life had suddenly crumbled without warning. Elise hadn't joined me, and I'd drifted on the edge of uneasy sleep until the bedroom door had creaked open a little after midnight. I heard her move through the darkness, then the shift as she settled on the edge of the bed right by my hip. Her hand had slid under the covers until it found my thigh.

I did it because I was so desperate to keep showing her that what we had was right and real. And I thought if only she could be honest with herself, with the world, then maybe this wouldn't happen. That she wouldn't leave. But she did leave, just a few hours after she'd held me as I'd climaxed.

The kiss eases and Elise goes still, studying me in that way she has which makes me feel like she already knows what I'm thinking before she asks the question. "What are you thinking about?"

"Everything." Perhaps stupidly, I add, "The last time we made love."

Her mouth quirks, and I don't know if she wants to smile or cry. I don't think she knows either. "I'm so sorry, for that last night. I shouldn't have done it. I needed you to know I loved you even though I couldn't stay. I just wanted you one more time, wanted something perfect."

"Was it perfect?" I ask before I can stop myself.

Her eyelashes flutter. "It was," she says, her voice tight and hoarse with emotion.

"Yes," I agree. "It was." Just as quickly as those thoughts intruded, I suddenly don't want to think about it anymore. I don't want those old emotions in my head. I want to focus on these new emotions where I know exactly what she wants but everything feels different, new, and exciting. I kiss her and force myself to let go.

Ellie lifts herself from my lap and I steady her with an arm around her waist before she settles herself on my fingers. She groans into my mouth. That sound, the sensation of her engulfing me sends excitement spiraling through my body, straight to my clit. I lift my hips, knowing even as I do it that I'm not going to find the friction I'm so desperate for.

She grinds down onto my hand, riding me in that frantic way that nobody else ever has, and thoughts of my own pleasure take a backseat. When we were together, quickies in the kitchen were frequent, but now that she's riding me to her imminent climax I realize I don't want that now. I want her in bed. I want to see every glorious inch of her spread out for me. I want to explore all the landmarks I already know but the memories of which have faded over time.

I manage, "Bed" around our kisses and the moment that word is out of my mouth she climbs from my lap and drags me up to stand. The guest room is closer than my room and we kiss our way through the house, dropping clothing and tugging at our remaining garments to loosen them so the moment we're inside the room we can drag them off. We're barely inside the door before we're naked and my fingers are on her clit again. She's gasping erratically, a sound I know all too well, the sound that means she can't focus on anything but what I'm doing to her.

I know she wants hard and fast right now, and I'm going to give that to her. But first, I just need a taste. I suck tight nipples into my mouth then kiss, lick, and suck my way over ribs, tight belly, pierced bellybutton. When she realizes my destination, Ellie pushes me further down her body, spreading her legs in invitation. She consents with a single choked, "Yes."

I want to dive into her, devour her, lick and suck until she's screaming with pleasure beneath me. But I also want to lick her slowly, slide my tongue through every crevasse of her and play with her clit exactly the way I know she loves. I'm so overwhelmed by all the things I feel and want that I don't know what to do.

And Elise, sensuous, pleasure-seeking Elise seems to know exactly what I'm thinking and knows how to take charge and guide me to exactly what she wants. Exactly what I want. Her fingers curl in my hair as she urges me downward. "Avery, please. Put your mouth on me. Just lick me."

I kiss my way up her inner thigh, then take a long moment to indulge myself in her scent before I close my lips around her clit. Ellie's light grip in my hair turns to a tug and then a sharp yank when I slide my tongue against her. Fuck, she's delicious and so aroused that her wetness coats my chin, thick and hot. I was going to take her fast and hard first, but the moment I taste her I decide I'm going to indulge myself. Just a little.

I make a slow pass through her labia, letting my tongue linger on the soft, warm, wet flesh, sucking and licking. Elise's exhalation feels like relief and the tight grip she's keeping on my hair releases. I want to stay here for the rest of the night, just tasting her, sliding my tongue along her folds and around her clit, teasing her until she comes in my mouth. But that's not what she wants right now. Next time…

There's not going to be a next time. But I still have this time.

When I run my tongue around the underside of her clit she bucks her hips into my mouth, pressing herself even harder against me. She writhes beneath me, restless and desperate, and that desperation flows to me. I want to feel her climax. When I poke my tongue against her entrance, Ellie's arousal coats my lips. She's almost hyperventilating, begging me to help her come, to fuck her harder. And I do. The moment I lightly flick her clit with my tongue she cries out, "Fuck me, please. I want you inside me."

I know exactly what those cries mean. I push myself up the bed, straddle her thigh and slide my fingers inside her again. She lifts her thigh, forcing that tight muscle against my clit and when I inhale sharply at the sensation, she presses harder. We're in time with each other, both of us moving at the same pace toward what we want. A distant part of my consciousness mulls over that, how it's happening now of all times. Sometimes when we'd make love, we would start off out of sync—one of us wanting hard and fast while the other begged for slow and sweet—and we'd butt up against each other like bumper cars, until something would finally fall into place and we'd be moving together again.

She wraps the leg that isn't currently driving my clit crazy around my waist, angling herself so I can get my fingers deeper. A bite to my neck, a suck on my earlobe, scratching nails on my back. "Oh god. Oh god. I—" Ellie lifts her hips, pressing herself more firmly against my hand. "I love it, just like that, please fuck me just like that."

The sensation of her tightening around my busy fingers tells me she's getting close. Her desire fuels mine and as I thrust inside her I keep riding her thigh, grinding my clit down against her. The sensation draws a moan from both of us. Fuck, I want her to come, want to feel it, want to know it was me who gave that to her again. But I want to draw it out, take my time to enjoy her, enjoy this. It's like feasting after a famine and I'm only going to have one chance to experience this.

With each thrust, my thumb glides lightly up and down over her clit until the pitch of her breathing changes to rapid, almost hyperventilating. She bites my shoulder hard enough to make me flinch and she doesn't apologize by kissing or licking the mark as she usually would. She's too far gone. Underneath me, she shudders, her back arching until she's pressed right against me. When I try to keep my weight from her, she holds me closer until I surrender to what she wants and let myself settle on her. Her small, tight nipples rub against mine and the added stimulation makes my clit throb unbearably.

I surrender again and rock myself against her thigh. As if she knows exactly what I'm feeling, Ellie grips my ass, pulling me harder against her. I almost buckle from the sensation and choke out a rough, "Ohmygod."

Elise is panting and when she speaks her words are hoarse. "That's it. Please, I'm going to come."

I'm trying to wade through my arousal to focus on her climax, the climax I know is imminent. She's so receptive, so responsive, and no matter how I fuck her she always reacts the same way just before her orgasm. That long slow shudder, the way she's desperate to touch me, the involuntary movement of her hands against my skin. She's so *so* close. I thrust deeper, slower and keep my thumb sliding against her clit until I feel the unmistakable sharp intake of breath and her groan of pleasure.

Ellie pulls me down for a fierce kiss, her teeth grazing my lower lip before she kisses me hard and moans her climax against my mouth. Her hoarse cries beg me not to stop, to keep fucking her as she comes. She tightens around my fingers, growing impossibly more wet. I suck her tongue and push deep inside her as she climaxes underneath me, around my fingers. Her nails dig deep into my skin as she repeats a single word, over and over and over.

Yes. Yes. Yes. Yes. Yes.

That word is in my ear. Against my skin. Under my skin. That word reminds me of every other yes she said to me, every time we made love, every time she agreed, every time she went along with me. And it makes me feel so suddenly pulled apart that I can barely breathe as I bring her down again with gentle strokes and soft kisses. Elise trembles, muscles quivering with her release and she's holding on to me as if she fears she might fall. She makes eye contact with me and that feeling of coming apart is so intense that I don't know what to do, what to feel. I have to kiss her or I'm going to say something I'll regret, or cry, or both.

Any thought of taking a moment to catch my breath and settle my own arousal so I can think beyond lust vanishes when Elise squirms from underneath me. With a hand on each thigh, she pushes me up slightly and wriggles to lie under my spread legs, before I'm pulled roughly down onto her face. Her hot tongue makes contact with my labia and she sucks hard, dragging soft flesh into her mouth, sliding her tongue through my folds until she finds my clit. I grip the headboard with both hands, desperately trying to stay upright as she expertly works me toward climax.

I'm so aroused, so wet, and ready to come. Her fingers dig into my trembling thighs. Her tongue is everywhere, sliding through my labia, licking my clit, gently poking my entrance. The stimulation from her thigh already has all my nerves firing and it doesn't take long until the first threads of my climax begin to unravel under her tongue's attention. Heat rushes through my body, spreading downward into my clit, and I come in waves of unrestrained pleasure.

It hits me so strongly and suddenly that my legs tremble and it's only Elise's grip on my thighs supporting my faltering grip on the headboard that keeps me from collapsing. I...I...

I'd forgotten this. Forgotten how much better it feels when someone else makes me come. Forgotten how much better Elise is than any other lover I've had at drawing every ounce of sensation from me. She's still lightly kissing my clit, dragging the lingering effects of my climax out in slow pulses of heat. After a few moments, she moves to kiss my inner thighs. Her lips linger against my skin, light and soft.

Then she speaks. "Thank you." Her voice is so quiet that it takes me a moment to realize what she's said.

I don't know what exactly she's thanking me for and I don't know how to respond. So I don't. I carefully climb off her and roll onto my back, sinking into the mattress. Elise props herself up on an elbow, looking down at me as if it's the first time she's really seeing me. She lowers her head, her lips brushing against my cheek. I close my eyes.

"I'd forgotten how beautiful your eyelashes are," she whispers. I feel the air blowing across my closed eyelids before she kisses them with the lightest touch.

I feel like I've just woken up after an odd and dimly unpleasant sexual dream, like sleeping with someone I would never sleep with. The inane, badly timed thought rattling around my head comes out in an attempt to say something that doesn't reveal how I'm feeling. "This bed is so comfortable. I can't believe I've never lain down on it."

"It really is." Elise's light fingers trace patterns on my skin. She makes a small sound, like she's testing the way a word might feel in her mouth, before quietly asking, "You didn't want me in your bed?" She sounds almost childlike, as if it's personal.

That self-consciousness and her obvious fear of rejection makes me want to soothe her, even as I know I should be trying to distance us, especially from this. But she's still Elise. And I still care about her. I sit up, dragging the sheet up to cover my exposed skin. "It wasn't that at all. I wanted you right away and this bed is closer." I catch myself before I tell her next time I'm going to fuck her in my bed.

There's not going to be a next time.

CHAPTER NINE

It takes me a few seconds to realize she's no longer in bed with me and another few to realize that I'm in my guest room. Elise's fearful question about me not wanting her in my bed echoes through my head and I suppress an anxious shudder. If only she knew how much I've wanted that almost every night when I'd go to bed alone. How much I wanted her to come back, wanted to love her in my bed again. But now, removed from what we did last night, I wonder if I'm insane for sleeping with my ex. I think I might be. I've done some stupid things but this probably tops the list of Avery Stupidity.

I lie still for a few moments, just listening, and hear her moving about in the kitchen. The sound of kibble being scooped into the metal dog bowl precedes the back screen door opening and Bennett's heavy excitement on the floor as he rushes in after his morning potty stop. I almost jump out of bed to make sure she's feeding him properly when I remember she knows what and how much the dog eats.

I creep out of the room, gathering my clothing along the way. My shirt is missing but I don't want to walk down the hall toward the kitchen to retrieve it in case I bump into Elise while I'm naked. The idea is ludicrous, given how many times she's seen me naked. But that's different. Last night was different. Thinking about the heated look in her eyes when she removed the last piece of clothing from my body is enough to send a fresh, slow roll of excitement through me. It was the exact look she used to get when she'd tear my clothing off like she couldn't stand the fact I was covered.

After half an hour on the treadmill to try and work out some of my discomfort, I take a shower, soaping myself roughly in a useless attempt to wash away the lingering sensation of Elise's mouth from my skin. I want to crawl into my own bed and slide under the covers to hide instead of walking into my kitchen to face Elise. The more I think about it, the more I know I've fucked up, and regret weighs heavily along with a hundred other emotions.

I don't regret the sex. I don't think anyone would regret going to bed with Elise. But I do regret my weakness and the confusion and everything I know that's going to follow on from it. Being horny and lonely and still in love with her isn't an excuse for jumping on her like I did, even if she did goad me into it. I ponder that thought. She did goad me, not that I needed much goading. I wonder about her reason for acting the way she did, for driving us both toward that moment. Maybe she was just horny and lonely too.

I take my time moisturizing, examining my face for wrinkles, tidying my eyebrows, and getting dressed until I resign myself to the fact I can't hide forever, as much as I wish I could. In the kitchen, Elise is playing with Bennie and when my dog spots me, his tail does its usual morning windshield-wiper-happy-to-see-me routine. But after his brief acknowledgment his focus goes right back to Elise who is holding his favorite elephant toy. She throws it down the hall and Bennie scoots past me to retrieve it. Nice to know where I stand. I don't blame him. He loves Elise. *Just like you*, my brain so unhelpfully reminds me.

Elise's smile is bright and for the briefest moment it feels like any other morning when we were together where she usually beat me to the kitchen. "Morning."

"Morning." I gesture at her neck. "You've taken the dressing off."

"I have. It felt awful and the Internet said removing it after a few days was fine." She smiles. "This morning was close enough to two days."

"Mmm." I lean as close as I dare to study the pinkish line on her neck. It looks okay, not inflamed or angry at all, just like a scratch really.

Elise holds up her mug. "Coffee's just brewed."

"Thanks."

She tosses the newly returned elephant toy down the hall. "Do you want me to make eggs?"

"No thanks, I'm good." Food is beyond my anxiety capacity right now and even as I acknowledge the anxiety I haven't managed to scrub away, I don't even know why it's there. We were consenting adults and it's not like we've done something illegal or immoral. But it still feels wrong. It feels like I've just dragged myself backward to immediately after the breakup. Maybe even further back than that.

"Have you seen the news?" Elise asks.

"Not yet."

"It's begun. Only one mention so far but I expect it to cascade into many mentions." She holds up her phone. "Elise Hayes threatened by overzealous fan on flight. There's one badly framed and badly focused phone photo of the…event, but no video thankfully. Also no mention of you, or the fact it was an assault not a threat, and with a lot of 'allegedly' throughout. It's interesting they're more worried about him suing them than telling the truth."

"Well, we knew it'd leak eventually, right? And isn't avoiding lawsuits practically a national pastime for any big corporation?"

"Right." After that single word, Elise is silent until I finally look at her. The moment we make eye contact she asks, "Do you want to talk about last night?"

I'm desperate to talk about it and talking about it is the last thing I want to do. I shrug and turn away to the coffeepot. I take my time filling my mug and adding almond milk but instead of moving to the table or checking up on news, I keep the counter as a barricade between us.

In the absence of my verbal response Ellie barrels on. "Clearly something's bothering you and I can only assume it's because of what we did last night." She clears her throat. "I don't regret it."

"I think I do," I say without thinking. It's the truth, but it's a cruel one and I should have tempered my response so it didn't sound so harsh.

Bennett returns with his elephant and drops it expectantly at Elise's feet. But instead of picking it up, she gestures that the game is done for now. He takes his elephant and wanders off to plop down in his bed in the corner of the room and chew. Ellie stares at her hands and after an eternal silence, finally looks up at me. "Why do you regret it?"

So many reasons swarm my brain and I try one on for size. "Because we're not together."

"Being together isn't a prerequisite for sleeping with someone, Avery."

"No, it's not," I agree. "But we broke up for a reason and sleeping together is…it's counterproductive to everything and it's going to confuse things even more than they already are."

"Counterproductive to what?" she quietly asks.

"To me moving on with my life." I set the mug down and wrap my hands around it. I don't know if it's fair or even worth it to tell her how her leaving me made me feel like I'd done something wrong, or that there was something wrong with me. But we shared so much of our life and it feels wrong to not let her know. More than that, the mean and childish part of me wants her to know just how much she hurt me, wants her to feel as bad as I did. But I can't find anything cruel to say, and the only thing that comes out is a hoarse, whispered, "Ellie…you left me."

Her expression softens. "Yes, I did. And I regret it more than I think you'll ever realize." The way she says it is tight, like the words don't want to come out and she's forcing them from her mouth.

"You left me," I repeat. "And you did it so suddenly and without any regard for my feelings or my thoughts on how we could have made it work. Having you here now is fresh torture for me because I've moved past it, moved past that fear that maybe there was something fundamentally wrong with me for you to have done what you did."

Her eyebrows shoot upward. "There was nothing wrong with you, *is* nothing wrong. I thought we'd talked about this, about the reasons why I couldn't stay."

"Did we? Like, really, I'm not just being facetious here. Did we actually discuss it? Because all I remember is you throwing a bunch of reasons at me before you packed up your shit and left."

Her voice lowers to soft intimacy. "Avery."

"Don't!" I take a shuddering breath. "Please don't say my name like that."

"Like what?"

"Like…like saying my name is going to make it all okay. Like just because you say it's fine that we can move past what happened."

"I'm not saying it's fine and I don't want to move past it. I hate it. You have no idea how much. Every day since, I've agonized over the choice I made. But it's done and there's nothing you or I can do about it but accept it and maybe try to move forward to some place where we can both be comfortable."

A slow panic rolls through me, followed by that same sickening dread I had when she said "I can't do this" right before she told me she was breaking up with me. I don't think she really gets it, or if she does—does she care? "Do you understand why this is hard for me? Why it's confusing and upsetting?"

"I do," she murmurs. "I'm sorry. I know having me here must be horrible for you but I don't know what else to say. I did what I did."

"Do you mean last night, or leaving me?"

She doesn't hesitate. "Leaving you. I regret that deeply but as I told you, I don't regret last night."

I pounce. "But you didn't *have* to leave me, Ellie. You chose to do it that way. You chose your life as an award-winning, universally loved, in-demand TV It Girl over me." That's the thing that's always stuck whenever I've thought about her breaking up with me. That I just wasn't worth it. That her career was more important than the life we were building together. The life together that I thought would be for the rest of mine because I loved her and loved *us* so much that I couldn't imagine trying to build what we had with anyone else.

Her mouth twists into something ugly and I don't know if she's angry or if the words taste bad. "You know why I left. Because…because I wanted to make sure I could keep paying for Steven's care. Because I was a fucking naïve idiot who listened to people I thought were supposed to have my back. Because Sandra and Bert told me over and over that I was getting too old and this was it, my big shot, and if I let it go because I was…" She air quotes. "*Stupid about my personal life* then I might never get a chance like that again, the lead role on a pilot. It was a dream for someone hardly known like me. I'd busted my ass for so many years that the thought of it all being taken away from me just because of who I loved made me feel sick. But I had to make a choice."

"It made me feel sick too." It still makes me feel sick. "And I know how hard you've worked, Elise. I was with you, supported your dream for five years. Five years of trying, of despondency and elation. Do you remember when you got the part on *Greed*?"

Her mouth opens, then closes again. A range of emotions flash across her face and I know she's thinking the same thing I am. The phone call where she was so excited she could barely speak, simply babbled nonsensical words that took me ages to decipher until I realized what she was saying and I could barely contain my pride and my excitement. I sat in the lounge at La Guardia and cried because I was so proud of her. On the way home from the airport I bought an expensive bottle of champagne for her to drink in celebration, then we made love and talked about the future until the sun peeked over the horizon. A brand-new day of a brand-new life.

What she can't know is how I felt in that moment. The hope and the promise and the feeling that finally something good was happening. That I'd found the one for me and she'd landed a life-changing role and everything was going to be amazing from that moment onward. That feeling only lasted a few months. When she doesn't answer, I keep talking. "I remember that moment like it was just last week. And every time I think about it I think about how perfect everything was up until those few months later when you started filming. And the way you just... came right out and said it. That it wasn't going to work, that you couldn't risk being out." She'd barely been able to speak around her tears, but I'd heard the words so clearly.

"Don't you remember a thing I said?" she asks tightly.

"I told you, I remember everything. Every. Single. Word." I want to forget those words, forget the feeling I have every time I think of them. But they're a persistent horrible niggle that sticks in my brain.

"Then why don't you remember the part where I said it wasn't fair to you to keep being hidden away, me not being true was unfair to you."

I almost choke on what she's just said. "I do remember that. And I remember how much of a slap in the face it was. Like you were trying to placate me with this...this...*add-on* of why you couldn't do it. A footnote after the main event of your career being more important than me."

It's obvious how much she's trying to control her emotion, but the tremble in her hands gives her away and she tucks them into her armpits as if trying to hide her feelings. "I didn't want you to have to deal with it and I thought it was better for you to not have a partner who you couldn't take out, and for you to be hidden. That seemed incredibly unfair to me."

"But it wasn't for you to decide. You didn't even ask me how I felt about it. You didn't talk to me about it, about how we could work through it or navigate it so we could stay together." I almost laugh at the absurdity of my last statement. We couldn't have navigated it because she was immovable on this aspect of her personal life.

"What do you want me to say?" she snaps. "That I made a mistake? That I hurt you? I fucking know what I did."

"It's not just about that. It's *how* you did it, without a single discussion. You *left* me, Elise. You made the decision. It was completely one-sided. You went without a backward glance and moved on to your new life. You made me feel like a pair of jeans you'd outgrown that you couldn't even be bothered donating to Goodwill, so you just tossed them in the trash." The breath I inhale doesn't satisfy me and I huff it out to gulp down another. "And you never once told me this, *us*, was going to be an issue for you when you became a big famous actress. I had no idea until you told me it was over. We were together for five years. Five fucking wonderful years. And not once during that time did I have any inkling you were going to do this to me. You never shared how worried you really were, how terrified you were of losing everything. Or why it had to be done then."

"I did it to me too," she says quietly, but her newly acquired calm doesn't assuage my anger.

"Right, because you really seem to have suffered since you left me. Award-winning star of an award-winning show. Hanging off the arm of every hot guy in town while you're out at your parties and award ceremonies and courtside games and hitting up the hottest restaurants. Yeah, that really looks like suffering to me." The sarcasm makes me sound bitter and angry and for a moment, I don't recognize myself.

"You of all people should know appearance is everything in this town and nothing is ever what it seems. You have *no* idea how hard it was for me to do what I did. How I agonized over it, second-guessed myself, beat myself up over it. I loved you, Avery. I still do. That didn't just go away because we broke up."

"If you did love me then you wouldn't have left me for the reason you did. You chose work over me, after telling me every day that you loved me. You took the coward's way out instead of standing up for what you believed in and what you wanted. It makes me sick."

I know I'm being cruel, that I'm oversimplifying it. I know why she chose her acting career, that she'd spent a lifetime trying to make it and being responsible for her brother's care was financially draining and her big break made that reality a lot easier. But all that knowledge doesn't make it any easier for me. It was 2019, not the fifties for Christ's sake. Nobody cares about LGBTQ+ celebs anymore. But she cared. She cared enough to hide who she really was.

Her mouth gapes before she finds words. "I thought we had discussed it. I told you repeatedly that I was afraid being publicly out might jeopardize my ability to find work, and you said you were okay with taking time to get comfortable."

"Get *comfortable*. Not just pack up and fuck off because I wasn't as important to you as working. It's like you made no effort to even see how being an openly out actress could fit into your life plan, like you just decided it belonged in the too-hard basket and bailed."

She looks incredulous, as if we're speaking different languages and pretending we understand each other. That look makes me pause. Maybe…maybe I hadn't taken it in and really listened to what she'd been trying to tell me, because I was so focused on the fact that I wanted her to be comfortable in her skin. Focused on the fact that I wanted to not feel like I was nobody. I wasn't chasing premieres and photoshoots and interviews. I was chasing…acceptance. Because by some warped thought process, maybe I equated her willingness to be out with the strength of her love for me.

Elise raises her hands. "I'm not like you, Avery. You were a lesbian from the moment you were born. It took me *years* to get comfortable with the fact I might not be straight, and then years again to maybe get brave enough to try dating a girl. To try dating *you*. You are the only woman I've ever dated, so please spare me your holier-than-thou bullshit, because you of all people should know that it's not a stroll in the park for some of us."

Bennett, apparently wondering what the hell is going on, gets up from his bed and wanders closer. He's looking between us, like he doesn't quite know what to do about our yell-fest. Elise and I have never yelled at each other, not even during our breakup. We'd rarely had even raised-voice arguments. He whines and I walk over to pet him. But then I'm too close to

Elise, close when I can't stand being near her, and I take a few steps back again. "I know that. And I'm sorry if my experience felt easier than yours, but a little credit please." My anger spikes. "When did I *ever* make you feel inferior or like you were just playing around because I was your first female lover? When did I ever not support you, not understand how hard it was for you?"

It takes her a few long moments to collect herself and when she answers me it's with a single, quiet, "Never." After a beat, her frustration breaks free. "What the fuck do you want me to say? That I'm an idiot? That I never loved you? That I *did* love you and leaving was the hardest thing I ever had to do? What do you want? Just tell me and I'll say it."

"I don't want any of that." I know she loved me. "I just want to understand why. Why you never said anything before. Why you didn't even try to figure out a way around it. Why you didn't fight for us. I thought what we had was something amazing, something real and lasting and ever since you left I've been trying to figure out if I was delusional all those years."

"You want to know why? Fine! I'll tell you." Her voice rises in pitch with each word, but before she can tell me *why*, Bennett growls low in his chest before letting loose with the scariest bark I've ever heard from him.

Bennett's hackles rise, sticking straight up from his hunched, defensive back like porcupine bristles. He doesn't move from where he's braced himself between us, but he's still barking deep authoritative barks and growling like he's trying his damnedest to stand up for himself and scare someone away. Elise's mouth falls open and she backs away from me.

I drop to my knees and open my arms to my dog. "Bennie. Hey, come here, bud." The barking stops and he glances first at Elise then regards me warily for a few seconds before coming right over to me. His posture is stiff, uncomfortable, and I run my hands through the fur on his shoulders, scratching him, soothing him. "I'm sorry, pal. I know, we were yelling and it was loud and scary. But it's okay. Everything's okay. I promise. We're not mad at you."

I rub his chest, his face, then keep massaging over his shoulders until he finally relaxes. When I tap my shoulder, he moves in to nestle against me for a hug and I keep scratching up and down his spine and along his sides, then hug him and kiss his head. "We're fine, pal, it's all good, you're all right. I'm sorry we scared you." He leans into me, snuggling down so his head is right under my chin and I keep cuddling him until I feel him relax further. I stand, leaning down to keep stroking between Bennie's ears and gently pulling just the way he likes.

He licks my hand, sniffs me then moves to Elise to give her the same treatment. She leans down to play with his ears as well and he pushes into her thigh as she rubs his head. I can't hear what she's saying to him, but I know she's crying. After a minute or so he leaves her to sit between us, watching us intently, his eyebrows dancing about as he looks from me to Elise.

Elise turns her tear-stained gaze to me. She raises both hands helplessly, fists clutching air. "You're right," she says quietly, sinking onto a kitchen chair. "I'm a coward. I wasn't strong enough to deal with the consequences of being out. I got scared. I made a mistake. I let people tell me how to live my life and I believed them when they said me being out would kill my chances of getting my contract renewed. And I've regretted it every single fucking day. I gave up everything for this career. *You* were everything. And now I don't even really know why I did it. It's not fair." She looks up at me, quickly wiping her eyes. "There. Are you happy now?"

"No," I exhale. I pull out the chair beside her. "Not at all. Why didn't you come back if you knew it was a mistake? We could have talked about it. Together. Maybe tried to work it out." If she'd done that, told me how sorry she was and that she would try to figure out how to live her life openly—not even right then, but just an acknowledgment that things would have to change for us to stay together—then I would have tried to work things through with her.

Elise laughs dryly. "Because I was too afraid of what you'd say to me. Afraid that you'd just tell me to fuck off. And I thought...I *knew* that I'd done something unforgivable. I don't forgive myself for that, not even now. So how could I have expected you to?" She rubs both hands hard over her face as if trying to scrub away the emotion.

"I'm sorry too, Ellie. I've been unfair. I guess I knew all this but I was so focused on my own hurt that I pushed yours aside."

She shrugs, as if acknowledging the statement without wanting to respond to it. "Do you want me to go?"

Bennett inserts himself between our knees and rests his head on my thigh. I play with one ear while Elise plays with the other. "Do you want to go? Do you have anywhere else that's safe to stay?"

"No, I don't want to go, but I could figure something else out if you want me out of your house."

My house. It used to be *our* house. My name was on the deed but we shared everything here, and her presence keeps reminding me of that. The bundle of anger and pain I've been holding on to is still there, but it doesn't feel so impenetrable. Maybe one day it really will open up, break apart, and leave me. "I want you to stay. I want you to be somewhere you feel comfortable and safe." I need that because even with everything we've just let out, the thought of her out there by herself and anxious about the Hayes Horde makes me so upset that I have to erase the idea as soon as it lands in my brain. "But...maybe don't kiss me again."

Laughing through her tears, Elise reminds me, "You kissed me."

I puff out a breath. "Right, I did. But you kind of made me do it. So if you promise to not do that again, then I promise I won't kiss you." This feels like the shittiest of shit vows.

Her laughter fades, but a smile keeps twitching at the edges of her mouth. "Okay then. It's a deal. No more kissing."

CHAPTER TEN

The excitement and enjoyment of having Elise in the house again has turned Bennett back into his squirmy, excitable puppy state. After his morning yard play time, he's still bouncing off the walls and continuously bringing both Ellie and me toys to toss for him, which makes me think he still needs to dispel some energy. I know how he feels, though my excitement and enjoyment is expressed perhaps with a little less zoomies and more with cautious, yet excited, trepidation.

He may still be anxious, because after his reaction to the fight yesterday morning, he's been super-needy—following both Ellie and I around the house and even trying to accompany me to the bathroom. At bedtime last night he came up to my bed three times instead of the usual once for his goodnight hand sniff, then sat by my bed for a while before eventually settling in his bed.

As soon as I'm done with my morning workout, I point at the basket of dog stuff by the front door. "Bennie, walk time. Get your leash. Leash. Just a walk this morning, no running,

I swear." He cocks his head. "Or you can come hike Switzer Falls with us tomorrow if you don't want to walk this morning." I gesture again and he rushes to the basket, snuffles around for a few seconds, pulls out his leash and drags it along the floor toward us. I had a feeling he'd choose a walk around the neighborhood over a four-and-a-half-mile hike.

Elise laughs. "I remember when we were teaching him how to do that."

"What was it you said? That a dog should take some responsibility for his life?"

"I didn't say that." She pauses, forehead furrowing. "Did I?"

"Mhmm. You really did." I take the leash Bennett's shoving against my leg and clip it to his collar.

Elise kneels and rubs the sides of his face. "That doesn't sound like me at all does it, Bennie? No it doesn't. I'm not a social dictator telling you how to live your life, am I?"

Bennett goes for a sneaky face lick but Elise jumps up before he makes contact. "Is it okay if I come too?"

The question is odd and unexpected. Though Bennie is my dog, he was part of the family we'd made and there would be no reason I'd ever say no to her walking with us. "Of course. You don't need to ask. And you know you can take him out whenever you want if I'm not here, obviously. If you're comfortable going out." She hasn't left the house, except to go into the backyard, since she got here three days ago.

She pauses to think about it, then echoes my thoughts. "I think I am. I mean it's not exactly an obvious place for me to be, and given the last time I was here was before I was well-known, it seems totally unlikely. And if I go out somewhere, with the emergency protective order in place, he can't come near me." Her forehead furrow is quickly followed by an eye roll. "Though of course, it's just a piece of paper."

Paper armor. Useless in the scheme of things. I don't want to agree with her that a restraining order means nothing to someone determined to make contact. And I also don't want to tell her that it's likely he lives in the city or close by, because that's what people like him do. "Have you heard anything more?"

Ellie avoids eye contact. "I had an email waiting for me this morning with some updates."

The fact she didn't mention it sooner is more upsetting than I'd thought it would be. I swallow the feeling and ask, "And? What's happening?"

Her voice and expression are carefully neutral. "Apparently his lawyer's a sweet talker because he was released on bail with a pinky promise that he'd return for other hearings and his trial because he's been a model citizen until this. They said he waived his right to a preliminary hearing?"

That catches my attention. Though I'm no lawyer, I have a *very* basic understanding of court processes. The only real reason I could think of for him to do that, and likely against his attorney's advice, is because he's going to plead guilty and he doesn't want anything that might come out in a prelim to get in the way of that. And he *wants* a trial. He wants to own what he did, he's proud of it, wants to wear it like a badge of honor. And like a disgusting bastard, he wants to force Elise to be present to hear about it. But if I tell her my theory, it's going to upset her. I swallow the bad taste in my mouth, but my words still come out croakily. "I guess he's a dumbass then."

Her mouth flickers but doesn't make it to a smile. "I guess. So it's basically passport surrender, staying with his parents in Malibu, promising to behave and stay away from me etcetera. But he's out. And with his dad's connections, they'll have a good shot of keeping it that way." She's trying to sound calm, but it's cracking at the edges.

It must be nice having a father who's a defense attorney with high-powered defense attorney friends. That rage simmers again and I have to clamp a lid down on it so I can talk. "Oh. What about the FBI's investigation into the cyberstalking stuff?"

"I don't know. They said that would take longer to bring to trial because all they have right now is him admitting he sent emails and pictures, and then the bragging about being part of the Hayes Horde. They need evidence to link him to them, access to his computer and phone. I don't know how it ties into the assault and everything else they charged him with from the plane." She pauses and seems to consciously force herself to reset and calm down. "I don't really understand it, if they're going to do the cyber stuff at the same time as the plane stuff or if it's two separate things or what. I just know that at some point I'm going to have to see him again, probably twice because I need to have the emergency protective order made more permanent. This system is *so* fucked."

"You're right. It is fucked." It's so inadequate, but it's the truth. "But…it sounds like they're on top of it."

"Yeah. Maybe he should have just murdered me. Then at least he'd still be locked up."

"That's not funny," I snap.

She touches my arm briefly. "Sorry. You're right, that was a stupid thing to say."

I set aside the unpleasant mental image she just put into my head. "What about your place? Is anyone keeping an eye on it?" As Elise mentioned, he undoubtedly knows where she lives and is probably watching her house. And if he wants to go for a walk, why would his parents stop him?

"Yeah. Rosemary texted to say they've hired private security to do drive-bys all day and night to make sure nothing seems out of place." She exhales. "It's going to be interesting when I move back home and go back to work."

"Right." I almost choke trying to hold on to my words. Inviting her to stay longer, as long as she needs to, is the obvious thing for me to do. The kind of thing a friend would do. But I'm still not sure where we sit on the friendship scale. Where is the spot on that scale for Broken Up, Slept Together, Trying to Figure Out How You Feel?

She flashes a brief, knowing smile. "Let me put on my sneakers and grab a hoodie."

To me, Elise looks like any other woman out on a Saturday-morning walk—ball cap and sunglasses, a hoodie, plain running tights and no makeup—but more than once, someone seems to do a double take as we pass. Probably to do with the story that broke this morning. But nobody seems *that* interested, which eases some of my anxiety about people gossiping that they saw her in my neighborhood. Despite her appearance being so different from her television character or even her public persona, there's apparently something that gives her away. I know what it is. Elise's natural magnetism draws people to her. Thankfully nobody does anything more than stare at her before walking right on by.

"Does the staring get to you?" I ask.

She glances up from her Pokémon Go app. "Not really. It used to, but I've become good at ignoring it. Is it bothering you?"

"They're not staring at me. So, no."

"They might be staring at you." Elise smiles and turns her attention back to her phone.

Bennett trots along beside us, occasionally grabbing the slack leash in his mouth and tugging as if to pull me along. Every time he does that, Elise laughs. He's always done it, like he must show some little rebellion for walking so well on a leash. And I'm caught in a time warp, where everything feels almost exactly as it did before the breakup. These moments make it so easy to forget we've broken up, because every moment with her feels so easy. It's always been easy. Until it was hard.

We've been walking in relative silence, except for the odd comment here and there or when Elise asks me to pause so she can catch a Pokémon or do some Poké-chore. Then she speaks out of the blue. She's quiet, contemplative. "Do you think it would have been easier on both of us if I'd left sooner? Like the moment I knew I couldn't keep on with us, that being in a relationship with a woman was going to apparently be such a big issue and career roadblock, that I should have told you then and we could have called it quits?"

The question, carrying over from our discussion the day before, doesn't upset me as I would have expected. "When did you know it was going to be an issue?"

"The moment I walked into Sandra's office for my first meeting as her client and she asked me straight out if there was anything that was going to cause an issue, like criminal history or my sexual orientation." Her expression twists. "As if those two things can be conflated."

I knew all this had something to do with her old manager. Elise had made a few off-hand comments about Sandra said this and Sandra thinks that—not to mention the one time I met her manager and she looked at me like I was a boil on the ass of humanity—but still, the idea of her putting that on Elise is sickening. As is the thought that Elise knew *we* might be an issue all that time and said nothing, because this conversation would have happened less than three months into our relationship. I manage a forced, "Right. Okay."

Elise's light touch on my shoulder startles me. "Avery."

I glance at her. "Mmm?"

"If you keep clenching your teeth like that, you're going to break one. And I don't want to have to hold you down so they can give you an anesthetic shot to fix it."

I force myself to relax my jaw, moving it side to side to ease the tense muscle. By the time we've reached the corner, all I've managed to come up with is, "I really hate her for doing that to you."

"Me too." Over the sound of suburban noise I hear her exhale. "And I think I might hate myself a little too."

That pulls me up. Literally. The moment I've stopped, Bennett sits by my feet, wedged in between Ellie and me. "What do you mean?" I quietly ask.

Elise slips around so she's by me instead of the dog. "I'm an adult, Avery. An adult who knows what's right and what's wrong and what feels like the best thing for me. And I still ignored all those gut feelings and did something just because someone said I should. I kept telling myself what Sandra said—that my private life was my own business but in this business everyone's business becomes public sooner or later. And yeah, I was scared of what that might mean for my career but also, I wanted this part of my life all for myself, for you and me, and I wasn't ready to be out and share that and be open to everyone having an opinion."

I gesture for Bennett to follow as we walk on. He grabs his leash again and moves just in front of us. "But doing those things, ignoring your gut and…staying in the closet, got you the part in *Greed*, the movie roles, awards and award nominations."

She's silent for a few seconds. "Did it though? Was that the only reason those things happened to me?" It's a musing question that still asks for a response.

"No, of course not. You got those things because you're brilliant, because you've worked hard and you deserve them."

"Right," she says. There's a hint of a smile in her voice when she adds, "Of course I'm brilliant."

"And modest."

"Funny." She gently elbows me. "Brilliance aside, I've spent the past year or so wondering if me being out would have had any effect at all on that career stuff."

"And what did you decide?" I'm almost afraid to hear her answer. On one hand, having her confirm that the heartbreak was worth it for her, that it really was the only way she could have gone forward, somehow almost makes *my* heartbreak seem worth it too. I've only ever wanted Ellie to realize her dreams, to become everything she always wanted. I just wanted to be part of it all.

Her inhalation is loud. "I decided no, it wouldn't have had any effect at all. Maybe some opportunities wouldn't have come my way, but knowing the team behind *Greed*, behind *Second Chance*, I'm confident I still would have landed those roles. So now I'm just sad and angry and frustrated that all the pain that came with leaving you was for nothing." She falters for a step as if tripping over a thought. "I love my job. I'm living my dream. I love my role in *Greed*, the movies I've done and the ones I have lined up, but there's still…a hollowness to it all, even with everything that's amazing. And I want to fill that hollowness."

She already knows how I feel about the situation, about our history sitting between us and why she left, so rehashing it now isn't going to help either of us. And asking her the question that fills my mouth might give me an answer I'm almost afraid to hear—that she wants to fill the hollowness with *Us*. So I decide to go for a little humor, and ask her the question I used to ask her when she'd come home despondent after another unsuccessful audition. "Yeah, but did you learn anything from the experience?"

She laughs quietly. "Nice one. And yes, I did learn something. I learned it pretty quickly."

"And what was it?" I prompt.

"That I shouldn't have left," she says immediately. "That it was the wrong thing, the worst thing." She entwines her fingers into mine, then as if she realizes we're in public, pulls her hand away again. "You haven't answered my question."

I have to drag my mind away from the sensation of that light touch so I can think back to exactly what the question was. Would it have been easier if she'd broken up with me right at the start of our relationship? It doesn't require much thought and I have to admit, "Yes, I think it would have been easier. Not easy. But easier. Maybe. I don't really know." I pause to collect scattered thoughts. "I'd already fallen in love with you by then. But having it happen after we'd had years to form a relationship that was built on trust and respect felt horribly cruel."

"I know. I fucked up and I'm sorry. How can I make it up to you?"

"You don't need to make it up to me. You don't owe me anything."

Ellie grabs my wrist and pulls me to a stop. She pulls off her sunglasses. Her eyes are wide and there's a burning intensity in her expression. "Yes, I do. I owe you everything. You showed me what real love, real connection, could be like. And then you showed me why I can't do without it."

Part of me wants to tell her I can't do without it either, that I need her like I need air. But those childish desires are foolish and pointless and are all mine, not something I want her to have to deal with. "What is it that you want, Ellie?"

"I want us to be friends." She slips her sunglasses back on and turns to keep walking. "I'm not naïve enough to think we're just going to slot back into the way it used to be, but I'd like to get as close as we could. Romance or not, I still care about you, Avery, and I love spending time with you. It would be amazing if we could find a comfortable place where we can hang out as friends, because right now I still feel like we've got a hand on each other's shoulder, making sure we don't get too close." She huffs out a dry laugh. "Except when we did get too close."

Remembering that *too close* sends a shiver of electricity through me. "Me too. And you're right." Despite our close quarters and that oopsie of sleeping together, it still feels like there's distance between us. I'm not sure if it's my caution or her remorse or a mix of both. "But it's only been a few days and there's a lot of stuff to accept and forgive if we're going to be friends." Stuff in both the distant and very recent past. After listening to her explanation, her obvious regrets, I feel less raw. Less raw but not fully healed.

"I know, but I want to make it work. I want to try being friends. This sounds kind of selfish, but I miss you and I need someone like you in my life."

"Who is someone like me?" I turn my head slightly so I can watch her as well as where I'm walking.

"Someone easy. Someone I never have to pretend around. Someone who I can be my real self around. Someone who's a safe place to completely drop all my barriers." She looks over at me. "I have *nobody* like that in my life. Even with those I trust, like Rosemary and Paul, I still feel like I always have some part of myself hidden away."

"That sounds awful," I say honestly. I can't imagine not feeling like I could just be myself, and I realize it's the first time I've ever really thought about what that side of being closeted means for her. "I—I think I'd like friendship. I've missed you too, even without the relationship stuff." Being with her now makes me realize that life without Elise is dull and gray. And besides, we're both adults, capable of compartmentalizing and keeping things friendly without letting other feelings get in the way. Theoretically at least.

"There's many benefits to being my friend, you know." There's a lilting, sing-song quality to her statement and I know the tone change is because she's feeling emotional.

Goddammit, I still know her so well. We still fit together so well even though we don't. We can't. I try to force the same lightness into my response. "Oh? Like what?"

"Endless marinara sauce, good seats at ball games, occasional free stuff. And best of all? I'll be able to play piano if you get married." That last one is clearly intended as a joke, but even

Elise with all her acting skill can't hide the fact she doesn't like the idea. The joke is tight, like she's forced it out of her mouth.

My own joke feels just as tight. "Well, if I ever feel the urge to get married, you'll be the first one to know about it so I can make sure you're available."

I've just taken a shower after returning from our please-get-tired-Bennett walk when I receive an unwanted text from work. I'm needed for a shift on my day off. Need aside, a day away from Elise might not be such a bad thing. I don't want to run away, but I do want some breathing room, and knowing Ellie, she does too. Instead of pulling on house sweats, I get dressed and put on makeup to suit today's "I'm Not An Air Marshal" disguise. Ellie doesn't bother to hide her dismay when I come back out in what she knows are work clothes. "You have to work?"

"Mhmm. Just got a call in. Sorry." I fasten my holster and pull a tailored blazer over the top, tugging to make sure my gun is covered. "My Saturday off has been trumped by someone's raging stomach flu. Hard to be inconspicuous when you've got bodily fluids coming out both ends." I probably wouldn't have agreed to an ordinary everyday mission flight, but we got word that a person of interest is flying today and we need to mobilize so we can track and possibly intercept.

Ellie forces cheer into her voice. "It's fine. You don't need to hang around and babysit me. I'm going to enjoy that newly tuned piano for a while and then I might even venture out for some errands. Maybe grab a few things from home if I'm feeling brave. I need more clothes." Smiling, she indicates my outfit and changes the subject. "Speaking of, who are you today?"

"Surly superstar who doesn't want to talk to fans." Jeans, fitted gray tee, Doc Martens, my blazer and oversized sunglasses.

Ellie nods slowly. "I believe it." She tries for casual and almost pulls it off. "Did you learn that one from me?"

For a fraction of a second I consider lying, only because for some childish reason some part of me still wants to make her hurt the way I did. But I can't do it. I don't want to do it anymore. "No. You're a lot of things, but never surly with fans."

"Maybe that's part of the problem," she says dryly.

"Maybe," I agree, trying not to smile at her tone. "I can teach you how."

Elise laughs. Not the practiced titter but her full-throated mirthful guffaw. The one that erupts from her when she watches *The Office*. "No you can't. You've never been surly either."

I join in her laughter. "No, I suppose you're right." As I collect the rest of my stuff I tell her, "Bennie will keep you company but you know he'll also be a really shit guard dog if anyone comes around. Except the opossum who keeps trying to get onto the back porch."

She laughs. "He really hasn't gotten any better with the whole protect your turf thing, huh?"

"Maybe a little? He's barked at the delivery guys a few times and he's chased the opossum. I *swear* he growled at someone walking past with their dog last month. But their dog was being a dick and coming onto our front lawn." Though he looks the part of a guard dog, Bennett is probably the most unlikely candidate for the job. Most mornings I have to nudge him or talk to him to rouse him from his sleep. He sleeps through pretty much everything, including a car crashing into a light pole down the street. My dog is many things, but menacing or aggressive are not one of them.

He *was* kind of protective of me when we were out on walks or runs, and had been with Elise too, but I doubt he'd ever attack anyone who encroached on his territory. His outburst during our argument had been so unexpected that it had startled me.

"So not really better with being tough then." Elise bends down to kiss between Bennett's eyes and he thumps his tail as she rubs his ears and tells him, "It's okay, my guy, I know you're a lover not a fighter." When she straightens, she's smiling. "It's okay, really. I'll be fine. Nobody except my team knows I'm here. I feel safe. I might even take him for another walk this afternoon to clear my head if that's okay?"

I doubt she will, just as I doubt she'll go out for errands or to collect clothes from her house without someone for company. But I want her to feel like she has control over her life and confidence in herself, so I say, "Of course it is. And I'm glad.

I'll have to go into the office afterward but I should be home in time to figure out what to do about dinner."

"Sounds like a good plan."

"Call me if you need anything. If I can't answer I'll get back to you as soon as I'm on the ground."

"Will do."

"And if anything feels wrong, you remember the number for 911?"

Her mouth quirks. "Hmmm, is it…911?"

"Smartass." I'm surprised at how easy things feel between us, especially considering everything that we've managed to cram into the last few days. Maybe clearing the air does make things easier.

Elise says something so familiar that my stomach twists. "Be safe up there."

My old response falls out of my mouth. "Always am."

CHAPTER ELEVEN

Fortunately, my flights are uneventful. Not so fortunately, I don't spot our Person of Interest and neither do the agents stationed at the bookend airports. Either the intel we received was wrong, our POI knew we'd be there, or he changed his appearance so drastically as to be unrecognizable. Hello, paperwork.

Also fortunate is that he's not classified as a priority one task, so there's no imminent threat to life or property, which would have made me seriously stressed about potentially missing him. Undoubtedly, we'll be mobilized again at a moment's notice when our next round of intel comes in. After I have a quick meeting over airport coffee at LAX with another Air Marshal I check my messages to make sure there's nothing from Elise, then head into the office for a few hours.

I've just about had enough of proofing a high-risk-person assessment report when one of my colleagues, Nicola, peeks into my office. "Avery, can you look at something for me?"

Thank you, much-needed distraction. I spin my chair around. "Sure. You too, huh? What did you get dragged in on a weekend for?"

"We picked up Eduardo Correia in San Diego. Finally." She makes a slam-dunk motion.

"Nice! Congrats on the catch. So, what am I looking at for you?"

Nicola closes the door most of the way and comes over to perch on the edge of my desk. "Nothing. I just want gossip. Did you really have an in-flight incident involving Elise Hayes on Wednesday?"

I bite back my sigh. "I did, yeah." I've no doubt about where this conversation is headed and it's going to end up there no matter what I do to try to steer it in a different direction.

Nicola blinks slowly and after an eternity of contemplation she manages, "Elise. Hayes. Holy shit." Elise has been at the top of Nicola's Hot Women Harem List since the *Greed* pilot. Talk about simultaneously awkward and amusing workplace dynamics.

"Mmm, that was pretty much my first thought too when I saw her." But my *holy shit* was definitely not in the same context as Nicola's.

"Sounds like a logistical nightmare. I mean, I take a few sick days and this happens. I'm surprised I haven't seen your face all over TMZ."

"It almost was, but some very on-the-ball cabin crew cleared the first-class space pretty fast and then curtained it off. Only other non-crew persons aside from…Ms. Hayes were my perp and a physician." The doctor who'd attended to Elise had barely spared me a glance and I doubted she'd spill that a Federal Air Marshal had intervened, if she'd even realized. She might have just thought I was a helpful passenger. With handcuffs. If she did put two and two together, it's not like she'd be able to pick me out of a lineup. I offer a smile. "My secret identity is safe."

Nicola studies me like I'm the world's most confusing puzzle. "What's up with you? If I'd met a famous actress, especially Elise Hayes, you would not be able to get the grin off my face."

"Yeah well, you're a wannabe starfucker." After a pause, where I have to force myself not to worry my lower lip with my teeth, I ask, "Do you really think Elise Hayes is classed as a famous actress?"

Nicola shrugs in agreement with my first statement and nods at the second. "She won an Emmy as the lead actress on a brand-new show and there's buzz that she'll get more Emmys, and a Golden Globe nomination too. Uh, yeah, I'd class her as a famous actress." After nudging me in the shin with her foot she asks me again, "What's up?"

I only just manage to hold back my muttered, "Brilliant" at the idea that Elise is famous with a capital F. Silently, I swivel side to side on my chair. "I've just had a weird couple days, that's all, the midair arrest of a celebrity stalker notwithstanding. My ex arrived on my doorstep that night, needing somewhere to stay for a few weeks."

Nicola gapes. Apparently my ex trumps her celebrity crush. If only she knew they are one and the same. "Whaaaaaaat? That's messed up. Why'd she come knocking on your doorstep? Did you say yes? Oh god, you totally said yes, didn't you? Averryyy," she whines. "Come on."

"Of course I said yes." The not-quite-truth comes easily. "She's got some issues with the place she's living and needed somewhere solid to stay. She's really stuck and I dunno, I felt like I should help out."

"And she knows nobody else in this city that she could stay with?" She echoes my original thought. "Hotel? Airbnb?"

"Nobody she trusts apparently."

Nicola verbalizes her thinking with a series of mmm's and hmm's. "Sounds like a recipe for awkward weirdness. My favorite." She flashes a sadistic grin.

"Yeah, pretty much. I mean, Bennett is in heaven—I always knew he adored her more than me because she spoils the shit out of him." I grab a pen, desperate for something with which to fidget.

"And you don't let him on your couch or bed," she points out. "What's with that? Maybe you should just give him to your ex."

"You've seen pictures of him. He's *huge*. I'd never had a dog before and I made a decision and stuck with it like training websites told me to. My brain was a little preoccupied at the time. And fuck off, he's my dog and I love him and he loves me. I'm not just going to give him to my ex because she loves him too."

"Love is letting them on the bed and couch."

"He's perfectly happy with all his deluxe dog beds where he can sprawl out as much as he wants. Can we maybe move past my alleged animal neglect?"

"Oh, you want to talk about your ex? Fine." She pretends to settle glasses on her face. "Tell me how you're feeling, what's the vibe in your house?"

I laugh at her therapist impersonation. "Like…on the surface it's all fine and we're getting along awkwardly but okay. But underneath it all my brain keeps reminding me of how great it was when we were together."

"You guys split because she wasn't ready to be publicly out, right?"

"Right." She knows the basics and I'd love nothing more than to lay it all out in detail. Nicola and I have been work best friends ever since she transferred to my office and as the only other out woman, we kind of gravitated toward one another. Between her divorce and my breakup with Elise, we'd cemented a solid friendship. But this friendship had sharing limits, especially when it came to Ellie. "I'm getting some solid hints that she really regrets what she did and is genuinely sorry for hurting me. Makes it hard to hold on to my hurt feeling."

"You're a better woman than I am. I've still got my divorce anger locked in a safe with chains welded around it. It's going to stay there for at least another decade."

"Maybe." I shrug. "Or maybe I'm just a sucker. I don't know. It's a weird situation all round because you know until we broke up, everything seemed amazing. And all that stuff lingers. Love and attraction. Lust. I'm still attracted to her. I never stopped loving her. But she left, and now she's back, and the spark is flaring more than it ever did. But the thing that caused the problem our first time around is still there."

"Did you sleep with her?"

I almost choke at her perceptiveness. "Jesus. Is it written on my forehead?"

Her mouth falls open and she coughs out an incredulous laugh. "Fuck me. I was just fishing about and teasing you. Way to fall for the oldest trick in the book. Idiot." She exhales a raspberry. "Damn. How do you feel about it? Fucking her when she's your ex that is."

"Felt amazing at the time." Understatement.

"Obviously. And then?"

"And then I felt like shit and the next day we had a huge argument about…basically everything. So, not so amazing."

"Damn."

"Yeah. It was our first actual argument, if you can believe it. We never fought. We bickered and had tiny disagreements but never any real arguments or fights." Our relationship was the definition of conjoined bliss with no rough seas anywhere on the horizon. Maybe that's why it all fell apart so spectacularly. Because I had no idea the rough seas were hiding beyond the horizon where I couldn't see them.

"Wow. I didn't even know relationships like that existed. My marriage was basically one great big fight for seven years."

Smiling, I assure her, "Oh they do exist. Both of us have—" I correct myself, "Both of us had enough stress in our work lives and it was so nice to know that going home was like a haven."

"Where are you two now? Still fighting? Or back to wanting to fuck?"

"Neither. Well. I mean, see above with the attraction and lust and love. So probably more toward the fucking but just… starting to learn how to be friends again I think."

"Interesting." Nicola's forehead wrinkles. "I'm trying to imagine it. Moving past a breakup, especially one like yours or mine." She doesn't need to elaborate. She was with me postbreakup when I was *not* an enjoyable person to be around. And from everything she told me, her divorce was messy with a capital M.

"Well, think about it. Like, even with the divorce, if you felt that way about Suzanne instead of wanting to kill her, and she turned up on your doorstep apologizing and telling you she made a mistake and then just…grabbed you and told you she wanted to fuck you senseless, wouldn't you go for it?"

"I guess. Maybe? I mean, I've gotten used to my singledom and all the self-pleasure perks that come with that. Maybe if I could get past the whole 'she cheated on me repeatedly then took our cats' thing? Which I'm not sure I could, even if she is smoking hot." She raises an eyebrow. "But nowhere near as hot as Elise Hayes. Come on, did you totally lose it when you saw her?" Nicola's thing for Ellie is kind of cute, in a weird way. My brain stumbles over the whole situation with Bridges and the million other people who I know think Elise is the hottest woman on the planet. Including me, I admit.

I offer a safe-for-work answer. "Not really. She's just a regular person. Nice, friendly, charming." My brain rattles off a list of other things about Elise that is definitely not safe-for-work.

"Is that why you jumped your ex? Because you'd just had an encounter with Elise Hayes and you had all this pent-up sexual energy from that?"

Oh boy, this is getting complex. And amusing. "Actually, my ex jumped me. What happened on the plane is something completely separate."

Nicola gapes. "You were inches from Elise Hayes and it didn't affect you at *all*? Do you not have eyes?"

There's no right answer here and I need to be careful. "Of course I have eyes. But have you ever thought about what it must be like for people like her? Knowing she has people lusting after her is one thing but then you add that whole stalker situation? And she can't do anything about it except know that there's creepy creeps out there thinking creepy things about her. I know I'd fucking hate it." And I know now that Ellie does too.

Nicola stares at me like I've just morphed into a person she doesn't know. "Not really, no, I haven't thought about that side of it. I mean, don't they sign up for attention and all that?"

"I don't think so at all. I think they sign up to act in a show or star in movies or sing songs or whatever. Not to have their personal lives intruded upon every time they try to get coffee or walk their dog."

Her expression is thoughtful. "I guess you're right. That *would* be a shit way to live your life. Flipside of the perks of fame I guess."

"Yeah." I toss the pen onto my desk. "I'm still not sure fame has enough perks that I'd ever want to trade them for being treated like a piece of meat with no feelings."

"True. Well, for what it's worth, I'm just going to keep admiring her from my safe distance of fandom where I think Elise Hayes is one of the hottest women I've ever laid eyes on."

I laugh and try not to sound relieved that Nicola appears to still be a regular "Elise is hot and a great actress" fan and not a "I'm going to stalk and attack you" fan. Not that it's for me to worry about who thinks Ellie is great. Right. I almost believe myself too. I swing sideways on my chair. "For the record? I agree Elise Hayes is one of the hottest women I've ever laid eyes on." I only just bite my tongue on telling Nicola what other body parts I've laid on Elise...

Whenever I come home, Bennett always rushes to greet me with an exuberant display of butt-shaking tail wags and bouncy play bows before zooming to the back door to be let out. So when I open the door after my impromptu workday and am met by no dog and no Elise, an uncomfortable worry tightens my stomach. Realistically, I know the likelihood of something bad having happened is tiny but the worry takes root and refuses to budge.

There are a few lights on, but the house is mostly dark. After I've divested myself of my bag and coat onto the kitchen table, I flip some light switches so I can go searching. I have to restrain myself from unholstering my firearm, and luckily the first room I go to provides all the answers. The living room is dim, only the lamp on the side table on, but I can still clearly see what is probably one of the cutest, and naughtiest, scenes I've ever witnessed.

Ellie has fallen asleep on the couch either with Bennett or he's jumped up to join her later. Given he knows he isn't allowed on the couch, my guess is she coaxed him up and then fell asleep before she could hide the evidence. I lean against the wall and stare. She's lying on her back with an arm slung over her head and the other hand resting on Bennett's head. He's settled on her legs, curled up to try and make himself fit. This is one of the reasons why I'd insisted he wasn't going to be a bed or couch dog—because he was going to grow up to be too damned big to fit with both me and Ellie on those spaces. He's too damned big for just him and Ellie, but somehow they're making it work.

Bennie's registered my presence but hasn't moved, aside from opening his eyes. His guilty look says it all, eyebrows dancing around as he studies me without lifting his head from Ellie's hip. Still without moving, Bennett looks at Elise's sleeping face before looking at me again, as if trying to tell me that it really isn't his fault while simultaneously wondering just how much trouble he's in. I know my dog and know just how much he wants to look away but he's staying still, staring at my face and waiting for me to tell him what to do.

Just this one time, pal. After taking a photo of the admittedly adorable scene I back up and after securing my gun, get started on dinner. Bennie joins me five minutes later, probably for his dinner too. He sits by my feet. "Did you enjoy your little couch vacation?" I ask him, settling my feet on either side of his butt so I can lean down and scratch his chest. He looks up at me, doggo grin telling me he did indeed enjoy it. I kiss the top of his head.

He's finished eating and is lick-pushing his metal bowl around the floor, trying to get the last bits of taste out of it, when Ellie emerges. She massages the back of her neck the way she always does when she has a tension headache then offers me a sheepish smile as she rubs behind Bennett's ears. "I guess you busted us, huh?"

I scrape julienned vegetables into the wok. "Eeeyep. Sure did."

Her shoulders drop. "Sorry, I know he's not supposed to be on the couch. I *know* that. I just wanted something to cuddle. He's always been so great for that."

You can always ask me if you need a hug is right on the edge of my tongue and I bite down lightly to stop myself from saying those words. "That he has. You want to talk about it?"

"Yes, I do. But later. I'm sorry," she says again. "It's disrespectful of me to break one of your house rules while I'm a guest." She climbs up onto the stool behind my breakfast bar and leans forward to rest her elbows on the counter. "It was totally all me. I asked him to get on the couch."

I make a noncommittal sound that I know she'll take for mild annoyance rather than anger, because I'm not angry. "Looked as squishy and uncomfortable as we'd always imagined it would be with him sharing a couch or bed with us."

"It was. But worth it. It won't happen again."

"It's…fine. I know these are extenuating circumstances." And once she's gone again, Bennett and I can go back to our regular routine of no dogs on my couch. Gone again. The thought sends a weird shudder down my back.

Elise's quiet, "Avery?" makes me look up from stirring dinner.

"Yeah?"

It takes her a few moments to frame her question. "Was lack of respect one of our problems?"

I really have to think about it, and even then I don't find a firm answer. I never felt disrespected by her, just not chosen or prioritized over her work. Was that disrespect? "I'm not sure. Maybe?" I blow out a breath. "Could have been we didn't respect each other enough to make it work. Didn't respect what we both needed. But is that actual disrespect as in its traditional definition?"

"I don't really know," she quietly says.

I frown at the plant-based faux chicken strips I've just liberated from their packaging. Really, when I think hard about it, it didn't feel like that. She gave me no choice because she couldn't deal with the career ramifications of *us*. There was no room for me to not respect her decision because she just left me. "I don't think I ever felt disrespected. Just…unwanted."

"I'm sorry," she murmurs for what feels like the thousandth apology.

"I know. So am I." The not-chicken joins the wok and I give everything a quick toss. "You're not sleeping well?" At her curious eyebrow lift I add, "Daytime napping?"

"Yeah. Can't sleep at night when I'm supposed to and then I'm just crashing after lunch."

"Anything in particular or just a culmination of insomnia-causing things?"

"Just a culmination of everything. Can't turn my brain off and I'm still dreaming scary shit. I was terrified when that guy had me, and I'm still terrified. But I'll cope." Her smile is tired and somewhat forced. "I've made an appointment to see my therapist on Monday after I go file the paperwork for this new restraining order."

"Good plan." When I'm satisfied dinner isn't going to go rogue on me, I face her. "If there's anything I can do to help, you know you only need to ask."

"I know. But you're already doing plenty," she murmurs. "You're giving me everything I could possibly need right now."

CHAPTER TWELVE

Because I'm a huge party animal I spend every Saturday night after dinner cleaning guns, regardless of whether I've fired them that week or not. Elise has been at the piano for an hour, playing mostly pop and rock, the full seventeen glorious minutes of Beethoven's "Moonlight Sonata" and the occasional Brahms. Her repertoire tells me her mood has shifted to relaxed and happy, so I leave her be and spread a microfiber towel over the kitchen table and set everything out. Each of the four guns—my work Sig Sauer P239, my personal Beretta 92FS, my custom-made Cabot S103 Southpaw 1911 and Grandpa's Colt 1911 that he carried in Vietnam—has their own special cleaning kit.

I've just broken down my work firearm when Elise strolls into the kitchen. She pauses, her mouth twitching into a smile as she stares at the four color-coded piles of cleaning equipment. "I'd totally forgotten about gun cleaning day." She sits to my right, at the head of the table, and shuffles her chair closer. "I don't know about you, but I love how familiar everything feels."

"Are you calling me boring?" I tease. I need to cover the emotion that's welled up at her sentiment. Everything does feel familiar, almost like we just had a minor disagreement, moved to different parts of the house for a few hours and now she's come back and we've made up.

"Never. Just…feels a little like I never left." Elise gestures to the most eye-catching gun on the table, a highly polished silver pistol with an ebony Fibonacci patterned grip and the coolest stars cut out of the trigger. "Is that the Cabot 1911?"

"It is."

"May I? I never actually saw it except for picking the different customization pieces on the website." Elise bought the Cabot for me as a thank-you for teaching her how to be comfortable and look natural with a range of firearms for her role in *Greed*. When she found out she got the part we spent hours at the range and she threw question after question at me, wanting to know everything about everything so she could look authentic.

"Of course." I make sure the weapon is safe and pass it to her.

She grips the handle, bouncing the gun in her hand. "Oof, it's heavy." Elise studies the Cabot, then me. "Do you…like it?"

"I love it." The Cabot isn't ambidextrous or partly customizable like some handguns, including my work firearm, but instead is custom made for southpaws—a perfect, redesigned 1911 just for lefties. It arrived on my doorstep six months after she left, like one last reminder of her. At the time it was not an enjoyable reminder.

I'd had no idea she'd even ordered the Cabot and I'd considered selling it when I realized how much she'd paid for it. But it really is a nice gun. Once my heart had settled into acceptance, I'd admitted to myself that it was even nicer that she'd heard my throwaway comments while I'd been teaching her to shoot and then decided to buy me a gift. I'd had to adapt to a right-handed gun world, with casings ejecting across my field of view from right-handed ports, and had also mentioned how much I loved Grandpa's 1911. It was a gift I couldn't use in my workplace, granted, but it was still a really nice gift. I'd always had conflicting feelings because this thing that was made just for me was all tied up in my ex-girlfriend.

Ellie turns the gun over, studying it from all angles. "God, it's gorgeous." She laughs. "But damn that grip feels horrible."

I grin. "Not for me."

She racks the slide. "Oh, baby, that is *smooth*."

My laugh bursts out. "Look at you, all gun-knowledgeable."

Smiling, Elise passes the gun back. "I had a great teacher."

"That you did." I place the Cabot back in its spot in the cleaning queue. "I was a little worried you'd been Hollywood corrupted."

"Just a little. I'm pretty sure I could still hit a target at…five paces." She props her elbows on the table. "I didn't even know you had the Cabot. I assumed you would have tossed it or sold it." Ellie's teeth brush her lower lip. "Why *did* you keep it? Why didn't you sell it?"

The rapid-fire questions give me no time to think or stall. "Like you said, it's gorgeous. And I'm not sure why I kept it exactly. Probably for the same reason I never sold Grandpa's piano. Sentimental reasons maybe? I didn't want to use it at first but once I'd gotten over my butt-hurtedness and learned to accept it for what it was, I realized how much trouble you'd gone to for me. Even when you were maybe dealing with other stuff." I gently grasp her wrist. "Thank you. I never got to say that. It's a beautiful gift, a beautiful gun, and not just to look at. One of the smoothest and most accurate pistols I've ever used. Like it was made for me."

Her smile is shy. "You're welcome. And it *was* made for you. I was going to give it to you for your birthday but then…stuff happened." She forces a smile and I know what she's thinking. And I wonder how many more times are we going to reference that horrible fucking time in our lives? Elise makes a subject change. "How did the office marksmanship pool go this year?"

"I won it." My grin is automatic and feels cocky. "Again. Top score across all national offices third year running."

Her laugh is loud and rich. "I don't know why anyone bets against you. You could hit a target with your eyes closed. I remember watching you shoot left- and right-handed with both left and right eye closed. Didn't you try both eyes closed just for fun and still hit the target?"

"Mhmm. Six times. I was just showing off for you though." Though Federal Air Marshals already have the highest marksmanship scores of anyone in law enforcement, I've always been ultra-competitive. When you're potentially taking a shot at someone in a space where there is *no* margin of error and little time to think, you have to know you can hit what you're aiming for no matter what—shooting with your dominant or non-dominant hand and potentially with some other part of yourself, like eyesight, compromised. I've thought about all of that since Elise's incident. I knew if I couldn't talk him down then I could draw my weapon, take the shot and end the standoff then and there. But all the what-if's crept in. What if he moved and I hit her instead? What if he didn't and Ellie was covered in pieces of him? What if this was my one-in-two-hundred miss?

"Well, you might be a crack shot but I'm not." She pauses, teeth worrying her lower lip. When she speaks again, she's rambling. "I could get a gun. Just in case. A Sig 226 just like I use in *Greed*. I'm comfortable with how it handles, even if it is just blanks. Even if I don't use it then it's still good practice for work." She gestures at the array of handguns laid out before us. "You could just let me borrow one of yours and we can go to the range but they're all set up wrong, except for your Grandpa's and I'd feel weird about that. So…I could get a gun," she repeats.

I take a few moments to think about how to be diplomatic and gentle about something that's obviously stressing her out. "Ordinarily I'd be all for it and marching you off to make sure your safety certs are up to date, get you licensed and then to a gun store. But, Ellie, I think for those who aren't used to shooting in real-life stressful situations and haven't trained for it, it's more harmful than helpful. Especially if you're disarmed. Then it's just fucking dangerous."

She raises a slow eyebrow which makes my stomach do funny things. "Are you saying my carefully crafted sets, blank rounds and extras who act predictably every single take aren't stressful?" Her tone is teasing but barely hides her worry.

"Ah, uh, umm…no comment. But I know what I see on screen looks like you absolutely know how to take care of yourself." I have to suppress the surge of anxiety at that thought, wondering if she really could take care of herself if absolutely necessary. "If you've got your heart set on having a personal firearm then I'll support that. I've registered my mild objection but ultimately, it's your choice. And I'd be more than happy to take you to the range and keep those skills up, and show you a few other tips for high-stress situations."

"Objection noted. And I take your advice on board. If you think it'd be more harmful than helpful for me to be armed then I'll forget about it. But I would like to go to the range, just for a little practice only, before I go back to work. Make sure I still look authentic."

"Hollywood authentic," I tease. "And sure. I can swap the mag release on the Beretta back to rightie's side for you."

"Thanks." She pauses, a smile working at the edges of her mouth. "You know, I can't think of anyone else who would happily take me to the shooting range, like just a normal day back in our dating life."

"No? Maybe you just need to date someone in law enforcement again. Or another actor who wants to practice lots so they look legit."

The smile wavers. "Maybe. Or maybe I just need to find someone, anyone, who I can connect with the way I did—" A quick headshake. "The way I *do* with you."

I think I know what she's hinting at, and the way she said it makes me think she wants me to probe further about what she's implying. It's not my place to ask, and I'm not even sure I want to know, but I can't stop myself from taking her bait. "You haven't dated since me?"

Her answer comes quickly. "I tried. And by tried I mean I just thought about it and all the associated shit that would go along with it. But honestly? After you, nobody held any appeal for me.

The thought of going back to a man wasn't... I just couldn't picture it. And I couldn't date a woman, not after leaving you."

"Why not?" Though I was the first woman she'd ever dated and slept with, Elise had never given any indication that she didn't find other women attractive.

She moves like she's going to grab Grandpa's 1911, then pulls her hand back. I know she wants something to fidget with but guns, even safe unloaded ones, aren't really fidget material. I hand her a jag from the Colt cleaning kit, and she takes it and immediately begins spinning the pointed end on the table like a toy top. "Mostly because I didn't think anyone would compare to you or that I could ever hope to re-create what we had. And I'm still not out. So, if I dated a woman it would just be secrecy all over again. Considering we broke up because I couldn't be out, I just...how could I do that to you? I couldn't be so unfair and cruel." She puffs out a rough breath. "And I couldn't do it to myself either."

I'm more relieved than I want to admit at her revelation. I'd thought about it after she left, that maybe she'd gotten involved with some other closeted actress, and I had kind of just accepted that it was the probability. What she's said makes more sense than that alternative, and I'm almost ashamed for thinking she left me to hook up with another woman. I set down the bottle of lubricant and sort through cleaning cloths, slowly, trying to put form to thoughts. "I'm not gonna lie, Ellie. I think it would have been doubly hurtful if you'd gone full hypocrite and jumped into a relationship with another woman. But I'm sorry you haven't found the space to feel comfortable being out, or a way to be with someone else."

"Me too." Her two-word agreement is a tight whisper.

"I'm just...not sure where we stand. I feel like we're hovering in some gray space where I don't really know where I stand or how you feel about this or what we're doing."

She takes a few moments to consider. "I think we're just learning how to exist together in this new dynamic of exes trying to be friends."

"True. How do you feel about it?" I know how I feel about it. Being friends with her is amazing but incomplete.

"Good," she says. After a beat she amends her thought to a smiling, "Mostly good. It's hard to feel this distance from you because we've never had that."

"No," I muse. "We haven't. It's not something I'm consciously doing, pushing you away. I don't want to feel like we're at arm's length from each other. But I guess some subconscious part of me wants to protect myself and is still trying to process everything that's happened. I'm scared if we don't consider things then it's just going to end up in a worse place than we were fifteen months ago. And I really don't think I could deal with that again."

"I don't want to be at arm's length either and I really don't want to feel the way I did in the months surrounding the breakup." She spins the jag hard and it wobbles and falls off the table. Elise leaves it where it's fallen. "I think…I think I've been making my way back to you for a while now and maybe trying to find myself at the same time. And when I saw you on the plane, I figured it was a sign that I was in the right place and this was the right thing and the right time for me to show you how much I regret what happened."

True, she wanted to talk on the plane before this all started. Kept hassling me until I eventually snapped at her to let it go. "How do you mean?"

Her eyebrows come together and she takes a little while to voice her thoughts. "I've thought about you in some capacity pretty much every day since I left."

"What about me?"

"Sometimes passing thoughts, like when I'd see the lines at Pink's and remember how you'd wait for ages for one of their hot dogs, or I'd go hiking with a friend who always forgets something and it made me think about how overprepared you are for every hike, or I'd play Beethoven and think about how it always makes you cry. Just random things that made it impossible to forget you." She shrugs and the movement shifts the too-big sweater from her shoulder. Ellie makes no move to pull it back up. "Mostly I just thought about how much I missed you, how I felt when I was with you and how desperately I wanted to feel that way again."

I have to stop myself from reaching over and fixing her sweater. "How's that?"

"Loved. Respected. Seen. Known. Wanted. All real feelings, not the fake ones that surround me every single fucking day." She blinks rapidly, swipes a hand across her eyes. "You just make me feel safe."

"Safe?"

"Mhmm. Not just physically, though you do inspire a certain confidence in that regard." A smile breaks through her tears. "More feeling safe to be myself, even when being myself was hurting you." The smile wavers. "Then I left and all I felt was just...sad and lonely."

"Same," I quietly admit. I wipe gun oil from my hands onto the towel and reach over to take her hand. "Do you still trust me? To keep you safe that is." I hold back the earnest, desperate promise that I'll do everything I can to keep her safe physically and emotionally and that she doesn't need to stress and worry about being armed, especially in my house or her house. Shoving those emotions onto her feels like they'd be smothering.

Her surprise is evident, as if it's the silliest question I could have asked. "Of course I do." She curls her fingers to trap mine against her palm.

"Good. Because that's really important to me, that you know that." My throat feels tight. "Ellie, I don't know what we're doing. I don't know if us trying to be friends is a good idea, if it's the right thing, if it's going to make things harder or easier or what. I just don't know."

"Me either," she murmurs. "But it doesn't make me feel like shit, I know that for sure. And feeling like shit has been a sensation overshadowing my life for a few years. So, I'm going with the *it's fine* for now."

"Me too." I gently extract my hand and rest my elbows on the table, careful to avoid gun parts. "I'm just worried that us being friends is going to lead us right back into our old life and it's going to be so hard to get out of that. Because we already know that we can't work."

"We can't work," she repeats, so quietly it's barely audible. "But what if we could?"

What if we could? It would be amazing. But we've had our amazing and then it was gone. And no matter how I look at it, I can't see it coming back unless Ellie changes a core part of herself and lets all her fears out into the open. And I can't see that happening either.

CHAPTER THIRTEEN

After a night of very explicit dreams about Elise, I wake on Monday feeling even more restless and unsettled than if I'd had a night of nightmares. It was like this after we'd broken up too, where I used to dream about her most nights then wake feeling like I'd barely slept at all. Though back then, it was mostly odd unpleasant dreams interspersed with those so sexually explicit I'd wake up on the verge of climax. Now it's mostly just pleasantly erotic.

We had a perfectly nice weekend, even with my emergency shift on Saturday. Sunday morning we went for our hike at Switzer Falls as planned, where I even managed not to fall into a puddle of nostalgia. Then we spent the afternoon doing housework before settling in for a movie Sunday night. An ordinary weekend. With extraordinary circumstances.

When I go to let Bennett out, I find Elise has beaten me to it. There's a note on the kitchen whiteboard telling me they've gone for a quick walk and the time she expects they'll be back. Enough time for me to have a workout. With no flights on my schedule for the day, I don't have to leave early for work.

Forty minutes later when I'm done in the gym, I can hear Ellie and Bennett out in the yard. I detour to the back door and stare through the glass door panel for a minute, watching them together. Bennie's tongue is flapping out the side of his mouth as he chases Elise around the yard, though in his case—chase is less chase and more just keeping beside whoever is playing with him.

Even from in here I can tell how much fun he's having. How much fun they're both having. It's going to break Bennett's heart when Elise goes again. And, I admit to myself, it's probably going to crack my heart a little too. I have no doubt she'd agree to meeting up for playdates with Bennett, which has the added benefit of me getting to see her as well. Maybe I'll suggest that.

I've just filled the coffee machine when Bennie charges into the house and straight to his water bowl. Elise follows at a more sedate pace, carrying his leash and a few dog toys. The moment she spots me, her face relaxes into a smile that makes my breath catch. Probably just residual dream libido. The morning huskiness of her pleased, "Hey" tells me it's not residual dream libido at all. It's real libido. Oh shit, this is problematic.

"Morning." I turn slightly away to check the too-slow drip of coffee. "Everything okay?"

"Yeah. I only took him for a short walk so figured he still needed a bit of playtime to tire him out for a day at home alone."

"Was the walk okay?"

Her eyebrows bounce upward in surprise. "Fine. He was perfect as usual." After a beat, she seems to catch on to what I'm trying to ask, and adds, "I was fine, a little wary but it was okay. Thanks." She walks past to drop the dog stuff in the basket by the front door then does an about-face. "I saw Mrs. Obermeier in her yard. She said she knew I was back because the piano music had started again. She asked me to keep up with the Beethoven and also play more Mendelssohn please and thank you."

"Ah, sounds about right. I spent months after you'd gone explaining what happened and apologizing that I couldn't play piano."

She pats my cheek. "Guess I have a lot of pianoing to make up then. Right. I'm going to take a shower."

"You're not having breakfast?"

Elise pauses by the fridge. "I'll eat once we're finished at the courthouse."

"Nerves?" She's going to file the paperwork for her temporary restraining order before the emergency one expires in a few days.

A quick smile. "No. We're hoping to get to the court right as they're opening up at eight, which means I had to bribe Rosemary with the promise of meeting a wonderful dog and then brunch. Both things combined just outweigh her dislike of getting anywhere before ten a.m."

"Ah. I admit to not a small amount of brunch jealousy. Do you need coffee?"

"I'll grab something on the way in, but thanks. In the unlikely event Rosemary is early, could you just park her somewhere and tell her I'll be ready in a minute. She'll probably just beeline for Bennie and stay there."

"Sure." I glance around the space, wondering if there's any visible evidence of me and Elise as Me-and-Elise. I can't see anything, but now I'm irrationally paranoid about it.

Ellie has obviously picked up on my alarm. "She knows about me, Avery. So does Paul. They've both known from the beginning." She blows out a noisy breath. "When I ditched Sandra and Bert I decided that my new team had to know the truth from the outset, because I was so sick of pretending to be someone I'm not with the people who're supposed to protect me and help me."

"That's great." The bitchy, still bitter part of me unhelpfully points out that she still wasn't comfortable enough to be honest with the world about us back when we were a couple. Remembering that feeling, dwelling on it, makes me feel like absolute shit. And I don't want to feel like that anymore. Right, Bitter Bitch. I don't need you anymore. Time to go. "I'm really happy you're comfortable with your team."

"Me too." An incongruous flash of panic crosses her face.

"What's wrong?"

"Nothing. Just uh, Rosemary likes to talk. That's all."

I know exactly what she's not saying—she's worried her manager and I are going to share stories. I'd never do something so personal and private without Ellie's approval, but her adorable attempt to seem like she doesn't care makes me want to tease. "Good thing I like to talk too."

"Great." She doesn't sound like she thinks it's great, at all. She jerks her thumb behind herself. "Right. Shower. I, uh... never mind."

Rosemary is indeed early and not at all what I'd expected. Elise's previous manager had been all sharp edges with her spike heels and power suits, fake Hollywood charm and passive-aggressive underhandedness. Rosemary reminds me of my mom—soft and warm, eclectic and eccentric.

The moment I open the door, she grasps both my hands in hers, her fingers squeezing mine. Rosemary's voice is high and slightly nasal, which only strengthens my comparison to my mother, and she smiles as she talks. "Avery, it is such a pleasure to finally meet you. I can't thank you enough for what you've done for Elise and not just during the horror of the plane incident but afterward and now. A good friend is exactly what she needs right now, especially with all the ridiculousness going on. Can you believe they just let him out on bail with a 'please behave and be sure to come back later'? Honestly, this system is so broken I don't even know where to begin."

She makes me feel so immediately comfortable that when I smile back, it's genuine rather than politely forced. "Great to meet you too. I know, it's ludicrous. And what are friends for, right?" And *finally*? I wonder exactly what's been said about me and how Elise and I know each other.

"Exactly." After another hand squeeze, Rosemary releases me to reach into her oversized purse. She extracts a compact and after a quick study of her reflection, stuffs it back. She lowers her voice. "How is she?"

"Okay, I think. I mean...you know, if you ignore the obvious of what she's dealing with." She really does seem okay. Scared and confused about what happened, what's going to happen, but coping with it.

"Right." She glances around as if checking for eavesdroppers. "You know I did offer to let her stay in my spare room because she really had nowhere else I could think of, or that I felt comfortable letting her go to. But she said she was going to come see her ex and see if she could help. Avery, I was so pleased and so relieved she has someone she trusts so much. Now don't get me wrong, I would have loved to have her with us, but I think being here is much better for her than with Irving and me. Plus, we did agree keeping work and home separate wasn't a bad thing."

I only just hold back my smile. Oh really, Elise? Didn't you basically say that I was the only person you knew who was available? It's so innocently conniving that I'm not even mad about it. If she hadn't made the first move then we'd never have had the chance to reconnect. And as much as I'm afraid of the hurt that'll come if she leaves again, or the confusion if she doesn't, I'm glad for the chance to finally get everything cleared and out in the open. "Ah, well I was happy to help out."

Bennett saunters in to interrupt with his usual "Who is this, are you allowed to be here, and if yes—will you pet me?" routine.

Rosemary's, "Oh, my darling" is a barely restrained whisper.

Bennett stops by my side and sits immediately at my hand signal. Rosemary glances at me. "May I?"

"Of course. He's usually a total teddy bear."

My permission to pet him turns her into a gushing grandmotherly type, and after carefully introducing herself to Bennett and receiving a hand nuzzle in response, she leans down to study him as she rubs the sides of his face. "Oh, you are so handsome, yes you are. My bastard ex-husband bred boerboels and I would bet a steak dinner one of his parents was purebred for sure." She spares me a glance. "Have you ever had him DNA tested?"

"Mhmm, Elise did not long after I got him. You're spot on. Boerboel, Rottweiler and a tiny bit of Lab because why not?"

She smiles as her attention returns to Bennett. "Did someone try to breed you to be a big growly boy? Silly people. Biggest sweethearts I ever owned were Rottweilers and boerboels. Loyal and protective to a fault when needed but so sweet otherwise."

Bennett's thumping tail is anything but growly. I scratch his neck. "He was my brother's dog. I kind of inherited him when he was just a puppy. But he's a great dog and pretty tolerant of me being away for work during the day. As long as he gets his walks and play time when I get home," I add.

Rosemary rubs Bennie's ears and he melts against her leg. "I bet he's a chewer."

"Oh yeah. Wears out heavy-duty toys in a month. When he's not people watching out the window, napping, or trying to get the opossum, chewing is his hobby." I gesture at the solid metal ring bolted into the wall just above Bennie's head height. The floor underneath the ring is worn out in an arc from Bennett's play. "I had that anchor point put in so I can tie a tug-toy there for him to play with during the day while I'm at work, and I leave him plenty of food-puzzle toys."

"Oh, that's a great idea." She laughs when Bennett attempts a cheek lick. "You are such a handsome boy and so lucky to have a Momma that loves you so much."

Elise emerges from the guest room in a whirlwind, still shrugging into a jacket as if she's afraid to let me and her manager chat for too long. She glances at herself in the hall mirror then moves to my side to join in the Bennett adoration-fest. Once she's finished showering him with goodbye pets, she looks to Rosemary. "Okay, are we ready?"

"Of course." She smiles at Ellie and asks a very motherly, "Do you have your paperwork?" Once Elise holds up a manila envelope, Rosemary gives me a soft, maternal cheek pat and Bennett a long, loving face rub before she slips out the front door with a lilting, "I'll leave you two to say bye."

When the door has closed, leaving Bennie to stare longingly at it, Elise turns to me. "Sorry, I hope she wasn't too…Rosemary."

"She was great. I like her."

"Phew," Elise exhales. "I should only be a few hours with this if everything at the courthouse goes to plan. And then after brunch we're going into the FBI office to talk with the agent in charge of my cybercrimes case. Rosemary wants to personally hand over everything she's been collecting—letters, photographs, emails. Especially the ones from Bridges and the Hayes Horde." The look she gives me tells me she knows it probably won't be as simple and easy as she's made out, and definitely not just a few hours. "And then my therapist's appointment this afternoon."

"Sure. I'll see you when I get home tonight. So far I've just got a day in the office. I'll let you know if that changes and I have to spend some time in the air and might be late. You can call if you need anything or if the FBI-speak is confusing."

Her smile is brilliant. "You bet. Be safe up there if you fly."

"Always am."

She sneaks a kiss, her lips just brushing the edge of my mouth. But despite not being a full kiss, her lips still linger, soft and warm. "I'll feed and play with Bennie to keep him happy until you get home."

At the sound of his name, Bennett's tail thumps hard on the polished hardwood floor.

My heart thumps in my chest.

After a tedious and tiring day, the moment I open the door, I hear music. Or more accurately—piano and quiet singing. After giving Bennett a hug hello, I follow the sound to the living room with him close behind. Ellie rarely sings when she plays, mostly because her go-to pieces are classical without lyrics but when she does, she's incredible. I'm not sure I'm hearing what I think I am, but after a few moments I realize it *is* Simon & Garfunkel. "Bridge Over Troubled Water" and the sound is haunting. She's always been able to take any piece of piano music and change the tempo and rhythm of it or even mix it with another style— Bach with a jazz lilt actually sounds pretty great—but in this case she's turned an already emotional song even more so, the rhythm almost off-kilter and falling apart even as she keeps it together.

I've forgotten her singing voice and I'm not surprised to feel the prickle of tears and a familiar tightening in my throat that has nothing and everything to do with her song. My brother always said his musical tastes were born twenty years before he was, and growing up, he would play Simon & Garfunkel, the Beatles, Cat Stevens, Fleetwood Mac, Led Zeppelin and dozens of other artists—all on vinyl of course—at top volume until either my parents or I would beg him to give us a break. After he died, I dragged out the vinyls and stereo he'd left for me and played every record as loudly as I could until I'd exhausted his collection and my grief. Then I put everything away and haven't touched it since.

I'm sure Elise has realized I'm there, but she doesn't stop. I lean down to scratch Bennett's chest then leave Elise to her restorative music. As I shower and get started on dinner, she flows through classical, pop, and rock before eventually emerging just as I'm setting the table.

"Hey," she murmurs.

"Hey yourself. How was everything today?"

"Fine. Court was surprisingly easy, as was the FBI visit. They were excited for all the stuff Rosemary handed over." Her smile is a little wonky. "And seeing my therapist was just what I needed to help me figure out my feelings about this. I'll probably go back again before Christmas."

"I'm glad." I gesture to the assorted bowls on the counter. "Great timing by the way. You missed out on all the meal prep I was going to ask you to help me with." The Vietnamese vegetarian summer rolls I made were fiddly but worth it.

Her grin tells me her tardiness is entirely intentional. "Thanks."

"You're going to be up shit creek when you go back to work and you have to cook every night instead of sharing duties with me."

"I'll be working most nights, and that's why they have craft services on set." She flutters her eyelashes. "Some nights if I'm too tired to cook, I hang around and steal some food before I go home."

"Sneaky."

"Very." Elise dips a finger into the lime dressing. "Oh that's yum."

"I know. Speaking of sneaky, Rosemary told me something interesting this morning."

"It's a lie," she says immediately. "I didn't really fall down the stairs in front of Ava DuVernay at an Emmy's after-party and get swooped up by her before I fell flat on my face. I just tripped as I approached her and I *did* manage to stay on my feet."

"I see. That's a story I definitely want to hear sometime. But that's not what she said. She told me she offered to let you stay at her place and you declined."

Ellie's expression is admirably neutral. "Right. She did, and I did."

"So when you said you didn't have anywhere to go…" I let the insinuation hang. I'm more amused than angry at her minor manipulation, but I'd still like to know exactly why she was so desperate to stay here.

She doesn't hesitate. "I wasn't exactly truthful. Yes, she did offer to let me stay with her and we did discuss it, but I thought I'd see if I could stay here first. I mean, I adore Rosemary and her husband but mixing work life and home life is not a good idea."

"Right."

I know by her expression that she's picked up on the meaning of my expression. Elise nervously fidgets with the mandoline I used to shred red cabbage. "Avery, when I saw you on that plane I felt like someone had just pulled my feet out from underneath me. It felt like a great big sign from the universe that what I'd been feeling and fighting was real, and that I really needed to do something about those feelings. And then the…the attack happened and you were right there, keeping me safe. And once I could breathe again, all I could see was the opportunity to maybe spend some time together and at least get back to some sort of friendship. So I decided to take it. But I really did need somewhere to stay. I didn't lie about that."

"I know you did." I smile and add, "And I know you didn't."

It feels like she thinks I don't believe her, and she keeps on with her rambling persuasion. "I needed somewhere safe, to be with someone I trust not just personally but also physically.

And I couldn't stop thinking about you after you walked off that plane. I felt like I just wanted to run after you, grab you and never let you go. And not just because of what you did."

"I know." I clear my throat.

Her tongue slides over her lower lip and her teeth briefly brush it before she seems to realize what she's doing and stops. "Are you mad at me?"

"Mildly annoyed, maybe. But not mad. And my annoyance is only because I would have preferred you to just tell me straight up why you wanted to stay here."

Both Ellie's hands come up in a placating gesture. "I was afraid you'd say no. I thought if you felt like you were my only real option then you'd be a little more agreeable to it."

"Do you really think I'd have said no after everything that happened that day?"

She pauses, face contorting as she considers. After almost a minute she murmurs, "Honestly? I didn't know what you would say. But my gut said you'd help me even after I left you and hurt you the way I did."

I reach for her, and am immediately soothed when she steps forward to take my hand. "Your gut is right, as usual. Even after all this time and all my feelings about it, I still—" I catch myself in time and hope she doesn't pick up on my falter. "—care about you."

But something in my voice, my expression, my words must have given me away. I'm not surprised, she's always read me better than anyone else. Ellie's gaze is steady, her voice measured and even when she tells me, "I still love you too."

CHAPTER FOURTEEN

It's *Greed* night! The mid-season finale has been at the back of my mind since Elise's arrival and I've been wondering if I can get her to not piano for an hour while I watch. I've also been wondering if she'll join me. She used to be ambivalent about watching herself on screen and the reason was usually something along the lines of her roles being blink-and-you'll-miss-me. Not anymore, Ellie.

The fact that the show is my weekly priority and not hers is evident when she drops a bomb on me as she's putting dinner on the table. "I was thinking we could go to the indoor shooting range after dinner tonight and get that practice in? Hopefully it'll be less busy around nine or ten p.m. and I can have a little privacy. What do you say?"

I can't believe she's just asked me that. "I say nope, sorry, I can't." At her look of surprised hurt I make sure to enunciate, "Elise. Tonight is *Greed* night, the last episode before Christmas break. It is *unmissable*. Any other night I'll be all over going to the range to practice with you, but tonight? My butt is going to be on the couch from nine to ten p.m. and the only thing that's going to move me is needing to pee during a commercial break."

Her face relaxes from upset into something more like pleasure. "Oh. It didn't even register that it's tonight." She bites her lower lip but her mouth twitches into a smile anyway. "You really do watch it? I thought you were just saying anything you could to get under his skin on the plane."

"Yes, I really watch it. I've watched it since the first episode."

She flushes then quickly turns her face away as if realizing she's revealed her feelings. "Why?" she asks as she spoons ratatouille onto my plate.

"At first I was curious to see this thing that was more important to you than us." I pause when I realize what I've just said sounds a little nasty. "Sorry, you know what I mean."

Her smile is knowing. "Yeah, I do."

"Then I realized how damned good the show is and how amazing you are in it."

My usually confident ex-girlfriend actually looks shy, almost embarrassed. "Ah. That's good. I'm glad you like it. I mean, objectively I know people do, but it always feels like that's separated from what I'm doing while filming it."

"They like it because of *you*, Ellie. You're utterly incredible."

"Thanks." Elise drops her gaze down to the casserole pot. After a few seconds she looks back up at me, now grinning wickedly. "I put extra eggplant in this."

"Oh that's going too far. You've really overstayed your welcome now," I drawl.

Still grinning, Ellie uses the serving spoon to pick a few bits of eggplant out of the ratatouille and, keeping eye contact with me, places them on my plate.

Not that I ever expect anything other than culinary genius from Elise, but dinner is wonderful—even the eggplant, which I admit I might eat again if it's like this. My stilted version of eggplant-praise earns me a beatific smile, a sneaky kiss then an even sneakier butt slap when I stand up to clear the table. I have half an hour to clean up and to prep myself for *Greed* and Ellie is obviously catching my glances at the clock. "Mind if I watch it with you? I don't think I've watched a full episode since the first season."

"Course you can, sweetheart, but I swear to god if you spoil any part of it for me I really am going to kick you out of my house. Eggplant is one thing but spoiling my favorite show is another level."

Her mouth twitches at my usage of *sweetheart*. "Can I take Bennett with me when you kick me out?"

"No."

"Shit. I'd better keep quiet then."

"Mmm, you'd better." I nudge the dishwasher closed with my foot. "This really is my favorite television event of the week, Ellie."

She leans into me, resting her face against my shoulder. Her words are slightly muffled. "You know I wouldn't dream of spoiling anything for you." She pulls back slightly. "Except the fact we've been renewed for another two seasons. But you didn't hear that from me."

I pretend to zip my lips. "Won't tell a soul. That's epic."

She smiles. "It is. I do love a steady paycheck." The smile wavers. "I just don't love some other things."

"Creepy stalkers and inappropriate fanboys aren't particularly lovable."

"No," she muses. "They aren't."

She tops off her glass of wine and pours me a berry kombucha. "All right. Let's do this. Do we get popcorn? Is there some special watching ritual or something?"

"Yeah. I park my ass, watch the show, and enjoy."

"Works for me."

I lower the level of liquid in my glass to won't-spill-while-carrying and grab an already open bag of Skittles from the pantry. "Ben! *Greed* time."

Bennett gets up from his bed right away and after a long stretch, saunters over to us. He's got his pleased face on, and his goofy expression—which is probably more just because he's been spoken to—sends Elise into a fit of giggles. "Oh no, really? Bennie's a fan of the show too?"

"Totally." I pat Bennett's butt and gesture for him to get settled in his bed by the couch while I turn the TV on. "Watches with me every week. He really hates Dimitri."

"Everyone hates Dimitri…"

I pour Skittles into my palm and stare at the sea of mostly yellow. Beside me, Elise is purposely still and seems to be deliberately not looking at me. I pop a few candies into my mouth. "How odd. I thought they'd figured out their flavor ratios but now it seems they're back to unusually high amounts of lemon in every packet."

"Odd indeed." She grabs the Skittles and after tipping some out, carefully puts all the yellow ones back.

"I missed a lot of things about you when you were gone, but I haven't missed being your yellow Skittles disposal."

"Things like what?" she asks quietly.

"Everything," I admit.

Elise studies me, her expression carefully neutral. The sound of Elise's voiceover from screen saying, "Previously on *Greed*" stops whatever she was about to say. "Saved by myself," she murmurs.

It's not as weird as I'd thought it would be, watching *Greed* with Elise. She's quiet and seems engaged in what's happening on screen, and after a few minutes settles to lie against me. With the first commercial break, Elise muses, "It's interesting to watch it, actually. Feels so disconnected from how I experience making the show without music or effects."

"I gotta know, who do you like playing more? Undercover Detective Jessica Meares, or Meares as Crime Boss Sloane Markwell?"

"Ten points for being the first person, ever, including every journalist, to ask me that one." She stretches up and kisses me softly, but quickly, as if she's scared I might move. No chance.

"If that's what I get for asking a ten-pointer question, what would I get for asking a twenty-pointer?" It's a dangerous question, dangerous innuendo.

Her smile is a little coy. "Maybe you should ask one and find out." Before I can think of a comeback she says, "I think Meares-as-Markwell. Because it gives Jessica the chance to let all those aspects of herself she usually has to hide out into the world. Every time I read Sloane's lines and slip into Sloane's skin, I feel like Sloane *is* the true Jessica. But Jessica's spent her life hiding that part of her nature, forcing herself to conform and fit into the box the world gave her. Sloane gives her the chance to just let loose and give in to that side of herself."

I'd suspected as much with Markwell not being just a covert role for Meares so much as an extension of herself, and always wonder how the show is going to play out and how far Meares is going to slip into Markwell. "Great answer." I pretend to scribble something down. "Thank you, Ms. Hayes."

Elise slaps me playfully. Then she says something I'd never expected, even though I'd been thinking it myself. "Playing the role is easy because I can relate. Jessica hiding Sloane away feels like me, hiding who I really am from the world but sometimes, with some people, I can just be who I really am." She grins. "Not saying you're a drug criminal, obviously. But you know."

"Thanks. And I do know." I brush my fingers over her cheek. "I'm so sorry, Ellie."

Her eyebrows rocket up. "For what?"

"For being selfish about you leaving, for making it all about me for this past year. I don't think I really appreciated how hard it was for you, being you, feeling the way you did and being so…stuck with your life that you had to leave our relationship. I was so focused on how broken I was that I forgot to think about you. I think maybe if I'd really listened and paid attention earlier then I might have seen what you weren't saying, or what you were trying to tell me. It must have been horrible for you."

"It was. I loved you, Avery, and that feeling never went away. You know I still do."

"I know." I want to tell her I still love her too, and I know she knows it, but it feels too sudden and soon. I'm saved from my overwhelming emotions by the commercial break ending.

The episode is as incredible as I'd hoped. Meares got badly hurt in a fight with one of the wives from the Dominican cocaine gang. Then when she went to find her handler-slash-partner he was acting super sketchy because he'd found out she'd shot Kanzi in cold blood last week. The episode left on a cliffhanger: Meares—dripping blood from an abdominal stab wound—facing off at gunpoint with her partner. Holy. Shit.

When the credits start rolling, Elise turns to me, her eyes comically wide. She enunciates every word in mock surprise. "Wow. That poor woman really can't catch a break. I wonder what's going to happen in the next episode."

"Don't you dare." I give her my best glare, which would stop a perp in their tracks, but just makes her laugh.

She raises both hands. "Wouldn't dream of it."

"Ellie, you're fucking amazing in this show. I can't say it enough."

She grins. "Good, because I can't listen to it enough."

Kissing her feels so natural that it's almost automatic when I lean over and softly brush my lips against hers. "I'm really proud of you." The sudden emotion makes my eyes prickle. I am proud of her, maybe even more so than when she'd just landed the role.

"I know you are," she murmurs. She kisses me again, then slowly runs her hand up my ribs, pausing before she touches my breast. The hand withdraws and Elise shuffles backward on the couch. "Sorry, forgot the rules."

I damned well forgot them too. After taking a moment to settle myself, I stand. "I'm just going to put the trash out." Bennett gives me some eyebrows. "You're safe from a long walk tonight, Bennie. Isn't it lucky Elise is around to play with you during the day, huh?"

"Lucky indeed," Elise echoes. "But you still gotta go out to pee later, Bennie."

Once I've set both lots of trash out, I glance up and down the street for strange cars. Then I take a look around to make sure nothing seems out of place with the exterior of my house. Everything seems perfectly normal on the street and with my property.

When I come back inside with a container of Mrs. Obermeier's strawberry-frosted vanilla cupcakes, Elise is on the phone. She's pacing slowly back and forth between the kitchen counters, letting her hip bump the counters before she turns. "Okay, great, yeah no that's good. It's with the lawyer?" She nods. "Yeah, I know. She called me at one a.m. once, so you got off easy with a nine p.m. call. Mhmm, okay, yeah that's fine. Just send me the calendar invite. Great." She laughs quickly, the sound a burst of light. "Me too. Bye."

I try not to look too expectant but it's clear from her excitement that something big happened. While I wait for her to tell me, I take a huge bite from a cupcake and offer the container to her. Elise takes one. "Thanks." She turns the cupcake around as if thinking and when she looks up, her smile is electric. "I got that part!" At my blank what-part-is-she-talking-about expression, Ellie lets me off the hook. "The one I mentioned on the plane where I'd just had the chemistry test in Chicago. Sorry, I don't even know if you remember it."

I hastily swallow my mouthful of cupcake. "That's fantastic! Congratulations. What's the role? Or aren't you allowed to say yet?"

"It'll be announced once things are signed, hopefully next week. I don't think someone—you—who has very little interest in the showbiz biz is going to spill. It's a book adaptation. Basically, a woman has signed up for a four-year psychological experiment for a bunch of cash. Total seclusion in this like, tiny farm in the forest and she's got no human contact except for checking in using a word-only message system with the people overseeing it. She's starting to have a bit of a mental breakdown then a woman arrives. It's kind of dark-ish but hopeful, a bit weird, then they hook up and then—" She grins. "I can't tell you because, spoiler."

The plot sounds incredible, if not a little weird, but I'm stuck on the "hooking up" part. A woman in seclusion who meets… another woman? My not-poker face makes Ellie laugh. "I know exactly what you're thinking. Am I worried this role is going to cause speculation?"

"That's actually not what I was thinking. My thoughts were more along the lines of imagining the 'hook up' part."

She feigns exasperation. "You have a filthy mind." Using just a forefinger she pokes me in the ribs. "Always thinking about me naked?"

I squirm away from her tickles and her too-close-to-the-mark remark. "We are *starved* for quality women-loving-women content, Ellie, and I know you're going to knock it out of the park." I decide to ask the question that's burning in the back of my mind. "Are you worried about it?" We could dive so deeply into the nuance of what the role means—personally and professionally—and if she's worried that being associated with a role like that might mean people start speculating about her sexuality which, if Nicola's constant speculation is any indication, seems to be the norm for any actress who kisses a woman on screen.

"About what exactly?"

"The woman-loving-woman part of it and what people might think and maybe um, project onto you."

"Ah. Well, Meares is openly bisexual and both her and Markwell have been with men and women in *Greed*." Her smile is gently indulgent. "So no, I'm not worried about my first fully lesbian role and what people might choose to extrapolate from it. I'm *super* excited for it. Not just the chance to play an openly lesbian character but just for the whole production. But thank you for checking in with me."

She seems so relaxed and as if it really is a complete nonissue for her that I believe her. "Then I'm excited for you." I lean against the counter. "So in this story, there's no people at the place at all? Not even calls?"

"Nope, nothing. Not even pictures in books."

"Fuck that. You couldn't pay me enough. Whoever wrote that sounds seriously weird."

Ellie laughs. "Yeah, you couldn't pay me enough either, but the script is amazing and the concept is incredible. Super twisty, angsty but not bad dark angst and…yeah."

"Are you the woman participating in the experiment or the intruder?"

"The woman participating." Her glee is palpable. "I'm really excited to work out how to play off nothing and nobody until my co-star arrives."

"Are there any accents? I nearly died when you got the part in that adaptation of *Jane Eyre*. I don't think I could take it again." She'd taken dialect lessons during her acting training and was one of those people who could slip in and out of accents with ease. In preparation for that role she'd worked with a dialect coach and had spoken in nothing but a British accent for months. Even in bed. Which made me want to drag her to bed even more.

Ellie's laugh is sudden and loud, as if she's recalling the exact same things I am. "Not from me, only my co-star."

"And do you know who's been cast as the intruder woman?"

Ellie's grin is sly and she waits for the most dramatic of beats before putting me out of my misery. "Isabella Barolo."

I groan, covering my face with both hands. "Brilliant," I mumble into my palms before dropping my hands. "You and the hottest Italian woman getting around are making a film together. With ladies-loving-ladies content. I might *literally* combust."

Laughing, Elise leans over to kiss me. "I'm sure you'll cope. Think of me, having to do sex scenes with her. I'm the one who's going to combust."

My brain finally remembers that most movies take months to shoot, which means Elise is going to be away working for a while. I shouldn't care, we're not *together*, but…I care. We've just reconnected and even if our relationship remains firmly in the "friends" camp, I like having her around. "When and where will you be filming these combustible scenes?"

"During winter hiatus next year, in Canada. It's going to be a tight tight shoot to get it all down before I go back to *Greed* in January, but I love that pressure."

"Why not film in the summer hiatus?"

"Isabella has another film shoot then, and it's almost impossible to get both done. You wouldn't even try."

"Hmm. So you'll get to enjoy some of that Canadian winter."

"I will. Might help keep me cool." She seems to finally remember she's got a cupcake, and after using a finger to scoop strawberry frosting into her mouth, says, "You could always come along, take some of your hoarded vacation time? Make sure I'm not combusting."

"I could," I muse. "Or I could see if Isabella Barolo wants to make me combust. Isn't she bi?"

"Do I have to snarl?" Elise deadpans.

"Do you want to snarl?"

"Yes."

I touch the tip of her nose with my forefinger. "Jealousy. Hmm. You know I never got jealous about you and your co-stars." We'd talked about it, because I'd been genuinely curious, if she had ever been attracted to anyone during work or had a reaction during sex scenes. And Ellie had laughed and said it's so not-private and so heavily choreographed that all sexiness is sucked out of the process.

"That was totally different, as will be my scenes with Isabella. It's work." Her voice gets tight. "What you're talking about is—"

"A joke." I exhale. "Ellie, from the moment we met, the only woman I've thought about is you. And after everything that's happened between us, you're still the only woman I want. Since we broke up, I've dated two women for about three seconds and every time they kissed me I clammed up because it felt so wrong. They were both really nice women, lots of potential chemistry. But they weren't you. And I thought it was just me trying to get used to someone new and if I gave it a good, honest shot, then I'd get past it."

I wish I could shut my mouth and stop admitting these things which are only going to hurt us. Acknowledging that we're still in love, that I still want her, that our spark is as strong as the day we met isn't going to overcome the massive barrier that stands like a ten-foot wall between us. Elise won't come out and I can't deal with being a cryptic footnote in her public life.

Her question is quiet. "Did you? Get past it, I mean."

I suck in a huge breath, trying not to think about the implications of what I've just admitted to her. "No. Come on, Elise. You know me. It took me three years to get over Julianne Moore replacing Jodie Foster as Clarice Starling after *Silence of the Lambs*. Did you think I was just going to move on from you in a heartbeat? There was no chance of it. I've accepted it happened and I really tried to move on. I did, honestly. But after those dating attempts, every single time I'd see someone I thought I was attracted to I'd think about her touching me or me kissing her and would get so anxious I'd feel sick. I just—"

She's against me so quickly that she cuts off what I'm trying to tell her. Her kiss is fierce, hungry, needy. She kisses me like she's afraid of what I might say and of what it could mean for us. The desperation makes arousal curl in my stomach and I pull her against me. Hands slip under my shirt and cup my breasts, then just as quickly, she pulls her hands and lips away. Elise presses her fingers to her mouth and slowly backs away. "I...I think I'll go to bed. Goodnight," she adds quickly before she rushes out of the kitchen.

"Ellie?" I call after her, barely able to get that word out around the tight knot of desire and anxiety taking up all the space in my chest.

She pauses and turns around, a smile already fixed in place. "It's fine, Avery. Really." Elise disappears into the hall.

It is so not fine.

CHAPTER FIFTEEN

Ellie is still in her sweaty workout clothes when she slips past, careful to not touch me, on her way to the front door. "Rosemary just called to say she's left some of my mail from home and the usual bag of fan letters she forgot to bring with her on Monday. She has to rush off for dinner with her awful in-laws otherwise she would have, and I quote, 'come in and smothered Bennett in kisses.'" After a glance through the peephole, she opens the door and pulls a huge duffel inside which she drops beside a kitchen chair.

I set down the vegetarian stroganoff ingredients I've just pulled from the fridge and stare at the bulging bag. "That's your fan mail? For a month, or..."

"A week." She drops a smaller stack of official-looking mail on the table.

"Wow. And you read all of it?"

"Mhmm, course I do." She pauses, smiles uneasily. "Well, actually, not *all* of it. I've gotten pretty good now at skimming and deciding if it's a genuine fan, someone wanting money or for me to endorse something, or a creep. The last two get tossed aside for Rosemary to go through and she decides if we need to put someone on a fan watchlist. Now, she's opening *all* my fan mail for me, and any creep letters or emails are going straight to my FBI guy." The uneasy smile wavers until it's a nonexistent smile. "She's warned me there's some photocopies of pretty nasty letters in this batch, and she's already forwarded the originals to the FBI."

I almost don't want to ask. "How many people are on this fan watchlist?"

"Last update a month or two ago was—" Her eyebrows dip, mouth twisting as she thinks. "—just over two hundred."

"Fuck." I'd been expecting her to say only a handful.

"Mmm. Some people have trouble with personal boundaries, as you know." We exchange a look that clearly says we both know some people, especially recently, definitely have a problem with that.

I try to sound casual when I ask, "Have you had any updates about Bridges?" I feel awful asking her about it repeatedly, especially knowing how long it can take to build a case, but I need to know someone is doing something.

"Yes, if you can call it an update. Basically just 'we're working on it.'"

I fight the urge to go comfort her and instead, try for a little levity. "I guess that's better than 'we're not working on it'?"

Ellie doesn't take my bait. "Mmm. As something to look forward to in the new year, I've got trial dates for the assault and my permanent restraining order because the temporary one will run out. So, I'll have to see him then. Twice. Can't wait," she grinds out. "And when we saw my FBI guy on Monday about the stalking stuff he said it's more of the same—gathering evidence, making sure the case will stick. But they couldn't get Bridges's computer because it seems he doesn't have one. Dumped or hidden is the theory, which looks super suspicious given his own admission that he's emailed me some lovely photoshopped pictures of myself."

"It does look suspicious," I say carefully. "Who doesn't have a computer?"

"Right. Meanwhile, I'm just stuck here thinking about what he's done, and unable to really do anything myself. It's fucked. Have I forgotten anything?"

"No…I think you've covered it all."

"I *hate* this waiting and worrying and not knowing. I just want to move on with my life instead of thinking about this every fucking waking hour."

"I know, sweetheart. It's unfair and it's wrong. But that's the ridiculous system."

"The system sucks." It's a perfect impersonation of a petulant kid.

"You're right, sometimes it does."

Ellie huffs out a breath and forces a resigned smile. She hoists the duffel onto a chair. "Well, at least I have something to occupy my mind for the rest of the night."

Elise has been reading mail for the last half hour while I listen to a gaming podcast as I create dinner. Bennett has had his dinner and is settled on his bed in the corner of the dining room, watching us both. It feels so normal, like we're playing happy housewives, when it's anything but.

We haven't spoken about last night, about both of us breaking the No Kiss rule, about how close we were to falling into bed again. I don't know if I want to talk about it but I feel like we should, even if I have no idea what we'd say. Oh yeah, we're still in love, still have insane chemistry and can't seem to stop touching or kissing each other, but we can't sustain a relationship so oh well, whaddya do? I'm not surprised by my reaction to her kissing me, not surprised by how much I wanted it. But I am surprised by how close I came to just saying *fuck it* and breaking the rules when it was me who insisted on the rules.

I've just put egg noodles into a pot of boiling water when I'm startled by a loud clattering over my podcast hosts debating next year's hottest wireless headset. I spin, yanking an earbud out in time to catch Ellie's tight, tense, "Avery? Can you come look at something for me?"

Her chair has been pushed back and toppled against the kitchen counter. Bennett has sprung from his bed and rushed to Elise's side. He noses her hand, pushing his head underneath it as if he thinks, in doggo-logic, something solid and soft will comfort her. She rests her hand flat on his head, fingers curling into his short fur as if she's trying to hold on to something. On the table to her left is a stack of opened envelopes, then two piles of paper and empty envelopes to her right. A single sheet of photocopied paper lies discarded, as if it's been hastily dropped. Ellie's shaking hand indicates that letter and I lean over to take a look.

Fury slides back under my skin. What I see makes me feel sick and I want to set fire to the paper, to burn the words so Elise will never have to see them again.

Our Elise,
We love you and we're going to make you see that. And if one of us fails, there's always someone to take our place. Troy sends his regards. And his regrets.
HH

I grind my molars, trying to chase away the bile rising up my throat. The words I want to say stick, like they know venting my anger is not appropriate, so all I manage is a tight, "I see."

"He can't do that, can he? Write me like this? I mean, he's not allowed to contact me or come near me or anything like that. Do we call the police or the FBI or a judge or what?"

I take her hand, squeezing firmly to stop her panic, and as calmly as I can, state the obvious. "Honey, this doesn't say it's from *him*. It's not really signed at all."

"Of course it's from him," she rebuts instantly. "How else would *they* know what happened?" She's obviously fighting to stay calm, and she's losing.

"Okay, okay. Let's just back up a step." If Bridges had some part in this then he must have gone home after being released on bail, told his cronies all about what happened, and one of them wrote this letter and posted it to her. Or he wrote it and is hiding behind this ridiculous Hayes Horde group façade.

I set the letter back on top of the pile. "Rosemary's already sent it the FBI agent, right? But…Ellie, I'm not sure it's actually from him. There's no concrete proof in this letter that he sent it."

"Isn't this concrete proof?" She points at the page. "His name is right there."

"Yes and no," I hedge. "It's just alluding, and his lawyers would likely argue that fact and also that he hasn't outright admitted to being one of them. And because there's not yet any evidence linking him to them, like email chains or phone calls or anything like that, our side can't yet prove he is actually part of it and not just bragging about it." By the time I've finished my explanation, I feel like I can barely breathe. And I wonder how many more times I'm going to have to tell her that this case will probably always be weighted against her, even if he's convicted.

"Okay, so if it's not him, then can *they* do this? It's like him contacting me, isn't it? It's right there, his name, alluding to what he did, like he's fucking taunting me." Her voice rises an octave with each word. "He can't do this can he? Not with the restraining order. Right? This is indirect contact and he can't do that." She sounds like she's barely keeping a grip on her panic.

I take both her hands and bring them to my mouth to kiss the knuckles on her thumbs before I hold her hands against my chest. "No, sweetheart, he can't. But we can't prove it was him, or that it's him behind this message. Unless he told this person to tell you this and again, there's no proof of that here, then it's not indirect contact."

"That's, that's…" She pulls her hands free to gesture helplessly. "That's fucking bullshit!"

"Yes," I agree. "It is. And the slippery legality doesn't make it right, and it *is* harassing you but again, it could just be that one of these guys saw what happened on the news, maybe recognized him or they'd discussed how he was going to do what he did and this guy decided to write the letter and mention him. I also think that's probably what his lawyers would argue, that it's not him, just someone in the Hayes Horde being a copycat because they saw what he did in the news, and Bridges is innocent." I feel awful having to tell her these things, that there are so many loopholes through which abusers can slip. "I don't think that's what happened. I think he *is* involved. But until the FBI gets proof of it, there's nothing we can do."

"Right. Right." Her breathing catches, her rising panic starting to run out of control. "I just keep thinking what if he knows where I am somehow? I mean, someone managed to hack the computers before. Why wouldn't he just do it again? Or get into my phone or emails or something? He could come here and find us and hurt us, all of us. He might even find Stevie. Why is he free?" She yanks her hands free from mine to fan her face, sucking in shallow, rasping breaths. "Oh god, I can't breathe."

I take her shoulders gently in both hands and shake her lightly, trying to get her to focus on me. "Ellie, you *can* breathe. You know how to breathe, just in and out. Look at me." I exaggerate a breath in and out, and relief replaces some of my worry when she tries to mimic me. "Good, sweetheart, and again. Breathe in and let it out. I'm here. We're safe."

After half a minute of coaching her, comforting her, she finally seems to take a full breath which she shudderingly releases. I squeeze her shoulders. "That's it, that's perfect. And then another one. I'm right here with you, sweetheart."

It takes another few minutes of me gently reminding her to relax for the wheezy panic to slide from her breathing. She dives against me, wrapping her arms tightly around my waist. When I pull her tighter, I feel the tremor in her body as her fear seeps out. "He's not going to come here, Ellie. He's not going to find you. He's not going to hurt you or me or Steven or Bennett." I kiss her temple, soothing her, and continue, "Didn't you say your management team has overhauled their online security? That an expert came in to help and it's locked down like Alcatraz. He'll never do that again. You also said you've got great security at your house. He has no idea where you are now. And when the time comes and the Feds have built a case against him, he'll go to jail."

She makes an indistinguishable sound and as I rub my hands up and down her back, I remind her, "You're safe here. You don't have to worry about anyone finding you or hurting you." Even as I say it, I hope I'm not lying to her. My gut tells me he would have no way of knowing she's here but even if he did, my house is more than secure enough.

"I know," she whispers. "I'm sorry. I know I'm safe. I know you'll keep me safe. It's just this feeling in the back of my mind that I can't shake and it's driving me insane."

I relax my grip slightly so I can see her face. "What do you need, Ellie? What can I do to help you?"

Before taking a step backward out of the circle of my arms, Elise shrugs—a short jerky gesture that conveys her turbulence. She crosses to the stove and yanks the lid from the rapidly boiling pot. "You always put the lid back on after you've put the noodles in," she quietly says, as if she's only just remembered this thing I do.

"I know." I blame my culinarily challenged mom who always did it and who influenced me to do the same.

She snags a dishcloth. "It doesn't make things cook faster, it just makes it boil over and causes a mess."

I smile. "Maybe I like cleaning up messes."

"Maybe you do," Elise muses. As she wrings out the dishcloth, I move to stand behind her. As if sensing where I am, she steps backward so her back is touching my front. Then she says, so quietly that I only just make out the words, "I'm sorry if I left you a mess to clean up."

She slips away before I've fully processed her words and can reply. A mess. The only mess she left me with was an emotional one. And I cleaned it up. I'm not sure I could clean up another one, but if she promised to never leave such an emotional pigsty in her wake, if things changed, maybe…

No. Maybe can't happen.

Elise stacks the mail at one end of the counter, nervously arranging and then rearranging the piles of letters and envelopes. She picks at dinner, which is usually one of her favorite meals, and abandons her glass of wine after a few small mouthfuls before she quietly excuses herself to take a shower. I break our usual "one cooks, one cleans up after" routine and tidy up the remnants of dinner while she's showering. When she reemerges, she's dressed in a threadbare tee and her favorite old pair of jeans, as if she's desperate for all the comfort she can find. Before I can ask her how she's feeling or if she wants to spend some time with the Steinway or watch a movie or just do something not-alone, she says, "I think I might just go to bed and have a mini-meltdown." Her wry smile tells me she's not entirely serious.

"Want some company for that?" My question isn't entirely serious either.

The smile flickers to amused for a moment. "I think I'll be okay. But thank you."

"Okay then. I'll probably be in the gaming cave if you need me."

"Thanks," Ellie murmurs. "For everything." She moves closer but stays outside my personal space. "I mean it, Avery. I'm not sure how I'd cope if I didn't have you around."

"You're welcome. And you won't need to worry about me not being around." The urge to touch her is overwhelming and I consider restraining myself for a second before I give in and take her hand. "You're strong and resilient and you're going to be okay. But I'm always happy to help a little around the edges when you need me."

A smile tugs at the corners of her mouth. "Strong and resilient. Hmm. Debatable." She leans in to kiss me lightly, then leaves. I let Bennie out, and as I watch him sniffing around the yard in the light cast from the garden spotlights I try to figure out what to do with my feelings. Killing pixel things should help vent some of the emotion until it's no longer pervasive.

I almost break the plastic wrap on *Assassin's Guild: Rhetra* but after staring at Ellie's face on the front, I change my mind. She was right—her being here, us interacting in our familiar ways has eased my reluctance to dive into the game. Now I have a sudden burning urge to open the packaging and jump into the game world. But I know myself. If I start playing, I won't want to stop. And I have work tomorrow. "I'll start you on the weekend," I murmur to myself.

"Sounds like I'll have to find a way to amuse myself for forty-eight hours then," comes the quiet and unexpected voice from the doorway.

Once I've un-startled myself I say, "It's not like you haven't done it before. Remember when *Prey* came out?" And pretty much every other game release with which I've been obsessed.

"I do. Vividly. I don't think I saw you for a week." She raises a slow eyebrow. "Except when you stumbled into bed at four a.m."

"Guilty. But I still maintain it was a great use of vacation time." She seems much calmer now, but my protective streak still flares. "How're you feeling?"

"Better." A wry smile. "I decided I didn't really want to have a meltdown after all."

"No? What do you want to do then? I can be quiet if you want to meditate. I promise I won't yell at the bad guys. Much," I add when her eyebrows rise in amusement. She knows that promise is one I'll break in about thirty seconds.

The amusement softens as Elise closes the gap between us, then carefully takes the game box from me and places it back on the shelf. "I want something good, something safe so I can forget about all this. I want you." The touch of fingers against my cheek is tentative and her thumb moves to gently trace under my lower lip.

Her caress makes me shudder inside. I know exactly what she means and I know *exactly* what she wants. What she needs. What she needs more than anything right now is to feel safe and in control, to know she's in charge and that nothing she doesn't want will happen to her. Fuck the rules. I can give her that. I'm going to give her that. Though I want nothing more than to touch her, to yank her against me and kiss her until she can no longer stand, I keep myself still and ask the simplest of questions. "Can I kiss you?"

Elise's forehead crinkles and I can see her trying to figure out why I'm asking. The edge of her mouth twitches. "Of course you can." Her voice is quiet and husky, inviting me in.

I lightly run my thumb over her lips and when Elise's mouth opens to suck my finger, my stomach muscles clench. I asked if I could kiss her but it's she who kisses me, leaning in to suck my lip softly before her mouth caresses mine in a kiss so slow and sensual that my clenched abdominals unclench themselves and turn quivering. Her hands slide under my tee and the sensation of her nails tracing a slow path down to my waistband sends goose bumps racing over my skin. I shudder. Elise's mouth is hungry, but her hands are not, and the sensation of hot, hard kisses and light, languorous hands is exquisite.

Her hands move to grip my hips and without breaking our kiss, she guides me out of the gaming cave and down the hall. Elise pauses at the door to the guest room but I keep moving, pulling her toward my room. She breaks the kiss to ask breathlessly and tentatively, "Are you sure?"

I nip lightly at her lip, then lick the spot of pain I've just inflicted. "I want you in my bed." Those last two words, *my bed*, catch in my throat.

Elise takes charge again to drag me to my bedroom. We've barely made it through the door before she pulls my shirt over my head and tugs at the string on my sweatpants. My underwear follows to puddle on the floor with the rest of my clothing. Now her hands speed up. They reach to cup my breasts, thumb my nipples, pinch them hard until electricity shoots down into my belly.

Ellie moves to pull her tee over her head, but I gently stop her. My question is husky. "May I undress you?"

After a long pause, she murmurs, "Yes." After a beat she adds, "Slowly." It's neither demand or command, but the no-nonsense tone makes it absolutely clear that she knows she's in control. Just as I wanted.

Slowly, I raise the shirt up her torso, letting my fingertips trace over her skin. I desperately want to let my fingers stray to brush the exquisitely soft skin of her breasts, but she hasn't given me permission to do that. Yet. I swallow hard. "Can I touch you?"

"Yes," Elise whispers.

I slide one hand up to brush underneath her breast. "Here?" She buries her teeth in her lower lip as she nods.

Though I didn't think she would deny me the pleasure of touching her, her permission floods me with relief. I cup her breasts, both the perfect size to nestle in my palms, and roll her nipples between my thumb and forefinger until she shudders. Her breasts beg for my lips and tongue, and I push her shirt up further to expose them to my hungry view. She's already given me permission to kiss her and touch her, but still I ask, "Can I put my mouth on you?"

It seems she's caught on to my intention of letting her lead the show and control this narrative, and she utters a hoarse, "Yes. Please."

After my first light kiss to each of her nipples, Elise cups the back of my head to hold me against her. Her fingers move restlessly through my hair and I play my tongue around her nipple before sucking it into my mouth. The other nipple receives the same treatment as I drag my fingernails lightly up and down her spine.

Elise lifts her arms so I can remove the shirt. I drop it to the floor before I drop to my knees in front of her. With my hands wrapped around to hold her ass, I slowly kiss her stomach, pausing here and there to lick or suck an enticing spot as I make my way along the waistband of her jeans. I unfasten both button and zip and slide the garment down thighs and calves for Ellie to step out and kick free. Kneeling with my face against her belly, I can smell her arousal and the musky scent makes my throat tighten. My own arousal rises fiercely, like something untamed, and I take a slow breath to settle myself.

A quick indulgence. I press my nose against her, inhaling the scent through her plain blue panties as both my hands glide up the back of her calves and thighs until I'm cupping her ass again. The movement of her hips against my face is subtle, but unmistakable. Her hand rests on top of my head, her fingers tugging my hair lightly. "Take them off," she says.

I break her rule of slow and with fingers hooked in the waistband of her panties, drag them down as quickly as I can.

The moment every beautiful inch of her is bared for me, I stand again and help her to my bed. She drags me down on top of her, scissoring her legs around the back of my calf. I let my hand rest against the thin strip of her pubic hair, careful to keep my fingers away from the place they're desperate to be. "How about here? May I touch you here?"

This "Yes" is a breathy exhalation, a sound of begging desperation.

I slide my fingers lightly through her valley, sampling her wetness before bringing my fingers back to glide over her clit. When I linger to lightly circle, Elise buries her face in my shoulder and her choked moan is hot against my skin. "More," she begs me.

I want to drag her leg up and around my waist, open her to my touch and fuck her deep and hard. But she hasn't asked for that. Yet. My light touch has her quivering and I keep up the steady rhythm, the barest pressure to hold her right on the edge. Her hands tangle in my hair, her mouth presses to my skin, her teeth and lips mark where she's been. The words muffle against my skin. "Please, that's so good, please."

I push myself up a little so I can see her. She's glorious, her skin flushed and sweaty and her complete unashamed, unabashed delight in the pleasure she's taking makes my own desire flare. "Can I taste you?" My throat tightens at the thought.

These words are not muffled. "Yessss. God, yes. Please. Yes. Put your mouth on me." Ellie pushes at my shoulders, my chest, as if she's trying desperately to convey just how much she wants me to go down on her.

I feast briefly on her nipples, taste her skin as I slide down her body to settle myself between her spread thighs. I take a moment to run my hands over her skin, up her thighs and across hips, over her tight belly and up until I'm cupping her breasts. Elise gasps as I pinch her nipples. The gasp turns to a choked moan when I cover her labia with my mouth. She covers my hands with hers, guiding my fingers to keep playing with her nipples as my tongue plays over her clit.

I lick her exactly the way I know she loves it, the way that's going to make her come quickly, not playing or teasing or trying to draw things out. When I press my tongue against her entrance, she bucks her hips against me and I'm gifted a fresh flood of arousal. I gather it on my tongue and take it back up to her clit. After indulging myself for long moments buried in her warm wetness, I drag my mouth away from her to ask, "Can I fuck you?"

Her answer is to take one of my hands currently fondling her breast and rolling her nipple back and forth and guide those fingers down. Elise arches up, pressing her clit into my mouth as she keeps pressing my fingers to enter her. Her arousal is so thick and wet that my fingers slide into her with the barest push. She spreads herself for me and as I thrust, I lightly suck the puffy engorged flesh around her clit, deliberately avoiding the thing we both most want my mouth to touch. That want can be set aside for now. Now I want to just hint at what's to come.

After a few thwarted attempts to press her clit into my mouth, Ellie seems to catch on and gives in to my teasing. The hands on mine relax, as if she's just taken a deep, soothing breath and surrendered to me. Her trusting me is everything. As I finger-fuck her, I make a slow sweep through her labia, suck tempting flesh and lick my way back to her clit. I have to force myself to be soft, to not fuck her hard with fingers and tongue. I want to draw her climax out in a long continuous wave of pleasure instead of a quick over-and-done.

"That feels so good." Ellie grasps a handful of my hair, gently holding me against her clit. "Keep licking me, please. I want to come with your tongue on me."

As I keep up my coordinated dance, Ellie's breathing grows more ragged, her grip in my hair tighter. She's restless, her body writhing as I lightly lick and gently suck her clit while my fingers play in and out of her heat. Her breathing catches. "Yes. Yes. I'm—" Her body tightens until her limbs are taut and trembling. She shifts slightly, raising herself up on an elbow. We make eye contact and she keeps up that intense, knowing gaze as she bucks and shudders through an endless climax.

The grip on my hair relaxes but that intense eye contact doesn't. She's slippery with sweat, her breasts rising and falling as she tries to catch her breath. Her lips part then quickly come back together as if she went to say something and decided against it. I have a pretty good idea of what she would have said. I softly kiss the skin below her bellybutton.

My arousal is loud, but not deafening, which makes it easier to drown it out. This wasn't about me or my orgasm. This was about Ellie. Tonight she needed me, needed something from me. And it was something I could give to her, something I wanted to give to her, something I want to give again and again. But I know I can't. What I want doesn't matter. I bury my face in the smooth warm skin of her thigh and try not to cry.

CHAPTER SIXTEEN

Elise pops into my periphery. "Are you busy-busy or just regular busy?"

I pause the game. "Not even regular busy. Just re-re-replaying some *Dishonored 2*. What's up?"

She exhales a slow breath. "I need to go home. I've had a parcel delivered there this afternoon and I should probably get some fresh clothes, water my plants, check things are okay and all that shit. Rosemary's been great, keeping an eye on things but it's so far out of her way and I feel terrible making her go up there just to make sure all is in order."

"I haven't been to your new place," I say inanely.

Ellie's left eyebrow arches. "No, you haven't. Would you like to?"

"Yes, I would."

"Great. Why don't you bring Bennie?"

"Sure." I pick up on what she's not saying and almost ask if she wants me to bring a gun. But I'm scared she might say yes.

Before she rented out her place and moved in with me, Ellie lived in Silver Lake and loved the funky, eclectic vibe of the suburb, not to mention the proximity to walking and hiking trails. Once she left me I assumed she'd go back there. She's close but has taken herself a little more upmarket.

From the outside, her place in the hills of Los Feliz is basically the one we had always agreed would be our perfect house in LA, if money was no object. It seems money isn't much of an object in Elise's world which she's worked her ass off to inhabit. Perched high enough that she has panoramic views over Griffith Park and the city—which looks amazing now at night—the space somehow still seems hidden and private. A seven-foot privacy fence with electronic codes for both pedestrian and vehicle gates surrounds the property, and the moment the sliding gate opens to admit us, floodlights illuminate the driveway and entrance. Security cameras and "Monitored by ADT" signs are peppered around the exterior of the house, which means in addition to the security Rosemary organized to do drive-bys, Elise has 24/7 monitoring in case an alarm is tripped.

Inside, I realize it really is the house of our dreams. Full of angular lines, interior glass, polished wood, and marble, the split-three levels give her plenty of space yet somehow manage to feel intimate. On the lower level is her living room filled with butter-soft black leather couches, a television that occupies most of the wall, and a grand piano standing on the opposite side. When we climb the wide set of stairs directly opposite the front door, I find the second level is for kitchen and dining. Her kitchen looks like a professional chef's heaven and once she flips on some exterior lights, I spot a pool and a gorgeous entertaining area with Elise's dream wall of plants on the rear retaining wall.

Sporadic dark-tile accents contrast with light walls—the whole house is modern without feeling cold, partly due to the design but also Ellie's personal touches like her piano and artwork, the colorful splashes of herself she's put through the house. The high windows would give her both an abundance of natural light in the daytime, as well as privacy—someone would have to be fifteen-feet tall to see through them.

Ellie beelines for the fridge. "Why don't you take a look around while I toss out a bunch of expired food?"

I can't tell if she needs some time alone, is embarrassed to witness me witnessing her personal space for the first time or if she just doesn't want me seeing what's in her fridge. "Sure. Bennie, stay here with Elise. Maybe she'll toss out some cheese and you'll get lucky."

His assent is a thumping tail wag.

The stairs to the third level sit in the middle of the second floor and are surrounded by the living area. As I walk up, I have an odd but not unpleasant feeling of being suspended in midair. There's a study and two bedrooms up here, all decorated in Elise's clean, modern style. The master bedroom and bath is basically as I'd imagined in a celebrity's house—big and fancy— and yet, it doesn't feel at all opulent. I'm weirdly relieved that Ellie is still Ellie, despite having obviously upgraded some aspects of her life.

The moment I see the size of her bed and the tall, padded headboard, my brain runs away to deliciously naughty places. The most predominant thought is that I could be the first person she fucks in this huge bed. As quickly as I think it, I try to unthink it. It would be a whole lot easier to tell myself we can't be in a relationship if I didn't automatically jump straight to relationship thoughts all the time.

Elise's call interrupts my runaway brain, probably for the best. "Avery? You okay up there?"

"I'm fine," I call back.

"Do you mind coming back down here? No rush, just whenever you're done exploring."

I jog back down the stairs. "I'm done exploring. What's up?"

Her smile comes too quickly. "Nothing. Just thought you might like a close look outside. Even if it's only by man-made light."

"Sounds great. Where's Bennett?"

"Wandered off after I gave him some cheese. Bennie!"

He comes lumbering up the stairs from the first level and, ever cheese-hopeful, goes straight to Elise. When he realizes she has nothing more, he sniffs around the kitchen floor. Elise gathers up a few bags of trash and again, it twigs what she's trying to say but isn't saying or can't make herself say.

I take one of the bags from her. "Ellie. You don't need to pretend with me and you don't need to use subterfuge to get me to do something. If you're worried or scared about something then you can just tell me." I kiss her gently. "I want to know how you're feeling. And it'll save you a lot of wasted roundabout words."

Her laugh is dry. "Should have known you'd see right through me." She takes a slow breath. "Okay…I'm terrified of being here. I don't want to go outside by myself, even though I know it's ridiculous. I can't even think of being here alone because I *know* that he must know where I live. And it's so fucked because this is my house, my personal space, my safe haven and I feel like I don't have that anymore. I just want to feel like I have control of this part of my life."

"You have a restraining order, Ellie. And they're working on the other stuff. We just have to be patient." It's not much, but it's the only thing I can think to say because she's absolutely right.

"Yes I do. And I also know that he can choose to ignore the restraining order if he really wants to, and all he'll get is a fine and a slap on the wrist and, if I'm lucky maybe a little jail time. But really, it's meaningless."

"It's not meaningless, Elise. It's an important step in the process which could lead to a conviction and jail."

The eyebrows-raised look she gives me clearly says she doesn't agree.

I take her free hand. "Tell you what. Why don't I stay here with you? Even for just a few hours, a night or two, whatever you want. I can even bring Bennie again, though…" Peering around the immaculate space, I realize it's maybe not a great idea. "This place is kind of upmarket for him. These floors will look like an ice-hockey rink after the first quarter of a Kings game."

That makes her laugh. "I don't care. I'd love to have him inside, doing zoomie laps, swimming in the heated pool, waging war with the opossums and coyotes."

"Oh shit, the pool. You're right. He'll die of happiness. I'll never be able to get him to come back home with me." I open the sliding glass door to the entertaining area and glance around, up the hill behind the retaining wall. Nothing there except a few small spotlights highlighting rocky ground and some sporadic plants placed on the hill to make it seem less sparse. Through the vegetation I can see another house about eighty feet away, set farther back up into the hill. Bennett rushes out and straight to the pool, and it's only my "Bennie, no!" that stops him diving in. I do not want a wet dog in my car and his screw-you glare is a small price to pay.

"I wouldn't mind having him stay for a while," Elise murmurs. "And you too, obviously. But I also don't want to disrupt your life any more than I already have."

Laughing, I hold up the lid on the trash bin for her. "Ellie, this is the good kind of disruption."

"Even with the crappier commute?"

"Even with that. But there are benefits that outweigh that inconvenience."

"Like what?"

I make a sweeping gesture. "As mentioned, the pool. Among other things. You've got all your great stuff, a bigger gym than me, that huge television, better couch. Need I say more?" I don't want to talk about her home security right now, which is better than mine, because I'd like to give her just a minute where she's not thinking about that.

Ellie offers an inscrutable smile, then moves away from the trash, leaving me to follow her inside. After Bennett's reluctant reentry into the house Elise locks the sliding door and I reflexively glance at it to double check it. She doesn't seem nervous so much as unsettled, flitting about like she can't quite decide where she wants to stop or what she wants to do. She finally settles by the sink. "Do you want a drink? I've even got one of those 'ridiculous in-fridge spring water and ice maker gadgets' and yes, as discussed years ago, it's frivolous, but I fucking love it and it was worth every dollar."

"Honey, if you want a fridge that spends its life quietly filtering your water and making ice and that also orders your groceries for you without you asking, then who am I to tell you it's creepy to let a computer decide when you need to order cheese and pickles."

"So you'll have extra ice then?" she deadpans.

I grin through my facetious, "Please."

When I suggest again that we could stay the night, I'm hastily vetoed by Elise. She throws out a handful of reasons, like she just emptied her refrigerator, I don't have things for work in the morning, nor do we have Bennett's breakfast or a bed for him, or…or…or. I don't push but when we're driving home I do hint that maybe she and Bennie could meet me here after work tomorrow and we could hang out at her place for the weekend. "Perfect swimming weather. Bennett will love you forever," I say lightly. "And I wouldn't mind some lazy time on a pool chair in the sun."

I catch her expression in the flickering streetlights and it's clear she's not keen. Her answer is a quiet, "Mmm."

"It's your call, Ellie, but if you'd like to start taking control of your life again, then this might be a good place to start." It's been just over a week since the incident, and while I don't want to push her, I can't keep her in my pocket forever. In addition to her house being just as secure as mine, perhaps even more so, the security patrols have seen no evidence of anyone hanging around who shouldn't be. "Ellie, I don't want to kick you out of the nest and say 'fly, bitch,' and *do* I want you to feel safe. But… at the same time, you're going to have to move home at some point. I think baby steps like being here for a few hours without me would help you."

It takes her another two blocks before she responds. "What time are you due home from work tomorrow?"

"You know, I think I might be feeling a little sick already so I might just come home early. Before dark." I glance at her and catch the hint of a smile. But she doesn't answer. When we pass a Burger King, I think of someone who might be able to make things a little easier for Elise, make it so she's safe while still having the confidence of being alone in her house. "I could ask a friend if they wouldn't mind a few hours sitting in a car outside your place."

"You know someone who'd do that?" There's a hint of surprise in her question.

"I know a few someones who'd do that." I grin at her. "I'm very charming and popular. They won't know it's you, I promise."

After a long pause, she agrees with a quiet, "Okay, thank you."

"I'll make the call now and be sure it's all set up. Can you pass me my AirPods please?"

Once I've stuffed them in my ears, I ask Siri to, "Call Brad."

Brad answers with his usual jovial, "Aviary! How are you?"

I don't bother correcting him because I know it'll only make him even worse with his deliberate mispronunciation of my name. My brother's old partner left Portland PD for LAPD not long after Tristan's promotion to Sex Crimes. Under threat of telling everyone about the time Brad ripped the ass out of his pants chasing a perp, he had been forced by Tristan to watch out for his little sister. Which translated to treating me like his little sister. "I'm good. You?"

"Alive and kicking. What can I help you with?"

"A favor." Brad was utterly trustworthy, and the furthest thing from a gossip I could think of. I knew I could trust him to watch Elise's house and never say anything about it.

"Geez, you save my life once and now I'm stuck with a life of servitude. Whaddya need?"

"Yeah well, don't have a cardiac arrest outside Burger King and I won't need to save your life and then you won't owe me favors forevermore. Giving you CPR for six and a half minutes translates to a lot of favors, Brad."

He grunts. "I know."

"Would you mind including a specific house as part of your daily traffic patrol tomorrow? I've heard there's a lot of people who speed along that street," I say slyly. "A couple of patrol cops in their car might discourage that."

He laughs and I know he's caught my meaning. "Sure. Can do."

"Perfect." I give him Elise's address. "In the course of your traffic watching, if you see anyone around that specific house who isn't me, feel free to intervene."

"Will do. Are you worried about someone going in, or coming out?"

"Going in. There's a roving private security patrol and I'll be there before dark, but I'd like coverage between me and the private security."

"Noted. Happy to help. Text me any other details you think are necessary. And bring us dinner, wouldya?"

"Sure. Thanks, Brad. I owe you."

"Nope, Aviary. I still owe you."

I end the call and pull the AirPods from my ears. "It's all set. My cop friend Brad and his partner will keep an eye on your house for a few hours until I get there. And I'll give you his number so you can call him and he'll be right in."

She's silent for the rest of the ride home and it's only when I've released Bennie's harness from the seat belt that she answers. It's quiet, not resigned exactly but there's still an undercurrent of reluctance. "Okay. You're right. Weekend at my place. I'll go round about two tomorrow with Bennett. And these cop friends of yours will just be watching the house until you get there?"

"They will be. And if they see even a delivery guy, they'll be on it."

Her shoulders drop. "Thank you. You promise you won't be late home tomorrow?"

"I promise I'll try not to be." I rub the Bennett head that's inserted itself in the gap between the front seats. "If I get called for a mission flight I'll let you know right away and you and Bennie can stay right here." And I'll have to figure out another way to try and help her get comfortable with being alone in her house.

"Okay. Deal. I'll give you a key. Will you bring your bikini?"

I arch an eyebrow. "I can't really swim or sunbake naked, can I?"

Elise brightens. "Says who?"

* * *

I decide to leave my car parked outside Elise's place in the hope that anyone who might come by will see someone other than Elise is here. I receive mock pouts from Brad and his partner because my healthy sandwiches-and-drinks dinner isn't another cardiac-arrest-inducing burger. After I thank them for their time and wave bye, Brad drives away, flashing his lights. I key in the code to open Elise's front gate and make sure it's securely latched behind me. Nothing in her front yard looks out of place, which I'd expected given Brad's presence.

Through the huge glass panels either side of Elise's front door I see Bennett waiting for me, his tail metronomeing back and forth. When I open the front door, the first thing I hear is Elise on the phone somewhere on the second floor, having what, if the tightness in her voice is anything to go by, an unpleasant conversation. I crouch down to say hi to Bennie and I can tell from his still-damp fur that he's only recently been dragged out of the pool. He's probably spent his whole afternoon in the sun-drenched heated pool, the lucky brat. When I climb the stairs and head to the kitchen, he follows me up and after detouring for a quick sniff around Elise's legs, plops onto his kitchen bed.

Ellie lifts her elbow and smiles by way of greeting then goes back to washing up while talking into the phone clamped between her ear and shoulder. "Mhmm, no that's fine, I'm happy for you to do that. Mhmm, yeah. No, I know. Sure, great. I'll wait to hear from you? Mhmm, yep, I'll let you know if anything changes. Okay, thanks, bye." Still up to mid-forearm in dishwater, she leans over to let the phone drop onto the countertop. "That was just the FBI agent," she offers without me even thinking of asking.

I slip around the island to the sink and after a moment's consideration, kiss her lightly hello. "Oh? Has there been some progress?"

"Not really." She leans in for another, longer kiss. "How was your day? Aside from long."

"That pretty much sums it up." Recognizing her redirect, I make another of my own. "He was just calling for a quick chat then?"

Ellie's tongue flashes out between her lips, so fast it's barely noticeable. "Pretty much."

Despite being an actress who can easily inhabit any character or say lines she doesn't necessarily agree with, during personal conversations Elise has a tell that always reveals when she isn't being entirely truthful or is withholding something—that quick lick of her lips. "What aren't you telling me?" Smiling, I touch my lips to indicate she's given herself away.

Her nose wrinkles. "Goddammit. Stupid face." Sighing, she drops the scrubbing brush. The long pause and tight set of her shoulders makes me think she doesn't want to tell me, but after almost a minute she admits, "I've had a bunch more letters from the Hayes Horde, all sent to Rosemary's office with postmarks from all over the country and all with basically the same message and a mention of...him. The FBI tracked one sender, a guy in Florida who said someone on that TinyTasker app paid him to forward a letter that was sent to him. Apparently he forgot he wasn't supposed to put his return address and was more worried about the fact he might get un-paid his five bucks from the app than that he's helping a criminal. And of course the original sender's account is now gone so they have to get more warrants to go digging through the app's data."

I try to act casually as I empty the contents of my pockets into the hand-blown glass bowl on the kitchen island that holds Elise's keys and wallet. "When did this happen?"

"They arrived in a clump over the last few days."

My stomach turns. "How many letters were there?"

She doesn't answer. Instead, she keeps her back to me as she pulls the plug and begins wiping down the counters.

"Ellie..."

"Are you ready to eat? I know it's a little early but I've got dinner in the fridge. I got bored so I made butternut risotto. Extra parmesan just for you."

"Elise!"

That makes her turn around. Her eyes are wide, too bright, as if she's trying to force herself to appear cheerful and relaxed. "What? You're not hungry yet?"

I take a slow breath and soften my tone. "Please stop avoiding the subject. Just tell me. It's okay. How many letters were there?"

She blinks hard a few times, like she's hoping to make me disappear. After an eternity, she whispers, "Thirty-seven."

I don't even know what to say. I manage a tight, "Oh. Fuck." A few slow breaths help me calm down. "Why didn't you just tell me this had happened again?" It makes me wonder what else she might be holding back from me.

"Because I didn't want to, Avery. I *hate* it," she spits out. "I hate that this is my life now and that you're involved in it too. Normally it's just…it's weird and busy and complex and hard to fathom, but at times like now? It's fucking scary. I don't want you involved." Her voice cracks. "I don't want you to get hurt because of me."

I go to touch her, but she moves away. Not far enough to put impassable distance between us, but enough to make it clear that she needs space. "I'm not going to get hurt."

Elise swipes angrily at her eyes. "You can't promise that. I don't want you anywhere near this but the thought of facing it right now by myself is terrifying. And then the thought of keeping you around and exposing you to all this and you getting hurt because of me makes me feel like I can't breathe." She inhales a deep shuddering breath but the words still come out broken. "I don't know what to do. Tell me what I should do, please."

I step closer and when she doesn't move away, I gather her close, soothing her. "I don't know what you should do, but I don't want you to shove me away. Nobody's going to hurt me, Ellie. I can handle myself."

Her response is muffled against my shoulder, but I think she says, "What if you can't?"

We stay like this for a few minutes, standing in the kitchen just hugging, until Elise carefully disengages from me and moves a few steps away. I don't chase her. "I wish you'd told me."

She nabs some kitchen roll to wipe her eyes. "I know. But the look on your face right now? That's why I didn't."

My face just feels like my face. "What look?"

"Like you want to charge right in and fix everything, no matter the cost. You had that exact expression on the plane too. And I don't want you charging in this time. It's too dangerous."

"The plane was just my job, Elise. You know that." I debate the thought that's in my head and decide I need to say it, even if it jeopardizes everything. "I...you can't have it every way you want. If you tell me that you want me to be around, that you want to stay with me, that you feel safe with me because of who I am both personally and professionally then you're telling me it's okay to behave the way I did on the plane. You know I'm here for you and that I'll protect you from whatever I can, however I can, because that's just me. But you can't cherry-pick the behavior you want from me."

Elise throws both hands up in surrender. "You're right. I'm sorry. God, I just feel like I'm walking a tightrope and no matter how I step I'm going to fall. Avery, I'm scared if you realize just how ridiculous my life can be, how different it is from fifteen months ago, then you'll run a mile. And I just...really need you around right now. I'm—I'm trying to figure out how I could maybe make all this work again and then shit like this happens and I'm thrown back to the beginning where I just don't know what to do."

"You really think I'd be scared or put off by all that? Ellie, come on, surely you know me better than that. It'll take more than some creepy crazy stalker fans to scare me off." I smile. "You'll have to throw some spiders into the mix if you want to really scare me."

She rewards me with a hint of a smile. "So noted. Fuck. Just...fuck all of this."

"I agree. Let's just walk the tightrope together, one slow and cautious step at a time."

"Okay. I can do that." Elise balls the paper towel into the trash. "Do you want dinner?"

"In a bit. First, I want..." I open my arms to her and she moves into me right away, wrapping her arms tightly around me as I pull her close. "It's okay, Ellie. I know this is fucked up and scary, but I'm here with you. You're not doing this alone." It feels a little like I'm making a promise and after a moment's thought, I concede I am. I'll stay with her. The minefield of navigating my personal feelings while keeping her safe emotionally and physically from the Hayes Horde is going to make it tricky. But I'm not going to abandon a friend, the woman I love, at such a horrible point in her life.

She burrows into me, snuggling her face against my neck. "I know."

By the time we're ready for bed, she's calmed down a little but she's clingy, wanting to be right near me and touch me constantly. Elise is such a tactile person and this has always been her stress response. I couldn't mind less that she's been resting against me with her fingers curled into my shirt while we watched television.

I assume I'll be sleeping in a guest room and after taking Bennett out, I head upstairs and brush my teeth in a guest bathroom. Elise's, "Avery?" calls me into her room, where she's at the mirror in her bathroom, engaged in her nightly skincare routine.

I still know the sequence so well that when I see she's using her spot correction treatment, I know she has about another seven minutes to go. Elise's twice-daily skincare routine outweighs mine by almost thirty minutes a day and when we first began our sleepovers I was transfixed by how automatically she went through her products, like she was hypnotized.

I once asked if she got bored—yes; if she ever thought about just skipping half the steps and going to sleep—fuck yes, especially after a day of shooting; and if she could claim all that expensive shit as a tax deductible—alas, no because having nice skin was just a side bonus that she could benefit from in her personal life as well as her professional.

I move to the empty sink beside her. "You know, when we're fifty, I'm going to look seventy and you'll still look twenty-five. We're going to meet up for coffee or something and they're going to ask me what my daughter wants."

Ellie snorts out a laugh. "That's the plan. I need to trick that bullshit ageist Hollywood machine somehow."

"Well, I suppose if part of my job description was literally 'look hot' I'd spend more than ten minutes twice a day on my face."

"I love your face. And yeah, if I didn't have to, I wouldn't go to this much trouble." She finds my eyes in the mirror and hers soften immediately.

"I love your face too. Almost as much as I love everything else about you."

"Mmm, kind of how I feel as well." She reaches for a jar of moisturizer and after unscrewing the lid, says, "Avery. What the hell are we doing? I mean, fucked-up stalker aside, I'm so confused."

"I don't know," I murmur. "I'm confused too."

As she slathers cream on her face, she keeps talking. "It's like we're magnets or something, stuck together or drawn together or whatever you want to call it. I love you. I know you love me. This…connection we have feels as strong as it ever did, maybe stronger." She pauses. "But me being in the closet isn't just about my career now, Avery. It's…everything. I'm so scared and I don't know how to navigate it. I don't know how to be out, how to have people look at me as Lesbian Actress Elise Hayes, instead of just Elise Hayes. I don't know how to have producers and directors ask if I'm okay with this mainstream straight role now that I'm not-straight, or maybe be passed over for roles because of bigotry and bias. I don't know how to deal with possible public backlash, or the religious right. I don't know how to be a role model. And I don't know how to get back to the place where you and I were happy. All I keep seeing is me failing and everything we're moving toward falling apart."

Agreeing with what she's said just feels cruel, because that inevitable heartbreak is only going to come from one place. Her. I love her more than I've ever loved anyone, and I want to spend my life with her. But I can't have her being in the closet hanging over us again. And if I'm honest with myself, I'm always going to wonder if somewhere in the future she'll make the same decision she did when she broke up with me the first time. "I know. And I don't know either."

"Should we just say no more now? Stop…whatever we're doing before we get too far in and it's harder for us to move apart again? Should I do what you said I should have done years ago? Finish it sooner rather than later, before we pass the point of no return. Should we say no to trying to be friends, because I'm not sure we're capable of being *just* friends." Ellie sifts through tubes and unscrews the cap from a small one.

I curse my previous answer to that exact question when she asked it during our walk with Bennett. Because the answer I gave then, that yes, it would have been easier to end it sooner, can't apply now. "Maybe? I feel like we're already teetering at the point of no return. And yeah, I'm not sure being just friends works for us." But I don't want to *not* be friends. Being with her feels like a flow diagram where every yes/no answer circles back to the same conclusion. We should be together. Except for Elise not being out, which I can't deal with. So we should just be friends. But we're trying to be friends and just keep falling back into relationship habits. So we should be together. But…

But…it will never work. Despite our past, our reconnection, our love and respect and desire and the mutual core of what we both want, Elise and I *can't* be in a romantic relationship. Even if we both want and need it, we have one basic issue that's always going to be a problem. I can't live like a dirty little secret, always afraid I might accidentally touch her in public and give her away, and I can't watch her drag man after man to every important event in her life. And I need to accept this is my reality, really accept it. Goddammit, I *had* accepted it.

"Mmm, I agree." Then she echoes my thoughts. "But the thought of not being friends feels fucking awful, even if all this wasn't happening and I wasn't feeling so hashtag desperate and needy."

I laugh at the Valley Girl that slipped in. "It does feel kind of strange to be worrying about us and a relationship with everything else that's going on."

"True." Ellie squeezes a small amount of yellow cream onto her fingertips and smiling, carefully smooths it over her face.

"But at the same time, it's giving me something else to focus on." She turns to me. "Tell me what you're thinking."

"I'm thinking…so many things. Mostly that I love you, Ellie. I love being with you in a partnership. I love how easy it is, how easy it always was. But I really can't go back to the relationship where you weren't out. It's not honest and neither is it healthy for us."

"I agree."

"But I also don't just want us to be friends with benefits, because that's also not fair for either of us either. As much as I love the benefits part."

She grins. "Again, I agree and agree."

"So where does that leave us? Friends who're in love with each other who need to learn to deal with it?"

"Pretty much. Just two people standing in front of a roadblock." She laughs dryly. "You know, usually the issues in relationships are things like people not being in love, not having things in common, stuff like that. Us not being in love was never the issue."

"No, it wasn't." Our dynamic has always been intense and electric.

"I just keep trying to picture how my life looks now. I'm going to have to deal with the fact things have changed and things are different." She eyes me. "And not just because of… Double-H. You're back in my life and it's different and the same all at once."

"You're right. But if there's one thing I know about you, it's that as well as your strength and resiliency, you're adaptable, Ellie. And I'll still be around in some way to support you."

"Some way," she echoes. It sounds as dull and hollow from her mouth as it did from mine.

Hearing her say it drives home the unpleasant truth. The truth I've been trying not to think about. All we can have is a distant friendship because being close friends will only keep trying to draw us together. It feels fucking awful. But it also feels better than her completely leaving my life again. And after a while I'm sure both of us will figure out where to put our feelings for each other. Maybe. And if I can't, well it's not like I haven't spent the last fifteen months in love with someone I couldn't be with.

I lean against the bathroom counter and watch her finish up. "Do you want me to sleep in the guest room tonight?"

"That depends."

"On what exactly?"

She lines up jars and tubes. "If you can keep your hands to yourself when you're in my bed."

"I can if you can."

"Good."

"*Good* isn't actually a 'yes I can keep my hands to myself' confirmation," I point out.

Laughing, she shakes her head. "You and your semantics." She studies herself in the mirror one more time then turns back to me. "I...think I might have a plan."

"Great. I love plans. Are you going to tell me what this plan is?"

"I will. When it's more formed and maybe a little more certain. I don't want to jump ahead of myself."

"Well, when you're ready to fill me in, I'm all ears."

She steps closer. "Good, because I'm all mouth."

"You're not helping..."

CHAPTER SEVENTEEN

Monday morning, we shift back to my place. Or more accurately—I go to work and Elise takes Bennett back home where she'll stay for the day. Because I can't ask for cop favors to keep them outside her house forevermore, we've decided to do a few nights at each of our places until she feels more comfortable being alone in her house all day. Then, we'll eventually segue into us moving back to our separate houses and be friends while her court cases are resolved. And then…and then I guess we'll quietly separate again. It's for the best, but it doesn't mean I like it. I think I hate it. And Bennett's probably going to be a destructive brat when Ellie's back at work in the new year and his daytime play pal is gone. Note to self: order him a super hardcore robust refill for his tug toy and lock up favorite shoes.

I've barely settled in my office chair when Nicola raps her knuckles on my doorframe. She launches right in. "So listen, I've spoken to everyone in the office and we've unanimously decided that we're just going to give you all the marksmanship pool money for next year's competition."

"You're too kind."

"I'm not finished. We give it to you to spare us the humiliation of losing to you yet again and in return, you take us out for a round of drinks."

"That sounds so fair," I drawl. "Let me guess, I'll drink sparkling water and lime and everyone else will have the most expensive alcohol the bar sells?"

"You know us too well. And we need something to heal our battered marksmanship egos." She smirks and claims the chair on the other side of my desk. "Speaking of egos, enough pampering yours. How're things with your ex?"

Well that was one way to deflate my ego and also remind me that I had no idea what I was doing. "Same I guess. Maybe more intense." I lean back in my chair, pushing until I feel it hit that perfect sweet spot of comfort right before it's about to topple over. It makes me think of me and Ellie, teetering and unsure which way we're falling. "I think we're starting to reach a breaking point and it's going to tip one way or the other soon."

Nicola frowns. "How so?"

"It feels like we *should* be back together, or like we basically are but are trying to pretend we aren't and that we should just be friends. But we don't work as friends, there's way too much spark and it just keeps on sparking. So we're stuck in this gray area where we can't be friends because neither of us can keep our hands to ourselves, but we can't be in a relationship because nothing's changed from when we split."

"Sparks huh. Have you two caught fire again?" At my blank expression, she laughs. "Have you slept with her again?"

I don't bother evading. "Mhmm, yeah."

"Good for you." She cackles. "Because when shit's confusing, why not make it even more so?"

"In my defense, she was having a *really* rough day and needed some uh, comfort."

"Zero judgment from me, my friend. I don't care if you've fucked her every day since she turned up. I just don't want to see you get hurt again." Nicola raises pointed eyebrows. "Because I have to assume what's not changed is the 'she can't be out' thing?"

"Not really. Maybe kind of?" I puff out a breath and find the truth instead of what I want to be the truth. "No, nothing's changed with that. But it's easy to see she's struggling with it, like I feel like she wants to come out. Maybe? But it's all tied up in her job, so she's stuck, fucked, and out of luck."

"Are they going to fire her for coming out?"

"I doubt it, but it could make her job harder moving forward."

Her expression transforms instantly to no-nonsense. "Like no promotions and stuff? If they screw her over, I know a great employment lawyer."

"You'd recommend your, and I quote your words back at you verbatim, *fucking bitch troll spawn-of-Satan* ex-wife?"

"Sure." Nicola grins. "As a person, she's the devil incarnate, but she *is* one of the top employment lawyers in the state."

"Noted. Thanks." Elise doesn't need a lawyer but it's nice to know Nicola cares enough to think about it.

"How long have you guys been back together but not back together?"

"She turned up late the night of the Elise Hayes thing, so…" I drag my mind back, trying to remember the date.

"Wednesday the second. Twelve days ago."

I lean forward so my chair levels out. "Wow. That's just a little creepy."

She raises both hands. "Hey, look. I only remember the day because I had a bikini wax."

"Weren't you out sick for most of that week with food poisoning?"

"I was. But I'd had that waxing appointment booked in for *months*. Ursula is a personal grooming goddess with a very full client list and you don't give up your spot unless you're dying. So I took my puke bucket, lay down and spread 'em. It was a memorable day, one you don't forget—me hurling while I got a Brazilian at the buttcrack of dawn, no pun intended, and you saving Elise Hayes on a flight."

"That's an image I'd rather not have in my brain."

"Well it's there now. Cherish it." She uncrosses and recrosses her legs. "So, what are you going to do? You don't want a closeted girlfriend, right?"

"It's more complicated than just me not wanting a closeted girlfriend," I rebut indignantly. It's not like I'm just being petulant about Ellie not wanting to be out—there are some very real consequences and I've already lived them once.

"Noted, sorry. I didn't mean to make it sound so flippant." Nicola actually seems contrite which is unusual for her.

"It's fine. Sorry, it's a raw spot that's only recently healed." I huff out a breath. "My current plan is to help her through this rough patch like a good friend, then kind of gently disengage and quietly sneak away to spend another year telling myself I don't love her."

Nicola snorts. "Like a lying-to-yourself coward?"

"Yes," I mutter in agreement. "Like a lying-to-myself coward."

A few moments after Bennett's greeted me at my door, Elise emerges, rubbing her eyes. She yawns in the middle of her, "Hey you."

"Hey." I nudge Bennie back into the house and close the door. "You run a marathon today?"

Ellie laughs. "I wish. Alas it's just been a day of Zoom meetings. I am not conditioned to stare at a screen allllll day." She quickly kisses the edge of my mouth. "How was your day?"

I grin. "I stared at a screen all day."

"Smartass." She looks me up and down, a smile twitching at the corners of her mouth like she's pleased about something. "When you're ready, could I talk to you about something?"

I pause unbuttoning my coat. "This sounds ominous. Should I be worried? Did you convert Bennett to some new and even fancier brand of dog food?"

"I've been trying but he's just not going for the thousand-dollars-a-can brand," she deadpans. "Lucky you."

"You think you're so funny."

"I don't think. I know." She pats my cheeks with both hands. "Whenever you're ready."

"Let me just put things away safely and I'll be right out."

I take my time locking away my work firearm and hanging my coat so I can smother some of my unease about this impending conversation. She could be about to tell me anything, like…she has to leave sooner than expected, she needs to stay for longer than anticipated, she— I shake the thoughts out, take a few deep breaths then leave my room to go find her.

The sound of the piano makes it easy. She's playing "Twinkle Twinkle Little Star" with just her forefinger.

"I think even I could learn that one," I say.

"Maybe." She turns around, grins at me like she's not sure I could, then turns around and starts another song, the short and batshit crazy "In the Hall of the Mountain King." When she's done, Ellie exhales like she's just had a huge stress-relieving scream and slides off the piano stool. "Do you want me to jump right in or do you want some meandering roundabout conversation first?"

"Let's get right to it."

"Phew. Because I am all out of meandering conversation." She sits on the couch and I follow to sit close to her, leaning back and crossing my legs. Ellie seems happy and relaxed, almost jovial, which eases some of my anxiety. If she's not worried then I shouldn't be either.

She pauses, then says, "I— Fuck. I've been thinking about what I wanted to say to you all day and now it's all just left my brain." She laughs and shakes her head, and I hear the trembling exhalation. "Avery…since I left, I feel like I've done nothing but think about what I did, even more so since I came here. And the more I think about it, the more I keep ending up at the same conclusion, no matter from what direction I come at it."

"What conclusion is that?" I murmur.

"I love you and I want to be with you. I have never been so certain of anything in my life." She inhales slowly and seems to gain some courage from it. When she speaks again her voice is strong and sure. "I want a go-around."

"Pardon me?"

"A go-around." She looks at me like she can't believe I haven't made some connection to what she's said. "Don't you remember the day we met?"

"Of course I remember that day." Vividly. I'd never felt so instantly drawn to anyone as I did to her. "I could barely focus on work because I was so stunned by how gorgeous and funny and personable you were."

She smirks, and that cocky, self-assured twist of her lips melts me as always. Ellie throws in a faux-nonchalant shrug for good measure. "Well, yes. Naturally. But don't you remember the go-around?"

"Course I do." I remember that all too clearly. She'd been terrified that the pilots were performing a go-around, aborting our landing to take another run at it. Nothing to suggest a major issue—just that they weren't satisfied everything was in place for a safe landing. A perfectly normal part of aviation. "It was a good one, nice and smooth and the second approach and landing was textbook."

"Right. Do you remember what you said to me? After you told me what was going on, that is." At my second nod, she reminds me, "You said I shouldn't worry, that it was common practice, that they trained for these things and it was the best thing to do in that situation and any moment, once we'd leveled again, the captain was going to come on and tell us everything was fine."

"And it was fine," I point out.

"It was. After I was scared shitless. And when I grabbed your hand, you didn't pull away. You held mine tightly, like you knew that I needed something solid and comforting at that moment. And you just kept talking the whole time like you were trying to distract me. Ever since that day, I've never forgotten what you said to me."

I recall the general conversation, the sensation I had being near her, the almost electric vibe that seemed to pass between us. But I can't remember exactly what I'd said to her. "Refresh my memory of these memorable words?"

Ellie's expression is earnest. "You told me the go-around was just a second chance to make sure everything was perfect. So…I want a second chance. I know what I did to you was wrong and it was selfish and cruel and cowardly and not how I should have handled the situation, but I'm not that person anymore. And now I want to try again to make things perfect for us."

My throat feels tight. "I know you're not that person anymore."

"Good." Her exhalation is a relieved rush of air. "I want to be with you."

"I want to be with you too, but, Ellie, I don't know if it's going to work. I *know* you've changed. I know you're sorry. I know we've both moved and grown as people. But one thing hasn't changed, and I can't go through a breakup like that again. I wanted to spend the rest of my life with you. I loved you so much and when you left I was completely broken. I've only recently unbroken myself." The moment I say those words, my brain trips. I thought my unbreaking, my healing, had happened months ago. But now I realize it only happened when she came back. So I needed her to come back in order to get over her leaving. Great job, Emotional Maturity.

"Me too," she whispers.

I fight for some steady ground. "I just can't walk down the same path again, knowing exactly what the destination is. I can't…sit at home and hide myself because you're not ready to be out. I'm not going to survive you casting me aside twice. I barely survived it last time."

She lightly thumbs the corner of my mouth. "I know. I wouldn't survive it either."

I gently pull her hand away from my mouth and the temptation of kissing her palm. "I don't want to give you an ultimatum because I tried it once and it felt horrible." Felt horrible doing it and felt even worse when she didn't choose me. "But…I don't see any other way. I'm sorry to do this again. And if you're still not ready then that's okay, it really is, Ellie. But I can't be with you. It'll be me who walks away this time."

"Don't walk away," she says instantly, and I hear the desperation in her plea. "You know me not loving you was *never* the problem. I just wasn't brave enough to stand up and tell everyone who I was. What I wanted." She swallows. "What I want. I've spent the past year realizing just how much I can't stand myself when I'm not with you. I've spent the past year learning how to be brave."

"What are you saying?" The answer seems so obvious but this isn't my thing, it's hers, and I wonder if she knows what I'm thinking.

It seems she does. She smiles then kisses me. "I've evolved. I'm going to show you I'm now the person you needed me to be then."

"How do you mean?" The possibility of what she's alluding to makes nervous excitement flutter in my stomach. But even as I'm thinking it, part of me knows it won't happen.

She doesn't hesitate, and even after all the build-up, she still says the last thing I expected.

"I'm going to make a public statement about my sexuality. I'm coming out of the closet."

Despite our recent reconnection and the fact that I've spent years wanting to hear those exact words from Elise, it still takes far longer than it should for my brain to sort through what she's just said. "You're coming out?"

"Yes. I've had a mass of Zoom meetings today with everyone I could possibly think of who might have some sort of say in this. I've laid down my position, told them what I'm doing and that I want to do it soon."

"Wow, it was that easy?"

"More or less. There was quite a bit of logistical discussion and whatnot on the timing and all that managerial crap but the outcome was sure, go for it, we support you and if you really can't wait then we'll deal with it happening now."

I can't sort through my tangle of emotions to properly articulate what I'm feeling, but I do manage, "That's awesome."

She studies me. "You don't seem particularly excited. I thought you'd be doing backflips."

Smiling, I remind her, "You know I don't know how to do a backflip." I take her hands, turning them over so I can kiss her palms. "I *am* excited. I'm pleased. I'm happy for you. I'm a million emotions all at once. But…that part of me who was so hurt back then is wondering what makes now so different?"

"Because I know what I have to lose now and I won't lose it again." She dips her head to catch my eyes. "Tell me what's bothering you. Tell me what you think I should do."

The two things are linked. "I can't tell you what to do, Ellie. I can tell you what I would like to happen and I can support your decisions all the way through from you thinking them to implementing them and then beyond. But I can't tell you what you should do. This is the one decision that is yours and yours alone."

"What if I'm doing it for us? Potential us," she corrects.

"Then that's amazing." I inhale slowly and steadily. "I just… if you do this for me then you're never going to be sure it was what *you* wanted. And I don't think I will be either."

"It's for me, Avery," she says instantly. "And the wonderful, unintended side effect of that is that it becomes for you too. For *us*. And if you're not on the same page then I'll still have being out, being authentic. I want—" Her forehead crinkles as she seems to sort through her thoughts. "No, I *need* the lightness of that. I've decided I even want the fear of being so open and exposed and everything that'll come with it. And I want to balance my fears with other people's acceptance. But mostly, I just want you."

"I want that for you too, Ellie. And of course I want us to be in a relationship again and for you to feel like you can be your authentic self. I want everything we had before and then more piled on top of that. I love you." I might need to relearn some trust again, but I don't need to learn to love her again. I never stopped loving her, even as I knew I should let her and us go.

"I love you too. Hence, this decision. It's the only way forward for us."

"Right… But this is huge. And once you do it you can never stuff it back into its bag. It's going to be out in the world for everyone to know. I just want you to be absolutely sure." The last thing I want to do is stop her, or discourage her, but I need to be sure that she really gets what it means to tell the world something so personal. For a regular non-celebrity it's a huge and frightening thing that makes us feel like we're sharing a piece of ourselves. For someone like Elise who spends her life under public scrutiny? I can't even imagine how much bigger and more intrusive it will be for her.

"I know that and I'm ready for it and I'm so sure this is what I want. I've always tried to imagine what it's like for you, how you've lived your entire life." Her forehead wrinkles. "You never seemed to have any doubt about any aspect of yourself, like you were born just…knowing who you were and what you wanted out of life. I want to feel that lightness, that certainty of who I am. That strength."

"I always knew who I was, yes. What I wanted, not so much," I offer, smiling as I think about it. She showed me those things, dangled possibility in front of me. "I had to learn that part. You taught it to me."

"And you taught me some things too." She crawls across the couch to kiss me, pressing me against the cushions. I wrap my arm around her waist, pulling her against me. Elise deepens the kiss, softly stroking my tongue with hers. Despite the lustiness of our kiss, it still feels less like we're about to get naked and more like we're reaffirming our connection. "So," Ellie says when she's done turning me to mush with her kiss. "What do you say?"

"I say… Let's go around. I'm all in."

CHAPTER EIGHTEEN

I have a vague idea of how much work goes on behind the scenes to ensure the public only sees what Elise's management team wants them to see, but organizing how she comes out to the world feels crass, even as I understand the necessity. An in-person meeting has been set up and I've been asked to attend. It's basically a planning session for how to release the information and what exactly will happen afterward. This totally counts as a personal matter and I've taken today off to deal with it, then enjoy the free afternoon with her.

"Bring Bennett," Elise tells me. "Rosemary's office is dog-friendly. She takes hers in all the time and she'll kill me if I don't bring Bennett in for a visit."

"Well that would be a damned shame right now when everything's about to get super great."

She laughs. "Oh, my sweet naïve darling."

"What?"

"It'll be great, but it's also going to be a shitfight."

I shrug. "I've dealt with many shitfights. I'm not worried."

"I am," she admits quietly, but she's smiling.

I've already met Rosemary of course, but not Elise's agent, Paul, and after our brief introduction, I decide immediately that I like him. He's quiet without being mousey and makes me feel at ease. He collects coffee and a plateful of pastries then sits in the corner, apparently content to watch, take notes and maybe interject if needed. After Elise offers profuse apologies for dragging everyone in at such short notice and during the lead-up to Christmas—to the apparently genuine nonconcern of the other three—they get right to work on probably one of the most confusing things I've ever witnessed.

Miranda The Public Relations Guru is a late-thirties woman who looks more like a receptionist than someone who can spin even the most nefarious things in a positive light. I'm not exactly sure who she works for—Elise, Rosemary and Paul, or the network—but when she eyes me over the top of her cat-eye frames I decide it doesn't matter. She's going to help Ellie and that's what matters. Miranda gets right to the point. "Elise, is there anything I should know up-front? Something hiding in the closet, pun intended, that might come back to bite us in the ass later?"

Elise's response is an emphatic, "No, nothing."

"Excellent. I loathe surprises. Now, about the timing." Miranda does an admirable job of covering her grimace after it sneaks out for a second. "Are you sure about it?"

"Absolutely. Rosemary and I spoke to the network execs and they're on board. Probably because the timing with *Greed* returning in the new year is a publicity delight." Elise glances at me, her mouth twitching like she's trying not to laugh. "But it's not about that. I want this done yesterday. This is something I should have done years ago and I don't want to wait a minute more than I have to."

"So I'm just a courtesy then?" Miranda says dryly. "I suppose I should be glad you didn't go off with some half-baked coming out with no prep time for us. That sort of thing gives me nightmares."

Rosemary pauses her adoration of my dog to snicker. "Everything gives you nightmares, Miranda. Nothing about this is problematic, so let's save the drama for Elise's scripts.

We've all known for a while that this could be a possibility, so stop acting so unprepared. The timing with the court case and that nutjob could be better, but we'll manage."

Miranda lets out an indignant snort. "I'm more than prepared. For Elise. But we have an unknown now. Avery."

Elise raises her hand. "Hi. Both Elise and Avery are here, adults, and can hear you discussing us."

Miranda's "Sorry" sounds genuine. She writes something on her notepad without taking her attention from me. "I suppose we should start with the basics, Avery. What is your job?"

"My job is…sensitive and I won't be disclosing it." I glance at Elise, who offers a small smile and nod in support. "Let's just make something up. Call me an entrepreneur, a self-employed businesswoman, unemployed, a landscaper, a bank teller. I don't care."

Miranda's eyebrows shoot up and she looks first to Elise, then to Rosemary and Paul. Paul looks impassive, which tells me he has no idea what I do for a living and that he's only going to step in if there's some sort of conflict. I know Rosemary doesn't know my job either and her expression is definitely telling Miranda not to look at her for an answer.

Ellie jumps in. "It's nothing salacious or disreputable." She pauses for a dramatic beat as her gaze glides from Paul to Rosemary and finally lingers on Miranda. "Not that we would care about that…right?" Her hand under the table moves to rest on my thigh and she lightly squeezes as if trying to reassure me.

"Right," Miranda mumbles, sounding unconvinced.

I can see they're going to keep at this like Bennett with a bone, so I decide to throw them a tiny one. "My job requires a very high security clearance, hence my lack of disclosure. That's how it is and there's no way around it. I'm sorry if it's problematic for you but I'm not budging on this one point. Everything else? I'm flexible."

Miranda's shoulders relax. "We can cope with high security clearance and will certainly exercise the utmost discretion. If you're a secret mob boss or something, then we're going to have issues." She studies me. "But you look like an accountant."

"I think that's a compliment."

Her smile is cheeky. "Mostly."

"Then let's go with that if you need to give me a job, and we can just hope nobody actually approaches me about doing their taxes."

"They might, simply to make a connection with you because you're associated with Elise."

Oh my god. I'd already known fans could go over-the-top, but that just sounds absurd.

Miranda's smile fades as quickly as mine had. She speaks as she types on her tablet. "Now. Elise has disclosed that you and she were in a relationship previously, so I'm sure you have some idea as to how things work with regard to media and managing public personas and what the public gets to know, which is a minor relief."

"Some. But—" I glance at Elise who smiles and nods, giving me permission to elaborate on things private. "That was a few years ago when she wasn't as big a deal as she is now. And I was hoping things had changed from then to now with regard to, uh, the ramifications of public figures being open about their sexuality."

"They have changed," Ellie interjects firmly.

Miranda nods. "Some things have changed. Other things, not so much. Regardless, you're going to face scrutiny and possible backlash, which in these cases usually stems from homophobia or fan jealousy. The negativity will possibly be journalistic, the religious-right press mainly, but most likely is that they'll come after you on social media." Miranda sounds as if she's reciting from a script and when she's done talking, her intense gaze falls to me. Her expression shifts, as if she expected mine to differ from what it is.

My answer is probably not what she expected either when I say, "I don't have any social media."

"You…what?" She sounds like I've just told her I have no blood circulating in my body.

"I don't have social media," I repeat. "I've never seen the need for it. My life is pretty boring, I don't have many friends and anything I need to know I can go to news sites for."

"Okay then." Miranda turns to Elise. "Then it's going to be all over yours, Elise."

Ellie shrugs. "Used to it." She grins at me. "I'll just be sure I read you any vitriol directed at you."

I take the hand resting on my thigh and bring it to my mouth to kiss her knuckles. "I can't wait. I hope you make them sound *really* nasty."

Miranda laughs. "It's good you guys have a sense of humor. You're both going to need it."

Once we've run over the plan, which includes beefing up security around Elise in case certain fans, like Bridges, take offense to her statement, and every step of the timing, and everyone is clear on what's going on—except me—we're dismissed. I've been hearing terms I don't understand for the last hour and a half and have no real idea of what's happening except Elise is making a coming-out statement. Before saying his goodbyes and exiting as quietly as he came in, Paul gives me a warm, firm handshake and tells me he hopes to see me soon. Rosemary finally lets us go but not before she's said a lengthy, affectionate goodbye to Bennett and given him one last sneaky dog treat.

He's staring longingly after Elise's manager and the bag of dog treats she stashed in her seemingly bottomless purse. When my usual verbal command has no effect I have to gently tug his leash to get him to follow. The moment we're outside the conference room, Elise slips her hand into mine. "I need coffee. Desperately. Mind if we take a walk and get some fresh air before we head home?"

"Sure. Where were you thinking?"

"There's a cluster of cafés and coffee places about two blocks from here."

I hold open the door leading out into the parking lot. "Lead the way."

She walks closely enough that her free hand brushes mine, until we reach the sidewalk and she subtly moves a step away from me. "Sorry," she murmurs immediately. "Just a little while longer then you won't be able to get your hand away from mine in public."

"S'okay, I get it." I grin at her. "And I can't wait for that day." It's a bland statement but the excitement of that possibility has my skin humming.

We walk quietly down the street, with Bennett doing his best to trip us both up as he jogs along in front of us with his leash in his mouth. Elise has been walking in total silence. It's a contemplative silence, not a troubled one, but I still prod her gently with, "What's up?"

"Just thinking about what's happening in a few days." She smiles over at me. "Not *re*thinking it, babe, in case you were about to ask."

"I wasn't going to ask that at all." I lean forward to kiss her, then immediately realize how in public we are, and straighten up again. Geez, just the hint of her being out and I've forgotten all my caution. "I *was* going to ask how you were feeling."

"Exhilarated, scared, relieved, cautious." Ellie's smile is rueful. "I'm not arrogant enough to think that many people care about what I do in my personal life but…having to make such a statement about it is still kind of scary."

"You don't have to do this, Ellie. If you're scared or worried or just…don't want to then it's okay. We can work through things together." I leave off the obvious part, that if Elise changes her mind and remains closeted, then we'll work through it as friends. I feel like a shit for being so unmovable on this point, but I've learned the hard way that her sexuality secret is bad for my mental and emotional health.

Her eyes widen, her expression one of utter disbelief. "Yes I *do* have to do it. I'm doing it for myself. I'm doing it for us. And if us doesn't work out again then we'll know that it really is just you and me that doesn't work, not that I can't let the world see you and the real me. I'm tired of hiding."

The relief of having her confirm what she wants and admit openly that she wants the freedom of being her authentic self makes me feel like crying. "Okay," I quietly say. "And you know I'm here for it, here to support you through this."

"I know. It's just…you're going to be hammered with some nastiness," she reminds me, as if I've forgotten the meeting we just had. "I hate that part of it. It's fair game for me, Ms. In The Public Eye, but for you it's just bullshit."

"I don't care. I never cared about that. You know that."

"I know." She pauses on the sidewalk outside a retro coffee shop storefront.

I lower my voice. "Those people have no right to what's between us. They can say whatever they want about me, and about us, but it doesn't change the fact that I love you."

"And I love you," she says quietly.

I gesture at the coffee shop. "You want to go in and order, or stay out here and hold Bennie?"

"I'll go in and order. I come here whenever there's meetings at Rosemary's office and usually nobody bats an eyelid at me." Her nose wrinkles. "And it's good practice for going out by myself again once this is all over. It's one thing to be at home alone with a cop outside, but being *alone* alone is another thing."

I alternate between reading news on my phone and checking the door while Bennett sniffs around poles and trash cans until Elise returns. She's holding a tray with both our cups and also a smaller cup labeled with BENNETT. I realize it's a coffee for my dog—what the heck? "What on earth is that?"

"A puppucino." She tilts it toward me. "Whipped cream in a cup for doggos. No coffee." Elise crouches to hold Bennett's treat and after a quick sniff he sticks his nose into the cup and gets to work.

"A…puppucino. Really? I've never heard of it."

"That's because you don't follow social media and haven't found out about the whole puppucino craze. Old news."

"Have I actually missed out on anything important by eschewing social media?"

She grins. "Not at all."

The glint of light on glass across the street makes my adrenaline spike and I move to block Ellie until I realize it's just some guy with a camera, not a rifle scope. That *some guy* is taking photos of us. I'm not sure how I feel about it. And I'm not sure how he knew it was Ellie. Though hers is an unmistakable face and an unforgettable beauty, like me, she can blend in when she wants to.

"There's a photographer over there," I point out.

Ellie doesn't look up as she turns the cup around to help Bennie get every last bit of cream from it. "Yeah? Probably hoping for some A-List celebrity photos so he can pay rent this month."

"Actually, he's taking photos of you."

"Us," she corrects, smiling as she stands. Elise rubs Bennett's head. "Unfortunately, pap-photos of me will only pay his rent for a week." The smile turns to a wicked grin. "Unless you and I kiss. Then I think he'd be set for rent for a few months."

Kissing her in public doesn't bother me at all. But the idea of someone profiting from it, of people thinking it's okay to intrude upon her life like that, does. Especially because we're not yet at Elise's Coming Out Day and a paparazzo breaking the news instead of Elise, when and where she decides—or her management team decides—and on her terms is wrong.

As if she knows exactly what I'm thinking, she bends down and kisses the top of Bennett's nose. "That's the only kiss of mine he'll make money from today." The smile she gives me is luminous and I wonder what caption will accompany these photos when they make it to the gossip pages.

Elise Hayes and a gal pal take Elise's handsome new guy out for coffee in WeHo. Does Tomas know he's been replaced by someone buff and super charming?

I also wonder who actually cares about these things. Except those who care too much...

Bennett takes a longing last look at his puppucino cup before Elise tosses it in the trash and as I slip my hand through the leash handle, I tell him, "Maybe Mommy E will make you one at home without all the sugar and whatnot I'm sure that thing was loaded with."

Elise's coffee cup pauses halfway to her mouth before she lowers it again. She stares intently at me. Her voice has the slightest tremble when she asks, "Mommy E?" *Momma A* and *Mommy E* were our dog-mom nicknames when we were together. Elise's idea, and usually so she could tell Bennie something like, "Mommy E wants you to have those leftovers, Bennett, but Momma A said no."

"Of course you're still his dog-mom, Ellie. You love him, he loves you."

"Goddammit," she mutters under her breath.

Not exactly the reaction I'd anticipated. "What?"

She inhales deeply. "That coming out statement. I...it's not live yet and so we can't...and I just want to kiss you so badly right now."

"Then let's go home and you can kiss me all you want."

"Deal." She pauses, her smile wavering. "Would you be okay with PDAs? When everything's out and official that is."

"Yes. I'm okay with pretty much anything." The idea of a PDA with Elise makes that excitement build again.

"Really? Even the shit stuff we talked about?"

"You know I am." I gently nudge her arm. "Hey, what's up? This feels like it's about more than just a PDA."

"It is, I guess. It's just...like...it's the people photographing you while you're just out buying tampons or trying to have a quiet brunch with a friend. Or when you're collecting your mail in your pajamas or arguing with the guy who keeps parking so he's *just* blocking your driveway. There's no privacy, Avery. And I know this is what I chose but it doesn't mean I have to like it. And if you're with me then that's going to happen to you too. There'll be speculation about Elise Hayes's new lady friend. And after the statement goes live..." She lets the implication hang.

"Does that bother you?"

"No," she says immediately. "But it might bother you. I know you're not enamored with having eyes upon you."

"No, I'm not. But I am enamored with having my eyes on you. We can deal with the rest of the stuff if and when it happens."

"It will happen," she assures me. "And I know they're going to dig to try and find out about you."

"Let them. We both know that nobody's going to find me on the Internet."

"I know. That was one of the things I thought back then, when I was trying to convince myself that I was doing the right thing for both of us." She pauses and her eye contact turns intense. "I wondered if you being publicly attached to me would piss your boss off. You shoving yourself into the public eye when you're supposed to blend into the shadows."

"I'm not my job, Ellie. I just do my job. You know we're allowed to have families and participate in things outside that job, right?"

"I know, it's just—"

"It's just nothing, babe. If I was a prolific social media user or ran some *Secrets of the Skies* blog or something under a pseudonym that a clever person could trace back to me somehow, then yeah I might have a modicum of concern. But as far as the world is concerned, I'm nobody."

"You're not nobody," she rebuts instantly. Her expression is focused, serious and though she lowers her voice there's still an intensity to her words. "You are the love of my life. You're my soulmate."

CHAPTER NINETEEN

Because of a gate holdup and delayed departure on my first mission flight, I'm running a little late for my flight back from Atlanta and board near the end of the first-class section instead of right up front as is preferable. I take my time walking to my seat, casually looking around at the other occupants of the first-class cabin. I decide nothing looks out of the ordinary. Except for a late-twenties blonde occupying the window seat of my row who eyes me like I'm her in-flight meal.

She doesn't bother hiding her glee when I slide into the seat beside her, especially when I smile at her. Without saying anything, I fish my book from my leather tote, open it, and pretend to read as I scan the rest of the passengers filtering through the plane. I can feel my seatmate's eyes on me as I'm reading and know she's seeing mid-thirties CEO-type businesswoman, and wondering where her opening will be. It doesn't take her long. "You don't like working on flights?"

Hmm, not what I'd expected. One point for originality. I turn away from my book and make myself look friendly. "Too cramped for me to concentrate. And I deserve a few hours off the clock."

"I think you deserve a lot of things," she purrs.

"You think so?"

The woman's voice lowers. "I know so."

The flirting is completely harmless, but something about it still feels wrong. Mercifully, she refrains from any more suggestive comments for the rest of the flight but once we've landed she leans in close, thankfully without touching me. "Why don't you give me your number? Then the next time we happen to be passing through the same town…"

She hands me a Mont Blanc pen and a small notebook. I pause, considering, then take the pen from her. If I refuse, it'll make a scene and all I want is to get off the plane and go home to Elise. I scrawl something on the page then close the notebook and hand it and the pen back. When she opens it she's not going to see a phone number, but a short message.

I have a girlfriend but thank you.

I have a girlfriend. I have a girlfriend. I have…a girlfriend.

Just as I'm leaving the airport, Elise calls and launches right in before my "Hi" is barely out of my mouth with, "I made pizza dough."

"That's great." Ellie's homemade pizza is the stuff of dreams. But she usually only makes it when she has time and is in one of two moods. "Are you stressed, or trying to get into my pants?"

"Yes." She laughs. "The dough is almost ready, but I realized I've done it all ass-backward. My brain's mush and I didn't check I had everything I needed for toppings before I made dough. Avery, please enlighten me as to why there's no buffalo mozzarella or homemade marinara sauce and just the bare minimum of veggies in your house? There's not even any turkey sausage for your pizza. What kind of culinary hellhole have you been living in?"

"The deepest of hellholes. The last time I made pizza from scratch was with you, hence the lack of ingredients. And you're the marinara master, not me. Also, we have tons of veggies in the fridge."

"Not the right ones for pizza. I am both shocked and appalled."

Since our breakup, I'd kind of forgotten how fun and funny she could be, and this ease with which we've slipped back into our relationship with all its silliness and amusement makes everything feel light and wonderful. "We can't have that. And might I remind you that you've had a couple grocery deliveries since you turned up, in each of which you could have added pizza things?"

She's quiet for a moment. "How was I supposed to know I needed to make pizza?"

"I think there's a difference between need and want. But I'm not going to complain. So, I guess I'm making a stop on my way home?"

"Mhmm. I'll text you a list. I won't have time to make sauce so it'll have to be premade, ugh. But the most important thing is to clean them out of plum tomatoes. I'm going to make jars and jars of pasta and pizza sauce while I have time before I go back to work." Which translates to Ellie stress-cooking marinara sauce. It was always my second-favorite way of her dealing with stress. The first being her asking for a massage which always ended with lovemaking. Stress equaled marinara sauce or sex. Either way, I won.

I make a mental note to detour to Paris Baguette to get her favorites—an almond croissant and some pistachio macarons. Her coming-out statement is going live tonight, and sweet treats usually improve her mood some. It's not going to ease all the worry she's trying to hide but it might help. "Yes, ma'am. Then I'll be home in an hour and a half or so."

"Hurry back. But also do it safely."

"Will do, Captain Contradiction."

"I love you. Don't forget the tomatoes, I'm talking like ten pounds or more."

"I won't forget your tomatoes. Love you."

Despite the fact Elise already fed him before I got home from work, Bennett is paying close attention to the pizza-making, hopefully watching the counter while I pull the insides from a turkey sausage. After a few minutes of mopey dog eyes, I break the bad news to him. "No sausage for dogs. You know it's got onion and garlic in it and I don't want you to get sick. We've had this discussion before. Repeatedly." I wash my hands and tear off a small piece of mozzarella for him. "Sit."

Bennett's butt hits the floor so fast he almost leaves a crater. I offer him the cheese and he takes it gently. "Good boy. So polite. Here you go, try this." When I hold out a slice of mushroom he takes that too but eats it with far less enthusiasm, like he wants to spit it out but feels like if he appears ungrateful the counter treats will stop.

Ellie laughs. "Poor Bennie." She tears off another piece of cheese and gives it to him. "There you go. That'll get the taste out of your mouth." After she pats him, she moves to wash her hands. Her back is still to me when she quietly says, "I had an update about...Troy Bridges today."

"Oh?" I force my shoulders to untighten from the instant tension the moment I heard that name. "And?"

She turns around and idly begins pushing the edges of pizza base dough. "Summary? He's still out on bail, still restrained by my temporary restraining order, behaving himself and adhering to the conditions of being released until trial."

"That sounds about right. The wheels of justice don't always spin as quickly as they do on television."

She smiles at my teasing dig. "Mmm, yes, I'm realizing that."

"Do you want to talk about it?"

"I think I'm okay, but thanks." Ellie sighs and it seems to release some of her tension. "I've made a decision." At my eyebrows-raised query of just what that decision might be, she elaborates, "I'm going to move past it until I have to allocate some emotional energy to it. There's nothing more I can do and thinking about him makes me feel so fucking awful. And this is not the time to feel awful and pinned down by those people who think they're entitled to the personal side of me. This is the time to feel free and easy within myself, not saddled with anxiety about things outside my control."

"I think that's a great way to approach it. I'm proud of you."
She leans over and kisses me. "Me too."

After dinner she stays in the kitchen while I clean up the sprawling mess. I think I got the raw end of the deal. However… Ellie's pizza is worth the mess. Elise is leaning against the counter mumbling to herself, "It's eight p.m. on a Friday night a week before Christmas. Nobody's going to be on social media. They're all out partying. It's a great time to sneak it through people. But I'm not sneaking, I'm being open and honest. Okay. Here goes." She taps and scrolls through something on the screen before holding it up for me to see the rainbow flag newly added to her profile. "Game on." Elise sets her phone on the table and pushes it away. After a moment she grabs it back and laughing, says, "I'm just going to mute notifications for a while."

"So now we just…wait?"

"Pretty much. I'll post the video in an hour or so and then it's done. I am officially out for all the world to see."

"Great." I pull her toward me. "How should we fill the time until then?"

"We could read. Watch TV. I could start my batch of marinara sauce." Elise fiddles with the hem of my shirt. "Or… we could have a make-out session to help relax me?"

"Tough choices. But I think I have to cast my vote for the last option."

She grasps my shirt and starts pulling me toward the living room. "Me too."

The make-out session might have relaxed her but it certainly hasn't relaxed me. Pent up from her teasing and anxious about the public reaction to her announcement, I drag Bennett outside to play some fetch and chasing games with me. From outside, unsurprisingly, I hear the unmistakable sound of Elise on the piano and call Bennett back so we can go inside to listen and have him settle.

Elise acknowledges me with a smile but continues playing without saying anything. Bennett flops panting into his bed by the couch to recover from his exuberance while I flop on the couch to enjoy being in Ellie's presence. In the hour since she quietly added her rainbow flag to her social media profile I've been watching the flurry of activity from followers throwing a barrage of comments at her. Using a pseudonymous handle, I signed up for Twitter and Instagram just so I could see the reaction to her coming out. I can already see how easy it'd be to get sucked down a rabbit hole of procrastination. I must stay strong. I must not follow anyone except @RealEliseHayes.

All in all, the responses seem geared more toward excitement and support rather than nastiness, which bodes well. My nervousness feels more directed at possible vitriol when she makes her official announcement, rather than at the spotlight her team assured me will shine on me when Ellie and I make our first appearance together, even if we aren't acting couple-y.

She's been playing everything from Beethoven to jazz to Rachmaninoff, while I've lounged on the couch and alternated between checking #EliseHayes on Twitter and reading a book that's not really holding my attention. I hear a tune I recognize— the opening bars to "Heart and Soul." She glances over her shoulder and grins at me without stopping. "Duet?" Duet is a loose term for what my contribution will be, but I dog-ear my page and walk over to stand at her right shoulder.

Ellie laughs and points to a key with her right forefinger, her left hand continuing the same notes over until I join in to play one of the few piano things I know—the most basic and well-known *dun dun dunnn, dun dun dun dun dun dun* notes of about ten bars of the song and that's it. When I'm done demonstrating my piano prowess, Elise laughs and takes over. When she's finished playing, she spins around on the piano stool. "You know…it's easier with you."

"That song?"

Ellie almost chokes on her laughter. "Uh, noooo."

I place my hand over my breast. "Ouch. I am mortally wounded that a classically trained Julliard pianist doesn't think my contribution to a duet is good enough."

"You idiot." She leans against my side, wrapping her arm around my butt and hip to pull me against her. Ellie rests her head against the side of my breast. "I meant *this*. Coming out." She makes a low purr when I run my hand through her hair and down to massage her neck.

"Of course it is." Leaning down I kiss the top of her head. "Everything's easier when we do it together."

I move back to the couch and leave her to continue playing while I go back to my book and my enjoyment of listening to her. More jazz and blues, a snippet of classical then she moves smoothly into the piano opening of "Bohemian Rhapsody." She plays it twice then stops abruptly, stands, and carefully closes the fallboard over the keys. "I think it's time to put my video up."

The little lurch in my stomach is excitement instead of dread. "Okay."

Elise comes over, carefully extracts the novel from my hand and leans down to kiss me. She sighs, radiating contentment, and manages to set the book down on the coffee table and straddle me without breaking the kiss. The moment she pauses for air, I ask a question my libido doesn't want me to ask, especially not after the make-out session's arousal hangover. "Is now a good time to start this?"

"It's *always* a good time." She smiles and her voice goes soft. "Just reminding myself of how important this is to me." After another kiss, this one less drag-me-off-to-bed intense, she disengages herself. "But you're right, I have to play publicity person. Hold those thoughts." She wanders out of the room with her phone in hand and returns a short while later. But she just stands by the entrance, leaning against the wall, watching me.

"All done?" I ask.

"Yep. It's social media official now. No taking it back." Her smile is forced and I know it's not that she regrets what's now out in the world, but that she's afraid. Even being as self-assured as I know she is, making a statement like this is daunting under normal circumstances. I can't imagine how she's feeling.

"Is it okay if I watch the video here now or would you prefer me to go lock myself in the bathroom or something?" I hadn't been present when Ellie recorded her coming-out statement yesterday, though she'd run a few things by me—like whether it was okay to mention me in the abstract and that she was dating—before she'd locked herself in my small, "acoustically excellent" gym to say what she needed to. She'd gone back and forth with her management team, who not only "approved" her script, but wanted her to record the video in a studio. The compromise for her looking authentic in an obviously home environment instead of a staged one was they had to approve the video. Which they did. After three recording attempts.

"Here now is fine. Is good." She bites her lip on a smile. "Do you need help finding it on the big, scary social media?"

"Ohhh, bite me."

"Later." Ellie blows me a kiss then moves to sit on the piano stool, facing me.

Less than two minutes after she posted it, the video already has a whole bunch of likes and shares and comments. Do people even consume this stuff or just react?

Ellie doesn't introduce herself, just launches right in, looking straight at the camera. It makes me feel as if she's looking right through me. She's smiling and seems relaxed and open. "When I was a kid, I was afraid of the monsters under the bed. And even though I knew logically that they weren't real, I was still afraid. When I got older I stopped being afraid of monsters, but I was still afraid of illogical things. Like being true to myself. Being afraid and hiding from things I knew to be true meant I hurt people I love, and I hurt myself." She exhales and the smile turns brilliant, genuine. "I've decided I'm going to try not being afraid of irrational things, so I'm just letting everyone know that I'm a member of the LGBTQ-Plus community and my pronouns are she and her. I've yet to find a label for my sexuality that I feel truly fits, but I *am* dating a woman." She pauses and the smile is still there. "I'm happy and comfortable in my skin and the only regret I have about coming out is that I didn't do it sooner. I'm excited to contribute to my community and look forward to engaging with you. Thank you for your support."

I know she has immense natural talent and can make you believe she feels any emotion, but in the video she was just a person telling someone their absolute truth. No bullshit. No subterfuge. She looked raw and she looked *real*. The prickle behind my eyes isn't surprising, nor is the intense pride and love and awe I feel at her bravery.

She looks as worried as I've ever seen her. "Was it okay?"

"It was absolutely perfect." I hold out my hand and when she gets up and takes it, I pull her close so she's snuggled in between my knees. "*You* were perfect."

"Thanks."

I rub my hands up and down the outside of her thighs. "How do you feel?"

She takes a few moments to think about it and her answer is a quiet, smiling, "Lighter."

"I can imagine. Are you going to tell them that we were dating before we…weren't?"

Her eyebrows shoot up. "I hadn't thought about it. I mean it's not really anyone's business."

"No. It's not. But if I was not me and I'd just seen that video, my first point of curiosity would be this mysterious person you said you'd hurt."

"Mmm. Good point. I don't think it's need-to-know information, do you?" She frowns. "I might contact Miranda and see what she thinks I should say. My instinct is to go with the good ol' 'none of your fucking business' brush aside."

"That's a good way to handle it. And no, I don't think it's anyone's business, unless you're trying to create a real-life *Second Chance* story."

Her smile is immediate. "Of course I am. Don't you know second-chance romance is Hallmark movie gold?"

"Oh? You want to star in Hallmark movies now?"

"Absolutely. If they catered to the women-loving-women market then I would be shoving other actresses out of the way. You know I love that cheesy romance stuff. Maybe I'll just write one for myself." Her smile fades. "But hopefully everyone adheres to human decency and general privacy rules and just… don't ask."

"How much faith do you have in human decency?"

"General public? Not so much. But you on the other hand…" Elise leans over so she's almost lying on top of me and kisses me slowly, thoroughly. Once we've finished casually exploring each other's mouths, she lightly nibbles my lip. "I have more faith in you than anyone else, so I know it'll be okay. And we already know there's a possibility people might be dickish about it, so we're prepared for that and all it entails."

"True." A text on my work phone interrupts before I can say more and I suppress my groan of annoyance. I don't want to work tomorrow. Elise settles back at her end of the couch while I wrestle my phone from my pocket. By some small mercy it's not Rowan telling me I need to take a shift tomorrow, or worse—get my ass on a red-eye now.

Nicola. *Elise Hayes just came out on Insta. I might die. Now I know I totally have a shot.*

Smiling, I tap out my reply. *Oh yeah, saw that. Good for her. Didn't she say something about being in a relationship?*

Minor detail. They could break up. Let me have my fantasy, you dream squashing bitch.

My laugh breaks free. I have no idea how my colleague somehow manages to be so on the money while simultaneously being so completely clueless. *Fantasize away. And good luck.* My laughter has alerted Ellie and she nudges me with her toe. "Something up?" The tone isn't nosy or controlling, but fearful. She thinks it's something about her coming out. Something not great. My suspicion is confirmed when she asks, "Oh god, are there memes about me coming out already?"

"No, sweetheart, that's not it at all. Basically, my workmate thinks Elise Hayes is the hottest woman on the planet."

Her expression relaxes. "Ah. Really?" She's trying not to smile, but I can tell she's pleased. Ellie isn't arrogantly vain, but she's not without a healthy ego and a realistic knowledge of her attractiveness. "That must be weird for you."

"Weird and amusing. Now she's seen your coming-out statement and is…very supportive and also seriously excited, because of course you being out means there's some distant chance of you being her girlfriend. She acknowledges this is contingent upon you breaking up with this mystery woman you're currently dating."

"I see," Elise muses. "Just out of curiosity, is she hot? I like to keep my options open."

"Not *my* type but might be yours." I reach for my phone again and pretend to type on it. "Should I let her know you'll be available once you're sick of me?"

Ellie pounces, pinning me to the couch. "No way." She takes the phone and leans over to place it on the floor. "I think we've established I'm not going to get sick of you."

"The feeling is mutual."

"Good." Ellie kisses the tip of my nose. "I feel like celebrating."

I reach up to push masses of chestnut hair back, holding it behind her neck in a loose fist. "How exactly do you celebrate coming out to the world?"

"By having hot sex with your hot girlfriend."

"Do you think you could fit any more instances of the word *hot* into that sentence?"

Ellie dips her head, her lips lingering a breath from mine. "Why don't you come to the bedroom with me and we can find out?"

CHAPTER TWENTY

In the six days since Ellie's very public coming out, it feels like we've rolled the clock back to when we first started dating and everything is fresh and exciting. But now, I'm also noticing a new easiness between us that hadn't been there before. It makes me realize the fear and worry Ellie must have been holding in all those years we were together, knowing eventually she might have to make a decision about her personal and professional lives intersecting.

Alongside the fresh and exciting is the feeling of comfort where we've skipped all the flirting and getting-to-know-yous and stepped straight into being together as people who know one another, care about each other, and are deeply in love. I'm also discovering this time feels lighter for me too. Knowing Ellie is out, being authentic, has me understanding that despite how often I assured both of us that it was fine, hiding our relationship made me feel heavy.

The response to her statement was basically as everyone expected—eighty percent supportive and excited, then twenty percent vitriolic-ish. Apparently, speculation is rife about who Elise's mystery girlfriend is and the photos of us getting coffee with Bennett after the PR meeting are being dissected everywhere, trying to figure out if I'm just some friend who is a girl instead of The Girlfriend. The consensus is that I'm The Girlfriend and that people wish the photos of me were front on instead of my back and a fraction of the side of my face. The whole thing feels ridiculous and I wonder why people care so much about something that doesn't affect them at all and are acting like Elise has given them a personal gift.

But Ellie's happy and I'm happy, so I set aside the weirdness of the whole thing to focus on us and settling back into the idea of sharing our lives again. Elise wants to give her brother's caretakers the whole Christmas Day off, and his roommates are spending Christmas with their families, so she's going over to Steven's first thing tomorrow for Christmas morning and will stay overnight. Which means Elise, certified jolly Christmas Elf, has decreed we're exchanging gifts at her place on Christmas Eve with her bigger and better, and not fake like mine, tree.

I'm the opposite of her Christmas Elf—Christmas for me is another day, but with presents that make me feel even more awkward than my birthday. When we were together before, I got better at being comfortable with accepting that's how things were. Better but not good. It was always a huge joke between us that Elise who loved gifting so much was dating me who was so awkward about receiving gifts.

It's always been that way. Like her, I love the pleasure of considering gifts for someone—the buying, the careful wrapping, the presenting of them. But give me something and I turn into a person who's so overwhelmed by someone else's careful thought and care that I get self-conscious about my expression of gratitude and turn into a mumbling idiot. And it's never changed.

Elise prepares a platter of antipasto which Bennett thinks is his Christmas treat, but once he's been given his actual gifts he settles near Elise's piano like the spoiled child he is to work on his new tough treat toy that she's stuffed with dog cookies. Ellie nabs her present for me before I've even had a chance to move toward the tree.

We're both sitting cross-legged near the tree and Elise looks like she's about to burst as I begin unwrapping a gift that's almost two-feet square. The moment I open the box I realize what she's done. I should have known it'd be one of Elise's Matryoshka doll gifts where she puts her gifts in empty box after empty box with a small gift in each layer before the actual main event gift in the last box. If we had a cat, they'd be in box heaven by the time I reach the main present. In between the layers of boxes I find a massage voucher, a PlayStation Store voucher and a super-hard-to-find *Rhetra* poster signed by the game developers. When I peel back another layer of brown paper wrapping and see a white box with SONY in the left corner, I grin. She's pulled one of her present practical jokes, and given me my gift inside her brother's PlayStation 5 box. It's only when I see the box is sealed that I realize it might actually be a PS5.

I break the seal and peek inside. It's a PS5. "Oh my god," I blurt. "You didn't. You did?"

Ellie looks like she's just given me the best gift ever, which she really has. "I did."

"How did you manage to get this so last-minute, especially after you already got one for Stevie?" A horrifying thought dawns. "Oh shit, this isn't his, is it?"

She laughs. "No, it's not his. I love you but denying my big brother the thing he's been asking for since he first heard about it would land me firmly on his shit list."

"Phew. Then do you have an inside guy at PlayStation who got you this one? Because if you do, I might marry you."

"No, but it sounds like I might have to get myself an inside guy at PlayStation if that's the benefit." She leans over to look inside the box, her expression confused as if she doesn't get why the entire world is turning themselves inside out trying to get this console. "I called around to see who had stock—basically nobody—until I found this tiny gaming shop who'd managed to get two extras on top of their pre-orders that they anticipated would sell out within seconds. In exchange for a console, I agreed to do an in-person meet-and-greet for *Assassin's Guild: Rhetra* at the store. They get publicity and revenue from sales. I get to make my girlfriend happy."

"So it really is all about who you know. Maybe I should start throwing your name around more. I could get faster coffee, great restaurant reservations, better parking, cheap movie tickets, a PlayStation Six when they make one in however many years. The possibilities are endless."

"Oh, so *now* you think dating a celebrity is awesome," she teases.

"Babe," I sigh. "Play. Station. Five."

"Yeah yeah, I get it," she drawls.

I lean over to kiss her and Ellie slides her hand around to cup the back of my neck, holding me in place. When we've satisfied our need, she releases me, but not before she's kissed the tip of my nose. I hug her, pressing my face into her hair. When I feel somewhat controlled, I release my tight grip. "Thank you. So much. This is so awesome." As always, my gratitude and excitement over receiving a gift feels stilted and entirely inadequate but Ellie knows me so well by now that she takes the awkward and makes it unawkward.

She kisses my forehead. "You're so welcome."

I begin the unboxing process. "Will you be all right with the game store meeting and greeting and talking and signing thing? Like, out in public where it's been advertised and…certain people will know you're there."

"Mhmm. I talked to Rosemary and Paul and they're totally on board. All that being out in public and reminding people I'm around stuff makes them both salivate. I think they nearly cried with relief when those pictures of us getting coffee with Bennett went up on the net."

"I'm glad to hear it, but that's not quite what I meant. It's not just you hating claustrophobic groups, it's about him knowing where you'll be at a specific time."

Her smile tells me she already knows what I mean. "It'll be fine. We'll have a couple of burly guys hanging around who'll have been given a photo of He Who Should Not Be There.

Organized events are easy. People approach me one or two at a time, we chat, I smile, sometimes there's photos and then I move on to the next person. No mobbing." She leans in close. "But, darling, I *would* brave a mob of gaming nerds for you and your PlayStation."

"I think that's the nicest thing anyone's ever said to me." I finally manage to expose the PS5 in all its glory. "Oh, she's beautiful. I love it. Thank you, Ellie."

"You know, that almost sounded not-awkward," she teases.

"Oh, be quiet."

Ellie grins. "You know, last Christmas and your birthday I was wondering if anyone was giving you gifts, and imagining you trying to say thank you and all your adorable overthinking about it. I missed it so much I almost came around with something, just for your reaction."

"That probably would have gotten you a *really* awkward response."

"True," Ellie muses.

It takes a big chunk of willpower to put the PS5 back in its box and collect my main gift to Elise from under the tree. "Merry Christmas, Ellie. I—" I have to swallow my emotion before I can continue, "I'm so happy we've found each other again."

"Me too." She raises her face to me for a kiss and once I've obliged, she starts carefully unwrapping her gift.

This first, bigger gift seems kind of lame in comparison to what she's given me and I can't deny my nervousness as she unearths the box of right-handed kitchen implements with a ribbon bow around each one. Smiling, Ellie holds up a can opener. "Are you trying to get me to spend more time in the kitchen?" She's attempting to sound light and teasing but I know she gets the implication of my gift, and her underlying hope and excitement is breaking through.

"In my kitchen, yes. In my house." I pause to take a steadying breath. "I'm not saying we should live together again right away, but maybe we could do it soon? I mean, we already know we can do it. I want to let everything settle into place first, but I also want you to know that's what I want." The thought makes me feel like crying, so I attempt a joke. "Plus, I'm not always going to be around to use my corkscrew for you so I figured you should have your own rightie one there. Among other things."

A slow eyebrow raise. "Is that so?"

"Yes."

"I want that too. Not the ability to use a corkscrew in your house but us living together again." She draws in a quiet breath, the rise of her chest measured as if she's taking in as much air as she can. "You're my anchor and my North Star, Avery. The thing that keeps me…myself, like I know exactly who I am when I'm with you. In my whole life I've never felt so off-kilter as I did this past time without you."

"Me too." The words are tight and I have to take a few moments to make sure I'm not going to burst into tears before I tell her, "I have one more thing." I fish a tissue paper-wrapped object from my front pocket.

She gives me a suspicious look as she takes the gift. The suspicion turns to understanding as she fingers the shape under the tissue. "Is this my bracelet?"

"Yes." I'd given it to her for her birthday our second year together, a kind of precursor to a ring. She'd left it on the kitchen counter in what felt like a final *fuck you*. I threw it in the trash and then the morning the trash bins were collected I'd sprinted out in panties and a tank top to fetch it again. At the time I'd just thought it ridiculous to throw away a two-thousand-dollar bracelet. Later, when I finally came to terms with her leaving, I realized my retrieving the bracelet was actually me not coming to terms with it then. "I washed the spaghetti sauce and banana peel off it."

She smiles. "You're so thoughtful."

"I know."

Elise carefully unwraps the bracelet then crumples the tissue paper. "You tossed it away?" She unfastens the clasp and holds the bracelet out to me. "And then un-tossed it away."

"That's right." I carefully fasten the bracelet around her delicate wrist and turn it so the clasp is on the underside. It looks gorgeous on her and I carefully trace the diamonds with my fingertips.

"I'm glad you did." She looks down to where my fingers are moving over the jewelry. "I love this bracelet, always have. I really didn't want to leave it and I knew exactly what it might imply, but I couldn't keep it. It just...it reminds me of you, Avery, and I knew every time I wore it or looked at it my heart would rip a little more."

"I get it," I quietly say. "And I mean, we got here in the end, scenic route and all."

She snorts out a laugh. "Scenic route with road blockages."

"True." I lie down and stretch out, resting my head in her lap so I can look at my gifts. "I've forgotten Christmas is kind of fun."

Ellie gestures to the PlayStation 5 box sitting proudly beside us. "Will you be gazing lovingly at that thing all night?"

I sit up and grip her hand, tugging her until she falls on top of me. "Not all night."

* * *

Bennett gives me a mopey look when he realizes he's spending Christmas Day alone in Elise's house because there's no point in backtracking to my place to drop him off before I go to Steven's. He's only slightly mollified by the bully stick I give him as a tasty chew treat, and stares at me as I sneak out the front door. It takes me over two and a half hours in Christmas Day traffic to get to Steven's place in Coto de Caza. His house is a modern ranch-style and as I knock, I feel unexpectedly nervous considering I've met him so many times before. From inside I can hear a muffled conversation between him and Elise before Steven opens the door.

Confusion flashes quickly over his face before it transforms to recognition then excitement. He's a little more stooped than the last time I saw him, but even with that loss of height he's easily six-one. The sibling resemblance is striking and the thick scar that runs from his right eyebrow and parts the hair all the way around to his right ear does nothing to diminish his handsome features.

I give him my friendliest smile. "Hi, Steven. Merry Christmas. How're you?"

Before I can fully reintroduce myself, Ellie appears behind him, wearing an apron and with a dishtowel over her shoulder. She reaches up to rest a hand on his shoulder. "Stevie, do you remember Avery?"

After a pause, he looks from Elise to me. A nod follows quickly. "She's your friend from before. Now your girlfriend."

"That's right."

He looks down at her. "Did she used to be your girlfriend? When she was your friend."

"She did," Elise confirms.

He seems to mull this over and then studies me again. "Okay. I thought so, even though you never said. She's still pretty." I suppress a laugh. I'd forgotten with his TBI he could be unfiltered, though he'd never said anything inappropriate to me. He grins his charming, lopsided grin, which is slightly more lopsided these days. "Come in, Avery. Welcome to my nice house."

"Thank you." A quick glance around tells me the nice house is open plan with minimal furniture and easy pathways for people to maneuver.

After Elise closes the front door, she snags my arm and pulls me toward her for a quick kiss. "Find it okay? How bad was traffic?"

"Easy-peasy. And I'll let you guess how bad it was."

Steven, having apparently noticed the small, wrapped box in my hand, asks, "Is that for me?"

Elise's admonishment is soft. "Stevie, come on."

"Why? What do you mean? Avery came to my house for Christmas so it makes a lot of sense that the gift is for me."

She pokes him in the belly. "Maybe it's for *me*. Did you stop to consider that?"

"No. It's too small to be a present for you. The only thing that small would be a ring and I think it's too early for you to be getting married. Maybe next Christmas."

I bite down on my laugh. "It is for you, Steven." I pass the gift to him. "Merry Christmas."

"Thank you. I didn't...get you anything. Elise didn't tell me I had to." His nervous glance moves from me to Elise who's gone into the kitchen to attend to something that smells incredible.

"It's fine, I swear. You absolutely did not need to get me a Christmas gift. I just saw this and thought about you and wanted to thank you for having me for Christmas. But if you're worried about not getting me anything, you can let me play a few games with you on your new console."

The anxiety melts from his face. "I can do that. Want me to beat you at *Overcooked*? Elise gave me a PS-Five for Christmas with my games all preloaded."

"I heard. Lucky you. I've been trying to get one of those consoles for months." I decide not to mention my PS5 in case it upsets him, thinking he wasn't special. "And I'd love to play some *Overcooked*. You never know, maybe I'll beat you."

His eyebrows scrunch. "Did you get better at that game since...before?"

Laughing I answer, "Probably not."

"Then you have no chance of beating me."

Elise interjects, "Games after lunch, please. You've been on that thing all morning, Stevie."

He turns slowly to face her. "How much longer until we... eat?"

"A little over an hour."

"Then we have time for games." Steven turns his attention back to me. "If you win, I'll set the table. If I win, you'll do it."

"Deal."

From the kitchen comes Ellie's exasperated, "No deal. Setting the table is your Christmas Day job, Steven. You don't make your guests do house chores. Especially not at Christmas."

He turns to me. "We can...do it together?"

I offer a conspiratorial nod then gesture to the small box dwarfed in his large hands. "Are you going to open your gift?"

"Oh, right. I forgot. Thanks. Can you get the game loaded?" He flashes me a charm-laden smile as he adds, "Please."

Elise interjects again. "In a minute." She points to a bowl on a sideboard, lowering her voice. "Darling, my car keys are in there. You can stash whatever you need to in my car. It's in the locked garage, door is the first one on the left down the hall." She makes a discreet thumb and forefinger gun.

"Thanks." My work firearm, required because I'm on call, will be safely locked in her car in the secure garage. Guns at social events are a real issue and I know my colleagues have rushed from unexpected overtime work to a barbecue or something and had to stash theirs on top of the fridge or a high cabinet out of reach of little hands. It'd been in the back of my mind that I couldn't leave it in the car parked on the street and having a hidden holstered gun during Christmas lunch was an annoyance I'd resigned myself to. I should have known Ellie would have thought of it. "I've just gotta do something, Steven, and I'll be right back."

The moment I return, he pounces. "My present now and then we game?"

I glance at Elise to make sure I'm not breaking some manners rule and when she nods, I agree, "Sure. Sounds perfect."

After he shows me where I can sit on the couch, Steven settles at the other end and begins carefully peeling back the tape on the small box. The present isn't anything exciting, but I know he loves Funko Pop figurines and after some reconnaissance from his caretakers and Elise, I got him an Emily Kaldwin from the game *Dishonored 2*. His mouth works open and closed, as if he's sorting through his thoughts. After a minute or so he stutters out, "Awe-awe-awe-some. Emily Kaldwin is...the rightful Empress of Dunwall. I love her."

I thank the universe that I've played through the game repeatedly and am intimately familiar with the storyline. "She sure is. Delilah sucks, right?"

"Totally." He leans over then pauses again. "Can I give you a...thank-you hug?"

"You can."

His side-on hug is tight before he gets up to place the Funko on the shelf with his others. He moves a few aside to put Emily

Kaldwin front and center. "Thank you, Avery. Now. You're going to lose at *Overcooked*."

I've no doubt I will. After checking Ellie doesn't want help with Christmas lunch, which she doesn't—and she's not just being polite or a holiday martyr, she really doesn't want any interference—Steven and I settle in for an hour of gaming. Ellie pops in here and there to refill drinks and snacks and assure me she's fine and happy in the kitchen by herself. It's a weird Thanksgiving and Christmas miracle that my parents were never around at the holidays when Ellie and I were together. I couldn't even imagine the clash of styles if my mother and Elise were trying to prep a meal together.

Mom is the epitome of stressed-out holiday housewife, which always felt so incongruous to me because in her job she's the coolest, calmest medico I know. But being a terrible cook means Thanksgiving and Christmas freak her out and she ends up begging for help after she's told us all that she doesn't want help. Ellie is like a cyborg, just calmly going through the motions to produce an amazing meal while shunning every offer of help.

The Christmas fairies are smiling on me and we make it through our meal without a single interruption. After Steven helps clear the table, Ellie shoos him back to his gaming so he won't be in the way while she's trying to clean up. She and I clean up together and once I've handed her the final rinsed plate I glance at the time. As much as I want to stay here with Elise and her brother, I need to begin the trek home. "I'd better get back and feed Bennie. Unless you need me here for something?"

"It's fine, but thanks." She passes me a foil-wrapped package from beside the stove. "Turkey for Bennett."

"You spoil him so hard."

"I know." She kisses me, not at all chastely. Her voice is low when she says, "And when I get home tomorrow morning, I'm going to spoil you too." Smiling, Ellie raises her voice to call, "Stevie, Avery is leaving now. You going to say bye or are you going to be rude?"

"Not rude!" is the returned call. Ten seconds later he lumbers into the kitchen. "Can you come back, Avery?"

"Of course. That'd be great."

"Will you come for burger night too? Elise eats salad on burger night. It's not salad night. It's burger night."

"I sure can and I'll eat a burger, not a salad."

"Cool. Thank you for coming to my house for Christmas. Can I hug you goodbye?"

"Course you can. And thank you for inviting me into your home."

He enfolds me in a warm hug, patting my back for a few moments before letting me go. "I'll see you very soon. Burger night is this next Friday. Don't forget."

"You got it. And I won't forget."

Stevie pats the tops of my shoulders then disappears without saying anything more. Moments later I hear his game start up again. Elise fixes my jacket collar, carefully smoothing the fabric then running her hand down my shoulder. "I'll let the caretakers know you're on the 'okay whenever Stevie is okay with a visit' list."

"Sounds great."

"He really loves burger nights. I like to think it's because he's spending time with me, but I'm pretty sure it's the burger. You being there eating a burger too will make him super happy. But if you're not up for it on Friday, I can talk him out of you being there."

"No way. That's my cooking night and there's no way I'm skipping a chance for someone else to do the cooking."

"Ah, the truth comes out." She kisses me lightly. "Come on, I'll walk you out."

Once I've collected my gun locked in Elise's car, she opens the garage door to let us out of the house. I stow Bennett's turkey treat on the passenger-side floor then crawl back out again and almost bump into Ellie. She's smiling, a secret, sly smile that makes me ask, "What?"

"You were right."

"Of course I was." I pause. "About what exactly?"

"Everything's easier when we do it together. Even mundane everyday stuff like this."

"It really is."

"I can't wait for years of mundane everyday stuff." Ellie grabs my hand, tugs me close and kisses me. She kisses me out in the open, on the driveway, where anyone could see us. "I love you, drive safe and let me know if you have to fly tonight. Are you going to stay at my place?"

"I love you too. And yeah, I probably will, just so I don't have to drive any more than I have to."

"Okay. Just let me know where you are tonight?"

"I will. Drive home safely tomorrow."

On the way back to Elise's I keep expecting my work phone to ring but it's mercifully silent. As I unlock the door, I can hear Bennett on the other side, excitedly waiting for his people to arrive. He sits, then bounces up on his back legs, then spins a circle. "Hey, pal. Merry Christmas again. I've got another present for you." I reset Ellie's alarm and dump my keys in the bowl on the kitchen counter, trying not to stumble over Bennett who is walking against me like he's trying to trip me. "What's up? You smell Elise's turkey, huh? Gimme a sec and it's all yours."

Bennie shadows me, still pressing himself against my leg. I give him a gentle nudge. "Personal space, Bennett. I'm not going to be able to feed you if you trip me up."

He waits until I've given him the okay to eat, sniffs the turkey, gobbles up a few quick mouthfuls then abandons his bowl to rush to the sliding glass door leading out to the pool area. He's tense, almost anxious, which is odd for him, even in a new-ish place. He's been mellow as anything about spending time in Elise's house, but now he's fixated on the patch of hill between her backyard and her neighbors to the rear.

"There a coyote up there? Found a new opossum?" I flick the lights to illuminate the entire entertaining area but can't see anything out of the ordinary, no animals skulking around in the vegetation. "You wanna go for a swim? Or do you need to go pee?" Bennie quickly noses my hand, then resumes his staring outside. After weighing it up I decide it's Christmas evening and if my dog wants a swim he can have a swim. The steam rising from the heated water is so enticing, I think I might join him.

The moment I unlock the door and slide it back, Bennett rockets outside. But he bypasses the pool and shoots up to the retaining wall at the back of the yard. After sniffing his way along the wall, he backtracks to look up the hill again. He's standing rigid, legs set apart like he's trying to be as staunch as possible. Something up the hill has him worked up to the point he's acting like a guard dog. But if it was anything serious he'd be barking, and the vegetation isn't thick enough to hide anything bigger than a coyote. Still, I collect a flashlight and quickly sweep the beam through the brush on the slope. Nothing.

At my whistle he reluctantly abandons his recon and comes back inside, but I can tell he really wants to be out there. A weird sensation slithers down my spine and I search the darkness again for anything that feels wrong. I see nothing. But my dog doesn't usually act like this and that alone tells me he's sensing something. I rub his head. "Let's take a look around the house."

Bennett and I take our time but I see absolutely nothing out of place. All the doors and windows are locked and I see no evidence that anyone other than the dog has been inside since I left that morning. I almost laugh at the absurdity of the thought. But still, I do another lap of each level until I'm satisfied that the only thing that's been inside today is Bennett. When I walk around the outside the house, I see nothing out there either.

But the dog keeps staring out the sliding door.

CHAPTER TWENTY-ONE

Ellie pops her head into her spacious gym where I'm stretching my glutes on the floor. She bounces her eyebrows. "Now that's a view."

"Hello to you too." I roll over and slowly change my position to stretch my other buttcheek.

"Tease."

Craning to look at her, I grin. "Always."

Elise settles on her free-weights bench. "Two things. Have you seen my lot badge? I'm trying to get back into work mode and just realized it's not in the mail bowl where I usually dump it after work."

The pass with her picture and the show she's working on that gets her onto the filming lot. "Sorry, no. I don't think I've ever seen it here."

"Weird. Maybe my cleaner moved it and forgot to put it back. Or I put it in a safe place until I go back to work next year, a place that's so safe it's unfindable."

"Probably," I agree. "What's the second thing?"

"I'm a space cadet and I totally forgot with all the coming out and Christmas yesterday and everything else between, but there's a Lakers' game tonight. You free?"

While skimming news and sports pages I've seen photos of Elise at Lakers' games, usually courtside with her not-boyfriend, Tomas, or other actors with whom she's friendly. The pictures always have Elise laughing and smiling, holding her companion's arm, gesturing at the players or expressing wild exasperation. Then there's the occasional picture of her sitting further back, usually alone and with a free seat beside her. Elise has been a hardcore Lakers fan most of her life and has had her two-seat membership from well before we were together.

I sit up, straighten my legs in front of me, and stretch forward to hook my fingers around my arches. "You...really had to ask me if I was free for that?"

"It's the polite thing to do. Next time, should I just say 'you, me, b-ball, now'?"

"Works for me. When do we have to leave?"

She glances at her watch. "Little under an hour."

"Should we shower together to save time?"

Her smile is part pleased, part leering. "It's like you read my mind." She offers me her hand to drag me from the floor.

The moment we're settled in our lower 100's seats, I turn to Elise. "Still hate courtside, I see?" I wonder why she hasn't upgraded her membership or asked for favors from famous friends to get courtside seats tonight. Not that I'm complaining about being at a Lakers' game again.

"Mhmm, I hate listening to the refs and players talking and can't get over my fear of a player colliding with me. I do *not* want to be responsible for breaking LeBron's leg. Nor do I want to spend the whole game worrying about getting an elbow to the face."

"I suppose that's as good a reason as any. And you know I like these seats." I lean forward. "You can see it all from here."

"Mmm." She slides her hand under my shirt to massage either side of my spine. "Speaking of seeing, it's highly likely a photographer will see us."

"I'm sure a lot of people will see us."

She pokes me in the ribs, lingering to tickle playfully. "Smartass. You know what I mean. See us and take photos of us which will likely be made public. We're not in the front row and I'm not Beyoncé or Obama-level famous obviously, but sometimes I'm all they can get in the way of *celebrity*."

"Baby, you're the biggest celebrity I know."

Elise leans in to speak low near my ear. "I think I'm the only celebrity you know." She slowly kisses the side of my neck, up to my ear. "And of course, now I'm out and in a public space where photographers are known to be, I'm fair game. Especially because I'm with a woman who I've been photographed with before." Another round of kisses, these ones light and staccato. "Are you okay with that? I know we talked about the whole you being part of the paparazzi scene but it can take some getting used to."

I suppress the shiver her kisses have elicited. "I coped with coffee guy, so I'll cope with this. And being photographed at a game where there's official photographers feels less icky than a guy on the street."

"That it does. But it's still not nice."

I turn to face her. "It's a small price to pay for being able to be out with you, to show people what we share."

Her laugh is dry. "I'll remind you of that when they run a picture of you with your mouth open taking a huge bite of hot dog outside Pink's."

"I'll be sure there's mustard and sauerkraut on my shirt too."

Elise grins. "Even better."

During the halftime break, the roar of the crowd takes my attention from court and it takes a moment to realize that Elise and I are on the Kiss Cam. Her expression is playful, as if she's both daring and soothing me all at once. She's telling me she wants me to kiss her, but I don't *have* to kiss her right here, in front of this stadium of basketball fans and whoever is watching at home. Her eyes tell me we can just laugh it off and everyone will playfully boo and the camera will move on.

But I want to kiss her. Mostly because I love kissing Elise, but also her utter nonchalance about something as monumental as kissing her same-sex partner in public is a huge deal. I wink and murmur, "Bring it on."

The kiss is soft and warm, intimate yet perfectly acceptable for the public eye in a venue filled with families. The cheering and applause rings through my ears. Elise lingers for a moment then pulls back. "Well," she says against my ear, "I guess there's no coming back from it now."

I turn to face her. "I guess not. Do you think Miranda planned that on-screen kiss for us? As in she asked them to find us in the crowd?"

Her eyes widen. "Shit. I...don't know. Maybe? But that seems weird and not really part of the plan. It's not like Kiss Cam hasn't happened before when I've been here with friends so, no I don't think so. Good publicity is good publicity but everyone in my team knows how I am about the private part of my life." The edges of her mouth are twitching. "Did it bother you?"

"Bothered is the least of what I am. I loved it. Loved how normal it was."

"Me too."

I lean closer to murmur, "In fact, I'm so unbothered, I think I'd like another."

"The Kiss Cam isn't on us."

"I don't care." Holding my cup aloft, I kiss her until I feel her melt into me. When we move apart, Ellie blinks hard a few times then reaches into her purse for some tissues. "Was the kiss that bad?" I joke, though her obvious emotion makes my throat tight.

She carefully dabs at her eyes. "No, Avery. It was absolutely perfect."

I hadn't told Elise about Bennett's weirdness on Christmas night but when he does it again after we get home from the game, I decide to mention it to her. Her apparent lack of concern seems forced as she reminds me about her regular opossum and coyote visitors, and then points out that if I'd found nothing out of place in or outside, and the security patrols saw nothing either, then that's good enough for her. I make another check around inside then go out to walk around the perimeter of her property with Bennett. I still find nothing unusual.

When I put the flashlight in the drawer, Elise asks, "No bogeymen?" The question is light but there's an undercurrent of worry.

"Nope. Not a Halloween villain to be seen. I guess he's just pretending to be big, tough wildlife-barking doggo."

"Probably," she agrees, her voice tight.

Bennett stares out the sliding glass door and barks once.

* * *

Coffee. I've just stepped out of my office when Nicola emerges from the elevator. She holds up two cups. "Thought I'd save you the trouble."

I take the one with my name on it. "Thank you, mind reader."

"You're welcome." Those two words are borderline manic, as if she's only just restrained herself from blurting something else. Knowing her as I do and knowing how much she adores the Lakers and gossip columns, I have a pretty good idea of what she would blurt.

When I do a one-eighty to head back to my office, Nicola follows me. I sip my coffee and steel myself for what feels like an inevitable interrogation. She waits until I'm settled at my desk before she sits in the chair on the other side of my desk, leans back and crosses her legs. "So...how was your weekend? You have a good Christmas?"

Oh, she knows for sure. We never talk about weekends or special days. "Pretty quiet Christmas with friends, didn't get called up thankfully. Bit of housework over the weekend, spent a little time with the PlayStation, took Bennett for a hike on Sunday. Usual stuff, nothing exciting."

Her response is a casual, "Right, cool, sounds great."

I decide to drag out her suspense. "How about yours?"

"Fine, nothing interesting. Christmas with my parents, watered my plants, watched the Lakers' game on Saturday." She's doing an admirable job of pretending to be casual.

"Yeah?" This is too fun. "I saw it too. Great game."

"Yeah. It was." She pauses for a millisecond before blurting, "You're dating Elise Hayes?" Her voice climbs an octave with each word of her question.

"Is this coffee a bribe? Like, you buy me coffee and I have to answer your questions?"

"You make it sound so sordid. But mhmm, pretty much, yeah, that's how it works."

"You're lucky I'm easily swayed by caffeine." There's no point in denying or dragging it out any longer when she's clearly figured out what's going on. "And yes, I'm dating Elise Hayes."

"Wow, you just came right out and said it. I thought I'd have to drag it out of you." She exhales a loud breath. "Just... like, fucking *wow*. How did that happen? Was she so grateful for what you did that day on the plane that she just slipped you her number afterward?"

"Uhhh...no, not exactly."

Nicola seems undeterred by my vague answers and keeps running away with her thoughts. "Fuck. That's incredible. You're dating Elise Hayes. How? Over a year of basically nothing, no serious dates and then, boom! Elise. Hayes. I guess things with your ex didn't really work out, huh?"

Smiling, I assure her, "Oh no, they worked out very well." I sip my coffee and wait for Nicola to connect the dots.

It takes about five seconds for her jaw to drop. "Wait. What? No. Fucking. Way. Elise Hayes is your ex? The ex who turned up at your house the day of the...uh, Elise Hayes thing?"

I feel not a little smug, and it seeps into my tone. "That's right."

"I—" She's doing a very good impersonation of a goldfish out of water. "That's fucking incredible. And confusing. And also probably one of the most romantic things I've ever heard. Full on knight-in-shining-armor shit to save her from a hostage situation and then wow. Just fucking wow."

"You're saying wow a lot."

She waves aside my comment. "How is it you never mentioned to me that Elise Hayes is your ex? How the hell did you keep that a secret for so long? You guys were together for five years."

"Because it wasn't my secret to tell."

It takes her even less time to connect these dots and she mock-slaps her forehead. "Of course. Your ex—Elise Hayes—left your relationship because she wasn't ready to be out. So nobody knew she was into women back then. So *of course* you couldn't say anything. Slow clap for Nicola."

"That's pretty much it, yeah."

Her expression transforms from manic to supportive. "That must have been really shitty. I remember how fucked up you were over the breakup."

"It really was shitty."

"I have a million inappropriate questions right now."

Laughing, I agree, "I'm sure you do."

Nicola straightens, raising her chin imperiously as if she's attempting to rise above her childishness. "But I'm going to be mature and respectful and not ask them." She gulps her coffee. "And also because I'm still trying to reconcile how you deal with dating an award-winning actress. For five years."

"Because there's far more to her than just her job. And when we first met and started dating she wasn't in *Greed* and with all the stuff associated with that. She was just Elise, a beautiful woman and fabulous actress who'd had some television guest roles and small parts in movies, working her ass off and waiting for the big break."

"Yeah, but—"

"Yeah but nothing. Aren't you and I the sum of all our parts? We're not one thing or another. Same with Elise. She's a brilliant person who just happens to be a brilliant actress."

"I guess." Nicola laughs. "I bet you've been laughing your ass off at me this whole time."

I move my thumb and forefinger close together. "Only this much."

"Sorry if I made it weird. It's just...wishful thinking."

"Oh I know. And it's fine. Kind of part of the gig I guess, knowing that half the country wants to sleep with your girlfriend."

"Right. How do you deal with that?"

I grin. "Because I know they don't actually get to sleep with her. I do."

Nicola chews the edge of her thumbnail while she works through whatever it is she's thinking. I expect her to say something deep or meaningful but instead she blurts, "Goddammit, Avery, you are the luckiest bitch I know."

My smile stretches my cheeks. "Trust me, I am well aware of that."

CHAPTER TWENTY-TWO

Since the day after Christmas, we've spent every night at Elise's place because it's bigger and frankly, waaay nicer than my place, which makes the crappy commute worth it. And, most importantly, she has the heated pool which has sent water-baby Bennett into a state of bliss. We haven't quite made it to let's-move-in-together stage, but it feels inevitable. Wonderfully so.

Hopefully she likes her really nice and really big house in the hills better than my three-bedroom in the valley. I've moved some of my clothes and essentials and at her request, the Cabot into her house. And every night I shift the 1911 from the safe to a drawer in the bedside table beside me. I don't love the system but it makes her feel secure and helps her sleep, which squashes some of my dislike of sleeping with a gun beside the bed.

Our New Year's Eve plans are quiet—a nice dinner, probably watch a movie and fall asleep before midnight the way we always have in the past. The best part of that plan is the relocation to bed from the couch always leads to ringing in the new year in a very sexy way. I finish up work early to battle traffic back to her place and as I'd expected, Elise and Bennett are in the pool.

I dump my things then go out to see them. Bennett acknowledges me with a glance as he paddles around with his floating bone toy in his mouth. After Elise pushes herself up on the pool edge to meet me halfway for a kiss, she drops back down to rest her arms against the edge, giving me a fabulous view down her bikini top. "You coming in?"

I straighten up. "Not now. I need to get dinner started first otherwise it'll mess with our movie plans."

"Boring." From her safe distance, she splashes water at me. I throw a pool toy at her and I'm almost to the house when that same pool toy skims past my hip.

I bend over to pick it up then turn around slowly. "You *really* want to start something with me?"

"Actually yes, I do." She pauses for a dramatic beat. "But maybe later." Her look is devilish and sends a surge of desire through me. Ellie blows me a kiss then paddles after Bennett. She does a duck dive, deliberately showing me her ass. Unfair.

By the time I've put dinner in the oven and showered, Ellie and Bennett have had enough of the pool. I leave Ellie to shower while I feed Bennie, set the table, and dish up the vegetarian lasagna. After dinner, we flip a coin to choose a movie and end up with *The Old Guard* which we've both been meaning to watch for months. I'm *always* late watching movies and Elise is usually so busy she doesn't get to new releases for months or more.

She settles against me on the couch, more on top of me than beside me, and the whole movie her fingers are busy against my skin. Not enough to cross the line and make me turn off the movie to have her right there, but enough that my nerves are sparking and a slow soft roll of arousal has been steadily building all night.

As usual, we fall short of ringing in the new year and decide 11:17 p.m. is good enough and it's time to go to bed. Bed. Not sleep. While Elise takes care of her Emmy Award-winning skin, I double check the doors, windows, and alarm as I do every night. By the time I'm finished, Elise is still not in bed. The covers have been pulled back and she's sitting cross-legged on top of the sheets, leaning back against her stack of pillows. Instead of her usual men's pajama pants and tank, she's wearing a black satin chemise edged in lace. Oh boy.

Bennett comes in to check on both of us as always before declaring all is fine for the night and sauntering out of the room and claw-clicking his way down the hall and stairs to one of his second-level beds. "Probably for the best," Elise comments. "Tonight is a closed door kind of night. I don't want him watching."

I close the bedroom door. "Watching...what exactly?"

Ellie ever-so-casually opens the top drawer of her bedside table. I know what she keeps in that drawer and anticipation makes my stomach tighten, my skin tingle. The slow roll of arousal turns to a quick hum of excitement. She settles back against her pillows, leaving the drawer open. "What do you think?"

I sit beside her, and after a peek at leather and metal and silicone, slide my hand up the inside of her calf, over her knee and thigh. I stop high on her inner thigh, my fingers softly stroking her skin. My voice is tight with desire. "I think you want to strap on and fuck me."

"That is exactly what I want." The low huskiness of her statement makes me tremble inside. She's going to be dominant, not rough, but demanding. Demanding not of what I give her, but what she gives to me. And I cannot fucking wait for it.

"Me too," I murmur. I stand, take the single step to the drawer and reach down to run my hand over the harness, gripping the leather to shake it. Buckles clink, leather hits the side of the drawer. I know how much she loves the anticipation of a strap-on session, that mental foreplay.

Elise inhales sharply, shifting on the bed. "It's all clean, just for you, just in case you said yes."

"Did you really think I'd say no?"

"It's been a while. I wasn't sure, but my gut said you'd be as excited as I am."

"Your gut is rarely wrong." I let the harness fall again then drop a knee onto the bed beside her hip. Even after a few moments to get myself under control, my response still comes out hoarsely. "I am excited. I've missed you fucking me with that toy."

Despite my exes before Ellie all leaning slightly toward the more butch end of the scale, she was the only woman who'd ever used a strap-on toy with me. Having her—gorgeous high femme—strap on and fuck me until I was a quivering puddle made me hotter than I could ever admit. She'd bought the harness and toy online six months into our first relationship and the shy confidence when she'd shown me, suggested using it, and described in graphic detail exactly how she wanted to use it had made me so wet that I'd begged her for it then and there. It was always hers to wear, kept on her side of the bed, and every so often she'd open the drawer and give me a suggestive look that had my insides trembling.

"I've missed it too," she murmurs. After a beat her tone changes to a forceful demand. "Now, take your clothes off. I want to see all of you."

I take my time and Ellie watches me strip, her eyes never leaving mine as I slowly remove clothing. Going slow goes against every instinct—I want to tear my clothes off and beg her to fuck me, but I know the anticipation is only going to make it better. The moment I'm naked she shifts until she's kneeling on the side of the bed. With a single forefinger, Elise glides her touch over my nipple before tracing a line along my collarbone, up my neck, along my jaw until she reaches my lips. That fingertip lightly traces my lower lip and I lean forward and teasingly bite it before sucking her finger into my mouth.

Elise's barely disguised moan makes my stomach twist. She adds another finger, gently opening my lips, and I suck that one too. Her pupils dilate as her lips part, almost as if she's thinking about kissing me. I run my tongue over her fingers and keep sucking as she carefully pulls them from my mouth. Both of those fingers move to my clit and I feel her slide over me before she sets one finger on either side and strokes up and down, gently squeezing. The touch sends bolts of electricity through me and I almost falter on quivering legs. "Jesus, fuck," I hiss.

Elise slips off the bed, roughly pulling me toward her. She kisses my neck, bites the sensitive skin near my ear as her fingers keep teasing through my wetness. "Fuck, indeed. You're so wet already. Are you thinking about me fucking you?"

I can barely articulate, "Please. Yes."

"Good," she murmurs, carefully withdrawing her teasing touch. "Then undress me."

I steal a kiss and if not for Elise pulling away with a strangled moan, I probably would have dropped to my knees, pushed her chemise up and taken her in my mouth. "Undress me," she says again.

I pull the garment off in one motion and throw it onto the antique accent chair in the corner of the room. Elise helps me remove her panties, stepping out of them quickly as if her own desperation has overwhelmed her. She sets her feet slightly apart and this demand is a low purr. "Put the harness on me. Leave the toy."

Ellie loves the sensation of smooth leather and cool metal buckles and I take my time sliding it up her legs, letting the straps and buckles glide over her skin. When I've tightened the last strap and tugged the harness so the crotchless opening is in the perfect spot, I drop to my knees and bury my mouth in her heat. She's so wet, so delicious. Elise grips a fistful of my hair, first pulling me against her so I can suck her clit and run my tongue through her folds, then pushing me away. "Wait," she murmurs. "Not yet."

Elise turns me and pushes me gently back to the bed then follows so she's on top of me. She indulges in a quick, heated kiss as she uses a hand on the inside of each of my thighs to spread my legs. There's a light touch, fingers gliding up and down my slit, brushing my clit and teasing my entrance until she crawls down my body so her shoulders are nestled between my thighs. Keeping eye contact with me, she drops her head and ever... so...slowly slides her tongue through my folds.

I gurgle out, "Oh, fuck" and struggle to draw a breath around the gasps her mouth is eliciting from me. She licks me slowly, thoroughly sliding her tongue up and down my labia until an eternity of teasing later she lightly tongues my clit. She lingers for the briefest moment before her tongue dances away, then comes back to slide up and over the top of my clit. "Ellie," I beg. "Please don't tease."

She stops teasing. She stops everything. After waiting agonizing seconds with her hot breath washing over my hotter flesh, Elise surges up my body, grips my hips hard and rolls us until I'm on top. She lightly slaps my ass and growls, "Turn around."

I know what she wants. I know what's about to happen. And the thought of burying myself in her wetness while she licks me sends a fresh flood of desire through my body. I do as I'm told and settle on top of her. The moment I'm in position, Elise grips my ass in both hands and yanks me down to her face. She wastes no time, diving in to devour me. I can barely think as her lips and mouth and tongue move over my sensitive flesh, driving my already spiraling arousal closer to breaking point.

I hold her thighs, trying to take some steadying breaths to shift my focus away from the heat in my belly and the throbbing in my depths. I pull the edges of soft, supple leather away from her labia and Elise moans against my clit as I cover her folds with my mouth and lightly tongue her clit. We know each other so well, have loved each other so thoroughly and so many times that giving her pleasure feels second nature to me.

My building climax is a ball of heat threatening to combust and my breathing hitches as Elise sucks my clit. I moan against her. She exhales a gasp and squirms underneath me, her legs moving erratically in the sheets. Ellie's mouth moves from my wetness and I feel her deep breathing against me. I wrap my lips around her clit, suck gently. Ellie gasps, "No no, stop. I want to come while I'm inside you."

Gentle teeth nip at the sensitive skin of my inner thigh and I drag myself away from her tempting flesh and carefully climb off her, rolling onto my back beside her. Elise leans over me, her fingertips tracing over my nipples then down the center of my belly. She kisses me, her tongue playing against mine for long, languorous seconds before she sucks my lower lip. Her grin is devilish. "Get comfortable, baby."

While Elise attaches her toy, I slide further up the bed and settle myself. Anticipation has my skin heating and the excitement of what's to come makes me even wetter. Ellie climbs back onto the bed and takes her time touching me, running her hands over my breasts, tweaking my nipples. Her mouth follows and her tongue loves all those places her hands have just touched until I'm nothing more than a big ball of desperate need.

She kneels between my spread legs, sliding the toy against me. My slippery arousal makes it glide sensuously over my clit, which feels so fucking amazing that I can barely draw in a breath. I feel selfish, greedy, but I know Elise and know she loves this as much as if I were sucking her clit and stroking her with my fingers. Ellie leans down so her breasts lightly brush my stomach and then her mouth is on my breasts, tongue and teeth loving my nipples.

My hands move erratically over her back, through her hair as I buck my hips against her, trying to convey what I want. The movement between my legs stills. "Do you want me to fuck you?"

"Please." That single word sounds desperate, needy. My arousal is hot and thick against the inside of my thighs and the thought of what she's about to do makes me feel impossibly more wet.

Elise smirks, a cocky knowing smirk before she drops her head to kiss me lightly. When she settles her hands beside my shoulders I grip her biceps hard, needing something to hold, something to ground myself as she slowly enters me with the toy. It feels so fucking incredible. I shudder at the sensation and have to take a few moments to calm myself or I'm going to come. Ellie's eye contact is intense. "You okay?" she asks quietly.

"More than," I rasp. "Please, fuck me. I want more." I wrap my legs around her ass, locking my ankles so I can pull her into me. She settles her hands on the bed and starts a steady rhythm. She's hitting every spot inside that makes me quiver and I have to force myself to relax and take a few deep breaths before I hyperventilate. Her slow withdrawal makes me groan and her quick reentry makes me gasp. She adjusts herself to rest her weight onto her knees and slips a hand between us. With every thrust Elise slides her thumb over my clit until I can barely think. I'm so close to climaxing, my body tight and aching with need, and I want it so badly I can't think of anything else.

Ellie settles back down on top of me, her body pressed full length against mine. Our mingled sweat makes us glide against each other. She fucks me deep and slow, taking her time to make sure I feel everything. And all I can do is hold on to her, suck her ear, her neck and keep my legs tight around her ass to keep her with me.

She raises herself up again, arms braced beside my shoulders as she thrusts slow and hard and deep. She's rubbing herself against me, seeking friction as she rocks forward on each thrust. As well as having the desired effect for her, it's pressing the harness against my clit and driving me closer and closer to release. I grip the leather at her hips, pulling her closer, pulling her deeper. "That's so good, Ellie, fuck me harder, please," I beg. "I'm so close. Please. *Please* I want to come." My words are disjointed, breathy as I try to focus on just one sensation at a time. But I can't and everything is so so fucking good that I give in and surrender to it.

An expression I recognize passes over her face—lusty and possessive. It's quickly replaced by another expression I recognize. She's so close herself, she wants to come but she's waiting for me. I pull her biceps, trying to get her to press herself to me. Elise drops down on top of me, sliding an arm under my shoulders. This kiss is fierce and needy and adds fuel to the fire between my thighs. I'm so close…so so close. The sensation of her inside me, against my clit, her nipples rubbing against mine, her mouth and tongue and hands and her whole fucking body is driving me insane.

She makes an extra deep thrust and I drag my nails over her ass and up her back. Ellie shudders, groaning into my mouth as she climaxes, and that sweet pressure against me, inside me takes me along with her. It's intense, explosive and when I arch up into her the pressure from the harness against my clit sets off a fresh wave of climax. Her mouth moves to my neck and she sucks hard, making me shudder again.

We're both panting and I pull her mouth back to mine for a kiss—deep at first before the kiss softens to gentle and sweet as she eases herself off me. Ellie unbuckles the harness and rolls over to drop it over the side of the bed. She rolls back and snuggles into me. Her lips make a path from my jaw to my ear before she murmurs, "Happy New Year."

I turn my face to her and indulge in a lingering kiss. "I think you mean happy new life…"

CHAPTER TWENTY-THREE

It takes me a few moments in my barely woken state to realize Elise is shaking me awake. "Avery." My name is a tight, urgent whisper.

"Mmm?" I reach for her, fumbling through the dark space for warm skin and willing flesh. "Again? Baby, you're insatiable tonight." Happy New Year indeed...

"Please don't," a vaguely familiar male voice answers in Ellie's stead. "It's sickening watching you touch her."

I instantly sit upright, my heart pounding and my eyes straining in the dark to find what I know is there. What should not be there. The questions I should be asking myself—how did he get in the house, what does he want, what should I do—are all clustered in the back of my mind, fighting for space while the most important thing rushes to the forefront. He must not get *anywhere* near Elise.

Great job, Bennett. Bridges must have tip-toed right past him like a goddamned cat burglar. A fresh worry pushes into my brain and adds itself to the current ones. Oh, fuck. What has he done to Bennett?

Elise turns on her bedside lamp, throwing light across the room, and after I've raised the sheet to cover her nudity, I ask, "How the fuck did you get in?" I really need to talk to someone at the LAPD or the FBI about their definition of "behaving himself and adhering to the conditions of being released until trial."

He ignores me to smile mockingly at Elise, poking the air with a forefinger as if putting in his PIN on an ATM. "Five-six-eight-two." He gestures around himself as if indicating the world. "So many sightlines for a good lens and binoculars with all these huge windows, and not to mention that conveniently placed glass paneling beside your door. Made it almost too easy to get your alarm system code."

Fuck. Bennett had known and he was trying to tell us that something was wrong. But we couldn't see it. I try for a slightly less confrontational tone. "What are you doing here? You're violating a restraining order right now and in a *serious* way. Not to mention the other charges. They'll send you to pris—"

He interrupts me with snarling, "Do you really think I care?"

Okay then. Confrontational is the name of this game. Without taking my eyes off him I quietly say, "Ellie, call 911."

Before she can move, Bridges holds up two cellphones. His right arm is strapped with athletic tape, not in a cast, but he's obviously still favoring that wrist I damaged. "With... what exactly?" Both phones are slipped into the thigh pocket of his cargo pants and he seals the Velcro fastening with slow precision. I see no obvious weapon on him and move for the top drawer of my dresser, but before I can even get my hand on the knob, he holds up a familiar-looking shape. "You won't find what you're looking for in there." Light glints off the polished silver of my 1911.

Fuck me. He's crept around in the dark *while we were asleep*, collected our phones and my gun. And god knows what he's done with my dog. I strain to listen for the sound of canine distress. But there's nothing. Bennie's a sound sleeper. Maybe he's just asleep. Elise grips my hand and the moment her fingers slide between mine, some of my anxiety abates. "That's a pity," I drawl, trying to sound bored.

His smile is sardonic. "Not for me."

Beside me, Elise draws in a slow breath. "I suppose this is where I ask you what you want?" Her voice is admirably calm. I wonder what it's taking her to keep the panic from her voice. Under the sheet, she's gripping my hand so hard her nails dig in painfully.

"You," he says simply. "I've told you that already, Elise. Repeatedly. But you won't listen to me, so now I'm going to make you listen."

"What about the other members of the Hayes Horde?" she asks. "I was under the impression you all worked in a team with everyone involved. I mean, if the private correspondence I've been receiving from all the other guys is anything to go by."

Oh, clever clever Ellie. I hope he takes the bait the way she's dangling it—that the members of his Creep Crew have been stepping out of line, not that she's interacting with them and not him—and redirects some of his focus and emotion. My heart rate drops fractionally at his expression. Rage, but not directed at Elise. Good. This is good.

"Fuck them," he snarls. "Inept. Idiotic. Too afraid to do anything but sit in Mommy's basement and think about what they want to do." Bridges pounds his chest with his left fist. "I'm the one who has the balls to take what I want. Me. Not them. They don't deserve to even look at you."

Elise's voice is conversational, relaxed as she says, "No? So why don't you tell me why *you* deserve to look at me and whatever else you think you're entitled to."

I can't listen to the foulness emanating from his mouth, so while Elise cleverly keeps him engaged with his ridiculous delusions and fantasies I study him more closely, trying to work out if he has a weapon, other than mine. I can't see anything— no holster, no knife sheath. Of course, that doesn't mean he isn't carrying, just that he's not carrying obviously.

I keep the assumption that he has a hidden weapon somewhere and set that thought alongside everything else I need to consider right now. At the moment, my most obvious obstacle is my Cabot. His grip on the 1911 is awkward but I can tell it's more than just that he's right-handed and nursing a sore wrist. It's obvious that he's not comfortable with guns and his lack of knowledge is further compromised by his right-handedness and his wrist injury. Good. Kind of. He's going to struggle with my left-handed Cabot. But probably only for a *very* short time. I only need a very short time. It might be my only opportunity and I need to be ready the moment the window opens for me.

In concession to Elise's anxiety at night, the Cabot lives in the drawer locked and loaded with the thumb safety off because I'm intimately familiar with using the gun, and it has a grip safety. So as it's configured now, it's ready to fire if he holds it correctly and properly engages the grip safety. I have to hope he doesn't.

Bridges stops speaking and for the first time, takes his intense gaze off Elise to give me more than a cursory look. His mouth works open and closed in spluttering rage. "You!" he spits at me. "I thought I recognized you from those photos with Elise. Now I remember you."

"I remember you too," I say neutrally.

The Cabot moves between Ellie and me. "So what's this? You moved in after you ruined *my* special day with Elise? Turned her…queer?" He says that last word as if it's vomit in his mouth.

I squeeze Ellie's hand as hard as I can, hoping she'll take my meaning that she cannot respond to his questions. She can't tell him anything personal about her sexuality that's going to send him off his course. Whatever course that is. I still don't know exactly how I should play this. Goading him and turning his focus from Elise to me worked last time but now he'd be wise to what happens if he falls for it.

I straighten up, angling my body so I'm partially in front of Elise. "I think you might have ruined your special day yourself. What you did wasn't very nice. Perhaps if you tried something less—" I almost say *violent*, but catch myself. I don't want him to think about violence. "—frightening and more gentle, then Elise might be more amenable to whatever it is you're wanting." Without turning away from him, I ask Ellie, "What do you think, Elise?"

Quietly she says, "I think I would probably agree with that statement."

He seems to turn this thought over. "What would make you happier?"

Ellie takes her time, pretending to really think about her answer. "For you to let Avery and me go."

"No," he growls. "You have to come with me, Elise. I saw you both tonight, saw you other nights. She's made you disgusting, perverted. That's not how you're supposed to make love. But it's all right, Elise. We can make it all right. I'll show you how we're supposed to do it." The thought he's been watching us, studying us, learning all our secrets, seeing us be intimate makes me feel sick. And the insinuation of him "making it all right" makes me feel even sicker and I have to swallow the bile rising up my throat. His attention turns back to me. "And *you*. You're not going to come back. I'm going to make sure of it. Get up and move over to the wall."

"No," I say flatly. There is no way in hell I'm leaving Elise here with him. He'll have to kill me to stop me. As soon as the thought enters my brain, my limbs go shaky. I think…I think that might be exactly what he has planned.

"Avery," Ellie hisses.

"Put your robe on, Ellie." To Bridges I say, only just restraining my snarl, "And you, avert your eyes. Have some respect. You don't get to see her without clothes unless she invites you to." It kills me to leave off the obvious, "And she never will," but saying that feels deliberately antagonistic.

To my utter surprise, he does what I told him to, dropping his head to stare at the polished floorboards underfoot. Elise tangles herself in the sheet to cover herself enough to reach for the robe slung over the back of the chair in the corner of the room. He's not looking directly at me and it's a perfect opportunity for me to act. But I'm too far away to do anything. By the time I've moved to tackle him, he will have time to react. Goddammit.

Now wrapped in her robe, Elise looks to me as if trying to gauge what we're going to do next. I move slowly over the bed, crabbing along on my butt until I can stand beside her. Then I move to block her from his view as much as possible. His eyes shift downward again, as if my naked body is offensive to him.

Ellie grips my bicep, pressing herself to my back. She's trembling and beside my ear I hear her noisy breathing.

"Please don't puke on me, Ellie," I murmur, hoping the teasing might ease some of her terror.

She sniffs out a sound of agreement, as a quiet sound from behind the door catches my attention. Scratching at the wood, then a low whine—the sounds Bennett makes when he desperately wants to go out into the yard after I've come home from work. Relief. Bennie. He's okay.

That relief lasts barely a second. Bridges seems to have registered that Bennett is on the other side of the door and after a nervous lick of his lips, he demands, "Elise, go stand by the door and turn around. Don't open it. Not until I'm done here and can deal with that dog."

Deal with that dog. Like fucking hell he's going to do anything to Elise or my dog. I turn my head slightly, keeping an eye on him. "It's okay, Ellie. Go stand at the door." If she's at the door she can open it and get out. I don't know what Bennett will do but I hope he follows her and stays with her because Bridges obviously knows I have a big, scary-looking dog and is afraid of him.

I reach behind myself and gently grasp her hip. She presses her lips to the skin at the base of my neck and I feel the soft breath as she whispers something that I can't hear. Both palms glide from my shoulders, down my back to rest just above my ass before she steps to the side and toward the doorway. I shadow her, keeping my body in front of hers.

Bridges points the gun at me, using it to gesture at the french doors leading out to the balcony off her room. "All right, you. Move, outside, out of the bedroom. I don't want her seeing this."

I register Ellie's quiet shriek at his statement, but I can't look at her. I can't take my focus off the man who has the gun. I don't move. Now I know exactly for sure what's going to happen. He's going to kill me so I'm no longer in his way. But there's no fear. Only anger. Focus. Determination. I make eye contact with him. "I have a name. It's Avery." I don't say it in the hopes of trying to get him to make some sort of personal connection, but because I'm sick of him calling me You.

"I don't care. Get outside."

So…he wants to kill me, but he doesn't want Elise to witness it. Why? That doesn't really gel with his behavior. I'd have thought he would want to show her that I was gone, that I wasn't an option anymore, that he was the only thing she had. But he seems to…care about it. Care about her. It makes me feel even more nauseated.

"No," Elise begs, her voice breaking around the word. "No, no no, please no." She's fighting to keep herself calm and her voice steady but she's failing, and her tears make it hard to understand the words as they tumble out of her mouth. "Please, don't. Don't. That's not going to help. You don't need to do this. I'll do whatever you want, without you doing that. Please don't hurt her. Please don't."

From the other side of the door Bennett barks a couple times. The sound is deep and loud and reminds me of the way he barked when Ellie and I were arguing. Now I look at her. "It's okay, Ellie. Really. It's okay," I repeat. I want to tell her I love her, in case this doesn't go the way I want it to, but I don't want to piss him off and make him act earlier than he's planned. She doesn't need me to say it. She knows I love her. I tell her without words every day. I showed her not two hours ago. What I need right now is for her to leave, to get out of this bedroom and run.

He snarls, "I said move. Fucking *move*! If I have to tell you again…"

Bennett responds with another bout of loud barking, then more frantic scrabbling against the bedroom door. Bridges's nervous tongue swipes over his lower lip. "Elise. Turn around."

Tears track down her cheeks and snot dribbles from her nose as she struggles to control herself. "No. I can't. I'm not leaving her."

His free hand clenches. "I said turn around. Do it now." The gun moves from me to Elise.

"Hey!" I snap, barely stopping myself from lunging at him. "Don't you dare!" I've never wanted to hurt someone as much as I want to hurt him right now. But I won't do anything while there's the slightest chance Ellie could be collateral damage. "You say you love her and you're pointing the gun at her? You *never* do that."

His hand drops immediately and stays by his side for a few seconds before it comes back up to level the gun at my head. Level is an optimistic word. His hand is trembling, from anger or fear, I don't know. Thankfully for me, his jiggling isn't going to accidentally shoot me—his finger rests lightly against the trigger guard. He uses the gun to gesture again, a quick wrist jerk toward the french doors. "You, move. To the glass doors, open them and go outside."

Now I do move, but not directly toward the doors where he's trying to take me outside like he's some executioner. I move diagonally, sort of to the doors and sort of toward him, but not close enough that he'll feel immediately threatened.

Elise cuts in and it seems she's managed to calm herself or at the very least, fake calm. "Avery—"

"Don't you use her name," Bridges snarls before his voice softens to address her again. "Elise, turn around. Please."

She doesn't. I take the opportunity of him focusing on her to creep forward another tiny step toward him. The tension and adrenaline in the room is so thick it feels like I could grasp it and wring it from the air. We aren't doing what he wants and I can tell that losing control of his narrative is making him even angrier. He affects a casual shrug. "Fine. Watch. Maybe you'll learn something."

He grips the slide in his left hand and tries to drag it back to cock the pistol, but all it does is eject the cartridge from the chamber. He tries again and I can tell right away that his clumsy fingertips just slipped under and engaged the thumb safety. The slide doesn't budge. He moves his hand forward on the slide, as if hoping more leverage might help. Nothing is going to move it except disengaging the thumb safety which is on the right side, not the left where he'd expect.

He exhales a frustrated grunt. As I'd hoped, he's confused that nothing is where it should be. The 1911 safety isn't a simple lever on the slide like most pistols, but on the frame and instead of stopping the firing pin, is an actual impediment to the slide moving.

"Do you even know how to use a gun? Seems like you're a bit of a fuckin' noob," I taunt, edging another step closer.

Bridges tilts the Cabot, studying it, his fingers moving over the grip and slide as if trying to work it all out. The concentration lapse is all I need. In one movement I grasp his wrist, shove my shoulder into his chest and use my momentum and his body weight to drive him backward and turn him away from the door. If he manages to get the safety off again and accidentally, or intentionally, fires a shot, I don't want it going anywhere near Ellie.

I almost can't believe he's fallen for basically the same trick from me twice and if this wasn't so horrifying I'd be laughing. Not to mention I'm naked and trying to wrestle a guy to the ground. But I can't laugh because I've fucked up. I didn't get enough momentum, didn't quite get my bodyweight right and he manages to stay on his feet and is still holding the gun, despite my twisting his injured wrist so hard he's yelling. But he's fighting me, trying to push me back with his left hand under my chin and I just can't…quite…get…my grip on him. Disarming people is second nature to me, something I don't even have to think about, but it seems he's learned a few things since last time because he keeps pushing me off balance and I can't gain the upper hand.

Dimly, I recognize Elise screaming, but I can't understand her words. Over the top of her shrieking is Bennett, who has clearly woken up to the fact something is *really* wrong on the other side of the bedroom door and is barking and growling furiously. It's unlike anything I've ever heard from my dog— deep and authoritative, frantic, almost feral—and I feel his desperation in the scrabbling at the door, the thud of his body against it as if he's trying to break through it.

I manage to hook a leg around the back of his calf and bring him to the ground but I'm unable to twist us. Rather than me landing on top, he falls heavily on me, pinning my left hand between us. The worst possible scenario. God-fucking-dammit all to hell. My right hand flails to get around his arm so I can push his head back, gouge his eyes, anything to make him get off me. He punches me in the face with the gun butt and the sharp pain sends bells and stars through my head. When I reach up again, all I grab is air and I swing my arm around, hoping to find his hair, his ear, something. I find nothing.

But I have to try.

He's yelling, shouting, screaming nonsensical things as he punches me in the face with the gun again and again. The pain is intense, consuming, searing, but I have to focus. Just for a moment. "Run! Call 911!" I scream it, hoping Elise hears me over Bridges's outrage. Did I scream? I think I did but my head feels like cotton wool and the high-pitched ringing in my ears makes it hard to hear myself. I can't see her. Don't know where she is or if she's still in the room or if she's okay.

But I have to try.

It couldn't have been more than twenty seconds since I first grasped his arm but it feels like an hour. Hot blood pours from my nose, drips from my lips and chin and I can barely see out of my left eye.

But I have to try.

I manage to get my hand under his chin and push his head back, trying to move him away. The gun barrel grazes my cheek and the panic I've been suppressing breaks free. I'm scrabbling, desperately trying to free my pinned left hand, kicking and twisting to get him off me. But I can't get free, no matter how much I struggle and squirm. I see his forefinger move up to where he accidentally put the safety on, then back down to the trigger, and I know in a fraction of a second he's going to feel that perfectly balanced trigger pull.

I know exactly how the gun will feel in his hand when he shoots me in the head.

Desperate now, panicked, frantic, I try to push his hand to the side, try to move my head, try to do anything to stop what I know is about to happen. But I'm in the worst possible position and no matter what I do with hand and legs and body, I can't shift him.

The explosion against my left ear makes me feel like I've dived into ice-cold water, a sharp shock that steals my hearing and sight. The searing pain through my face is immediate and unlike anything I've ever felt before.

I know he's just shot me. In the face. Somewhere. My right ear rings so loudly I can barely hear on that side and my left ear is completely deaf. When I try to open my eyes, only my right one cooperates and even then it's barely cracked open.

Fuck. Oh fuck.

But I'm thinking. I can move. I'm alive.

Thick blood runs from the left side of my face, over my neck, my ear in a river of sticky warmth. The distant part of me that is allowed to think about things like being shot in the face, losing my hearing, losing my eye or even dying comes to the forefront for a panicked moment, and I can't do anything except try to deal with the intense pain that radiates like a flame across my face.

Then I remember Ellie. Ellie. I can't hear her. Can't see her. I still don't know where she is, if she's called emergency services, if she's somewhere safe. I think I call out to her but then I realize I might have just imagined it. I need to do something other than bleed out all over the floor. Oh fuck, help me, please, I can't just lie here until he shoots me again.

But I don't. I can't. I can't do anything.

His weight shifts off me and a moment later comes the muffled sound of screams and yelps, the vibration of his shoe heels thumping on polished wood. Free of him, I bring my hand to my face to cover whatever he's done to me and with the blurry vision of my right eye, try to see what's going on. I can barely hear anything and the loss of sensation sends a fresh wave of panic through me. Rolling over, I try to bring myself up onto my knees so I can stand but my legs give way and I fall onto my stomach, winding myself. But I can move my head. Just. And when I see it, I can't believe I'm seeing it.

Bennett has Bridges pinned with his full weight on his chest. He's snapping and snarling, biting whatever he can like a rabid, possessed werewolf. Bridges is flailing, punching, doing everything he can to shift my very large dog. Bennie yelps, then continues growling and snarling and biting. The glint of polished metal breaks through my haze and I crawl and fall and stumble to the gun lying on the floor just out of Bridges's reach.

The gun. It takes a lifetime to get there and my fingers keep slipping when I try to grasp it. Another lifetime and I finally grip it, run my thumb over the shape I know so well and know immediately that it's ready if I need it. I have it trained on him but my hand is shaking so much my target is bouncing from center mass to head to arm to leg to center mass. And my dog. My dog is still there. I can't risk it. I would never risk him. "Bennie," I gasp. "Here."

It takes a few seconds but Bennett finally seems to register my hoarse command and abandons his attack. But he's still snarling and barking, dancing forward and back like he's warning Bridges to stay away as he lashes out wildly with arms and legs. The shape of my dog is a trembling blur and I can't tell if it's him or me shaking with rage.

Where's Elise? I want to find her, want to call out for her but after calling Bennett off, I can't make my mouth work again to call out and I can't leave Bridges, who's bleeding from his face and hands, choking out something as he struggles to his knees and unsteadily straightens up. I grit my teeth, ignore the fuzziness and pain and blood swamping my left eye to keep the gun trained on him.

The single word comes out of his mouth on a spray of blood. "Bitch." Swaying unsteadily, he reaches behind himself.

The moment I see the shape of the object in his hand, I pull the trigger.

CHAPTER TWENTY-FOUR

I know I'm in a hospital, I've had surgery, I'm okay. I also know Ellie and Bennett are okay. I've been dimly aware of her presence in some other time and space, and knowing she's there helps ease some of my fear. I think it's her who's told me all these things, over and over as if she's chanting them to me or herself. I don't know. The only thing I know for sure is I hurt so badly it's stealing my breath.

I hate lying on my back, but every time I've tried to move and get more comfortable I've had a painful reminder of how bad an idea it is. My entire body feels like it's been steamrolled and the pain in my face and head is like I tripped into an acid bath. I decide again to try rolling slightly to lie on my hip and realize immediately I'm going to fail, and with a grunt of frustration and discomfort, give up.

"Avery?"

Cracking my right eye open produces no nausea this time which is a small win. My left eye is welded shut and won't open no matter how I try. I can see, kind of, but it's only out of my right eye and nothing more than a blurry mess of shapes with little depth perception. I feel and hear Elise coming closer.

"Hey," she says, gently squeezing my hand. "Hey, baby. It's me. You're okay. Everything's fine and we're safe." The words echo as a memory of things I've said to her before. Her touch moves up my arm. "How're you feeling?"

I try out my voice, which was touch and go earlier when I'd talked to the doctors. It's a little more go this time but still coarse and gravelly and my tongue feels like it's too fat for my mouth. "Like…some fucking bastard incel shot me in the face, broke my nose, a rib and two of my fingers." I close my eye again. The movement is accompanied by sharp pain through my skull.

"Strange." There's a tiny smile in her voice. She gently brings my hand to her mouth and kisses the base of each finger and my thumb. "Because that's exactly what happened to you, darling."

"Are you…okay?" That question has been screaming through my brain from the moment I first saw him in her bedroom. I thought it when it was done, as I crawled across the bedroom floor to try to find her again. I thought it as I was trying to stay conscious. I thought it as I felt myself pass out. And I thought it the moment I regained consciousness.

There's a long pause, but I know she's still there. Eventually Ellie murmurs, "I will be. I'm not hurt. Physically."

It's her *evasion for now* response and I know we'll come back to it. But I also know it's not a lie. If she says she's not hurt then I believe her. Talking with my eyes closed is disorienting and I open my right eye again but it's even worse than keeping my eyes closed. "I'm sorry. I want to look at your beautiful face but my eyes aren't working."

"I know, sweetheart. It's fine."

"How's Bennie?" I know he's okay too, but I wonder if his okay is like Elise's.

"I picked him up from the vet a couple days ago, he was pretty pleased to get out of there." She laughs quietly. "Probably wondering what he did to deserve that torture. There's no actual wounds or anything broken. Just soft tissue bruising, the vet says. He seems fine, maybe a bit quiet but he's eating okay and he's been sleeping in his bed in your bedroom with me. I think he's missing you."

"I miss him too." I inhale a cautious deep breath and let out an even more cautious one. "I still can't believe he did that. It was incredible. Protective Bennett was a badass." I swallow hard, not knowing how to verbalize exactly what I'm thinking. I wouldn't be here if he hadn't done what he did. If Elise hadn't opened the door to get out or let him in or whatever she did.

"It really was incredible." I feel the emotion in her pause. "I…didn't see it all, just a little, at the end." Elise inhales shakily. "But I heard it. He loves you. Even though you don't let him up on the bed or the couch," she adds facetiously.

"I think he loves *you*. And maybe I'll let him on the couch and bed now. He's a hero." After a pause to collect some dropped thoughts I add, "We'll need to get a six-seater to fit all three of us on it."

She laughs. "I think he's happy with how things are, he's got everything he needs. Or he will when you come home." Ellie turns my hand over and kisses the underside of my wrist, my palm. "I spoke to my lawyer and he says home defense laws apply with Bennie, so nothing's going to happen to him. The city might keep an eye on him in case he has a complete personality change and decides to terrorize the public. I told my lawyer that based on the dog I know, that would never happen."

I'd suspected as much, but hearing they aren't going to take my dog sends a flood of relief through me. And given I killed a man who'd assaulted me with the intention of murdering me, the same laws apply to me. "Can you hug him hard for me? And give him a ribeye or whole brisket or something tonight? And take a photo for me, though fuck I won't be able to see it properly."

"You know I will," she assures me. "Did they say when they might let you out of here?"

"Not sure." I don't even know how long I've been here. Maybe a week? "Not until the swelling has gone down enough and they're sure I'm not going to need a glass eye I guess." Somehow, I managed to get my head out of the way enough that instead of shooting me through the forehead, the bullet grazed a path right along the side of my face and skull near the top of my cheekbone, taking the top of my ear with it. Thankfully it's just a hardcore flesh wound.

As well as the trauma surgeon, I've had groggy conversations with a plastic surgeon and neurosurgeon and they both seemed to be trying to outdo themselves with the "You'll be fine and look and act just the way you did before" speeches. I think the fact Elise has been around probably has something to do with the fawning level of service. She turns my hand over, gently moving each of my fingers. "Are you in pain?"

I won't lie to her. "Yeah. The worst is in my head, like I have an eight-out-of-ten headache but it's a face ache too. Can I have some water please? Talking hurts."

"I'm so sorry, darling." Her voice is tight and I can tell her grip on her tears is tenuous. She presses the straw against my lips, keeping her hand against mine as I clumsily try to hold it in place.

After I've taken a few cautious sips, I try to reassure her, "It's not your fault, Ellie."

"Debatable. It *was* about me, so..." She laughs dryly. "But that's something for us to talk through later when you're not in a hospital, and for me to spend fifty therapy sessions digging through."

A quiet knock on the door interrupts my response. I crack open my eye and vaguely see a pale-blue figure. A nurse. "Hi, Avery." I know this one's voice. Belinda? Brenda? I can't remember and I can't focus on small nametags. I dub thee Belenda. I close my eye as she approaches. I hear electronic beeps and feel her moving things attached to me before she asks, "How're you feeling?"

I've exhausted my limited supply of lighthearted responses, so go with a truthful, "Pretty shitty. More pain than yesterday and just like...tight in my face still."

"Hmm. The swelling is actually easing. Slowly. The pain is to be expected I'm afraid but I'll talk to someone about managing it if what we're giving you isn't cutting it. What would you rate the pain?"

"About six, seven."

"Liar," Elise interjects. "You literally just said you had an eight-out-of-ten headache."

Goddammit.

Belenda laughs. "I'll go talk to your doctor. All your vitals look great and everything seems to be progressing as it should. It's just a matter of letting yourself heal. I'll come back soon."

"Thanks," I mumble.

When Belenda's gone, Ellie asks, "Is it just me, or do the nurses come into your room a lot?"

I'd laugh if I wasn't so afraid of the hurting. "My sweet little cookie. They don't when you're not here. I only get the regular checkup treatments then, not these 'my famous girlfriend is here' treatments."

"Dammit, I specifically asked them to give you famous-girlfriend treatments all the time." She exhales a faux-indignant snort. "I'll have to speak to the manager about this, mention all my famousness and awards and shit." She's trying to be light and easy, using humor to deflect how upset she is and I decide I'll play along. We'll have plenty of time later to unpack everything we've been through in the past few weeks and more specifically, these past few days.

I smile and regret it. "Don't be funny, it hurts too much. No jokes until I don't feel like a water balloon."

"I'm sorry, baby."

I reach up with an unsteady hand to touch my cheekbone which feels like Tyson punched me. Repeatedly. "Well, I guess I won't be getting an Emmy with this face."

Her laugh is rich and I feel some of the tension ease from the room. "It's okay, I'll get another one for the both of us."

"I think I'm worth at least an Oscar, Ellie."

"Deal." She brushes the lightest kiss on my uninjured cheek.

"Seriously, I feel like a water balloon that's about to burst. How bad does it look?"

"Better than it did a few days ago." The sound of her phone unlocking is sharp. "Here." When I open my right eye, she's holding her phone up in front of me.

"What am I looking at?"

"Yourself." Elise moves the screen closer until I nod that it's vaguely focused, then treats me to a swipe-show of me unconscious and intubated right through to what I assume is this morning. It's weird seeing myself like this, almost as if it doesn't seem like me. It might not be me, given the uncertain status of my vision.

I fumble for her hand. "Are you *sure* you're okay? I'm trying to remember exactly what happened. Everything still feels kind of fuzzy and unfocused. Like the events are there but they feel a bit surreal. I was trying to talk to a cop the other day but I'm pretty sure I was in Lollipop Land riding a hippopotamus around and trying not to fall into lava, so it was probably not very coherent."

She laughs. "Mhmm. They tried to interview you the day after and I told them to leave you alone for a bit."

"My protector." I run my tongue around my mouth. "Can I have another drink please?" I hear her shuffling around and then the touch of a straw against my lips. After a few delicate sips, I push the straw out of my mouth. "Thanks."

Ellie pauses and when she speaks again it's a quiet, "Do you want to know what happened?"

"If you know what happened and if you're okay telling me, yes I would. Please." I make a helpless gesture. "I think not being sure, trying to piece it together is just making it worse in my head and giving me anxiety about it."

She takes my hand in both of hers, her fingers moving up and down the back of my hand as if it's helping her relax. I sense rather than hear her preparing herself with some deep breathing, and when she starts talking her voice is calm and steady. "We know what happened when we were there but he left notes at his house which have filled in some of the blanks, like his surveillance of my place so he knew my security codes and how he got a gun. He stole his dad's Glock, thinking he could use it to control us if necessary, but apparently he wanted to…kill you with yours, like some sick poetic justice."

"Guess his surveillance wasn't that great if he didn't realize the Cabot was a Southpaw. Lucky us. And lucky us again that he was such a firearms novice."

"Guess so." Ellie's fingers on my hand still for a few moments then start up again. Her voice is neutral, forcibly so. "It was basically what he said. Kill you, take me and…have me, make me his."

My chest feels so tight that I struggle for a breath and when I speak it's strained. "It's okay if you don't want to talk about it, Ellie."

"It's fine, you're right, you should know what happened. Turns out, the Hayes Horde was a one-man band. It was all him."

"What? But he was talking about them." My incredulity makes my voice squeak.

"All delusions, probably something to make himself feel stronger like he had a team behind him. He was sending all the letters, all the emails. So it was a little bit of mental illness and a little bit of psychopathy."

"I can't believe it. Fuck." I take a few moments to process what she's said. "So I guess it's really all over then? No him, no Hayes Horde? Hopefully some of the truth gets into the news so all this shit withers and dies."

"I hope so too," she murmurs. "I'm sure there'll still be fanboys and girls, but I'm hoping this makes them realize there's a line. I wouldn't wish this feeling on anyone." She clears her throat. "They also found my missing lot badge and some of my stuff—underwear, scarves—at his place, so he was a thief as well as a creepy stalker."

"Gross."

Elise murmurs a sound of agreement. "I…I was by the door and you two were struggling behind the bed and I couldn't see you and I just didn't know what to do. I could hear you yelling at me but it was just a roar of noise. And then the gunshot and

I—" Her voice cracks. "I thought you were dead and I didn't know what to do. I wanted to get to you, Avery, I swear, but I couldn't make my legs work and I heard you choking and saying something but I didn't know what and Bennett was just going nuts and I thought I heard you say *run* so I was going to run down to the neighbors because I don't have a landline and I didn't have my phone but as soon as I opened the door, Bennie rushed in. He knocked me down and he just went straight for him like he wanted to kill him." She swallows. "If I didn't know Bennie, he would have terrified me."

"You did exactly the right thing, Ellie. You did exactly what I wanted. I was trying to think of what to do and it was just this constant looping thought of needing you to be safe. If you hadn't opened that door? I think it would have turned out differently."

She's silent for a long while, just stroking my hand. "Then it was the second gunshot and I had no idea if it was you or him and I thought I was just going to kill him myself if he'd shot you again and killed you this time. But then I came around the side of the bed and saw both of you and it was the most indescribable feeling when I saw him and then I saw you and there was so much blood all over your face and hair and the floor and I—I'm sorry. I don't think I can talk about this part anymore." She's trying to hide it, but she's crying.

"It's okay, Ellie. It's all okay." If not for the greater fear of pain, I'd let my own tears loose.

"And I had to touch him and get my phone so I could call 911 and…Avery, I was so fucking scared. You were bleeding so much and Bennie was still out of his mind, growling and snarling and he wouldn't leave us. When everyone turned up I had to lock him in my bathroom and I felt awful but he was so protective and was growling at the paramedics and I was scared he'd do something again."

I squeeze her fingers. "You did the right thing to keep him safe and I'm sure he's forgiven you."

"Mmmm." Her voice relaxes and a touch of amusement creeps in. "My *favorite* part was how the strap-on harness and toy were still on the ground by the bed when every single law enforcement and medical person in the city turned up to deal with the situation. Like, it's a crime scene and I couldn't move it. Thanks, TV job, for teaching me that. As it was, I had to tell them I'd touched him to get my phone. And now there's crime scene photos of one of our sex toys living in a box somewhere for the rest of time."

I have to take a few slow breaths to calm the mirth at that image. Laughing will make my head feel like it's about to explode. I manage a controlled, "Oh no."

"Oh yes. So now most of LA's cops, paramedics and detectives know what we get up to in the bedroom."

"I'm sure they'll be discreet."

She sounds both amused and mortified. "I'm sure they will be but still, I'd hoped to keep *some* of my personal details private."

"I know, honey. But oh, I would have given anything to be there and witness that. Just to…support you I mean."

"Sure," she drawls. "Support." As if sensing I'm about to ask, Elise offers me some more water.

"Thanks." I close my eye and relax into the pillows. There's a lot to unpack, and when I'm functioning a little better I'll have to take some time to process it all. But for now, the only things that matter are that she's safe, Bennett's safe, I'm safe. The rest of it is just background noise. "Are you back at work? I'm not sure what day it is."

"Almost. It's Wednesday, just before midday. I'm back at work on Monday."

"Oh. Okay. Good. Sorry I'm not around to keep you company."

She carefully picks hair from my face and smooths it back. "We're managing, just. Bennie and I have been keeping busy with some house hunting."

"Are you running off with my dog?"

She laughs quietly. "No. I'm selling up. Once they're finished with the house as a crime scene and the crew comes to…clean him off the floor and repair the broken window and bullet hole in the floor, I'm hiring someone to get all my stuff out and putting the house on the market. I don't ever want to go back there again." She pauses. "I want us to live together, either we stay at your place, or we find somewhere close to both our workplaces where there's heaps of room for all our shit."

I stifle a laugh as I remind her, "I can't afford a house closer to my workplace."

"You could if you married me."

My brain stutters to a complete stop and takes a few long moments to reboot. I force myself to keep my right eye open, even though it's painful and disorienting. "Marry you? Are you serious?"

"Yes, I'm serious. Avery, I—"

I decide to spare her the feeling of being forced into something just because of guilt or a fear of loss or any of those things that can come with traumatic circumstances. "Ellie…you don't need to say it."

"Say what?"

"That me being hurt, this whole thing has made you reevaluate your priorities and now you can't imagine spending the rest of your life without me."

"I wasn't going to say that at all. I'm not asking you to marry me because of what happened. I'm asking you because I love you and I knew way before this that I wanted to spend my life with you, Avery." She sniffs. "Do you know what I thought the first time I said *I love you*? It was the day you drove us up to San Fran because I'd heard that antique store had an old Edwardian mahogany piano stool, and even though it was my thing not yours you were still *so* excited for it. And I said it on the way home, at the truck stop taqueria in Lost Hills after you'd just taken a bite of your taco, because I was watching you eat and was just hit over the head by how much I was in love with you."

She doesn't wait for me to answer. "The moment I said those three words I thought, 'I could marry her, I want to marry her.' And that thought stuck with me from that moment until this moment, even as I was running away from myself. And I can't see any reason that you shouldn't know that. But for the record, I *am* so relieved and happy and everything else that you're okay."

"I'm relieved and happy and everything else that I'm okay too." I move my tongue around my dry mouth. "So did you get me a ring or is this totally unplanned?"

"No ring, yet. I have a few on my shortlist but I kind of moved my timeline up a little so I haven't bought one." She runs her thumb over my left ring finger. "You still haven't answered me."

"I didn't think I had to. Of course it's yes."

"Phew. You know this is all conditional on you bringing your grandpa's piano with you. If we buy or build a new place, I'm going to have a room of amazing acoustics and just fill it with pianos."

"Weird hobby, but okay."

"Says the video-game collector." She leans in to kiss me and the soft touch of her lips feels soothing. "Speaking of video games, I'll have to leave soon to go see Stevie. I've spoken to him a few times, told him what happened before he saw it on the Internet but he still wants to *see me* see me. He's pretty upset." Her smile flickers. "About what happened and also that he might lose a video game pal. And that we had to cancel burger night."

"I love his priorities."

Ellie chuckles. "Same."

"Shit. If I move, we'll to have to drop by every week to put out Mrs. Obermeier's trash. Or maybe we can hire someone to do it for her. And you'll have to record some piano playing on a CD or something so she doesn't miss you. Goddammit, I'll lose my weekly sweet treats. Will you bake for me?"

She smiles indulgently. "We can do all of that. And yes, I'll bake for you."

"Phew." I squirm against the pillows. "So what happens now? Is everything just over?"

"Almost. I still have to sit down properly and talk to the detectives." She exhales a sigh. "And go over everything with the FBI just to tie up loose ends. But given there's no real threat from the Hayes Horde because he's…" Elise wavers to a stop and I hear the uncertainty in her voice.

"Dead," I finish for her. "He's dead and he's never going to hurt you." I move my hand, fumbling for her and am relieved when her fingers curl into mine. "It's okay, Ellie. I know what I did and I would do it again without a moment's thought in the same situation."

Her voice is tight. "I know you would. I just hope you never have to do anything like this for me ever again."

"Me either." I try a smile. "And just think, if we can come out of this okay, then I feel like everything will be smooth flying from now on. This is an anomaly, Ellie. Sure, there might be a few things that pop up, but it'll be nothing compared to this."

"You're right." She exhales. "And no matter what happens, we'll be flying together."

EPILOGUE

I study my reflection in the full-length dressing room mirror. "Shouldn't I be in a dress?"

Elise steps in behind me, resting her hands on my shoulders. "You should be in whatever you want, darling."

"I just don't want people to look at us as a couple and think we're conforming to the heteronormative ideal of dress and suit when we appear at official filmy things together."

Ellie's hands move around to smooth down my lapels. "I think the only thing people are going to think when they look at us is how smoking hot you look in a suit and tie with those heels."

From behind us, Elise's stylist's sigh is the perfect mix of boredom and exasperation. I empathize. I have no idea how Ellie does this day in and day out. Smiling at the stylist, I offer a helpless, "Sorry. New to all this."

"I can tell," is the droll reply.

Ellie shoots her a look and the stylist offers a genuine, "Sorry."

I run my hands down the front of the suit jacket. "Can't we just get both options and I can decide if I'm feeling suit or dress the day of the award ceremony?"

"No!" Elise and the stylist blurt out at the same time.

"Whoa, okay then. Sorry."

Ellie's smile is apologetic as she squeezes my hand. "I did warn you about how preplanned this stuff was. Deviation is unacceptable."

Turning sideways, I look myself up and down. My hairdresser is a marvel and the scar in my hairline is completely hidden. The one on my face, not so much, but…makeup. Ellie is studying me in the mirror and I find her eyes, which soften instantly as we make eye contact. I smile. "Just checking—will we have to do this all over again for your role in *Alone*? Like…for Cannes and other film festivals and then when you're nominated for an Oscar and every other award possible for that performance? Like, repeatedly?"

"Mhmm." She bounces her eyebrows and I know that she's trying to say she knows it's bizarre and annoying but this is how it is, without offending the stylist whose job is to make us ceremony-ready.

"Great," I breathe. "So every few months I'm going to have to decide what I'll feel like wearing at an event weeks in the future."

"Pretty much. Speaking of, are we going to spend the next six months with you trying to decide if you want a suit or dress for our wedding?"

My eyebrows shoot up. "Of course not. I already know."

"And?"

"And nothing," I answer. "You'll find out when I meet you at the altar."

The stylist interjects, "Please do not pick a wedding outfit without input. Either of you. If you want any chance of selling those photos to pay for your honeymoon, then all the publications need to know what they're buying."

Selling wedding photos. Sometimes I forget what a weird world my fiancée inhabits. And then someone says something like that and reminds me. Elise grins, first at me, then at the stylist. "Maybe we'll just sneak off to Vegas in disguise."

The stylist sighs. "Please don't do that either, for my sake. I'm desperate to style a wedding between two women. You're both so gorgeous you could go whatever way you wanted to and get away with it. Dual dresses, dual tuxes, one tux and one dress."

"Thanks," I murmur. "I think." I turn back to the mirror. "I guess this is fine. I look okay and I feel okay, so if this is what you want, Ellie?"

"I just want you to be comfortable."

The stylist gathers her things. "I'll give you both a few minutes to argue about it. Let me know when you've made a decision."

The moment the door's closed, Ellie turns to me. "I mean it, wear whatever makes you comfortable." With a laugh she adds, "From the approved lists of outfits that is. Everything at premieres is so weird and hectic and I really do just want you to feel good in your skin."

"How hard can it be? I've watched YouTube videos of you at premieres. If you can do it then I'm sure I'll manage to look hot and confident and charming and witty and—"

She cuts me off with a firm kiss. "Smartass." Elise strokes my cheek, reaching up to push my hair from my eyes. Her thumb brushes along the scar that runs from the edge of my left eyebrow and disappears into my hair. Her light touch on the sensitive skin always makes me shudder, yet she still does it, almost as if reminding herself, reassuring herself that despite the scar I'm still here. "A wedding," she whispers. "Every now and then I forget about it and then it just jumps into my consciousness as a great big bundle of excitement."

"Yes, Ellie. *Our* wedding." I take her hands and hold them against my chest. "It's going to be amazing. Especially now that Nicola has realized you're just a normal person, so she won't be gaga during the ceremony."

A thought pings into my head and I try to tamp down my manic grin. "Do you remember when you told me you'd be there to play piano at my wedding?" I unbutton the tailored suit jacket and hang it up. "So...will you?"

She laughs, long and loud. "I did say that. And sure, why not. But only if you'll duet with me."

"Are we playing 'Chopsticks,' or 'Heart and Soul'?"

Elise kisses me. "I don't care. The only thing that matters is that we're doing it together."

"Yes," I drawl. "That is the exact definition of a duet."

"You really are a smartass. Can't you just let me have the last loving, emotional word?"

"Fine. Sorry." When she doesn't say anything, I make a come-on gesture. "Gimme this last word of yours."

Ellie leans close and after a light kiss, murmurs against my ear. "Ladies, this is your captain speaking. Thank you for your patience and your bravery during that bumpy period. I'd just like to let you know that we've had a successful go-around and it'll be nothing but clear skies and smooth travels from now on."

"Nice one. That's a good last word. Maybe not what I would have said, but it was pretty good. Eight out of ten."

Ellie rolls her eyes. "What would you have said?"

I grin. "Not sure. Probably something like, uhhh..." I lean in, letting our lips brush softly. "Ladies...we've arrived."

Bella Books, Inc.

Women. Books. Even Better Together.

P.O. Box 10543
Tallahassee, FL 32302

Phone: 800-729-4992
www.bellabooks.com

9 781642 473254